I0577834

ABOUT BROKEN TRUST

I'm what some people call the bogeyman. Most people have the good sense to be afraid of me. Unfortunately, my best friend's little sister is NOT most people. She's not afraid of me at all. But she should be. She doesn't know the secrets I'm hiding.

Look, Lucia Demarco is a handful. She's stubborn, gorgeous, a magnet for trouble, and sets my blood on fire. Ignore that last part. I can't have her. I promised my best friend on his deathbed that I'd always take care of her. And I have...never you mind about the thoughts that plague me at night. The point is, she's been poking her head where it doesn't belong and now some idiots are about to find out why they call me the reaper.

I hear former hitmen make the best bodyguards. True story!

I'll keep my word and keep Lucia safe. And I absolutely refuse to give in to her sunny smile or sharp wit.

I can be strong. Or will I risk just one taste?

BROKEN TRUST

M. MALONE

NANA MALONE

CONTENTS

PART 1

Chapter 1   3
Chapter 2   11
Chapter 3   16
Chapter 4   27
Chapter 5   37
Chapter 6   49
Chapter 7   58
Chapter 8   65
Chapter 9   72
Chapter 10   80
Chapter 11   87
Chapter 12   98
Chapter 13   105
Chapter 14   114
Chapter 15   121
Chapter 16   126
Chapter 17   132

PART 2

Chapter 18   141
Chapter 19   150
Chapter 20   158
Chapter 21   166
Chapter 22   173
Chapter 23   183
Chapter 24   190
Chapter 25   198
Chapter 26   206
Chapter 27   213
Chapter 28   221
Chapter 29   228
Chapter 30   235

Chapter 31   242
Chapter 32   249

PART 3

Chapter 33   261
Chapter 34   270
Chapter 35   279
Chapter 36   288
Chapter 37   296
Chapter 38   304
Chapter 39   312
Chapter 40   320
Chapter 41   326
Chapter 42   334
Chapter 43   344
Chapter 44   350
Chapter 45   355
Chapter 46   362
Epilogue   370
Epilogue   377
Another Epilogue   384

About the Authors   391
Also by M. Malone   393
Also by Nana Malone   395

BROKEN TRUST

PART 1

CHAPTER ONE

Noah

"How do you want to play this?"

I tugged the baseball cap I wore lower over my forehead before responding to the voice coming through my earpiece. "The usual. Unless he refuses our invitation."

"You think he'll come easy, mate?"

Matthias, the insanely brilliant and also incredibly annoying tech god that I'd had the good sense to hire/rescue years ago had never been the most optimistic guy. One of the reasons we got along so well.

"Do they ever?"

I glanced at the row house across the street currently housing our target, William Chamberlin. There was nothing special about this guy at all, just another asshole who needed a reminder that stalking was illegal. We handled several of these a month, and while they weren't particularly interesting, there was something satisfying about these cases.

Jonas's voice came through my earpiece next. "If he doesn't, then I'll change his mind."

I had to smile at the predictable reply. Opening my own security firm had given me financial freedom and the stability I needed after my chaotic early years, but it also brought a world of headaches.

Namely, keeping the merry band of past criminals I employed on the straight and narrow.

"Just don't kill him."

Jonas made a sound that could have been a laugh or a snort. "First it was 'don't sleep with the clients.' Now you're telling me I can't kill people? You're no fun lately."

"When has he ever been fun?" Matthias interjected.

That actually made me smile. If someone had told me years ago that I'd be the voice of reason, hell, the responsible one, I'd have thought they were on something. But that was before Rafe died.

That was before Lucia.

Thoughts of her always carried a range of emotions from protectiveness to the sharp pang of desire, and of course, there was the guilt. Always the damn guilt. I'd promised Rafe that I'd look after her, and I'd done that. It was the least I could do for the man who'd pulled me out of the gutter and shown me a better way to live. I'd upheld my oath and honored the memory of my best friend every day.

But while I'd done my best to shelter her over the past few years, I could never truly be honest with her. She'd never look at me the same way if she knew what I was truly capable of. What her beloved brother had been capable of. It was a quandary with no solution. There was nothing I could do about that. So I'd keep doing what I did best... *Lie, cheat and kill?* No. Damn it. I shoved the errant thought that slid in on the shoulders of my guilt aside. I would protect her. Just like always.

"Let's get this fucker."

I kept my head down as I approached the building, noting that the street was empty and there was no movement in the house. I knew Jonas would approach from the back to prevent any possibility of the target slipping through our grasp. This was a standard job, just letting the guy know that it was best if he stayed away from our client. I wouldn't call it threatening. Threaten was such a harsh word. This was more like a conversation, but it was a fine line we walked. We did what was necessary to keep our clients safe and most of it was borderline as hell. Just like the rest of my life.

"Guys, we've got a runner. He's going out the back." Matthias sounded as annoyed as I felt, his British accent coming across as clipped. Suddenly, I could hear him in my other comm unit, on the secondary channel. "Also, you should probably know, Lucia broke routine this morning."

My chest tightened at the mention of the one woman who could twist me up. The one woman who would never follow the rules I set up for her.

"For fuck's sake. Get someone to tail her and make sure she's okay."

"Already done. Um, Oskar said she was talking to some guy."

Son of a bitch. If I wasn't chasing assholes, I was making sure some grab-handy dipshit didn't get his grubby paws on my best friend's little sister.

"I'll deal with her when I see her." I quickened my pace as I heard the sound of Jonas's breathing in my other earpiece and knew he wasn't in position yet.

"Jonas, he's probably going to cut over to the next street. Go around and cut him off."

"Got it."

I could hear a variety of sounds that were hard to decipher: Jonas's breathing, the clang that could be a metal fence, and then the unmistakable sound of scuffling. A few muffled curses later, it was quiet.

When I rounded the corner, Jonas already had the guy on the ground with one arm twisted behind his back.

"Good work. I didn't really feel like sweating today."

Jonas made a face. "Fuck you, Noah. These shoes were not meant for running."

The guy on the ground craned his neck, trying to see over his shoulder. When he caught sight of me, he struggled against Jonas's hold and got a knee in his lower back for his trouble.

"What the fuck, man? Get off me!"

I squatted next to him and then pulled out a small picture of a pretty redhead. Clara Spencer. Although she looked nothing like Lucia, it wasn't a mystery to me why I took these cases so seriously.

Lucia was a good girl; Nonna DeMarco had made sure of that. But even good girls had to grow up some time. And since Rafe wasn't here to protect her like a big brother, I would have to do it. There would come a day when Lucia started dating seriously, and just the possibility that one of those fuckers might treat her like this dickhead, terrorizing her with the threat of what he might do, made me want to put my fist through a wall...or this douchebag's face.

What if something had happened to me? What if I'd died the same day as Rafe? Lucia might have ended up just like Clara Spencer. There were so many girls out there with no one to stand for them. It was my pleasure to stand for as many of them as I could.

I flipped the photo around. At the sight, William blanched and then started struggling anew. Jonas twisted his arm higher until it was clear that he wasn't going anywhere.

"Do you recognize her? Hmm? I think you do." I spoke softly, having learned over the years that a soft voice could often convey menace more convincingly than a loud one.

"No. I've never seen her before!"

"You're a terrible liar, William. Almost as bad as you are at listening. Because Clara has told you several times not to contact her again. Since you didn't seem to be getting the picture, we thought we'd stop by and make sure we're all on the same page."

Casually, I reached in my pocket and pulled out an apple. Then my knife. I ignored the other man's whimpers and sliced a bit of skin off the fruit.

"Now there are several ways this can go down. Option number one: You agree to stay away from Clara. My buddy over there—" I pointed at Jonas with the edge of the blade. "—goes home and finishes jacking off to Ariana Grande videos."

"Fucking hell," Jonas mumbled under his breath. "You know I prefer Rihanna. Always liked a little ass."

"And I go home and pretend I didn't spend my morning in the shittiest part of the city waiting on you. But honestly, I'm feeling a little cranky and you don't look that bright. So we're going to stop wasting time and just get on with option number two."

"I didn't do anything, I swear," William mumbled, his face half pressed into the ground.

"I know. And we're going to make sure it stays that way."

I sliced off the last bit of skin and then took a bite out of the apple before handing the knife to Jonas.

William let out a low whimper. Once he realized that there was no way to escape Jonas's iron-tight grip, he went slack and a dark spot appeared on the front of his jeans.

I sighed. This was about to get messy.

———

Lucia

There was nothing like the sound of New York City in the morning.

Between the honking cars, the cursing and the never-ending rush of voices, just walking down the street was an assault to the senses. To everyone else it sounded like noise but to me it was a raw kind of symphony. It was a reminder that despite everything I'd been through, I was still here.

I was still here and *still* late.

Already I was out of breath as I hurried across the street, narrowly missing being hit by yet *another* cab. Unfortunately, I didn't do the delicate, charmingly breathless thing. Oh no. Sweating caused my overly curly hair to stick to my forehead and I didn't pant for air in a sexy, Marilyn Monroe kind of way, either. Instead it was more like gasping out my last breath. My job as a fashion assistant for *THE* up and coming fashion line didn't leave much time for anything unnecessary like sleeping, eating or going to the gym. I made a mental note to start taking better care of myself and filed it along with the ten thousand other things I did not have time for.

Dodging traffic counted as a workout, right?

My phone vibrated in the pocket of my skirt, the early morning humidity and my sweat already making the fabric stick to my legs. I pulled it out while trying to balance the tray of coffees I held with my other arm.

My handbag, a sample from a new designer that my friend JJ had given me just last week, banged against my hip as I trotted through the crosswalk while reading my texts.

JESSICA JONES

Where the hell are you? Adriana is losing her shit!

I groaned and walked faster. It had taken me longer than expected to get the coffee and I was cutting it way too close to being subject to one of Adriana's famous tirades. If I'd known I'd be running across town perhaps I would have worn something other than four-inch heels. Perhaps the adorable ballet flats I'd borrowed from the sample closet just last night. However, this was the only chance I'd have to stop by the records office today so I'd have to ignore my already throbbing feet.

When the Southampton records office told me they'd sent some of their archives to be held in the city, I'd assumed my research had hit a dead end. It had taken me years to piece together the information I had, and it had been a long shot anyway. After all, what did I expect?

I gulped down the huge knot that always rose in my throat when I thought about my brother. Rafe had been gone for six years now, and there were still days I woke up thinking I was fifteen years old again and my favorite person in the world would be in the kitchen making pancakes.

It was a knife to the gut every time my mind cleared and I remembered he was gone.

The details of that day were still not entirely clear, but I'd managed to piece together where the shooting had taken place and had used every spare moment over the past year to find out more about the owners of the property. It was a struggle to find anyone who remembered anything about it, which was strange in a town where everyone knew everyone.

But my tenacity had paid off because I'd gotten a name and had looked up the deed. It had been sold multiple times since then, and the local records office had only digitized their files the prior year. Somehow, some of the files related to the property had been sent off to archives accidentally.

I looked up at the sign over the drab gray building that housed the New York State Archives. My heartbeat danced in my chest. Whatever I found out today could either shed light on the worst day of my life or lead to another dead end. The heavy glass door opened and as I tried to move out of the way, the coffee tray tilted slightly, leaving a wet, brown spot on the front of my white silk blouse. *Awesome.*

There was no way Adriana would miss that.

"Sorry!"

I nodded absently as the man who'd been in such a hurry continued down the sidewalk without taking a second glance back.

"Good day to you, too."

I pulled the door open and let out a sigh of relief when I saw there was no one else inside. The gods of karma were taking pity on me finally.

"Hi, Brent. I got your message that you have something for me?"

The man behind the counter glanced up from his computer and smiled. Average height with dark hair and a nice smile, Brent was a nice guy. *Nice* seemed to be the only word I could think of to describe him, actually. He'd helped me fill out an official request the last time I was there and had promised to look in the archives personally. The fact that he'd flirted with me made me feel a little guilty. I had never been the bat-my-eyelashes type and I had no plans to start now. However, I was willing to take any help I could get at this point.

"Hi. How's your day going so far?"

I set the tray of coffee on the counter between us and hitched my bag higher on my shoulder. I gestured at the brown stain and grinned. "Amazing! As you can see."

He chuckled, although his eyes lingered on the swell of my breasts a bit longer than was strictly polite. I cleared my throat and his eyes finally snapped back up to mine.

"You said you found something?" I prodded.

"I did. Sorry it took me so long. I'm not sure what happened when the files were transferred, but a bunch of files were in the wrong boxes. Though, as luck would have it, I finally found the deed of sale from the time period you asked for. I made a copy of it for you."

He reached under the counter and pulled out a yellow, legal-size envelope. With shaking fingers, I pulled it across the counter toward me. I lifted the flap with the tip of my index finger but then closed it again. Tonight was soon enough to go down that rabbit hole.

"So, I was wondering if, maybe, I mean you might not be into it..."

My phone buzzed in my pocket again and I pulled it out, smiling apologetically at Brent who didn't even notice. I glanced down at the text message from JJ. It was marked as *Urgent*.

JESSICA JONES

Remember that painting on the wall of Rocco's when we were there for dinner last week? Adriana wants a swatch of Belgian linen in the exact same shade.

I glanced up at Brent, who was still droning on, before quickly typing an answer.

> Belgian Linen in a shade of blue that I barely
> remember. That's it? You can't tell me anything else?

JESSICA JONES

> You know how she is. Just get back here. Fast!

After stashing my phone back in my pocket, I picked up the envelope and threw it in my bag. It was only when I looked up again that I realized Brent was staring at me.

"So, what do you think?" he asked.

"Um, sounds good?" I had no idea what he'd been talking about and then instantly felt guilty for not listening, especially after he'd been so helpful. But I had to magically cross town in less than ten minutes and also conjure up a fabric that looked like something my boss had seen in a restaurant last week.

"I hate to cut and run but I'm late. So, I guess I'll see you later." I picked up the tray of coffee, wondering if I should take it back to the office before going back out for the linen swatches.

"Really?" Brent clapped his hands, the loud sound startling me so badly I almost dropped the coffee entirely. He ran a hand through his hair and let out a loud sigh as if he'd just run a marathon. "I mean, that's great. I've been wanting to try this place for a while and I think you'll really like it. So I'll pick you up at seven, if that's okay?"

Wait, what?

I laughed nervously when I realized exactly what I'd missed while engrossed in my phone. I forced a smile while Brent opened a new contact on his phone and then typed my number in. A minute later I was outside on the sidewalk with cold coffee and a date.

It wasn't the worst thing ever, to go out with a nice guy. Although, I had a feeling Noah wouldn't feel that way when he found out. I winced, imagining how that would go over. But he wasn't my daddy or my brother. Just a family friend who was way too bossy for his own good. Maybe I wouldn't tell him. Or I could text him. He couldn't yell at me over text message.

And what happens if you don't tell him?

I considered that for a moment. Just because he saw himself as a big brother type, didn't mean I had to give him access to my life.

Besides, what was the worst that could happen?

CHAPTER TWO

Noah

I watched the date from the comfort of my SUV. All the while silently fuming.

What the hell did Lucia think she was doing? My team hadn't vetted the guy. They didn't know anything about him. So far, she'd broken all of the dating rules I'd given her.

For the first date, always meet at a designated location. And of course, she'd let this doofus pick her up for their date. As if I hadn't told her a million times to do the exact opposite.

I'd also been very clear not to get in the car with strange men. So that was rule one and rule two broken right off the bat. As if I hadn't trained her on how to be careful and what to watch out for. But *oh no*, Lucia didn't listen to shit. Every time I turned around, there she was, careening headfirst into trouble.

Maybe she didn't see her date as a potential threat, but dammit she needed to be more careful. What the hell did she even know about this guy?

"What the hell kind of name is Brent anyway?"

I hadn't even realized that I'd spoken out loud, until the voice in my comm unit laughed. "Last I checked, Brent is a perfectly normal name. Lots of guys have it."

I barely restrained a growl. "Matthias, when I want your input, I'll give it to you."

There was a chuckle on the other end of the line. I made a mental note to give Matthias some really horrible surveillance duty for the next month. This wasn't funny. This was Lucia. They all cared about her well-being.

Maybe you more than the others.

Yeah, so what? I cared about her. And maybe it wasn't the easiest thing in the world watching her date loser after loser. But it was my job, no strike that, it was my *responsibility* to look after her. I owed Rafe that much. But how the hell was I supposed to look out for her when she kept making it so damn difficult? Lucia was obstinate, infuriating, pigheaded, and—

Beautiful.

No. She was like a little sister to me. Yet somehow my dick couldn't seem to get with that program lately. More and more frequently, some very *unsisterly* thoughts wormed their way into my consciousness.

"Matthias, give me something on this Brent guy. Aren't you supposed to be some kind of super-hacker?"

"You better believe it. But, there's nothing on him. Everything is normal. Boring. Most interesting thing about this guy is he likes adventure sports. He skydives, bungee jumps, that sort of thing. Does some triathlons. Maybe he's some kind of adrenaline junkie. But there's nothing else on him. No flags. He lives here in New York in the East Village. No roommates. Rent isn't exorbitant. Works for the city. No large withdrawals of cash. Good credit. As far as I can tell, he's clean but that's just his electronic trail. Maybe you're right on this one and he's a little too clean. I mean, there's not even an online dating profile on him. To me, that's weird. Who doesn't have an online dating profile? Tinder, Bumble, Hinge?"

I chuckled and then lifted my binoculars again. Lucia was laughing at something. So Brent thought he was a comedian, huh? What the hell was so damn funny? There was too much interference to use the boom mic, otherwise I'd know.

Brent reached across the table and took Lucia's hand, and I nearly chipped a tooth from grinding my teeth so hard. I could see Lucia's eyes go wide. Was that surprise? I hoped it was disgust.

Did she actually like this guy?

My gut clenched at the thought. *Perfect, just what I need. Lucia liking this fucking idiot.*

It wasn't that she hadn't dated before. She had. Mostly in college. Most of those guys had merely needed a strong reminder to mind their Ps & Qs with her. But this guy, this guy was random—unknown. Which meant it would take more work to scare him off. But I was up for the challenge.

Lucia deserved to be happy, just with somebody vetted and approved. After the shit she had survived in her life? The girl needed some happy endings.

Fuck. Not happy endings.

I groaned and turned my attention back to the restaurant. Brent raised a hand and signaled their server. Shit, they were leaving. The real trick was guessing where they were going. I'd put a tracker on her phone, so if I guessed wrong, I could always follow. But what if something happened to her before I could get there?

"Matthias, turn on the listening device on her phone. I'm heading to the house in case that's where they go."

There was a beat of silence. I could almost hear Matthias's silent condemnation. "The thing is, Noah, she's not going to like that."

"The thing is, Matthias, I don't care," I muttered using the same singsong tone.

Yeah, I knew I sounded like an asshole. But this was Lucia. If she wasn't going to take care of herself, that left it to me to do it for her. We had one simple rule: I vetted all her dates. And sometimes, without her knowing, I'd scare them off. But that was really beside the point. It wasn't my fault she couldn't pick a decent guy.

I made a left turn on 10th Ave, right near the USB Theater, then I sped through Chelsea before making a left on 28th Street, heading toward Chelsea Piers. I made a right at the stop sign, turning onto her quiet street. The street was lined with lofts and new apartment high-rises, all boasting a name with Arms, or Manor.

Before she'd moved, me and my team researched the building's owners and the neighborhood crime rate. Everything to make sure she would be safe. Well as safe as she could be in Manhattan. It also didn't hurt that I watched her every move.

Not in some creepy, stalkery way, but more like a big brother way. *Sort of...*

Never mind that. I drove past her building and around the back to the lot I paid for specifically for these kinds of situations. Yeah, so maybe I also paid most of her rent. She thought she'd gotten extremely lucky with a rent-controlled apartment in the heart of the city. In reality, I paid most of the tab. I also paid for two parking spots. Not that Lucia had a car. But in case she ever got one, she'd have somewhere safe to park it. Somewhere right next to the damn elevator. I paid almost as much to secure those spots as I paid for the apartment.

My spot was in the darkened shadows somewhere she'd never think to look. I didn't mind though, because in most scenarios, I was the thing that went bump in the night.

"Matthias, talk to me. Where are they headed?"

"They're stopping for ice cream at Benny's then he's going to take her home."

Okay, so I had about ten minutes. Benny's was a local mom-and-pop ice-cream place about five blocks away. I jogged along the parking garage to the side stairs. While I'd insisted that she get a building with a doorman, there was no accounting for the additional exits and entrances into the building. Luckily, this one was exit only. Only confirmed residents had keys. Unfortunately, even your average guy could pick these locks, and I happened to be better than average.

In less than a minute, I was through the door and took the back stairway up to her apartment. She'd listened to me and employed the deadbolt. Problem for her was I had a key.

In seconds I turned off her security alarm. Well, at least she'd turned it on this time. Lucia had been so against it in the first place. At least she'd finally realized that a woman living alone needed *some* security. I glanced around and noted that she'd changed a few things. Was that a new pillow?

Matthias spoke into my earpiece. "You've got about five, boss. They've stopped outside the apartment. I'm going to go ahead and turn off the mic on her phone now if that's okay with you."

More judgment from the youngest member of the team. Whatever. I'd deal with that later. Now, the real question was where to wait for her.

What if she brought the guy in here?

Oh hell no. The mere idea of it had me gripping the edge of the countertop. She had better be coming in alone.

Damn it, this was their first date. She was supposed to make the guy twist in the wind for a bit first.

How many one-night stands have you had?

No. I was not going to think about that. It was different. That's all. Besides, Lucia was a good kid. And there was no way Nonna DeMarco would approve.

I'd give her a few minutes to run the guy off herself, and then the two of us were going to have another conversation about dating and personal safety.

She couldn't really be interested in this guy, right? He was boring. *Unlike you?* I grimaced. Yeah well, she didn't need to date anyone like me either. If she did, I would have to employ more drastic measures to keep her safe.

No. Lucia needed a nice guy, but someone more interesting than a records keeper.

Okay, if I was going to give her the chance to send Brent packing by herself, I needed to wait somewhere other than the living room. If she caught sight of me first, and if she was carrying that Taser I'd given her for Christmas, I might end up as fried toast. I jogged down the hallway and turned left into her bedroom, gently closing the door behind me.

I hopped onto her bed, bouncing slightly and leaned back against the pillows. *I've always loved how girly she is,* I thought, enjoying the scent of her perfume in the room and looking around at the four-poster bed, the soft colors, and all the ruffled pillows. I also loved that when she completely lost her temper her curls went flying and her eyes snapped with anger.

It was probably why I enjoyed pissing her off so much.

Something caught my eye as I lay back against the pillows, readjusting them for my comfort. Her bottom drawer was open.

Do not open it. Leave it be. She won't appreciate — Oh fuck it.

I pulled it open and took out my phone, shining the flashlight directly inside.

"Well, well, well. What do we have here?"

CHAPTER THREE

Lucia

This is a date. You should be having fun.

I fixed my lipstick in the mirror at Benny's. I didn't need to use the bathroom. I was stalling.

Stalling for time.

Stalling for composure.

Whatever.

I wasn't sure what I was doing. Brent was really trying, but I was giving him a half-assed date.

It wasn't like he wasn't interesting. He was. Yeah, okay, maybe he had no edge. But, there was more to life than edge, right? The guy skydived for the love of God. I should be totally into this. He ran triathlons, so that meant a great body. In theory, anyway.

Then why are you hiding in the bathroom? I swallowed hard.

I fluffed my curls, gently winding a couple of the loose strands around my finger to give them more bounce. Next, I fixed a nonexistent smudge of eyeliner.

Get back out there. He won't bite.

Maybe if he did you'd be more into this.

Stop it. Good Catholic girls don't want to be bitten.

No, but fun *Catholic girls do.*

What was wrong with me? He was cute. And God knew I needed

a life. Hell, make that a sex life. It wasn't like I never had any other takers. I'd dated some. But no one who interested me in that deep primal way.

Except for Noah.

And go ahead and mark that under, *Never. Going. To. Happen.* Noah had been my brother's best friend and fashioned himself responsible for me. He was also the biggest pain in the ass I'd ever met. He was always there, invading my life, my mind, my decisions — my family.

I couldn't throw a stone without running into him or one of the men who worked for him. Ever since Rafe had died, he'd made himself my surrogate big brother. Problem was, as sexy as he was, most of the time I found it hard to look at him in a brotherly way.

Not going to happen so I needed to get that out of my head.

Besides, Brent was...great. He was the kind of guy I *should* want. He was the kind of guy I *should* be thinking about. Not some guy who was too sexy, too cocky, and too damn good-looking.

Everything about Noah Blake screamed, *Danger, Will Robinson, danger.* He was the kind of guy that I didn't know how to handle. The kind of guy who wanted a woman who knew what she was doing. And I was not that woman.

Forget about him. Focus on the guy who wants you. The guy sitting outside.

With a deep breath, I squared my shoulders. I could do this. I could play sexy vixen. For once, I didn't want to be the good girl. For once, I didn't want to be the one who was overlooked.

I wanted to feel sexy. I wanted to be *wanted*.

I slid my gaze down to my purse and the manila envelope sticking out of the corner. *Are you sure you want him? Or do you just want what he can give you?* Yes, I'd agreed to go out with Brent, because well, he'd helped me. But he *was* good-looking. And interesting.

Who are you trying to convince?

Yes, I needed the information he'd gotten for me. If it would help me track down who owned that house, and eventually my brother's murderer, then I was going to take it. Because that was all I'd ever wanted. Some answers about what happened to Rafe. I deserved those answers.

More importantly, my grandmother deserved closure.

Rafe had always looked out for me. If something had happened to me, he would have torn the world apart looking for justice.

But for the first time in a long time, I'd accepted that I couldn't make Rafe my whole life. He'd been gone for six years. It was time to move on. The envelope could wait. Right now, I had a date and an ice cream waiting. Besides, Rafe wouldn't begrudge me a life. He may not be so thrilled about the *kind* of life I wanted, but he'd want me to be happy. Maybe Brent could give that to me.

Not likely. He's not Noah.

Dammit. I had to get Noah Blake off the brain. Lately it had gotten worse. I'd started to imagine heated glances from him. Whenever I was at his office, and I caught him looking at me, I would swear I saw...longing in his eyes. But that couldn't be right. Maybe more of an intensity? What the hell did I know?

All I knew was every time I caught him looking at me like that, I thought about using one of those toys JJ got me as a gag gift. The ones in my bedside drawer that no one knew about. The same ones that I put in a shoebox under my bed every time the cleaning lady came by.

I still flushed at the thought of the ridiculous party favor I'd gotten at that bachelorette party the prior month. The thing was insane. No one on earth was that big. It just wasn't possible. Though it wasn't like I had anything to go on.

If you want something to go on, stop hiding in the bathroom.

Checking my appearance one more time, I forced a smile on my face. I was going to do this. I was going to go out there and have a good time and let Brent take me home. Then I was going to let him kiss me good night.

For once, instead of overthinking it, I was going to see where things went.

More resolute, I pushed open the door and grinned when I saw Brent standing there with two strawberry ice cream cones. He handed me one, and when some melted on my finger, he took my hand and gently licked it off.

I fought the immediate urge to snatch my hand back. *Relax. He's trying to be cute. Not creepy.*

"Come on, let's head back," I said. We'd opted to park his car and just walk back to my place.

As we walked and ate our ice cream, the balmy summer breeze lifting a few of my curls, he said "I'm glad you agreed to go out with me. Although you should know, I wasn't above begging."

I took another lick of my ice cream. "You're sweet."

He shrugged. "Not that sweet. I've seen you walk by the Café on fourth before. You can imagine my surprise when you walked into my office. I had to take a shot and ask you out."

I wasn't used to quite so many compliments. Oh sure, *at first* guys were interested, but then something always happened to make them cool off. Most of my dates never went past date one. I was starting to think I was really bad at this.

JJ said I just needed to date a few more frogs. Though, it seemed to me that I'd had more than my fair share of them.

In the five blocks it took to reach my apartment, Brent regaled me with stories of his last bungee jumping trip.

"Okay, if I agree to go bungee jumping, where do you suggest I jump first?"

His answer was instant. "Over the Zambezi River in Zimbabwe, hands down."

I laughed. "Wait, I have to go all the way to Zimbabwe for my very first jump?"

"There's nothing like it with Victoria Falls thundering behind you. It'll be awesome."

"Okay, maybe I'll book that trip. But maybe, just maybe, we could try something closer to home first."

We reached my apartment just as I finished the last bit of my cone. I shifted on my feet nervously. This was it. The moment I was waiting for. Do or die. Well okay, not do or die, but close.

Brent stepped closer. "Thank you for agreeing to go out with me. And just so you know, I'm going to kiss you in a second. But first, I want to ask you out again. Don't worry we'll take it slow on the thrill rides. But I do want to see you. So what do you say...go out with me again?"

No. "I'd like that."

Despite everything in my body telling me that this was not the guy, I was deliberately ignoring it. He was nice. I couldn't wait for perfect. Sometimes nice and good-looking would just have to do.

He leaned forward, shifting his hand to cup my cheek, and stroking it gently. When he dipped his head down, I had to force myself to hold still. He gently brushed his lips over mine. His lips were firm but undemanding. As if he was waiting for my permission.

He pulled back with a smile. "I'd like to be a gentleman and walk you upstairs if that's okay?"

Upstairs? As in, inside my apartment? My heart thundered but not from desire. More like pure unadulterated nerves.

I could do this, right? Just because I didn't feel anything when he kissed me, it didn't mean anything. Maybe I just needed more time to get into it. This was the kind of guy that most girls would be drooling over. What was wrong with me?

I took his hand and smiled up at him. "Come on up."

The elevator ride was tense. Or maybe it was just tense to me because I had no idea what was going to happen. More kissing probably. But I had no idea how to do any of what came next. All I had to go on were a few heavy make out sessions and most of those were in high school.

JJ kept telling me I needed to have a one-night stand to just drop the V card already. And that way, I'd be a lot less nervous about it. Maybe she was right. Brent seemed to actually like me, so he was far better than a one-night stand.

Except, you're totally not into this.

Okay, that was beside the point. When the elevator doors chimed, a shiver stole up my neck, making the fine hairs stand on end. With a wan smile, I led the way to my apartment, pausing at the door. There were those shivers again. Like an alarm. Like a warning. Maybe just nerves?

"This is me." Turning the key, I let myself in and went to turn off the alarm, but it was already off.

I frowned. My brain mentally rewound the day's events. I could see myself arming it. Or had I? Was my brain just replacing a memory from yesterday for today?

I closed the door behind us. "Would you like a drink?"

Brent shook his head. "No. All I want is you."

———

This was the part where I was supposed to feel the butterflies. Every brush of his fingers was supposed to feel as if I had electricity coursing through me. This was the part where I moaned into his embrace, right?

Except none of that was happening. Not even when he pulled me close, pressing our bodies together.

This was ... *nice*. Perfectly pleasant. Maybe even a little warm. Warm was good, right?

Head in the game DeMarco.

I started slowly, leading him back toward the bedroom. Maybe if I got him there I'd get more in the mood. I'd have all the nice-smelling girly things in there which hopefully would feel more romantic.

He easily followed my lead. He made a moaning sound deep in his throat, and I only wished I wanted to make such a sound. A tiny annoying voice spoke up from deep in the recesses of my mind.

Are you sure you want to do this? You want your first time to just be ... fine?

No. I wanted hot. I wanted sexy. I wanted to tingle. I wanted to feel like a supermodel who'd found my accompanying rock star. But not everybody got a rock star. Sometimes nice was good.

I opened the door to the bedroom, and he continued to kiss me. But the more his tongue slid into my mouth, licking inside, the more I wanted to turn my head. I drew back, angling my head away slightly. He took that to mean that I wanted him to kiss my neck. With a little groan, he slid his lips along my jaw, then the column of my throat. But I was having a hard time getting into the mood.

All I kept thinking about was if I was doing this right. And getting out of my shoes because they were pinching my toes. And those growling noises he was making were actually kind of funny. When had I left my blinds open? While I was at it, I really needed to get some damn groceries.

This is not what you're supposed to be thinking about.

There was something wrong with me. Here was a perfectly nice guy wanting to rock my world and I was thinking about my damn blinds and groceries.

I bet you wouldn't feel this way with Noah.

Just like that, heat raced through my bloodstream and my breath caught. Just thinking about him was enough to make my skin tight and itchy. Those butterflies I'd been concerned about, there they were, fluttering rapidly inside, making something deep in my core pull tight.

Still, I fought it. There was no way I was going to think about Noah at a time like this. But, maybe that wasn't the end of the world. It was just a fantasy. My brain latched on to what my body was craving. And the image of him in my mind formed and solidified.

Suddenly, it wasn't Brent kissing my throat, it was Noah. But his lips weren't quite as soft. They were firm. Sure. Knew exactly what he wanted and exactly how to get the right response from me.

There was no thinking about anything else when I was with him. Only the sensation of being in his arms. The sensation of my heart hammering so fast it nearly beat out of my chest. The feeling I sometimes got when he looked at me and all my bones felt like jelly. That was how it was meant to be with Noah.

A little dangerous. Definitely bad for you. But oh so good.

I slid my hands into Noah's hair, tugging a little. He muttered a soft curse against my throat, his hands holding me flush against him. Through his jeans I could feel the pulse of his erection against my center.

Yes. This was much more like it.

His kisses grew more frantic. His hands less patient. They skimmed over my hips with a strong grip. Before sliding his thumbs up over my belly and over my ribcage, just under my —

"Okay, Romeo. I think that's enough."

I squeaked, then jumped away from Noah — err, Brent. *Right Brent.* My date.

Noah, was on my bed.

"Wha–What the hell are you doing here, Noah?"

He lay back against the pillows. His feet were on my bed with his shoes on, I noticed with irritation. He looked comfortable. Completely relaxed, as if he belonged there.

Wouldn't you like that?

"Well, it looks like I'm just in time to interrupt."

Brent stared between me and Noah, then back again. "I thought you said you didn't have a boyfriend."

I turned my attention to him and placed a reassuring hand on his arm. "I don't. The intruder on my bed is my wannabe big brother. *And he was just leaving.*"

Noah shook his head. "No such luck, princess. You don't know this dude from a can of paint. We had a deal. You let me check out anyone you want to go out with. You seem to have forgotten that."

"We never had a deal. You just seem to think you can dictate to me. You can't!"

Brent interjected. "I should probably be going."

I gripped his forearm harder. "No. Stay. *He* is going. Aren't you Noah?"

Noah grinned, his devilish smile bringing a mischievous twinkle to his eyes. Looking at the two of them in close proximity, I could see clearly that there was no competition. Noah had dark sooty lashes that framed those intense moss-colored eyes, high cheekbones, a straight Roman nose, and full lips that tilted crookedly when he smiled. The man was gorgeous and he knew it. Which was a problem, because he often used it to get what he wanted.

Brent, in comparison, also had dark hair, but not as dark as Noah's. It also didn't fall in disarray where some parts looked styled and other parts unkempt, but mostly looking like he'd just rolled out of bed. Or he'd rolled out of bed *with someone*. Brent's eyes were a pale blue. Kind. He was cute in that boy-next-door kind of way. He didn't look like he belonged in a fashion magazine, not like Noah did.

Feeling a little uncharitable for comparing Brent so unfavorably with Noah, I had to concede that he was at least tall. Not as tall as Noah, but few men could compare to his towering height. Besides it wasn't about looks, or height, or charisma, anyway.

Annoyed, I closed my eyes, hoping maybe this was all a bad dream, but when I opened them again he was still there. With Noah in the room, it was hard to breathe. He dominated everyone and sucked up all the air, silently pulling me toward him with his gravitational force alone. It was like poor Brent wasn't even there.

"Now, Lucia, I know you'd like to think you're in charge right now. But you're not. You don't know this guy. And you invited him back to your place? I thought I taught you better than that."

Brent tried to make an escape again. "Lucia, why don't you deal with this guy? We'll try this again later."

"No. You're not going anywhere."

Noah pushed himself to a seated position on the edge of the bed.

"Oh yes he is. Because you and I need to discuss what the hell this is for." He held up the gift from the bachelorette party.

Oh no. Oh no. Oh no.

In that moment, I prayed to every saint my grandmother had ever forced me to pray to. Prayed to the Virgin Mary then to Jesus. Heck, for good measure I added Buddha in there too. Just in case. But nothing happened. The ground did not open and swallow me.

Instead, I stood with my hand on Brent's arm, staring at Noah as he held up the largest purple dildo I'd ever seen in my life.

Brent's mouth fell open but no sound came out. As mortified as I was, I couldn't really blame him. The stupid thing was over a foot long, and thick. Really, really thick. Like thicker than a cucumber. I'd certainly never used the thing. It was a gag gift.

"How dare you go through my things!" I squeaked.

Noah shrugged. "I didn't go through your things. The drawer was open. The thing was practically sticking out of it. Making its escape."

Brent shifted his gaze to me.

"That's not mine," I whispered. "I m-mean it is but I've never used it. It's a gag gift from a bachelorette party." I swung my gaze to Noah. *"Put that down."*

"Not a chance. I mean, this thing is fascinating. I'm no stranger to toys myself. As far as I'm concerned, they can always enhance the situation. I'm not one of those guys that feel jealous or threatened. Matter of fact, I'm all for a little solo play. But this thing..." He held it up and shook it around. "Even I've never seen anything like it. And I've had a lot of practice."

He turned his attention to Brent. "No disrespect to you, but I don't think you can live up to this. It vibrates *and* rotates! Even I feel a little frightened by this thing."

Screw the ground opening up and swallowing me whole. Just shoot me now. That would end this quickly. Shoot me. Send my little behind to heaven. Because I was done. Noah was bending the dildo around as it wiggled in his hands. He pushed the button, and the damn thing rotated on its own, making a whirring sound. *Oh God.* Could this get any worse?

Brent fixed his gaze on me. "I'm going to go."

"No, please don't go."

I lunged and grabbed at the dildo, tugging when Noah refused to release it. The silicone material bent in ways I was sure weren't intended as we fought over it. This was easily one of the most undignified moments of my life, but I just couldn't take it anymore. Noah's smug face as he watched me struggling to get a better grip on the wiggling, gyrating piece of plastic only made it worse.

"Ugh, let go!"

In a fit of sudden anger, I kicked him in the shin. In his surprise, Noah let go of his end of the toy. The next few seconds would forever play in my mind in slow motion as I watched the toy fly end over end and hit Brent directly in the face.

"Ouch!"

I covered my mouth in horror as the toy fell to his feet. The silence that followed was only broken by the sounds of the still-running toy, wiggling over the carpet.

Noah guffawed. "My bad. Did I get it in your mouth? Don't worry, it doesn't mean anything. What's a little dick in the mouth between friends, am I right?"

"I have to go."

"No, wait!"

But Brent didn't wait. All I could hear were his footsteps as they echoed on the hardwood floors, down the hall, into my living room, then kitchen, and then the front door opening and slamming shut behind him.

With a deep breath, I whirled on Noah.

"I swear to God I will make you pay if it's the last thing I do. You are going to pay so hard. What the hell is wrong with you? *You are completely shameless!*"

He grinned as he stood and then knelt to grab the toy, pushing the button on the dildo again. "I'm looking forward to it. This is the best laugh I've had in months."

He moved toward me, his gait smooth and predatory. He paused about a foot away, and I could smell the scent of sandalwood. I fought the urge to inhale deeply.

When he leaned close, I held my breath.

"Next time, *I* check out the guy. And pick somebody tougher. If he'd stood up to me, I would have respected him more."

I couldn't help it. Frustration was taking over as the blood boiled under my skin. And the urge to hit him overwhelmed me.

"I hate you," I whispered between clenched teeth.

He took a step, bringing us so close we were almost touching. When he leaned over me again, I nervously licked my lips as my belly flipped.

His voice was low and sultry as he whispered. "No. You don't."

CHAPTER FOUR

Noah

It shouldn't have hurt so much to hear her say those words.

I hate you.

Especially when I knew it was just a reaction to finding me in her room. But even knowing that, it cut through me with all the precision of a knife and I was left with the curious sensation of a widening in my chest.

"You could never hate me, Princess."

Lucia's eyes flashed and I would have laughed if I wasn't afraid she might actually try to attack. There wasn't much she could do to me, but more than likely she'd hurt *herself* in the attempt and I couldn't allow that. Despite what she thought, everything I ever did was to protect her. Especially keeping her away from guys like the one I'd found attempting to suck off her face just now.

Disgust had me glancing down at the monstrously large dildo in my hand.

"Did you really think that guy was going to get the job done if you're used to this?"

Lucia screeched and whacked me right in the middle of the chest. "I told you it's not even mine! Not really. It was a gift."

"What the hell kind of friend gives you a dinosaur dildo as a gift?"

"None of your business."

She tried to grab it, stretching on her toes as I raised my arm overhead. The position put her off balance and I instinctively held out an arm to steady her when her legs gave out. Her breasts crushed against my chest, and the soft curves I'd tried so hard to ignore were suddenly front and center in my brain, along with the enticing summer scent of her hair. She placed a hand on my waist as she straightened, and I knew a solid sixty seconds of true fear as all my blood shot below my belt.

I could not throw wood around Lucia. *Stand down. Stand down.* I chanted the order, praying the relevant pieces of anatomy would get the message in time.

Lucia took advantage of my distraction and jumped, managing to snatch the dildo from my hand while simultaneously fulfilling every late-night fantasy I'd ever had about her.

"And for god's sake put it down!" She threw the still-rotating dildo on the bed before turning back to me, murder in her eyes.

"Okay, okay. I was just playing around."

Lucia pointed to the door. "Outside. Now."

I backed up, allowing her to push me out of the room and into the hallway. The evidence of what I'd only been able to hear earlier was all around us. The sky-high stilettos she always wore kicked off by the front door. Her jacket was discarded in the middle of the floor, torn off in a fit of passion, perhaps? I ground my jaw at the reminder of that guy's hands all over her. He wasn't anywhere near good enough for her.

And you are?

I shook off the thought. No one was good enough for Lucia, especially not me, but it was the least I could do to help her weed out the obvious losers. It was what Rafe would have done.

Hell, Rafe probably would have thrown that guy over the balcony for pawing his sister that way. Seriously, it was their first date and that asshole had actually thought a rushed screw was appropriate? Lucia was the kind of woman who deserved flowers and chocolates and candlelight. Not some frantic fuck against the wall.

Though shit, just the idea was fucking hot: Lucia, sweaty and panting, me behind her lifting her skirt—oh and what do you know, my erection was back in full force.

I was so caught up in my thoughts, I barely noticed where she was pushing me until she had the front door open and I was in the hallway.

"Give me back my key." She held out her hand, her lips pursed into the most adorable pout.

I knew she was really pissed but couldn't resist tormenting her a little bit.

"Do you really think I need a key to get in here?"

Her deep breath told me how close I was to getting smacked again. But then suddenly her face changed and she shook her head sadly.

"You just don't get it, Noah. This is my life and no one is going to stop me from living it. Not even you. I have to grow up sometime."

"I'm not trying to stop you from living. I'm just trying to keep you safe."

"Safe, I understand. But this...this is too much. You're out of control. I have the right to my privacy and having you show up in the middle of my bedroom is kind of a buzzkill to my sex life, you know? So maybe next time we'll go to his place."

The fuck there would be a next time. I'd kill the asshole first.

There you go with your killer instinct again.

"Lucia...Don't do anything crazy."

The thought of her at some guy's place, possibly somewhere I couldn't get to her if things went wrong, made me feel like I was having a heart attack. I put a hand over my heart to make sure it wasn't actually going to jump out of my chest the way it felt.

"Crazy like showing up in someone else's bedroom holding a dildo? I don't think you should be giving me advice in this particular situation. Although, I suppose I should thank you for finding that for me. Since Brent and I were interrupted, I guess I'll need it tonight."

Before I could process her words, the door was coming at me. I took a step back mere seconds before it would have hit me in the face.

I stood there for a few more minutes, listening to the sounds of her moving around the apartment before I finally left. She was upset right now, but she'd come around. She always did. Although I couldn't deny that something about tonight felt different. Not only that she'd actually stood up to me and thrown me out, but what she'd said about using that sex toy later.

She had to have been joking about that, right?

There was no way Lucia was that kinky. And, oh so helpfully, my brain offered an image of her, on her bed, legs splayed, head thrown back in ecstasy as that dildo worked its magic.

Fuck.

As I was descending the stairs, I hit the first speed dial on my cell phone. Matthias answered immediately.

"Hey, did you kill the surveillance on Lucia's place yet?"

There was a moment of silence before Matthias responded. "You mean did we just see you get your ass handed to you? Nope, no idea what you're talking about."

I cursed. I could hear the muffled laughter coming through the line which told me Matthias wasn't alone in the office. Great. This was what I got for hiring a bunch of anti-social loners. They didn't have anywhere else to be on a Friday night either.

There was no way Jonas was ever going to let me live this one down.

"Whatever. I'll be in the office in a few."

I hung up and shoved my phone back in my pocket. Once I reached the parking lot, I looked up to Lucia's window. I watched as her shadow moved around the apartment before the light in the front went dark. Over the years, I'd been so many things to her as she grew up. Surrogate big brother. Protector. A shoulder to cry on.

But I'd never felt like I was on the outside looking in to her life.

I'd spent years knowing this time was coming. That there would be a day when she'd meet someone, a man without screwed-up ethics and a boatload of secrets. Someone who could love her the way she deserved and give her the things she needed. All the things I couldn't do. I thought I was ready for when that day approached, but I had no idea how fast the years would go by.

I have to grow up sometime, she'd said, with no idea what those words meant to me.

Yeah, I thought, *but not yet*. I couldn't bear to lose her yet.

———

Lucia

I stood in the middle of my living room for a moment, trying to process what had just happened. I rubbed my temples. Maybe if I pretended it hadn't happened this would all go away. But the evidence was all around: my jacket on the floor and my lucky shoes by the door, the ones I only wore when I had a date.

My lucky stilettos hadn't been so lucky tonight.

I groaned before stooping to pick up the shoes. Things had definitely not gone the way I'd expected. Poor Brent. All he'd done was have the misfortune of asking me out. How was he to know I had a crazy, over-protective pseudo-stalker who'd show up and cock-block him before he even got to second base?

I winced, imagining what he must think of me now. I hadn't even wanted to go on the date at first so I couldn't consider it too much of a loss, but damn, it was still embarrassing. Well, at least I didn't have to figure out a way to let him down easy.

Noah had taken care of that for me, I thought bitterly.

I cleaned up the living room and cut out all the lights before heading back to my room. My face flamed at the sight of the large purple dildo on the bed. It was still running, the lights on the base blinking furiously as it moved around on the comforter. I picked it up, and after mashing a few random buttons, I finally managed to turn it off.

Just looking at it made me angry all over again.

The anger had nowhere to go and because it made me want to scream, I picked up my phone and hit the second speed dial. The fact that Noah had programmed himself in on the first speed dial annoyed me all over again.

JJ answered on the first ring. "Why are you calling me? You're supposed to be on a date."

I sighed. "I *was* on a date. He's gone now."

"Already? Please tell me you got laid at least?"

"I was close. Then Noah showed up."

JJ was silent for a moment. Then she exploded in laughter. "You have got to be fucking *kidding* me? Noah showed up in the middle of your date? Wait, go back and tell me everything."

I settled myself on top of my comforter as I relayed the story. By the time I got to Noah showing up in my room and the dildo hitting Brent, JJ was laughing so hard she was wheezing. As much as I wanted to stay mad, I couldn't after retelling the story. It truly was the most ridiculous thing ever.

"So, he got nailed in the face, no pun intended." There was a pause as JJ tried to rein in her laughter. "Then he just ran out?"

I felt a sudden burst of shame on Brent's behalf. He really had just ditched me without looking back. Although considering how menacing Noah could appear at times, I couldn't really blame him. That was a battle he couldn't possibly win.

"What else could he do? Noah was in my room, *on my bed,* like a jealous ex-boyfriend. You know how he gets."

"Yes, I do. And so do you. Which makes me wonder why you don't just bone the guy already and put us all out of our virtual blue balls."

My friend's words brought a rush of conflicting emotions. The usual denial mixed with an uncharacteristic blast of heat at the thought of getting naked with Noah. I wasn't sure when my thoughts about him began to change. One day he'd been good old Noah, the surrogate big brother who annoyed me one minute and delighted me the next.

Then one day I'd looked at him and everything was different. He was suddenly the smartest, most handsome, most masculine presence I'd ever been exposed to, and everything inside of me had taken notice all at once. It had made me feel both awakened and unsettled to discover that I could feel these things for someone who had been a part of my life for so long.

"It's not like that between us. You know that."

JJ made a rude sound. "So you keep saying, but I have eyes. That man is insanely sexy. There is no way you can be exposed to that kind of grade-A testosterone all the time and not feel anything. I don't believe it."

"Well, believe it. He's like another brother."

"I guess."

JJ didn't sound convinced, which only increased my agitation. Noah had never looked at me as anything other than the annoying young girl that he had to look out for. I was an obligation, a tie to a former life that he'd probably rather forget. As soon as I had the thought, I was ashamed. Noah had idolized my brother Rafe, and I didn't really think he wanted to forget about him. It would just be nice not to feel like an old debt that he was paying off.

"He only does this because he feels like it's what Rafe would do if he were here. But this time he's gone too far. He can't just break into my apartment whenever he wants."

"Well, it sounds like it's time for a little payback."

JJ was known for her creative and diabolical thinking so if she had a plan, I was all in. It would be nice to feel like I had the upper hand with Noah for once. Maybe even give him a little taste of what it was like to have someone butting into your life at the most inopportune moment.

"What do you mean by payback?"

JJ chuckled in a way that told me she already had an idea. "I have just the thing."

Immediately, I had second thoughts. Did I really want to start a war with Noah? Not that I ever thought for even a moment that he would hurt me, but JJ had a tendency to be a little...inappropriate. Following her advice for payback would be like adding gasoline to a fire that was already dangerously close to raging out of control.

Then I got a mental image of Noah holding that stupid dildo and waving it around. I wrinkled my nose. No, he'd brought this all on himself.

"What do you have in mind?"

JJ chuckled. "Do you have anything against public nudity?"

———

Later that night, I was snuggled under the covers when I finally remembered the envelope. It was hard to believe, but in all the hustle and excitement of having a date and then the showdown with Noah, I'd completely forgotten that I might have finally found the information I'd been searching for these past few months.

Throwing the comforter back, I swung my legs over the edge of the mattress and stood. My handbag was still out front where I'd left it on the couch. I walked slowly, navigating the apartment in the dark. My fingers fumbled over the lamp on the side table until I was able to turn the switch, and the room filled with light. My bag was still right where I'd left it. It was kind of amusing that it was still in the same spot after the wild events of the evening.

The thought brought back everything that had happened with Noah. *What the hell was wrong with him lately?* He'd always been over the top, but this was somehow different. I ignored the nagging sense that it was different because *I* was different. The same things that wouldn't have bothered me in the past were suddenly excruciating in light of the annoying, completely inappropriate feelings I'd been having whenever he was around.

Just let it go already.

I slung my handbag over my arm and then turned the light off before retracing my steps back to my room. The envelope had gotten slightly smashed under my wallet and keys so I gently smoothed it with my fingers before taking it back to bed with me. Under the covers, I hesitated before pulling up the flap. Now that the moment was here, part of me wondered if it wasn't better to leave the past in the past.

When I'd first started searching for more details about my brother's murder, I'd still been completely mired in grief. My mind had been focused solely on getting answers and filling in the gaps that my own memory refused to fill. Now that so much time had passed, I'd finally settled in to a life of my own and things were good.

Did I really want to know what had happened that day? What if I couldn't handle it? It wasn't as if knowing who was responsible would bring my brother back.

But it would give me some closure, wouldn't it? At least I'd know why. Even if it wouldn't bring Rafe back, it would mean something to me to know the people responsible for my brother's death had been brought to justice. I wasn't as much of an idiot as my brother and Noah had assumed. I was aware that he hadn't always lived his life on the straight and narrow. But no matter what he'd done, he didn't deserve to die the way he had. No one deserved that.

Wiping away the tears that had spilled over on my cheek, I lifted the flap of the envelope and pulled out the piece of paper inside. It was a copy of a deed of sale.

HoloCorp, Inc.

My heartbeat stuttered for a moment and then hammered against my ribcage. It was just a name, but it was more than I'd ever had before. And this time I had exactly what I needed to follow the breadcrumbs.

More like exactly *who* I needed, I thought as I grabbed my cell phone and scrolled through my contacts list. When I found the name I was looking for, I tapped the screen before I could change my mind.

"Lucia? Is everything okay?"

I smiled. Matthias always sounded worried when I spoke to him, something I found endearing. It was interesting that the same words from Noah made me feel smothered, but they just seemed sweet when coming from Matthias. Then again, he was a gentle sort of guy, always more worried about what I needed than himself.

The fact that he had a bit of a crush on me was part of it, too. In all honesty, he was a much better choice for me. He was cute. It was kind of ridiculous actually. Like Noah put "No Uglies" on the job description. And Matthias was sweet. No way would he ever invade my privacy.

Then why *not* Matthias? The answer was simple. He wasn't Noah. He was missing that raw sexual edge.

"I'm fine. How are you?" The sounds in the background got abruptly louder and I giggled when I heard what sounded like sighs and feminine moans. "Are you guys watching porn over there?"

There was a beat of silence. "No! Uh, that was just Jonas being an asshole." After a brief pause, all the sounds receded. "Sorry about that. Uh, what's up?"

"I need a favor."

"Of course. Anything for you."

"Um, a favor you can't tell Noah about."

He was quiet, and I felt even worse. I was asking him to choose me over his friend and boss. It normally wasn't something I'd ever do. His crush on me was an open secret amongst our group, and I had always made an effort to be considerate of his feelings. I wasn't the kind of girl who considered a man's feelings a weapon to use against him. But in this particular case, it was a risk I'd have to take in light of what I was asking him to do.

"I normally would never ask you to do that but...I wasn't sure who else to call."

Matthias sighed. "You can always call me. You know that. What do you need?"

"To track down the owners of a corporation. All I have is a deed to a property purchased in the corporation's name. That's probably not enough, but it's all I've got."

"It's no problem. Send me what you have and I'll see what I can do."

Suddenly, I heard Jonas's voice in the background. "Why are you hiding out in here? Are you sexting?"

"No, I'm not sexting. It's Lucia."

"Why are you sexting with Lucia? I'm telling…"

"*No one is sexting*," Matthias shouted, sounding exasperated.

"Hi, Lucia!" Jonas yelled.

Matthias groaned. "Dude, stop yelling in my ear."

"I'm just trying to say hi."

"She heard you. I'm pretty sure everyone in the building heard you."

I covered my mouth to keep from laughing. All the guys on Noah's team were like family at this point. Family that fought and bickered constantly, but would walk through fire to protect their own.

"Tell him I said hello."

"She says hello. Now go away." Matthias relayed the message in a grumpy voice.

"Okay. Well, I know you guys are busy so I'll go now. Thanks for your help, Matthias. And remember, don't tell–"

"Yeah, yeah. Don't tell Noah. Got it."

Right before I hung up, I heard Jonas's voice again. "Don't tell Noah? Good luck with that. He's for sure going to find out about your sexting."

As I turned out the light, I could only hope we wouldn't need luck.

CHAPTER FIVE

Noah

I checked my phone to see if there were any messages from Lucia. Nothing. It had been a few days since I'd seen her and she was still pissed off at me. Whatever. It was for her safety.

Are you sure about that?

I shoved away the thought and dragged my attention back to my workout. Angrily I pushed the button to increase the speed on the treadmill. Outside the window, I watched the throng of passersby and tourists on the streets down below in Midtown as police attempted to direct traffic.

Man, did I love this city.

As a thief on the streets below, I'd never thought I'd end up here now. It was a long way from where I'd started. And I didn't take any of it for granted.

Bouncing around from foster home to foster home, I got to see a lot of the city. Unfortunately, I spent most of that time picking the best marks. And nowhere was better for marks than Midtown. Times Square.

But now...now instead of looking at them as targets, I saw them as the people I protected. *Sometimes.* Other times I was the bad guy.

But that's not who you are anymore. That's not what you do.

Back then, when I'd saved Ian's life, I hadn't considered where that one action would lead. The dark and twisty path it would take me on. That path had exploited my best skills and nurtured my darkest ones. Despite that, I considered myself lucky. I'd helped people. Saved them. But saving those lives came at a cost.

And when the cost got too high, I'd gotten out.

I pushed myself on the treadmill, running until my lungs burned and my eyes watered. Until my heart thundered against my ribs, begging for mercy. When I finally hit the stop button and the treadmill slowed, I dragged in deep breaths, completely unaware that I wasn't alone.

Then I turned and startled when I saw Jonas leaning against the glass doors of the gym.

"You're going pretty hard there," the other man commented as he pushed off the doors and walked closer.

"*Jesus Christ*, Jonas. You're a silent motherfucker, you know that? I may consider putting a bell on you."

Jonas just shrugged his big shoulders. "You're welcome to try."

I grabbed a towel and wiped my face. "You want to tell me why you're standing there staring like you got a crush? Or do you want me to guess?"

Jonas chuckled and shook his head but still didn't say anything. Jonas knew me better than anyone. He was my oldest friend.

"What's up, Jonas? You're creeping me out."

"Well, I was sort of hoping you could tell me. You've been out of it the last week. Lucia still not returning your calls?"

I knew a loaded question when I heard it. For years, Jonas had pestered me about Lucia. Jonas was the only one who knew how I felt about her.

"No, I haven't heard from her. She'll settle down. See it my way eventually."

"You sure about that? Either date her yourself, or cut her loose to do what she wants to do."

"You know I can't do that. I'm supposed to be looking out for her. So if she can't choose wisely, then I'm going to make a nuisance of myself until she learns."

Jonas rolled his eyes. "How's that plan working out for you?"

Like shit. But there was no way I was telling him that. "It's working fine. Get the team ready. I'll need five for a shower."

After a quick shower, I joined the assembled team in the conference room. Matthias sat with his two laptops and an earpiece in his ear. Jonas was at the other end of the table lounging back in the chair, his feet kicked up, gleaming loafers on display.

Oskar sat in front of his laptop looking irritated. But then, that was Oskar. The German rarely smiled. That was probably a good thing given the number of female clients who openly stared at him in interest. If he started smiling back at them, it might be pandemonium.

Ryan and Dylan rounded out the group. They were the newest additions. So far they'd proven themselves on assignments, but I was still testing them out.

"Okay guys." I shook out my hair, wiping away the last remnants of water. "We had a few new clients come in and a few repeat requests. Alana Brooks, the singer, is coming back to town and has an open spot for bodyguard duty. Ryan, you worked with her before. You willing to do it again?"

"Yeah, that's fine. Though if she insists on going to a mall again, I'm backing out. Those teenyboppers are scary."

Everyone laughed. Even Oskar.

"You're afraid of a couple of teenagers?" Dylan asked.

"Laugh all you want but those girls can be dangerous. One jumped on my back in an attempt to climb over me and get to her." He shuddered. "That shit was terrifying."

Matthias laughed. "The great Ryan Delaney taken down by a couple of teenage girls."

I knew the kid had a point. There was nothing more frightening in our world than an unknown variable. A screaming girl determined to get to the object of her affection definitely qualified because you could never predict how far they'd go to get what they wanted.

"Okay, I'll put you down. We've also got the Boynton Corporation. They want us to take a look at their security setup. They've had a couple of internal break-ins."

Jonas nodded. "I can do the initial intake if you want."

I nodded. With our current caseload, I'd been relying on Jonas more and more. Maybe it was time to give him a raise.

We reviewed a few additional new cases. One for the FBI, who wanted to borrow Matthias's skills. For that one, I would do initial intake myself. I didn't trust the Feds.

After going through the rest of our new cases, I brought up the last item on the agenda. "So, we've got a few pro bono cases on the docket."

Oskar groaned. "How are we ever supposed to make money if you keep taking pro bono cases?" Taking jobs that didn't bring in money made the German twitchy.

But he hated scumbag abusers more than any of us. Which was why, even though he grumbled, he was usually first in line for ass-kicking duty.

Besides, I had used my buy-out from ORUS to start this place, so we weren't hurting for money. I'd put that money to good use. Oskar had helped me invest wisely, and those returns went to running Blake Security. That didn't mean Oskar wasn't wired to obsess over the bottom line.

"For every three jobs we take a pro bono one. That's how it works. You want to let this latest scumbag roam free?" What I didn't say was that I felt like I needed to do the penance.

Oskar harrumphed. Crossed his arms and sat back. "Whatever."

I fought a grin. That was his way of saying 'Fine. Who do we have to save now?'

I nodded at Matthias, who put up the picture of our new client, a smiling young girl with a long brown ponytail.

"This is Ella Wielding."

Matthias popped up another picture, this time a man in his forties. Dark, greasy hair, scraggly beard, beady little eyes.

"This is her neighbor, James Thorne. He's been following Ella. Ella's mother has gone to the police about his inappropriate interactions with her daughter. Ella insists that she's seen him at the mall, when she's at soccer practice, and out with her friends. So far he hasn't touched, but that's just a matter of time. I want everything we've got on this guy."

Oskar sat forward, his brow furrowed deep. "What's our endgame?"

Everyone knew what he was asking. Oskar wanted to know if we were going to hand out police justice or street justice. One of those would land James Thorne in the East River.

I didn't flinch. "It depends on what we find. If he's done this before, repeatedly, I'd like to permanently *rehome* him somewhere he'll never hurt anyone again."

Oskar nodded his approval, but Jonas pinned me with a level gaze. Ryan and Dylan looked unperturbed. Matthias didn't even look up from his computer. They were all okay with it if guys like this no longer walked the planet.

While Oskar could be downright savage if it meant saving an innocent, Jonas believed in truth, justice and the American way. But even he had seen way too much injustice as of late. Jonas knew who I was. What I'd done before I opened Blake Security.

The guilt that I carried around.

He acted as my conscience. But if James Thorne turned out to be the lowest of the low, then I might let my old self out to play.

Because sometimes you just had to take out the trash.

"Matthias, find us anything you can. Then we'll decide what to do with James Thorne."

———

Lucia

I eyed myself in the full-length mirror attached to the closet door. Mentally I ran through the checklist of things Nonna was sure to scrutinize and chastise me for.

Skirt length, check.

Blouse tucked in, check.

Hair smoothed back into a simple clip, check.

Earrings in, check.

I sighed. Because God forbid I didn't have earrings on when I went to see my Nonna. I loved my grandmother. I really did. But she had antiquated ideas about how a woman was supposed to present herself at all times.

Once I had made the mistake of not wearing proper undergarments to bed as a teenager, and I'd thought my grandmother would faint from distress when she'd woken me for school the next morning.

I had asked her what the big deal was about not wearing underwear to bed. Plenty of my friends did it and claimed it was more comfortable. What was the worst that could happen?

All Nonna had been able to get out between pinched lips was that it was improper. And what would happen if there were some emergency and we had to evacuate our building in the middle of the night?

I hadn't had the nerve to point out that in the event of an emergency, I doubted anyone would care if I was bare-assed beneath my nightgown.

Growing up, Nonna had also had specific requirements about how a young lady should dress. Particularly, skirt length. Nothing above the knees, as it was vulgar. Blouses should always be tucked in to minimize sloppiness. Plus they must also not be too tight, in order to minimize generous curves.

I looked down at my boobs. Yeah, no minimizing those. And the hair. Well, Nonna had never been particularly happy with that either. We'd spent hours upon hours trying to smooth out every last hint of curl.

As I had gotten older, I'd let some of those things go. I secretly loved my wild curls and thought I looked better with my natural hair anyway. Besides, who had time for blow-drying? Not me. Especially not with my job.

The job was another point of contention. Nonna did not approve of fashion as a profession. Or even as a hobby. Which meant I had been forced to sneak in my *Vogue* and *Vanity Fair* magazines. I'd hidden them under my mattress like I supposed some guys would hide dirty magazines. She'd been far less concerned about the salacious romance novels JJ had asked me to hide, since Nonna devoured them, too.

I figured I couldn't complain too much. JJ's mom had been a renowned snooper. There was no getting anything past her. Nonna, while occasionally self-righteous, didn't look very hard. Under the mattress was a decent hiding place in my house. Lucky for Rafe. I smiled thinking of my brother. He'd always been a handful but he'd been so much fun. The best big brother a girl could have.

Outside of the aging brownstone in Queens where I'd grown up, I tugged open the creaking glass door before turning the brass knob of the main door. Damn, it was unlocked. My grandmother really needed to tighten up the security around here.

Awesome. Now I sounded like Noah and that was the last thing on earth I wanted. That meddling self-righteous asshole.

With a deep breath, I stepped into the house and was instantly greeted by the scent of garlic and tomatoes. It smelled like home. I missed being here. I missed knowing that no matter what, Nonna was always going to be cooking and fussing about how I didn't eat enough. And at the same time fussing about my figure.

I found my grandmother in the living room dusting.

"Nonna, what are you doing? You're supposed to be recovering from pneumonia. Besides, I got you a cleaning lady so that you wouldn't have to do all this bending and reaching to clean."

Nonna wrinkled her nose. "You know I don't like someone poking around my house."

"Well, I know for a fact that she comes every week because I've been paying her. What does she do if you don't let her clean?"

A slight flush tinted my grandmother's cheeks. "Okay, so sometimes I feed her. The poor thing is so skinny. How is she going to get a good husband if she doesn't eat?"

I could only sigh. Okay, new rules and a new cleaning lady, this one older. Someone Nonna couldn't push around so easily.

"I do these things so that you can be taken care of even when I'm not here. You have to let me help."

"Nonsense. I can take care of myself."

I crossed my arms. "Do I need to remind you that you've been very ill? You should be resting. Let someone else take care of you for once."

Nonna waved me off. "I'm a grown woman. I'll tell you —"

A knock at the door stopped the argument mid-flow.

"Are you expecting anyone?"

I held up a hand to prevent her from going to open the door. Nonna shook her head in amusement.

"Yes, actually, I am expecting someone. I have a life, too, young lady."

I laughed. What was wrong with me? I'd become nearly as paranoid as Noah. After peering through the peephole, I opened the door to find a dark-haired man on my grandmother's steps.

"Can I help you?"

He smiled broadly showing straight, blindingly white teeth. "I'm here to see Rosa DeMarco. I'm a doctor."

He didn't look like my Nonna's doctor. I glanced back at my grandmother. "Nonna?"

My grandmother grinned, pushing me aside to open the door and welcome him.

"Antonio! I'm so glad you were able to come by to check on me."

Nonna stepped back to let him by and he walked straight into the living room as if he knew his way around. I had no choice but to follow them both. My grandmother sat on the couch watching with avid interest as he pulled out a stethoscope and blood pressure pump.

I watched the two of them with mounting suspicion. "So, how long have you been my grandmother's doctor? Do you work with Dr. Erlichman?"

Dr. Antonio opened his mouth to answer, but Nonna answered for him.

"You remember my friend Esther? Well, this is her grandson, Antonio. While he's home helping her out for a month, he agreed to check on me. Especially since I was ill. He wanted to make sure that I was following all my doctor's orders."

Antonio nodded. "It's no trouble. My grandmother lives three doors down. So after I check on her, I look in on your grandmother." He flashed another grin.

I licked my lips. Something was up. I could feel it. "Well, I am grateful. Nonna doesn't usually let anyone help her. She's very independent."

He chuckled. "Oh, I'm well acquainted with her. That's why I was so surprised she asked me to check up on her every now and again. I'm sorry I was late today. I got held up with a friend in Brooklyn."

I cocked my head. "Oh, did you guys have a set appointment? I would've taken my time getting here if I'd known that."

I got the distinct impression my grandmother wanted me to arrive just when I had. Just in time to meet Dr. *Antonio*. Who, for all intents and purposes, was very good-looking. Tall, lean, thick dark hair. Everything about him screamed, 'I'm a good Italian boy.' But I was in no mood.

"Okay then, I'll leave you to it. I have phone calls to make anyway."

The old lady thought she was tricky. Damn, I'd had to run out of my office, change in the building bathroom, hop two trains and a bus just to get here at the specific time my grandmother said she needed me. Under normal circumstances, I would have come on Saturday.

But my grandmother said she'd been feeling weak since her illness, so of course I had wanted to check on her.

You've been played.

Thirty minutes later, after Dr. Antonio came into the kitchen to say goodbye to me, I faced off against my grandmother.

"You think I can't recognize a set up when I see one?"

Nonna rolled her eyes. "Lucia, all I'm trying to do is introduce you to some nice Italian boys. Who knows the kind of people you're meeting in the city? Antonio goes to church. He's a doctor. You could do worse. Honestly, you act like I'm trying to force you into an arranged marriage. All I'm doing is introducing you. He thinks you're very pretty."

I threw my hands up. "Nonna, that is not the point. I'm sure he is a very nice guy." But not Noah. I shoved that thought far aside. "I'm just not looking to date anyone right now."

My grandmother scoffed. "Instead, what? You're running around playing sleuth? Trying to find out what happened to your brother? That's not the kind of life I want for you. I want you to be married and have babies, not skulking around in the dark looking in places you shouldn't be."

It was an old argument. I turned to the stove and turned on the kettle. "I appreciate what you're trying to do. I know you just want me to be happy. But you can't rule my life. Between you and Noah, I could use some breathing room."

I reached for the tea but the box on the counter was empty. I spotted a large tin behind the flour. Maybe Nonna had started putting her teas in there. I pulled out the can to open it. But instead of tea, there was a wad of cash.

Holy hell.

"Nonna. What is this?"

My grandmother snatched the container out of my hand with more force than I had ever seen her use. "It's just something I keep for a rainy day."

"That must be some rainy day you're expecting. Is there a tsunami coming? That's a lot of money, Nonna. There must be thousands of dollars in there."

Nonna closed the lid quickly and shoved it back behind the other canisters. "Yes. I've been saving for years. A little bit here, a little bit there. I find ways to save money. That's money I use just in case." She squared her shoulders. "I'm an old lady. I'm entitled to some secrets."

I chuckled. "As long as those secrets don't include more men for me to meet, that is fine."

But even as I made my cup of tea and one for Nonna, I wondered what other secrets she was hiding.

———

My feet were killing me. By the time I got home, the penny loafers had pinched so much I was convinced I'd never walk right again. Nonna didn't approve of stilettos and high heels. Which was a real bummer because they were pretty and, well, my boss insisted that I wear them.

The shoes my grandmother would prefer I wear were uncomfortable as hell. Once I got home, the first thing I did was kick them off. I tossed the mail onto the counter and then limped over to the couch and plopped down. I quickly checked my emails on my phone.

I grinned when I saw the confirmation for the surprise I'd set up for Noah. He would be livid. But he was the one who'd started this little war, so turnabout was fair play. And this was perfect because I would also get back at the gang at Blake Security for that little prank they'd pulled on me last Halloween.

Whoever thought acting out *The Shining* in a warehouse building was seriously sick. I blamed Matthias. He might look sweet, but he was secretly devious.

If this surprise didn't get Noah off my back I didn't know what would. I relaxed against the cushions of the couch, allowing the tempting pull of sleep to close in around me, but then I turned my head.

No. I needed food first. And food was all the way over there—in the fridge.

Food was overrated, right? The more I gave any credence to the thought the more my stomach rumbled. "Okay, fine. I'll get up."

I pushed to standing and winced with every step as I padded into the kitchen. I pulled together the makings of a quick soup and preheated the oven for some bread Nonna had sent home with me. It wasn't much, and it definitely wasn't fancy, but for now it would do.

This week I'd been so busy I'd been flying by the seat of my pants as far as meals went.

I stared at the pile of mail and sighed. Eventually, I started sorting through the stack. Mostly bills. A few magazine subscriptions. That had been my major indulgence when I moved out on my own, openly getting a magazine subscription to every major fashion magazine. Eventually it had started to add up so I'd pulled back to just a few, but they were still my guilty pleasure. I was lucky I'd found a rent-controlled apartment so I could afford the little splurges like this.

I methodically went through the bills, putting most of them away to deal with later while making a mental note to call the student loan office. Then I was down to one last envelope. Plain manila. My address typed.

No return address.

I frowned. No postmark. Could it have come from the Housing Association? They would occasionally send leaflets or notices. Most of those were mailed, but it was possible they'd decided to hand-deliver something. It must be pretty urgent. I flipped over the letter and there were no markings or logos on the back. Just a plain envelope. Putting a finger under a small gap, I peeled it open and pulled out the letter inside. As I unfolded it, I noted there was only one line of text:

Stop. Digging.

A cold chill ran up my spine as the letter floated to the counter.

Oh shit. Did someone know what I was up to? How was that even possible? Who would care? I'd been careful and wasn't advertising what I was doing. Why would my getting answers now be a problem for anyone? Did that mean I was finally on the right track?

I'd gone with my brother that day as he was in a panic to stop something from happening. But what? For the past two years, I'd become obsessed. I'd written down everything I could remember but not a single memory cast any light onto that day.

I'd even tried hypnosis once. That had backfired. While I'd been very relaxed at first, I'd burst into tears as I'd tried to force my mind back to that memory.

That day in my life was like a big black hole.

At least I had the first memory of the day with Rafe on Coney Island. Anything after he got that phone call was a complete blank until the next morning when I woke up expecting to see my brother, but instead was told by Nonna that he was gone.

I'd been looking for clues ever since. I *needed* to know what happened that day. Because if I didn't, how would I ever mend the hole in my heart? *Keep pushing and you won't have a heart anymore,* I thought as I looked down at the message. Were the answers I needed worth dying for?

I picked up the letter. Maybe I did need to let go. Maybe for once I needed to listen to Noah and Nonna and just get on with life. Is that what Rafe would have wanted? Could I just walk away and let it go?

My eyes glanced back at the sheet of paper. What if this time, it didn't just affect me? What if it affected Nonna, too?

I didn't need any more persuading. I ran back to the couch, picked up the phone and typed out a quick message to Matthias.

> That thing I asked you for? Never mind. Just leave it alone. I don't need to know anymore.

I tossed my phone on the couch and scrubbed my hands over my face. Maybe this was for the best. Rafe would want more for me than a life of looking over my shoulder.

CHAPTER SIX

Noah

Lucia still wasn't talking to me.

Most days when I woke up, I wasn't thinking about anything in particular. I'd always been a light sleeper, useful when you never know if you'll wake with a gun to your head. But even once Rafe had taken me in, I'd always started each day as a blank slate. I wasn't happy or sad, just resigned to do whatever was necessary to make sure I survived to see the next morning.

But that day I'd woken with a cloud of foreboding. It was a strange thing to feel so much when you weren't used to giving a shit about anything. I hadn't really understood how familiar I'd become with Lucia's gentle intrusion in my life. Her soft glances and constant questions had started out as annoying and then became reassuring. Somehow I'd grown accustomed to someone caring about me.

But for the last week I'd had an abrupt return to what life was like before. No Lucia stopping by the office to bring me a home cooked meal. No calls to ask if I'd come by and fix something or kill a bug. No hugs that made me feel like a heart still beat somewhere within me. She was angry with me, and although she'd been mad at me before, this was different.

Maybe this is the new normal, I thought as I walked into the office over two hours later than usual. I'd overslept for the first time in years and it only added to my cranky mood.

The first clue it wasn't going to be a typical day was seeing that Matthias was waiting for me in the common area.

"Yes, he just got here." Matthias hung up then, looking exasperated. "Did you forget we had a new client intake this morning?"

Damn. I never fucked up with clients. "Sorry, I overslept."

By the twitch in his eyebrow it was clear Matthias wanted to call bullshit on that, but wisely he didn't say anything. I walked past him and into the conference room.

"My apologies, we can start now. I'm Noah Blake and I hope the others have already introduced themselves."

The men sitting around the table nodded and smiled. They all looked extremely young and more likely to be on their way to a frat party than a business meeting. I looked down at the new client form that Matthias placed in front of me. Apparently they owned and operated a chain of fitness centers.

Suddenly, the awful orange spray tans and more muscles than your average desk jockey made sense. This should be a pretty easy intake all around. Which was a good thing, since I was exhausted and definitely not functioning at full tilt.

"So, tell me what brings you to Blake Security gentlemen."

"Actually, we came by to deliver a message," said one of the men sitting directly across from me. "Jason, hit the music!"

All three of the men stood suddenly and ripped their shirts open, revealing oiled-up chests and six-pack abs. Rock music blared from somewhere that I couldn't identify.

What. The. Fuck.

Two seconds went by in complete, stunned silence before there was an explosion of movement and multiple weapons aimed in every direction. Next to me, Jonas had his Glock 9 pointing at the new client directly across from him, and I had my Sig Sauer aimed at the man across from me. Oskar had the other guy in a headlock. His face was bright red and going nearly purple.

The man across from me held his hands up slowly. "Well, this isn't the usual response to a birthday-gram."

"Wait, what?" I asked through clenched teeth.

He held up the card in his hand and wiggled it. I indicated with my head for Matthias to go get it. Matthias took the card gingerly and opened it. Suddenly he snorted. He walked over to me and held out the neon green card.

"It's just a birthday card."

"I thought they said they had a message for us?"

"We do," one of the guys interjected. "A message from Lucia. Can we put our hands down?"

"Yes." I nodded at the others to let the men go.

As soon as all our weapons were sheathed, the men glanced at each other and then one by one they ripped off their slacks, the tearing sound of fabric startling me so much I almost drew my gun again.

"Happy Birthday, Noah!" They screeched in unison and then proceeded to sing. Every time they sang "Happy Birthday," they shimmied and gyrated in unison until their extremely tiny banana hammocks were dangerously close to giving up the fight.

Oh. Fuck. No.

Just what I needed on top of a night of no sleep; a room full of dudes with their dicks hanging out.

I opened the card and immediately recognized Lucia's handwriting. Just the sight of it brought a jolt of unexpected warmth to my heart. Until the three men approached, gyrating and rolling their abs as they finished the song, flinging their arms up at the end. In the silence that followed, the only sound was their breathing and Oskar's muffled laughter behind me.

Jonas clapped and Matthias joined in.

"Thank you. This has definitely made things more interesting around here, and it's not even my birthday," Jonas boomed.

"Or mine," I added under my breath, coughing when Jonas elbowed me in the gut. "Yes, thank you." I bit out the words, figuring if I played along they'd leave faster than if I explained the whole thing was a mistake. Okay, not a mistake — a prank.

"Oh I almost forgot!" One of the guys held up a small noisemaker. The others, once they saw his, pulled out similar ones. They all blew at once, releasing a chorus of loud honks and streams of glittery confetti that exploded in the air around us.

I blinked as confetti streamed all over me. I watched as the men waved happily and then grabbed their clothes before filing out. A piece of confetti tickled the edge of my nose and I sneezed suddenly.

When I opened my eyes, Jonas stood next to me, his hand covering his mouth.

"Don't even say it," I growled.

"I wasn't going to say anything." Jonas held his hands up in surrender.

Wordlessly, I walked over to the garbage can and brushed as much of the confetti off as possible. Glitter stuck to my shirt and hands, and I'd probably be washing it out until next week.

Jonas helped me gather the confetti streamers and stuffed them into the garbage can next to the conference table. Then he laughed suddenly. "I can't believe she got you a stripper-gram."

I had never been so pissed and simultaneously amused. How was it possible that I wanted to spank her and kiss her all at once?

The funniest part was that she'd no doubt thought the strippers would embarrass me in some way. Maybe she thought this would even the score between us, her embarrassment countered by mine. It only showed how little she actually knew. You could only be embarrassed if you had any shame left.

I'd lost what little shame I had back on the streets.

"That girl has balls, that's for sure." Jonas handed over the folder he'd been carrying under his arm. "At least she's not pretending you don't exist anymore."

"I'm starting to think I'd prefer being invisible." I pretended I didn't see the look of pity Jonas threw my way. I definitely wasn't going there today.

Matthias stuck his head around the door. "Is it bloody safe to come in?"

Jonas snorted. "Scared of a few shlongs in thongs?"

Matthias's only response was the middle finger he waved in Jonas's direction. However, I noticed he didn't say anything until Jonas left. It was rare for us to keep secrets from each other; after all, our safety often hinged on the entire group being fully apprised of every possible future scenario. Which meant something was up.

"What's wrong?"

Matthias shrugged. Then he glanced over his shoulder at the open door. "It's Lucia," he said in a low voice.

Fear lanced through me. "What do you mean? What's wrong with her?"

"Nothing. She's fine. Fuck, I probably shouldn't even be telling you this."

I took a deep breath and struggled to keep my temper under control. Raging at one of my best friends wouldn't help the situation. "If something's going on with Lucia then you need to tell me. I know you...care about her, too."

It was as close as we'd ever come to acknowledging our shared fate of loving a woman that neither of us had a chance with.

Matthias flushed. "I do. Care, I mean. That's why I originally agreed to help her."

"Help her with what?"

Matthias pulled out his phone. A few thumb taps later he held it out so I could see the image on the screen. My blood went cold when I recognized the house.

"Where did you get that?"

My voice didn't even sound like my own, and I cleared my throat trying to get some composure back. But it was impossible to be unaffected when the past came back to haunt you. My time with ORUS wasn't something I could ever forget, but I'd tried too damn hard to keep it in the past where it belonged.

Now it was rising like a specter to remind me that I'd never be free.

"Lucia asked me to help her do some research. She sent me a deed to a house and asked for info on finding the owners. All she had to go on was the name of the corporation on the deed."

"*Lucia* asked you about that house?"

I closed my eyes. This was so much worse than I'd thought. It wasn't just the past coming back to haunt me, it was the past reaching forward with icy fingers trying to snatch the only person I'd been able to save that day.

Matthias was watching me closely. "It's weird because the name on the deed didn't actually match the corporation name. It's a fake. But I had the address so I could do some digging of my own. Then suddenly she said never mind. That she didn't need to know anymore."

"That's not like her."

"No, it's not. It's also not like her to ask me not to tell you about it. Which probably means she's doing something she shouldn't be."

I grunted. "She's mad at me right now."

"I figured that. But it's Lucia. She's always mad at you."

"Not like this."

I sighed. There really wasn't anything I could say to explain. I wasn't entirely sure what was different about this time. All I knew was Lucia was gone even while she was still there, and I'd never felt more empty.

When I didn't say anything, Matthias knocked on the edge of the table. "Mad or not, she's family."

The truth in Matthias's words rang through my head. That day, that horrible day, had almost stolen everything from me, but I'd managed to keep the vow I'd sworn while bathed in blood. To pledge my life to Lucia and Nonna DeMarco. To protect Rafe's family.

To protect *my* family.

"Tell the others I'm taking the day off. I have to take care of something."

————

Lucia

He was smiling.

I closed my eyes, soaking up the late summer rays and reveling in a rare afternoon spent with my big brother. Rafe was always lecturing me on how I needed to get better grades and work hard so I could take care of Nonna. He was always so serious but not today. For once, he was smiling and everything was wonderful.

A shot rang out.

I flinched and then the scene shifted. Suddenly, I was in our car and Rafe was trying to leave me. Where was he going?

"*Stay here. No matter what, okay?*"

He always looked so fierce. I nodded, sure he was just being his usual overprotective self.

"*Okay, fine. But really, where am I going to go?*"

"*I'm serious, Lulu.*"

He leaned over me and popped open the glove compartment. I gasped at the sight of the gun and then went still when he picked up my hand and pressed the gun into my palm.

"Take this. If something happens...you drive out of here as fast as you can."

"Rafe, I can't drive yet."

"I've taught you enough. Just drive, Lu. As fast as you can."

A shot rang out.

"Rafe!"

I reached out for him but he was already falling. There was so much blood; it was on my hands, in my hair. Then I raised the gun in my hand and fired. And Rafe's body dissolved in my arms.

"I love you. Come back," I sobbed, trying desperately to hold on to his body but it flowed through my fingers like water.

A shot rang out.

I bolted upright on the couch and then squeaked at the sound of a fist hitting the front door. It was hard to separate what was real from the dream, but as the knocking continued, I figured someone really wanted to talk to me.

"Okay, I'm coming." I pushed my hair out of my face irritably. I was still wearing my yoga clothes and hadn't showered. The damn dreams...It was getting harder and harder to sleep at night knowing what I'd see when I closed my eyes. So I'd been staying up later, reading, cleaning and just subsisting off of caffeine and adrenaline. It was finally catching up to me.

I leaned forward to check the peephole before opening the door. Noah stepped through as soon as the door opened, brushing past me and then closing and bolting the door behind him.

"Come on in. Make yourself at home," I grumbled.

"You don't get to be mad today. Not when I'm going to be washing glitter out of my ass crack for the next month after that little birthday production you ordered up for me."

The thought of Mr. Tough Guy finding glitter in unmentionable places made me feel a little better.

"Just a little payback. I hope you guys enjoyed the show, though."

Noah chuckled. "I don't know about that, but I was impressed at your creativity. It was just the right combination of cheerful and maddening."

"You taught me well."

Noah settled on the edge of the couch and leveled that stare at me.

The one that always made me feel like I'd just been called to the principal's office.

"I did, which is why I want to know what the hell you're up to. Matthias told me about what you asked him to research."

My heart sank. "Bunch of tattletales you've got working for you."

He shrugged. "I think he wouldn't have told me except he says you called it off. Knowing how stubborn you are, he figured you wouldn't do that without good reason."

I kept my eyes on the floor.

"Lucia. If something happened, you need to tell me. Right now."

My shoulders slumped. "Okay, but you have to promise not to freak."

"I think I can keep my head."

I walked back to my room and pulled the letter out of my night table drawer. It was still in the original envelope. When I got back to the living room, Noah was pacing in front of the window. Nothing was out of place, but I could tell he was on edge. Wordlessly, I handed him the envelope. He opened it and pulled out the sheet of paper. Instantly, it felt like the temperature in the room dropped twenty degrees.

I had a feeling I was going to pay dearly for not showing this to him right away.

"When did this arrive?" he asked softly, his voice perfectly calm.

"Last week."

His only response was a soft grunt. "Last week. Of course it's been a *week*. Of course you've been walking around for a week with minimal protection and no regard for your own safety. *Of course!*"

He shouted the last two words and I jumped. Then I backed up as he advanced on me, backing me against the wall, leaning over until all that surrounded me was him. Instantly, my heartbeat accelerated and my stomach dropped. Noah would never hurt me, I had no doubt about that, but I'd never seen him quite like this. Wild. Untamed. Undone.

Captivating.

"You don't know how vital you are, do you? Not just to your friends and your family but to *me*. If something ever happened to you, Lucia..."

He dipped his head, his lips brushing against my hair. In that moment, everything inside me went liquid and I let out a soft sigh, suddenly aware that I'd been holding my breath the whole time. His scent was all around me and I wanted to rub up against him.

"Nothing is going to happen to me."

"You're damn right it's not. I won't let it. From now on, I'm not letting you out of my sight."

Ah, the man was infuriating. I shoved him, annoyed that I could be so easily distracted by him when he was busy trying to take over my life. Again.

"I don't need a shadow. This is my problem and I've got it handled. You aren't my father, and I'm not a little girl who needs a babysitter."

He let out a low growl, the sound so insanely sexy that it brought a blush to my cheeks.

"Believe me, I know you aren't a little girl."

He tipped his head and our faces were so close...so close, that I could feel the warm whisper of his breath on my skin. Then suddenly he pulled me up on my toes and his mouth covered mine. His tongue slid into my mouth and over mine, making lust pierce through me.

I melted against him, my limbs turning to jelly. He kissed me until I couldn't think or move or even breathe. My hands slid into his hair of their own volition, twining through the thick strands to hold him against me. He was my only anchor in a storm of sensation, and I hung on for dear life. By the time I had to break away to take a needed gasp of air, he allowed me to slide slowly down until I was standing on my own two feet again.

"I have to go, but I'll be back in a few hours."

"Why are you coming back?" I barely recognized my own voice. That lazy, husky sound couldn't be coming from *me*, could it?

Noah tipped up my chin until I met his gaze. "Because as of right now, you have a roommate. I'm moving in. I hope you don't snore, princess."

He left me standing against the wall in my living room trying to figure out how I'd lost complete control of the situation.

CHAPTER SEVEN

Noah

I staggered outside Lucia's apartment, slamming the door behind me.

Holy shit. What the hell just happened? One second, we were fighting, the next my lips were on hers and it felt like...bliss.

I was well aware of the location of the cameras, so I waited until I was past the camera right outside her door and before I was within range of the camera at the end of the hallway. My own personal blind spot. I leaned against the wall and tried to collect myself. The blood still rushed in my skull and her scent still permeated every cell of my body.

Fuck, I could barely stand.

What the hell had I been thinking? *You know what you were thinking.* I ignored the raging lust in my blood. For years, I'd managed to ignore the temptation. How I'd managed to ignore it for so long and then break it in one moment, one *ill-advised* moment, I had no idea.

This was a disaster.

I'd just been so *pissed*. It was a familiar feeling lately. I'd felt the same way watching her dating guys who weren't worthy of her. For once, it was time to get past the bullshit I'd been telling everyone about her being nothing more than a little sister to me. I'd been *ill* watching her out on a date with another guy. I'd hated the fact that anyone else's hands were on her.

But it wasn't like I could have her myself. There would be no happy ending for the two of us. I was not the kind of guy she could take home to her family.

Never mind that Nonna had practically helped to raise me, or had at least seen me into adulthood. That was hardly the point. She deserved someone way better than I was. She deserved a guy who would take her to church on Sundays, rub her feet on Wednesdays and make polite love to her on Fridays.

A guy who wasn't a killer.

A guy who wasn't so damn good at it.

I pushed away from the wall and inhaled a deep breath. I needed to get my shit together. First things first, I needed to make sure that Matthias scrubbed the surveillance footage. The last thing I needed was the guys giving me shit about this. I sure as hell didn't need Jonas with his knowing gaze tracking my movements. I loved him like a brother, but that shit was annoying.

I needed to sort this out and quick. Step one, keep Lucia safe. Her safety was all that mattered. Step two, never, *ever* kiss her again. How hard could that be? I'd managed not to touch her for years. I just had to remember all the reasons why I'd stayed away from her all this time.

Next, I needed to figure out who the hell had her in their sights. Because I may not have been able to save Rafe, but there was no way I was going to lose Lucia, too. She and Nonna were the only family I had. And I owed her.

I made the drive uptown back to the office in surprisingly little time. The moment I walked in the loft, I went straight for Matthias. His shit-eating grin told me he'd already seen the video feed.

Matthias winked at me. "I have always loved must-see TV."

I was in no mood. "I need you to scrub all the surveillance from Lucia's place today. All of it."

Matthias's brows drew down. "Noah, you set the rules. Standard procedure is we keep the footage for a month, and then we archive it. Just in case anything comes up. There might be something on there we may need later, especially given everything we know now."

I ground my teeth together, pretty sure I was going to crack a molar any second. "I said, clear the fucking footage."

Matthias stilled, and his eyes went wide. I saw that hint of fear, and it made my gut curl. Even after everything, I couldn't escape what

I was. No matter how far I'd come, I was still the thing that went bump in the night. My own men knew enough to be wary. Why didn't Lucia? How could she look at me with that sweet adoration and blind trust?

I took a breath and relaxed my expression. I needed that footage gone, one way or another.

Matthias may have been a little afraid of me, but he wasn't backing down. "No. I'm not going to clear it, mate. I'll clear the segment of you and her in her place. But everything else stays." He shrugged. "Sorry, boss. They're your bloody rules."

The guy gave me a look that was all steady steel. And not for the first time, I was reminded of why I plucked Matthias out of ORUS with me when I left. There was a cold center to the kid that could come out when pushed, and I hadn't wanted that cold to grow and take over completely.

I nodded. "Fine. Just erase that footage then."

Matthias hesitated. "Is now a good time to mention Jonas has already seen it?"

I paused on the way out and muttered a string of expletives. "How the hell is that possible?"

Matthias shrugged. "Well, you were pretty pissed when you headed over there. None of us have ever seen you that angry before. He wanted to make sure you didn't kill her."

I turned to Matthias, working the muscles on my jaw. "I would *never* hurt Lucia."

Matthias grinned. "Oh we both know that. We mostly wanted to see if you'd finally snap and kiss her. For what it's worth, I said no way. Jonas made a cool twenty bucks off of me." He shrugged again. "That's what I get for loyalty."

Jesus Christ. I was going to kill Jonas. And then when I was done with Jonas, I was going to kill Matthias. Was it so obvious to everyone? How desperate I was for her? That I was fighting a losing battle with myself?

"Find Jonas. Tell him to get his ass to Lucia's until I can get there."

"He's already on his way." Matthias was the only other one besides me who stayed at the loft. He hadn't wanted to at first, but I knew the big bosses at ORUS were less than pleased about losing their best hacker. I'd wanted to keep the kid safe. Kind of like Rafe had done for me.

I had to remember though, that while Matthias might be young, he wasn't defenseless. The kid was good. Too good.

Kind of like you.

Besides, there was safety in numbers. The penthouse was a fortress. But one day, someone might come looking for us.

"Whatever." I padded across to my room, my angry stride eating up the concrete. When I reached my private quarters, I slammed the door behind me.

In the solace of my own space, I leaned against the door, my brain replaying every moment of the last three hours. I needed to rewind. Go back to that moment before I kissed her. Because I was never going to survive if I kept thinking about it. So for now, I would just continue like I always had done.

Needing to work off some of the tension, I changed quickly and headed for the treadmill in the gym. After forty-five minutes of a grueling pace, I hopped in the shower, not allowing myself to linger. Routine. That was what I needed.

Once showered, I finally paid attention to the grumbling in my stomach. Unfortunately, when I opened the freezer, there were signs of Lucia everywhere. All the food she'd brought over. She knew I was useless in the kitchen. Lasagna. Wedding soup. I spent a good deal of my time deliberately making her crazy, but still she took care of me. Because that's what you did for family. And like it or not, Lucia was family. I would do whatever was necessary to protect her, even from myself.

I closed the freezer and decided to start packing. After retrieving my laptop from my office, I carried it to my bedroom. I grabbed enough clothes to last for a week and shoved them in a duffel bag. When I opened the drawer beside my bed, my heart stopped. Right on top sat a photo of me, Lucia, Rafe, and Nonna. It had been taken nine months before Rafe died. We looked happy. We looked like family. Back then, I'd been too young to know what I was getting myself into.

Too young to know what I was doing to my soul.

With a curse, I shut the drawer on my past, the guilt gnawing at me. Because of my choices, *my ego*, my friend was dead. If I couldn't forgive myself, how could I ever expect Lucia to?

No. She was better off with someone else. Someone who wouldn't get her killed. I knew what I had to do. Protect her with my life and keep my hands off of her.

———

Lucia

Noah Blake was simply the most infuriating man I had ever met. How dare he think he could just dictate my life?

Infuriating. Annoying. Bossy. So damn bossy. But damn could the man kiss. He'd left over thirty minutes ago, and I still couldn't calm my heart rate.

Thinking about Noah crashing his lips to mine as he backed me up against the wall made me ache in places. Ache and *tingle*. Because while something low in my belly pulled at my center, my nipples peaked. My skin itched, as if it was too tight over my muscles. And my lips, well, I wasn't talking to them.

Who are you kidding? It was the best kiss you've ever had in your life.

That was what was missing from my date with Brent. That was what was missing with every guy I ever attempted to date. That heat, lust, longing, need. All of those things. But why, why did it have to be Noah? I always pictured myself dating a great guy, the kind of person I could bring home to Nonna, but who still also made me feel tingly all over. The kind of guy who wanted to meet my friends and hang out having picnics in Bryant Park.

Yes, I maybe watched and read one too many romantic comedies. But that was beside the point. I wanted a *normal* dating life. Where I would call some guy, chat for hours, and then argue about who would hang up first. Wasn't that how it was supposed to go? JJ was my only real marker for these kinds of things, and JJ was more of the *'play hard to get and then screw the guy senseless before leaving him wanting more'* kind of girl.

I couldn't do that. And dammit, Noah was all wrong. There was always an edge to him. A hint of danger.

Rafe had been his mentor of sorts where they worked. Back then, I'd been completely dazzled because he was the only one who had the nerve to swear in front of me. He was older, so yeah, of course there was an inappropriate crush.

But I was older now. I got it. I understood that guys with edge, guys with hidden tattoos, who rode motorcycles and checked every movement with their shrewd eyes, those guys were dangerous. Those were the kind of guys that had killed my brother. I wanted nothing to do with that type of man. Especially not now. I'd been serious when I said I was going to back off. It wasn't worth my life. Rafe wouldn't want that. But that didn't mean I didn't feel the pull to Noah like the gravitational force of the sun. Every time I was in a room with him, I couldn't help but track his movements, be aware of him.

Did he feel the same way I did? As I struggled to pin down exactly how I felt, something caught my eye on the coffee table. Noah had left his phone and someone was leaving a message.

Probably one of his many women. Did they know he was busy kissing me? Okay, I needed to stop thinking about that kiss. Because every time I did, my body betrayed me.

I picked up his phone and saw the notification.

ALARM

All secure. Movement in living room.

I stared at the message. What the hell? The rational part of my brain tried to reason with the irrational suspicion bubbling in my blood. *It can't be what you think.* As I stared at the phone, I knew I was about to cross a line. I'd seen Noah enter his password so many times that I knew it by heart but entering it now would be breaching his trust. Then the phone flashed with another notification.

Oh hell. I entered the code and then gaped at the picture that had just come in. A clear image of my living room.

I dropped the phone and did a quick circle around the room. Holy hell. He had cameras in here? Throughout my house? I shuddered. Sometimes I understood why he was so protective of me, but to have a surveillance camera in my damn house? I was going to kill him.

My brain scrambled to come to grips with the messages I'd just seen. Murder was the only solution. That was the end of that. I'd hated violence ever since Rafe had been taken from me, but this required bodily harm.

Take a deep breath. Remember what he taught you. Be systematic.

I'd always thought Noah was being crazy when he taught me to look for bugs; when he'd taught me to put a little piece of tape up above the door so I would know if someone had come into my place unannounced. Even if they hadn't touched anything.

He taught me all sorts of ways to be sure I was safe. Except I wasn't safe from him. I stared at my front door, checking the doorframes and the peephole. After that, I systematically moved to the walls. I checked all the picture frames, picking them up off their hangings, inspecting the frame, looking for anything that could be a camera or that looked 'off.' One by one, I rehung the pictures and then moved over into the living room to the bookcase. After a thorough scan, I found what I was looking for. Right dead-center of my bookcase, was the picture frame Noah had given me for Christmas last year. In it, I'd put a picture of me, Noah and Nonna from Christmas breakfast that morning.

In the picture, my grandmother was squeezing me tight, leaning up to give me a kiss on the cheek. On my other side stood Noah, smiling but somehow a bit separate in the image. He was somehow always there, always a part of my family. But not really. All this time, how long had he been watching me? And why? It was time for some damn answers.

But first, I was going to find the rest of it. I wanted all the surveillance gone. I knew everyone thought I was so innocent and needed to be sheltered. I might not know exactly what Noah did, but I knew the kind of man he was. Protective. Strong. But this? I stared down at the picture. This was going too far. I spent the next hour meticulously searching my house. I didn't want to tamper with the security system in case that was actually necessary. But the moment he was back, I would have him remove anything that was in there.

After a thorough sweep, I found two cameras, in the living room and kitchen. Luckily, there were none in my bedroom. Thank God, but that didn't let Noah off the hook. He was going too far. I knew he felt like he had to take care of me after Rafe died, but this...this was another level. I wasn't going to stand for it.

As soon as he got back, he was going to have some serious explaining to do.

CHAPTER EIGHT

Noah

Matthias paused in the doorway. "Boss, have you heard from Lucia?"

I stopped in the middle of shoving clothes in a bag to glare at Matthias. "What the fuck are you talking about? You saw me get kicked out of her place not two hours ago. Speaking of which, is Jonas there?"

Matthias licked his lips. "Yeah, he's there, but listen, something's up with her."

"What's wrong?"

Matthias shrugged. "I'm not sure."

"What do you mean?"

"She's being weird."

I finally lost my patience. "What the hell does that mean? What is she doing?"

It took a moment, but Matthias finally said, "Not sure. She's moving things around. I guess she's redecorating but it's really difficult to see what's going on. There's all this crap in front of the camera now."

My mild panic started to recede slightly. "You're sure Jonas is outside?"

"Yeah, of course. He just checked in, right on schedule. I don't know, something just seemed off. It might be nothing, but I figured you'd want to know before you walk into that."

I finished grabbing underwear and a few toiletries before tossing my shaving kit on top of it all. "You know how she is. Antsy when she's annoyed. I'll fix it when I get back over there."

It took me much longer to get my things than I'd anticipated. By the time I got back to Lucia's apartment it was almost midnight. Luckily, Jonas had been able to stick around and keep an eye on things until I could get back. Moving in with Lucia sounded easy enough in theory. But once I'd started packing up, it had become clear just how much stuff I relied on every day.

The thought brought to mind *the people* I relied on every day. Maybe by the time I went in to work tomorrow I'd have figured out what I was going to say to explain my new living situation. Matthias already knew, of course, since he was usually the one monitoring Lucia's surveillance feed. But I could already hear the bullshit I'd get from Jonas when he found out.

That was the problem with hiring your friends. They knew you too well for you to bullshit them, and they always had something to say about what you were doing. Especially since they knew what Lucia meant to me. It wasn't something I'd ever admitted aloud, but it was one of those things that was so obvious it didn't require explanation.

I knocked and shifted my duffle bag to the other shoulder. While I waited, I looked up and down the hallway. Most of Lucia's neighbors were older, one of the main reasons we'd gotten her into this building. The location wasn't exactly convenient to my office, but a longer commute time was no big thing in the long run.

It would be no small feat to run my business from another location, but there was no doubt in my mind this was the right move. The *only* move. Lucia was more important than anything else. There weren't too many things in my life that I'd gotten completely right, but taking care of her and Nonna DeMarco were at the top of my list.

I could only hope that if Rafe was looking down on us, he'd be proud.

I wasn't a religious man, despite Nonna's best efforts, but I took my oaths seriously. I'd promised Rafe that I'd take care of them if the worst ever happened, and I'd lay down my life to keep that vow.

Especially since my best friend couldn't have known that the worst thing out there was me.

I knocked on the door again and then stood back so Lucia could see me through the peephole. She'd gotten much better about not opening the door without checking first. It had killed me that living in this neighborhood had made her soft for a while. After a few minutes of standing there, I started to get impatient. I let my duffle bag fall to the ground. There was a dull clank as all the electronics jostled against each other. I'd probably brought more tech gadgets than clothes.

"Lucia, open up!"

There was no sound inside. I frowned. Jonas would have let me know if she'd left. She'd been pissed at me earlier but it wasn't like her to be petty. She was way more likely to open the door and yell at me than leave me outside making a scene in her hallway.

I knocked once more for good measure and then pulled out my key. Once inside, I disabled the alarm. As soon as I flipped on the lights, my hand instinctively went to the Sig Sauer holstered on my hip.

What the hell?

The place looked like it had been trashed. Every couch cushion was on the floor, and the chairs had been knocked over. The bookshelves were swept clean, the books and knickknacks littering the floor. My blood went cold as I realized that something was very wrong. There was no way this kind of mayhem could have occurred without our surveillance picking it up. If someone had circumvented our security measures then I had no idea what I was walking in to.

A soft sound drew my attention, and I walked quickly and quietly down the hall to Lucia's bedroom door. It was quiet, but then I heard her voice. She was on the phone. She didn't sound upset or even frightened. Confused, I pushed the door open.

Lucia was reclining on the bed with one hand under her head and her phone in the other. The only light in the room came from the small lamp she'd left on next to the bed. A single picture frame rested on the comforter next to her. The picture frame that I'd given her for her birthday last year.

The frame that housed a pinhole camera. It sat next to my phone. I must have left it behind.

Lucia mumbled something and then put the phone on the bedside table. I holstered my weapon.

"Is everything okay?"

She gave me a murderous look. "What do you think?"

I wasn't sure how to answer. Maybe it was a coincidence that she had that particular frame out. "Were you doing some redecorating?"

"Seriously? That's all you have to say to me?" She gestured to the frame on the bed next to her.

I hung my head. "Fuck."

———

Lucia

I watched warily as Noah moved closer. My friends would probably describe me as calm, levelheaded and in control, which made the feelings of rage swirling inside me even harder to take. When I'd found the camera, it was like a switch had been flipped and a new, never-before-seen side of me emerged.

Over the years, I'd tolerated a lot from Noah. He thought I didn't understand him, but I truly did. He'd been my brother's friend, protégé, and more like family than anyone else in my life. So even though he'd never spoken about *that day* with me, I already knew why he worked so hard to take care of me and Nonna.

Rafe had been extremely protective of the women in his life, and I had no doubt that somewhere along the way, he'd tasked Noah with watching over us if he wasn't around to do it himself.

Only someone who'd known my brother would understand just how hard it was not to give in when Rafe wanted something. Even when I'd been a young teenager and chafing under the supervision of my extremely chauvinistic big brother, I'd had a hard time being mad at him. There had just been something about Rafe that made you want to let him handle things. He'd had that sort of aura, the kind that made you want to trust in his leadership and work extra hard to make him proud.

So I got it. I understood.

But there was a line that had been crossed somewhere along the way, and Noah seemed to have forgotten that not only did he have a responsibility to Rafe, but one to me as well. I was the one he talked to every day. Rafe had been his best friend, but I was one of his best friends now. Or so I'd thought.

Because a friend wouldn't do this. A friend wouldn't violate my privacy without a second thought.

"I guess I don't have to ask if you know what that is." Noah gestured toward the picture frame resting on the comforter between us.

"Since you're the one who taught me how to spot a pinhole camera, no, you don't. My question is, when did you switch the frames?"

Although I asked the question casually, I was truly interested in the answer. The camera hadn't been there when I'd gotten the frame. I would have noticed it. Which meant he'd waited until I was used to seeing the frame on the shelf and then swapped in a dupe at some point. It was clever, and damn if that didn't make it all worse. Noah was brilliant and diabolical. Traits that I'd never thought he'd use against me.

"I waited until Easter."

I shook my head, furious when tears sprang to my eyes. "Nice long game. So you've been spying on me ever since. Funny if I hadn't seen the text alert on your phone, I never would have known."

He ran a hand over his hair, tugging at the dark strands in frustration. I'd never seen him look this unsettled.

"You don't understand, Lucia. If something ever happened to you...this was for your protection."

"What are you so worried about? What aren't you telling me?"

For a moment he stared at me and I thought, *finally he'll confide in me.* There were so many moments when I could tell he was holding back, and all I wanted was to be the one person in his life he didn't keep secrets from.

"Nothing. I just want you to be safe," he finally said.

The same standard answer he always gave when I asked why he was so hyper-vigilant about my security. The disappointment covered me like a shroud. In that moment I realized it was never going to happen. He would never trust me or see me as anything but someone to protect.

Never a partner, never his equal, and certainly never his soul mate.

The loss hit me all at once, and suddenly I was as heartbroken as I was furious.

I stood up and went into my closet. When I came out holding my suitcase, Noah's eyes flared with anger. He grabbed it from me.

"Why do you have your suitcase? You're not going *anywhere* right now. I know you're mad at me, but we have bigger things to worry about right now. Like whoever wrote that note."

Furious, I tugged on the handle until he let go. I suspected I only got it away from him because he was surprised I'd fought back. I'd barely gotten it open before he was right there zipping it back up.

"Get out of the way, Noah! You can't tell me what to do. You're *not* my boyfriend. One kiss doesn't give you the right to interfere in my life."

"What about two kisses? Does that give me any rights?"

He stepped in front of me, blocking my access to the suitcase, and all the blood left my head. I swayed, and of course the bastard used that as an opportunity to pull me against his chest. For a moment I rested there, taking in the scent that was uniquely his and the sultry, sandalwood notes in the aftershave he'd used for years. It would be so easy to forgive him and let him cajole me into submission. But that wouldn't change anything. He'd still see me as an obligation, and I'd still be pining for something that could never be.

I pushed away from him, fighting against his hold when he tried to keep me in his arms.

"You wish. You're lucky you got one kiss. And it wasn't even that good!" I added that last part in a rush of anger, hoping to make him feel as unsettled as I did.

Got him, I thought, watching his eyes narrow at the insult.

"I'm pretty sure you were into it at the time. Want an instant replay?"

Before I could process his words, his hand slid up my back and under my ponytail, holding me still. His lips covered mine and I froze in place. It was just as explosive as the first time, as everything in me responded to the dominant way he took what he wanted. I gasped and when my lips parted his tongue slid against mine in an erotic dance that made me even more lightheaded.

My entire universe contracted to that moment; my body pressed against the muscular frame that had haunted my dreams for years while the man I loved desperately kissed me stupid.

Noah slid one leg between mine, and the contact of his hard thigh against my core made me cry out. I'd never known I could feel like this; hot and cold, furious and elated, damned and blessed, simultaneously.

"That's it, princess. God, you're so perfect. Everything I should never touch." His whispered words didn't even make sense in the moment, but the soft rasp of his breath against my neck as he kissed his way down my throat sent me soaring.

My eyes opened briefly, and while he was busy doing things that felt amazing to my collarbone, my eyes landed on the picture frame on the bed.

Noah had never said these sorts of things to me before, and *I knew him*. I knew how he operated. Everything I'd discovered today had proven that he'd use any skills he had to get his way.

Even seduction.

I shoved him away and then picked up the frame from the bed. He ducked just in time to avoid getting clipped in the forehead when I threw it at him.

"You aren't going to distract me by pretending to want me, Noah."

He blinked, his eyes looking lazy and seductive, the way I imagined he'd look when he woke up. Or after lovemaking. I shook my head, trying to clear my mind.

"You think I was pretending?"

Noah looked down, and I followed his gaze to the huge bulge in the front of his jeans. *Oh my god.* My breath left my lungs in a rush.

"It doesn't change anything," I protested weakly.

Noah walked forward and I tensed, worried that if he kissed me again I wouldn't have the willpower to resist a second time.

"It changes everything, princess."

He leaned forward and I closed my eyes, bracing for another erotic assault. Then my eyes popped open at the gentle kiss on my forehead.

"Go to sleep. Before I give you what your eyes are asking for."

I watched as he strode out of the room, pulling my door closed behind him.

CHAPTER NINE

Noah

I should have never kissed her. Because once that line was crossed, there was no going back. No pretending. She'd been there, she'd felt the desperation I had to keep touching her, to keep holding her, pressing my body into hers. It was unmistakable. My only option right now was to attempt to bring us back to normal. To before.

My dick twitched against my thigh as if to say, *yeah, good luck with that.* I groaned and turned onto my side, flipping the pillow under my head. As big as the couch was, it was still just a smidge too short. My feet were dangling off the edge. The blanket I'd pulled out of the linen closet covered my feet but not all of my chest. Plus, I usually slept naked. Somehow, I didn't think that was going to fly with Lucia in the next room. Then again maybe she did, too.

Do not think about Lucia.

Do not think about Lucia lying naked in bed.

Not that I would ever know whether Lucia slept naked or not, but either way, it didn't matter to my dick. Damn thing hadn't gone down since I'd gotten a taste of her.

I rolled over again and stared at the ceiling.

How did you end up here?

Because you insisted you knew best.

I'd intruded on her privacy. I knew it. And the thing was, I wasn't sorry. I'd been keeping watch over her for years. Keeping her safe. Keeping her from finding out about ORUS. About Rafe. About myself. Allowing her to keep her air of innocence for as long as possible. Allowing her to live the kind of life that was only possible when you were oblivious.

But now, when there might be real danger, I had no idea how the hell I was going to keep her safe. I had no idea why she had started digging into Rafe's death again. Or maybe she'd never stopped. I wasn't even sure exactly what she'd found. Suddenly her date with Brent made sense. Whatever she'd asked the pencil pusher to look up, someone didn't want her asking questions about it.

I had Matthias digging for any traces of that company name she'd given him, but so far he hadn't found anything. I just prayed that whatever she was doing, I could still keep her safe. She was messing in some dangerous waters, and I couldn't let her get too close to the man that I'd been before. Because then she would be in real danger.

I considered all the things I'd kept from her for years. How would she react if she knew the truth? If she was pissed off now, I could only imagine how she would feel about me then. She would run out of my life and never look back.

I shook my head as if I could dislodge the unsettling thought. I couldn't allow that to ever happen. If she knew what kind of man I was, *the things I'd done*, she would never speak to me again. She would never even look at me. Right now, she was mad. But she would eventually see I had her best interest at heart.

If she found out the truth, it would be over.

There would be no more family dinners at the DeMarco house anymore. No welcoming arms, even when she was irritated with me. The one constant in my life, gone.

After what I'd done, I deserved worse. But I didn't want to lose her. That could never happen. I wouldn't *let* it happen.

In a perfect world, one where I wasn't a natural born killer, I could have a girl like that. Sweet. Sunshine practically pouring out of her. A completely normal life filled with all those silly things that couples did. Brunches at Bryant Park, walks around the city talking about nothing, horseback riding in Central Park. All that stuff I'd always seen as cheesy and stupid. But cheesy or not, they were things I would never have. That was family. That was love.

That's not for you.

No. I knew that. I'd learned that lesson a long time ago.

From her bedroom, I heard a low buzzing noise, kind of like her phone was ringing. I immediately rolled over to my side, and picked up my phone off the coffee table. I'd paired our phones together. *Yes,* without her knowledge, but it was for her own good. Whatever, I'd swallow the guilt on this one. But there were no incoming calls, or text messages. What the hell?

When I rolled back to my side and my dick throbbed again, I suddenly had a very good idea of exactly what she was doing in there and it made my blood run hot. My muscles bunched as I tried to force my brain to think of anything other than Lucia using that monster dildo on herself. Legs splayed wide, eyes rolled back in her head, panting.

No. Stop it now.

I couldn't have her, so I wasn't thinking about her like that. That was just a recipe for — *Jesus Christ.* The buzzing was still going on.

With a growl, I called out, "You'd better not be using that monster vibrator in there. You know I can hear it."

Immediately the buzzing stopped. She was silent. Quiet as a church mouse. Her happy drawer went against everything in my mind of exactly who Lucia was. The problem was that in a twisted way, that knowledge only made her more interesting. And even more untouchable. With a frustrated moan, I sat up.

"Hey, DeMarco. Just wondering, does that thing stand up and tap dance too? Inquiring minds and all that."

Yeah, I was giving her shit. Being an asshole. But I needed her to stop using that thing. It was bad enough I kept thinking of all the myriad ways I could use it on her. Those dirty thoughts weren't going to help either of us sleep.

I called out again. "What's the matter? Pussy got your tongue?"

My brain was working against me. Now all I could do was think about my tongue between her legs.

"You know, I hear you can go blind if you use those things too much."

I lay back against the pillow and smiled into the darkness when I heard one of her drawers slam shut.

If I wasn't getting any sleep tonight because of my raging erection, then neither was she.

———

Lucia

Number of attempted orgasms: 1.
 Number of setting changes on battery-operated boyfriend: 4.
 Number of hours of sleep obtained: 0.
 Number of attempts to stop thinking about Noah: Infinite.

I had slept like a monkey's ass, and my mood was not made any better by Noah with his tight-shirted workout that morning. I managed to stumble out of my room, bleary-eyed and in desperate need of coffee, only to find him doing push-ups in my living room. Beads of sweat clung to his hair and his muscles were clearly defined under his clothes. And the worst part was, he looked—delicious.

There, I said it. He looked amazing. Sweat had molded the T-shirt to his ridiculous body. I may or may not have spent a good couple of minutes counting his abs. Or licking them in my mind.

No. Stop it. Noah is the devil. I hated him. Okay, so not exactly *hated,* but he pissed me off like no other.

And infuriatingly, the asshole totally caught me staring. Like a man with too much sex appeal for his own good, he'd given me one of his shameless cocky grins. As if to say, 'Yeah, I know what I look like. Were you dreaming about this last night?'

I'd have had no other choice but to say 'Hell yes.' I *had* been thinking about him. And no, it hadn't gotten me anywhere. Except to Frustration City.

By the time I made it into the office after being jostled on the subway for thirty minutes, I was ready to rip someone's head off. This morning, Matthias had been my escort, and he'd been perturbed at my refusal to get into the SUV. But he'd had no choice but to follow me onto the subway. After all, what was he going to do, throw me over his shoulder? First, he wasn't the type. Unlike the others who worked at Blake Security, he wasn't a caveman. I wondered about him sometimes. There was no way Noah would have sent him with me if he didn't know how to protect me.

Luckily, JJ was already there. She was always guaranteed to put a smile on my face.

"Morning sunshine. You excited? I'm so stoked about my first fashion week. I know you've been to a couple of these now with Adriana, but I can't wait. I get to sit in on the final strategy meeting for hair and make-up. I guess you're getting the final model list today?"

After fashion school, JJ had been apprenticed to a makeup artist. I'd already managed to score a gig here at Adriana Patterson Fashions so when JJ had been looking for change, I recommended her. It was awesome getting to work with my best friend, but maybe not first thing in the morning before my second cup of coffee and after a night of no sleep. JJ was just far too chipper for eight o'clock in the morning.

"Yeah, sounds great."

"What's up? You're extra grumpy today."

The guilt hit hard. "Sorry. It's not your fault. It's freaking Noah."

JJ sat on the edge of my desk. "What? The strippers were a perfect idea. Did they not show?"

I groaned. "Oh, they showed all right. Noah was *pissed*. And the company sent me a video recording of them singing happy birthday. I have digital proof of Noah at the center of a confetti storm. That part is awesome. What's not so awesome is Noah in overprotective mode."

JJ laughed. "What? Did he decide that you must be somehow dating one of the strippers and do a background check on the guy?"

I rolled my eyes. "He thinks he's protecting me. What he's really doing is being an ass. I don't have a father or big brother anymore. I don't need him volunteering."

JJ sighed. "I have told you a million times that Noah isn't volunteering as tribute. He does this shit because he wants you. Sooner or later you're going to need to see that. But I digress. What's his problem this time?"

I checked the time and stood. "I need to go get Adriana's coffee. Walk with me and I'll fill you in?"

"Yep, let me get my purse."

We headed out of the building toward the heart of Soho. Adriana had a very specific coffee order that only one coffee cart vendor in the city carried. And he didn't open until 8:30. So this was part of the routine. What was *not* part of the routine was JJ peppering questions about what Noah was doing at my place. Or the shadow I knew had to be following me.

"Okay, you know how I've been looking into the situation around how Rafe died?"

JJ nodded. "Yeah, I remember you said that you might've found out who owned the house. From Brent, the records guy? He gave you the information, right?"

I nodded. "Yeah, he gave me what I was looking for, and I sent it off to Matthias to look into on the lowdown. But then a couple of days later, I got a letter in the mail telling me to stop digging."

JJ stopped dead in her tracks. "Excuse me? Is there a reason you don't have an armed escort right now? Why aren't the cops following you around? You know, skulking behind corners trying to act like hidden bodyguards? Ooh, even better, a young Kevin Costner?"

I dragged her along. "I swear to God you sound just like him. I don't *need* a bodyguard. Anyway, once Noah found out that I'd asked Matthias for help and then got this note, he insisted that he was moving in. So, there he was this morning, working out or whatever, and looking hot in a T-shirt."

JJ grinned. "Oh, I see. You're getting a little hot and bothered under that buttoned up collar. That's totally normal. You realize he's doing it on purpose right?"

I frowned. "What?"

"Honey, the guy has a gym at his place. As if he needs to work out in your tiny ass living room. Besides, if he's so worried about you, why didn't he send you with an armed guard to protect your ass?"

I groaned. "Who says he didn't?"

We slowed as we reached the coffee cart and took our place in line. I angled my head to the northwest where a black SUV sat, with Jonas in the driver's seat. He winked at me.

I rolled my eyes and turned back to JJ. "Jonas is on duty this morning. He's been following us since we left the office. Matthias accompanied me on the subway because I refused to sit with Jonas in the car. So I do have armed bodyguards. I just don't want them."

JJ laughed. "Somehow, this is not the hot sexy bodyguard scenario I was picturing in my head. I mean, they are sexy as hell, but I was picturing more of you and Noah in a forced proximity kind of thing."

I rolled my eyes.

"So, what are you going to do? I mean are you going to stop looking into Rafe's death?"

I shrugged. "Right now I don't really feel like I have a choice. Noah could help. He has resources. But he doesn't want me digging into any of that stuff. Keeps telling me if I go digging, I might find things I don't want to know."

"Maybe he has a point, sweetie."

"How can he say that to me? To be quiet and not worry my pretty little head? At the same time, whatever my brother was working on, he was killed because of it. I still have nightmares. So for now, I'm letting it go. Because all I've ever wanted is normalcy. If someone doesn't want me to look, it may be a good idea to lay low for a while."

"So you're listening to Noah for once?"

I smacked her on the arm. "If you tell him, I swear to God I will shave you bald."

JJ laughed. "Whatever. I could totally pull off a pixie cut. Okay, look. Maybe you need a night out to forget about all this stuff for a bit."

"How? I'm not going to be allowed to go anywhere without my oversized baboons following me. They'll never let me out of their sight. Let alone go somewhere that's going to be hyper crowded. They'll probably escort me right back to my place tonight. No detours allowed."

JJ scoffed. "C'mon, it's Friday night. And I feel all right."

I laughed "I wish. But even if I could shake them, they have this uncanny way of always finding me. They're probably tracking my phone."

JJ chewed her bottom lip as she thought it through. "Well, what if you left your phone here? You don't need it while you're with me. I have my phone. If anything weird happens, you can call Noah. He may not be too thrilled, but you're still perfectly safe with me."

I considered the idea. Noah would be pissed. But he had bugged my place, so he deserved to have me give him a hard time.

"Okay, let's say we do it. Exactly how am I supposed to ditch Thing One and Thing Two? I see Jonas. But I know Matthias is around here somewhere. I just can't see him."

JJ grinned. "You leave that to me."

I lifted my brow. "Why do I have a feeling that we're going to get in trouble for this?"

"Oh, ye of little faith. You know the girl in Accounting, the one with the curly hair? She matches you enough in looks and height that if you change clothes, they'll follow her back to your place. Or at the very least follow her onto the subway. Which is just enough time for us to get into a cab and go party."

I stared at JJ. I'd always loved my friend's more adventurous side, but this...this was diabolical. "You think it'll work?"

JJ gave me a brisk nod. "Noah and crew will never know what hit them."

CHAPTER TEN

Lucia

I tossed back my first and only shot of the night and wiggled my hips to the techno beat blaring through the club. This wasn't usually my scene, but after how tense everything had been, I had to admit that JJ was right. Alcohol and dancing were the cure for almost anything.

"Are you having fun?" JJ yelled over the music. As usual, my friend looked amazing, even while sweaty and tired.

I pushed back a curl that had escaped from the high bun I'd eventually pulled my hair into. No matter how I started the night my hair always ended up in a bun. It was the only way to contain the frizz.

"I am. This is exactly what I needed," I yelled back.

JJ smiled but her eyes kept going to something over my shoulder. I turned and saw a tall, well-built blond guy near the bar who was staring at JJ.

"That guy is cute. You should go talk to him."

JJ shrugged. "Maybe later. Gotta make him work for it." But even as she said the words, her eyes slid back over to the bar.

Suddenly, I realized why she was being so blasé. You don't ditch your friends. Since it was just the two of us, JJ wasn't going to leave me alone. Which made me feel guilty. Just because I had no sex life, it didn't mean that my friend should have to suffer.

"Go talk to him. I'm fine. Actually I'm going to head out anyway."

"Are you sure?" JJ bit her lip and glanced back over at the bar. I turned around too and then laughed when the guy winked at her.

"Yes, I'm sure. Go!" I pushed JJ in his direction and then grabbed the small clutch I'd abandoned on top of the table when we started doing shots. I watched wistfully as JJ approached the bar and climbed onto the stool next to blondie.

I'd give anything to have JJ's confidence but truthfully, it probably wouldn't even matter if I did. My heart had been lost years ago to a grumpy, overbearing asshole. On that depressing thought, I walked down the stairs separating the bar area from the main dance floor. The club was packed and before long I was overheated and slightly nauseous from being bounced between all the people.

Suddenly, someone grabbed me from behind. I twisted frantically and screeched as adrenaline flooded my system. But in the midst of the crowded dance floor it was impossible to move away.

"Get your hands off me!"

The music was so loud that no one paid any attention as I was picked up and carried through the crowd. I went slack, forcing my attacker to carry the full brunt of my body weight. To my surprise, he just turned me around and threw me over his shoulder. I got only a glimpse of Noah's pissed off expression before I found myself hanging upside down.

Shock made me compliant. How the hell had he found me?

Finally we reached a dark part of the club. Noah set me gently on my feet and put his arms on the wall on either side of my head to keep me from escaping.

"How did you know where I was?"

Noah glowered at me. "I have my ways. What the hell is wrong with you, Lulu? Do you think this is a game?"

His use of my old nickname sent shock through my system. No one had called me that in a very long time. Not since Rafe died.

"I'm not playing games. I'm just trying to live my life. A life that doesn't include you."

"Is that really what you want?"

"No. None of this is what I want. What I want is for my big brother to be alive and for him to be here annoying me right now instead of you. So go away and leave me alone."

"That's not the world we live in. And since we don't live in fantasyland, there is no way I'm going to leave you alone, ever. I failed him but I will not fail you."

"What does that mean?"

Noah sighed and bowed his head. He wasn't going to tell me. It always came back to this, his inability to let me in.

He moved to block me when I tried to walk away but at my evil glare, he allowed me to pass. It took quite a bit of maneuvering to get to the door past all the sweaty, moving bodies, and I had no doubt that Noah's hulking presence was the only thing that got most of the people to move. *What a metaphor for the rest of my life,* I thought with amusement. Noah had always been like that, largely unseen in the background of my life until I needed him.

Outside, I took a big gulp of fresh air. It occurred to me that this was the perfect time to make a run for it. If I surprised him, there was a chance I could catch a cab and get in before he could catch up. As if he could guess my thoughts, he leaned over and whispered "Don't even think about running."

"There you are! I saw you get grabbed..." JJ suddenly appeared on the sidewalk next to me. She looked between us with a knowing smirk on her face. "I should have known. Hi, Noah."

He nodded in her direction. "Hi, JJ. Do you need a ride home?"

"No, I'm good. There's a sexy Viking inside who's going to plunder my spoils tonight. But thanks."

Noah grimaced, unsettled as always by JJ's bluntness. "Great."

JJ was aware that she wasn't his favorite person, and it had never bothered her. Instead she took the opportunity to needle him every chance she could.

"Heard you've been playing with dildos. I can get you one of your own if you want."

"No, that won't be necessary." Noah looked almost green now.

"Okay, if you're sure. I get a discount so it's no biggie. Hope you enjoyed the stripper-gram the other day. That was my idea."

I snorted behind my hand, the events of the week and the long night of dancing suddenly catching up with me. The street swam before me and I would have fallen over if Noah hadn't caught me.

"That's our cue to get home." Noah flagged down a passing cab.

JJ stood back as he bent and scooped me into his arms.

"Wait. Noah, she was really hurt by whatever happened between you guys earlier. Will you...just be careful with her, okay?"

"I would never do anything to hurt her."

Then it occurred to me that JJ didn't know that I'd been drinking virgin margaritas all night. She probably thought I was drunk. I almost lifted my head to tell them both I could take care of myself but then stopped.

I was finally where I'd always longed to be. In Noah's arms.

My heart pounded so hard it felt like it was trying to escape my body as I curled my fingers in the front of his shirt, wishing I had the right to do this all the time. But for now all I could do was rest my head on his shoulder and absorb the feeling of being safe and secure in his arms.

Anything else would have to wait.

———

Noah

The ride home seemed to take forever. The entire time, I looked down at the sleeping angel in my arms and wished that things could be different.

Lucia deserved the kind of guy that could be honest with her and tell her his darkest secrets. Share everything. But that would never happen. My darkest secrets would break her, and that was the absolute last thing I would ever want to do.

The cab pulled up outside her building, and I shifted slightly to pull out my wallet. I handed over a few bills, not even caring if I'd overpaid. All of my attention was on taking care of Lucia. I'd never seen her the way she'd been tonight. For an hour, I'd stood in the shadows watching as she drank and danced and looked more lost by the minute. Maybe no one else would have been able to tell, but I could see the sadness in her eyes and it killed me to know I'd put it there.

I'd broken her trust, and I'd do it over and over again. There was no possible happy ending to this scenario. She'd only be hurt more deeply the closer she got to me.

Lucia stirred only when I had to set her on her feet to open her apartment door. Even then, she leaned against me, almost melting into me, looking up with achingly big gray eyes.

"It's okay, princess. We're home."

As I whispered the words, I'd never wished more intensely that they could be true. That this could be *my* home and that I could belong here. It had been so long since I'd had a true home.

She closed her eyes and leaned against me again as I carried her inside. I didn't bother with the lights since I knew every inch of her apartment just as well as I knew my own place. I settled Lucia on the couch and shrugged out of my jacket. After a moment of hesitation, I took my holster off as well. I was going to have to wake her to get some water in her and she hated to see my gun, always had.

I walked into the kitchen and retrieved a bottle of water from the fridge. After opening it, I took a swig myself. Even though I hadn't been drinking, I'd spent an hour sweating bullets wondering where she was before finally tracking her through JJ's phone. I wasn't sure if Matthias had done something illegal to find out where she was, and I wouldn't ask.

I walked back into the living room and knelt next to the couch where Lucia had burrowed into the pillows.

"Lucia? I need you to drink some water."

She sat up slightly and took a few sips. Her eyes stayed on me the whole time. After draining about half of the bottle, she set it aside.

"Let's get you into bed."

She shook her head. "Not yet."

I swallowed hard as I watched her. She was so damn beautiful. The curtains had been left open and moonlight illuminated the living room. There were several shoes kicked off by the door, like she'd had trouble deciding which ones to wear that morning.

I eased her onto the couch and pulled a throw over her. Unable to help myself, I watched her sleeping for a moment. If I could I'd memorize the lines of her face and the adorable way she moved her lips while she slept, like her mind didn't stop working, even in sleep.

When she suddenly opened her eyes, I wasn't ready for it. We stared at each other, naked emotion on display for a few seconds before she shocked the hell out of me by tugging on my hand until I sat on the couch next to her. She scooted over to make room for me.

"How do you do it?"

Her voice was soft in the quiet of the room but still penetrated all the way to the deepest part of me.

"What?" I asked gruffly.

"How do you live without knowing why?"

Surprised to see her eyes wide open and completely alert, I wasn't prepared for her to ask *that*. "That's not really a middle of the night conversation, princess. Go to sleep. You'll feel better in the morning."

Lucia sat up in bed and crossed her arms. "I'm not drunk, Noah. I was drinking virgin drinks all night."

"I saw you do a shot."

"Yeah. *A* shot. As in...one. I was able to fool JJ into thinking I was partying before that but then she wanted to do shots. I couldn't really ask the bartender for a shot of apple juice."

I laughed. "Why do you hang out with her, anyway?"

At that, Lucia glared at me from the corner of her eye. "Maybe she's loud and brash and occasionally pushes me to do things outside my comfort zone but you know what else she is? *Honest*. With JJ, what you see is what you get. She would never lie to me. That's just not how she rolls."

I closed my eyes. "You're still angry with me."

She had every right to be pissed but it wouldn't change anything. I still couldn't confide in her, and I was still going to annoy the hell out of her by hovering.

"I miss him so much."

When I looked at her again, I was shocked to see tears streaming down her cheeks. Lucia was an emotional person but carried herself with such dignity. I'd only seen her cry the day of Rafe's funeral. She'd put on a stoic face as she consoled her grandmother that terrible day and every day since. But apparently Lucia was as skilled at hiding her true feelings as I was.

Moved by her emotion, I moved closer and gently thumbed away the tears. She sighed and pressed her cheek into the palm of my hand, and I knew with certainty that I'd never love anyone else quite like this.

"I miss him too, princess. Every fucking day. I'm always thinking about what he'd do in a situation or what he'd say if he were here."

She looked at me pleadingly. "How do I let this go? If I stop looking for answers, it feels like I'm letting him down. Because he'd never stop searching for justice for me. Never. Even if he was afraid of what he'd find."

Not caring that this was far too intimate, I pulled her to me. Lucia let out a sob and clung to me, her arms wrapped around my neck so tight I almost couldn't breathe. I welcomed the discomfort. I'd take any pain for her. Anything but telling her the truth that would devastate her so completely.

"I can't stand to see you cry," I whispered.

Lucia glanced up at me and then slowly raised her hand to my cheek. I was shocked when she drew it back and her fingers were wet.

"I don't want you to be hurt either," Lucia said. Then she curled her hand behind my neck and tugged me closer.

I should have pulled back. I should have turned away. But, the only thing I could do in that moment was allow her to guide my lips to hers. The first brush of our lips jolted me to the core. The kiss was soft, sweet, and it filled me with a sense of rightness that I'd never felt before.

This woman was my sun, my sky, and my reason for existence.

"I love you, Noah." Her whispered words sent me soaring, and then just as quickly, crashing again.

She couldn't love me. She didn't truly know me. If she did, she wouldn't be looking at me with her heart in her lovely gray eyes. A good guy would tell her that.

Then Lucia smiled and kissed me again, and I was lost.

CHAPTER ELEVEN

Lucia

"Lucia?" he murmured against my lips.

I stared up at Noah. He was asking permission. Or maybe he was asking if I'd lost my damn mind. I wasn't sure. All I knew was that I wanted his lips back on mine. I didn't want him seeing me as a little sister. Not anymore.

I reached up and cupped his cheek gently before sliding my hands into his hair and pulling him down to me. As he leaned over, I could see the torment in his eyes, the confusion. As if he waged a war with himself.

I had no clue what I was doing. All I knew was I liked this feeling. This tingly, too-hot, desperate feeling. I liked being in his arms. I didn't know what that meant, but I didn't want him to stop.

He growled low in his throat and I was no longer in control of the kiss. His lips crashed on mine, pouring heat and desperation and desire into me with every lick of his tongue into my mouth, with every graze of his teeth on my lower lip.

Noah angled our bodies, until I lay back against the arm of the couch. As we shifted to get more comfortable, he moved so that he partially lay over me, his full weight resting between my thighs.

Oh God. Yes, please.

His lips were expert. Equal parts gentle, but demanding, coaxing a response out of me with his tongue, with his hands, which teased at the hem of my shirt.

His thumbs gently grazed my skin in slow circles. All I could do was hold on and dig my hands into his hair. He slid his hand over my skin, teasing the lower ribs, making me tingle.

Involuntarily, I raised my hips in a desperate attempt to get closer to him. Before I knew what was happening, his strong hands picked me up and over, lifting me until I straddled him, bringing my center right onto his —

Oh. My. God. He is huge.

And that felt—amazing. His hands gently gripped my hips as he kissed me, rocked me over him. The motion made me cry out.

Noah dragged his lips off of mine, kissing along my cheek and then my jaw. His hands were in my hair, tugging my head back. He brushed his lips against my throat, murmuring, "You are so fucking beautiful."

I felt beautiful in his arms. Sexy. Wanted. I rocked over him again, his strong hands guiding me, showing me exactly how to move. He nipped at my throat, gentle love bites, followed by teasing licks to soothe the tiny wounds.

I tried desperately to drag air into my lungs but all that came out were tiny pants, hardly enough to stay conscious. Screw it. Who needed consciousness? I loved this buzzing, floaty state with Noah. This alternate world. One in which I was sexy and he wanted me more than his next breath. I didn't want to go back to reality. Not yet. I just needed—more.

Noah dragged his lips away from my throat, and somewhere in the room there was a low whimpering sound. Wait, was that me?

Noah chuckled. "So you want more, do you?"

He took my hands, and slid them over his shoulders, into his hair before bringing his lips back to mine; giving me those heady kisses that put my brain into a coma and made my heart thump and my body tingle.

As he kissed me, his hands slid up under my shirt again. When his thumbs grazed the undersides of my breasts, I gasped, automatically arching into the caress. Against my lips, I could feel his smile. He knew exactly what he was doing, how he was making me feel. And I didn't care, I wanted more.

"I think we can get rid of this," he whispered.

I looked down at the shirt he tugged on, and nodded my head briskly. "Yeah. Who needs this old thing?"

He gave me a lopsided smile as he tugged on the hem. I raised my hands to make things easier for him, and up and over it went, making barely a sound as it hit the coffee table behind me.

Noah stared, his eyes pinned on my bra as he licked his bottom lip. Impatient, I rolled my hips again, riding along the edge of his erection, and his gaze snapped back to mine. "You feel what you're doing to me without even trying?"

Breathlessly I asked, "Am I doing anything?"

He gave me another patented Noah Blake grin as his hands slid up my back to support me. He leaned into me, gently kissing along my ribs on the left, and then across to the other side. Kissing the underside of my bra, and then my sternum. Teasing. Promising, but not delivering. Driving me crazy. He was doing this on purpose. He knew the effect he had on me. Knew that any second, I was going to burst into flames.

"Noah—"

"Easy, princess. No way in hell I'm rushing this."

Damn it. I needed—more.

Through my bra, Noah blew a hot breath directly on my nipple. That tore a low moan out of my chest. *Holy cow. That was so—*

But he wasn't done yet. With one thumb, he drew gentle circles over the opposite nipple, even as he wrapped his lips around the now hardened bud. He grazed gently with his teeth, then lapped at me with his tongue.

"Oh my God. Jesus."

Behind me, his fingers flicked and I felt my bra strap release. The next thing I knew, his mouth was on me. *Hot. Wet. Slick.* With every pull of his tongue and lips, my core contracted. I involuntarily rolled my hips, seeking more contact, more friction, just *more.*

Apparently, Noah had plans to torture me as he moved to do the exact same thing to my other nipple. With an expert flick of his tongue, pulling and tugging, he made me beg.

Noah Blake completely owned my body.

With his lips still around my nipple, he made a muffled sound as his fingers slid down my ribs, and my torso, past my bellybutton to where I rode him. Oh so gently, he ran his thumb over the heat of my core through my leggings, and I bucked.

With a hand firmly on my ass, he kept me in position and continued to tease me with his teeth. His thumb drove me closer and closer to the edge of bliss and destruction. One stroke up, one stroke down, then a slow, teasing circle.

Ooh God, I was going to die like this—hovering on the edge, not knowing what it would feel like to—suddenly my body bucked and shook, and stars exploded around me. The rush of heat and heaven and pure pleasure flooded my bloodstream.

"Oh my God, Noah."

Against my nipple, Noah muttered, "Yeah, princess. That's it. Let go for me."

I thought he might stop, but he kept up the onslaught, dragging me right back up the mountain only to push me over once more. When another wave of pure bliss washed over me, I sagged.

Noah finally let up with his thumb. He gently released my nipple and kissed up to my collarbone, then my jaw, and gently kissed my lips. "My God, I love how you do that."

I flushed. "I don't think I've ever—"

But I didn't get to finish, because Noah was kissing me again. Gentle, unhurried, but deep. Against my core, his erection still throbbed as if begging, 'I'm still here. Please don't forget about me.' Not that I could.

He gently lifted me so that my legs wrapped around him, and he carried me through the living room and down the hall to my bedroom.

He gently set me down on the bed before reaching for my leggings and dragging them off in one fell swoop. Then he reached behind his back and dragged his T-shirt over his head. With only moonlight streaming in through the edges of the blinds, all I could do was make out the shape of his broad shoulders and the ridges of his abdominal muscles.

He was—wow. I held my breath and waited for him to finish undressing. Geez, we were really doing this. And despite the fact that I'd never done it before, I wasn't scared. Quite the opposite. I wasn't worried at all.

Except, well, he was *huge*. But I wanted him. I wanted *this*. I'd wanted Noah Blake from the moment I'd first noticed boys, so there was no stopping this train. I was running past go, and I was going to collect my $200.

Noah undid his buckle, shoved his jeans down and stepped out of them easily. Before he tossed them though, he reached into a pocket and grabbed his wallet, taking out a condom and tucking it into the back of his boxer briefs.

He climbed on the bed beside me and tugged me to him, pulling my body flush against him, and the hair on his chest made my nipples tingle with awareness again. He flipped us over so that I lay on top of him.

Against the juncture of my thighs, his erection pulsed, begging for freedom. I brushed my fingertips along his stomach, his muscles bunching and shifting with every trace.

When I reached the edge of his boxers, Noah dragged his lips from mine and cursed. "Lucia?" he asked, his voice gravelly as I teased my fingertips along the edge. When his hips rose, he muttered a string of things he'd never said around me before.

"Yes, Noah."

His breath hitched. "You know you're driving me crazy, right?"

I was driving *him* crazy? I was the one who felt like I was on the edge of desperation. Now I wanted to play a little. "Am I?"

Another hip roll from him. "Yes. You can't tell?" His voice was barely audible as his muscles tensed.

I lifted my head to watch him carefully as I traced my finger over the soft cotton. Deliberately, I traced my fingers along the length of him. Noah hissed, but he didn't stop me. I grew bolder, wrapping my fingers around him and squeezing gently. Wanting more, I released him and then slipped my hand into the waistband.

Noah sat up. "Lucia, wait."

I froze. "Am I doing it wrong?"

He gave me a sharp chuckle even as his brows furrowed down. "Wrong? Fuck no. But if you—"

I wrapped my fingers around him again, feeling the softness of his skin, the throbbing pulse as the blood that ran through his body concentrated in one organ. Gently I pumped him, fascinated that I was having this kind of effect on him.

"Oh, *fuck*, Lucia. Jesus. I won't make it. You have to—"

I traced my fingers to the tip, spreading the drop of moisture that had pooled. "Is this okay?"

Noah groaned but didn't stop me. Instead, he dug his hands into his hair and tugged while he let me play. His body twitched and bucked under my exploration. But he didn't push, nor did he stop me. I raised my gaze to meet his. He was watching me with a half-lidded look of desperation in his eyes. I turned my attention back to what I was doing. My tongue snaked out of my mouth as I wondered what those pearly drops of moisture tasted like. I licked my lips.

Noah cursed. "Oh, no you don't. If you put your mouth on me, I'm not going to make it. And I think I owe you at least a couple more orgasms before you put me down for the night."

I had no idea what he meant, but damn he was fast. Before I knew it, he had me flat on my back with his lips on mine again. With both my hands safely trapped in one of his, he kissed me deeply. When he pulled back, he nipped at my bottom lip.

"I think that's enough playing for now. You can play more later. Right now I'm too on edge."

He took the sting out of taking my new favorite toy away by giving me something he knew I liked. He lowered his head to my nipple, sucking, licking, driving me back to that brink of heaven. But this time, instead of just stroking me through my underwear, he took his hand down to the juncture of my thighs, parting me gently.

I had to remind myself to breathe, trying to remember how to do the simple motion I did every day, all day. It was too difficult with Noah teasing me. In and out.

Noah teased the skin where the elastic of my underwear met my thigh and then nudged the fabric aside. His thumb found me slick, and wet, and one of his fingers gently teased my entrance, probing, testing.

Against my breasts, he muttered, "Fuck. I could do this all day." Then he slid a finger in deep.

I never stood a chance...especially when he curled the finger inside me, pressing gently.

Holy Mother of God. He pressed again gently stroking back and forth, and then I was sailing over the cliff, happy to dive without a parachute. My body quaked, tightening around his finger, desperate to hold it inside.

"Oh my God, Noah."

He hooked his thumbs in the elastic of my panties and tugged them down easily. And then, he splayed my hips wide with his broad shoulders, tucking his hands under my ass, lifting me to him. The first stroke of his tongue made me moan. He stroked me again and again, and soon one orgasm rolled into another, and I had no idea where Noah ended and I began.

With every stroke, lick, gentle flick of his finger, and penetration of his tongue, I was flying into the void.

I collapsed against the pillows, my body limp, unable to move. Noah kissed his way up my thigh even as he chuckled. He rolled away to shuck his boxers. Then I heard the tearing of foil. When he rolled back, he settled over me. I lifted my hips impatiently.

"Lucia, you're supposed to let me take my time."

No way that was happening. I lifted my hips again. I wanted him. I wanted this. He was taking too long.

Noah growled deeply before sinking in to the hilt. I hissed. *Oh God.*

Noah muttered, "Fuck. You're so tight."

"Noah—"

He pulled back a little, and I wrapped my legs around his back. No way was he leaving. He dropped his head to my throat and nuzzled me gently as he sank back in. Another curse.

He repeated the action, small movements, until the sting and burn were replaced with something far more intense, far more pleasurable. Once again, Noah was dragging me to the edge of the cliff, but this wasn't a race for something fast and fleeting like a fireworks. This was stronger, more tangible somehow.

Noah dropped his forehead to mine. My fingernails dug into his shoulders, and I blinked rapidly as I tried to hold on tight. His gaze met mine and held. Then he made love to me. His hips rocking in and out; slide, retreat, slide, retreat, never breaking eye contact.

I matched him thrust for thrust, rocking my hips into his, seeking more contact. My fingers clutched desperately at his shoulders, trying to pull him deeper. "Noah, please," I whispered.

Something broke, and it was like the tether on his control snapped. He rocked into me again, harder this time, his pace increasing. No longer gentle, he bit his lower lip and his motions became more desperate. His hand tightened on my hip, almost bruising.

His lips were a demand on mine, his hand in my hair under the nape, angling me so he could kiss me deeper. And then it happened again. I broke all the way down to my soul, and I squeezed my legs around him, unwilling to let go as my body convulsed.

"Jesus, what the fuck..." His pace increased, almost punishing, he was no longer in control. He was chasing me. Chasing bliss. Chasing something more.

When he came, his body went rigid over mine and he threw his head back as he roared. I dug my nails into his shoulders, and he gripped me tight.

And as I looked up at him, I knew I would never be able to get him out of my blood.

———

Noah

A faint sound from the other room woke me with a start. I reached for my gun holster and realized I'd left it in the living room with my phone. I was used to being ready for action at a moment's notice. One damn night with Lucia and I was forgetting critical shit?

Rookie mistake, dumbass.

The phone chimed two more times, and then after a brief pause, started again. I had to get that. Lucia's body curled into my side. The sheet had slipped, exposing her bare shoulders, and I wanted to kiss one of the freckles I saw there. But if I did, I'd want to kiss more. And if I was right, my old life was calling.

I slipped out of bed without waking her, quickly padding into the other room to grab my phone before the noise woke Lucia. I entered my passcode and then stared at the string of text messages I'd just received. To anyone else they'd look like a string of random letters and numbers, but to me, they were a reminder that my past was never too far away.

What the hell did Ian want? The series of messages told me who the anonymous caller would be. It was a system we'd worked out at ORUS. A series of secure text messages sent through relays, pinging across several countries. We'd learned every agent's signal as a matter of course.

Three minutes later when the phone rang from a blocked number, I answered, "Ian, what's wrong?"

Ian's voice was mellow, calm. But then, that was Ian for you. Nothing ever ruffled the guy. Not the years of wet work. Not the time he'd almost bled out in an alley with no help for three days, save a scared sixteen-year-old kid.

Ian didn't particularly seem to enjoy his job either, but that didn't make the dude any less eerie.

"Noah, you sound well. You almost sound like you were sleeping."

I ran a hand over my hair as I stood naked in Lucia's living room, talking to a ghost. "Well, I sleep much better now but you know the drill. I still never sleep through the night. What do you want, Ian?"

My old friend hesitated a moment, and that pause made the hairs on my arms tingle. Something was very, very wrong. Ian didn't hesitate about shit.

"Look, I'm calling out of respect. For you. For Rafe."

Fuck. "Spit it out, Ian."

"There's been a call put out for a job. It was assigned to me, but I'm feeling a little sluggish today. I don't really know if I want to get out of bed for anything less than 200K. So a job like this, no skin off my back to give you a call and a heads up."

My skin went cold, clammy. They were finally coming for me. Or after two years, were they coming for Matthias? That was the only thing I'd done to truly piss off our superiors. I'd known the kind of people I had worked for. It had been a risk taking the kid, but I'd had to. Besides, ORUS were supposed to be the good guys...as assassins went. They only went after the worst of the worst. The ones who had managed to evade local and international laws. The things that went bump in the night. Why were they coming after me now? Why did what I'd done to free Matthias matter after two years?

I was so lost in thought, I almost missed what Ian said next. "It's the girl. We got a call out for Lucia."

My whole world stood still as the icy tundra pushed away all warmth, all feeling, all sunshine.

"Job came in about thirty minutes ago, right before I texted you. So it's fresh."

"What the fuck happened to you guys being the good guys?"

"*You* guys?" Ian asked incredulously. "You forget, once you're one of us, you stay one of us."

My chest constricted as I looked toward the bedroom. If they were coming for Lucia, they'd have a hell of a time getting through me first. I needed to get her to the office. The place was a fortress. Except, shit. I didn't want to scare her. Didn't want her paralyzed with fear.

We needed a plan. For starters, no way was she going anywhere without an armed guard. Probably two. Fuck it, three. I dragged my attention back to Ian.

"Why call me? You know how that will look. And do you want to fucking explain to me how taking her out is for the greater good?"

There was another brief hesitation before Ian answered. "Let's just say I'm keeping to the respect thing. Besides, I don't think you were wrong for leaving. ORUS, what we do here, it's not for everyone. But we are concerned with the greater good, even if you don't see it. The kid, she's turning up stones that will get a mess of people killed."

"Did you send the letter?" I demanded.

There was a pause. "What letter?"

"She got a letter a couple of days ago that told her to stop digging. You guys fucking with unarmed civilians now?"

"I know nothing about it. Look, if you can keep her safe, and you can get her to stop looking, maybe this shit goes away. Either that, or you take her and the money you have squirreled away and you run."

"I'm not fucking running." That came out as more of a growl.

Ian sighed. "I know. It was worth a shot. If you want, I can find out more about exactly who wants the hit. I'll try and keep it discreet. Orion's still salty about Matthias."

"Thanks, Ian. I owe you one. After the way I left..." I let my voice trail.

Ian cleared his throat. "You saved my life once. Besides, you saw a way to save your soul and you took it. I can't be mad about that. Someone like me, I'm too far gone, if I ever had a chance in the first place."

I had to get the fuck out of here. I had work to do. "Any way you can buy us a day or two?"

"Not likely. Orion makes sure there are fail-safes on each job. Since you. Since Rafe. Not much chance of holding him off. But I'll see what I can do." My old friend took a deep breath. "Look man, watch your six."

"Will do." I hung up and immediately called Oskar to come and take guard watch. Then I began snatching my clothes off of Lucia's bedroom floor like a co-ed at a frat party. I spared her only a small glimpse before leaving. I'd fucked up last night. Gotten way too close.

She was a bright ray of sunshine, and I, well, I was all darkness and shadows. I may not be worthy of her, given my past, but I could sure as shit protect her.

I would start by never touching her again.

CHAPTER TWELVE

Lucia

My eyes flew open and for a moment, I didn't know where I was. The sound of a gunshot echoed in my head. I shivered and my fingers curled around my comforter, clenching the fabric so hard it hurt. As my eyes adjusted to the darkness, the dream receded and the panic that had put my heart in my throat faded a bit.

I was home, safe in bed.

With a soft moan, I buried my face in my pillow, grateful tears welling in my eyes.

Breathe in.

Breathe out.

I focused on slowing my breathing until I was calm enough to open my eyes again. It took a few seconds for them to adjust to the darkness, but then I was able to pick out the shape of the table next to the bed and the chair by the window where I always threw clothes when I was deciding what to wear. It was comforting to focus on the familiar shapes that told me I was home.

Not back in the courtyard of an unfamiliar building with my brother's dead body on the ground next to me.

I sat up, dragging the sheet around my shoulders. The nightmares were becoming more frequent. Before this week, it had been a few months since the last one. Was it really accurate to call it a nightmare when it had really happened? It was more like my memories deciding to torment me. If I concentrated hard enough, I could feel the cold weight of steel in my hand and the blast of pure rage that had fueled me as I pulled the trigger. Certain details were so vivid it was like a painting I could reach out and touch. But no matter how hard I tried, I couldn't see his face, my brother's killer. The man I'd shot in a rage, desperate to protect my brother and myself.

Thinking about that always led me down a rabbit hole of depression that took weeks to crawl out of. After years of self-reflection and a short bout of therapy, I'd learned that it was best to stay positive. I'd lost my brother but I had survived. There was nothing to be gained from lamenting the way things had happened in the past when I couldn't change it.

Staying in bed staring at the ceiling after a nightmare had never helped me fall back asleep so I decided to go watch a movie in the living room. When I tried to stand I sucked in a sharp breath.

"Oh, whoa."

Moving slowly, I sat back down on the edge of the bed. The dull throbbing between my legs brought back the more recent memories of what had happened right here in this very room. The fact that I was completely nude was also a dead giveaway. I'd slept with Noah. How could I have forgotten? Only a nightmare could have distracted me from the most monumental event of my adult life.

I smiled remembering how wild and passionate Noah had been and how...*intense* it had been to be completely one with him. It had been overwhelming but in the best way.

"Noah?"

I waited to see if he was in the bathroom or perhaps had gone to the kitchen to get a drink. When there was no reply, I stood again, dragging the sheet around my naked body like a toga. The hallway was dark but I could make my way from memory. I flipped on the light in the kitchen. It was empty. I got a glass down from the cupboard and filled it at the sink. After taking a drink I walked into the living room.

Where the hell was he?

I swallowed against a rising tide of panic. He wouldn't just leave me after last night, would he? I curled a hand around my neck and rubbed the knot of tension at the base of my nape. Maybe he was walking around outside just to make sure we were safe. I opened the door and poked my head out in the hallway.

One of the bodyguards Noah had hired last year stood across the hall. I had only seen him around the office sporadically but thought his name was David. Or was it Derek?

He straightened up, and then his eyes slowly widened as he took in what I was wearing.

"Um, hi. Did you need anything?" He asked while keeping his eyes somewhere over my left shoulder.

When I glanced down I almost choked as I realized that my toga-style sheet had slipped and was exposing an extreme amount of cleavage. I blushed so hard it felt like my cheeks were melting. Freaking perfect. No wonder the poor guy was so uncomfortable.

I was going to kill Noah for this.

"No, I don't need anything. Sorry about...well, whatever. See you later...Derek?"

"It's Dylan," he said with a small smile.

"Right. Dylan. Well, see you around."

I backed up and then closed the door, careful not to catch my sheet. The last thing I needed was a wardrobe malfunction. We'd both spontaneously combust from mortification.

I stood there for a moment, unsure of what to do. Noah had left. He'd just...left. What did that mean? Things had been so great, hadn't they? At least they had been for me. Maybe it wasn't good for him?

Feeling completely lost, I walked back to my room and picked up my phone. Then put it back down. I wasn't going to be some needy girl who called him crying because he'd slept with me and then bailed before I woke up. I was a modern, independent woman and I could handle this. He was the one missing out because I was *awesome.*

I climbed in bed with the sheet still wrapped around me and snuggled beneath the covers, an angry tear escaping. A few seconds later my hand shot out and grabbed my phone. It only rang twice before JJ answered in a sleepy voice.

"Hello?"

"It's me. I slept with Noah last night and then he was gone when I woke up. What does that mean?"

There was a pause before JJ answered. "*Motherfucker*. I'm coming over."

———

Noah

"Knock knock. Is it safe to come in?"

I looked up to find Jonas standing just outside. Normally he would have just barged right on in. Any of them would. But everyone had been giving me a wide berth that morning. I was as prickly as a bear and starting to get on my own nerves.

"Come in."

I waved a hand absently for Jonas to take a seat in one of the modernistic metal chairs in front of my desk. Everything in the office had been designed to be efficient, functional and easy to clean. That was exactly what I'd wanted at the time, but in my current mood, the stark atmosphere wasn't helping any. That was one of the side effects of spending the night wrapped up in Lucia's softness.

It had been like ascending to heaven, only to be dropped back into hell a few hours later.

How was I supposed to walk around in the world after an experience like that? She'd been so sweet and so damn eager to please. I gripped the paper in my hand, no longer able to see any of the words on the page. All I could see was Lucia's lush curls tangled on her pillowcase, the hesitant but trusting expression in her beautiful eyes when she'd taken me deep for the first time.

That look in her eyes had smashed me over the head at about five o'clock this morning. I'd been in the middle of rearranging the caseload for the next month so I could have all available agents covering Lucia. One minute I was seeing the scheduling system on the computer. The next, all I could see was her beautiful face and that damn look of blind trust and love.

"Damn, you have it even worse than I thought," Jonas muttered.

I looked up to find my friend watching me with a mixture of pity and disgust.

"Don't even say it."

"Fuck that. I'm the only one who has the balls to come in here and confront you, but somebody has to. What the hell are you doing, man?"

The softly spoken question hit the target, making me feel even more like shit than my own conscience had been able to. Worst of all, I had no answer. There was nothing I could say in my own defense.

"This is not the time, Jonas. I know I fucked up. Believe me, I am fully aware."

"Are you really? Because if you don't want us all up in your business, maybe you should have Matthias kill the video feed beforehand."

I groaned and pressed the heel of my hands against my temples. I regretted reinstalling the camera over Lucia's door. I'd been singularly focused last night, first on getting Lucia home safe and then protecting her from the newest threat. Nowhere in all of that had I even considered that the entire team would witness the aftermath of my monumentally bad decision-making.

"Fucking hell," I muttered.

"Luckily, we couldn't see that part," Jonas said. "But we all saw Lucia wandering around this morning wearing nothing but a sheet. We all saw her face as she was looking for you and finally realized that you weren't there."

It broke me to imagine my sweet princess waking up to discover that I was gone. For her to have to face the fact that she'd given herself to the worst sort of man. All those guys I'd driven off, and I'd been unable to protect her from the worst predator of all. *Me.*

Jonas seemed to sense my inner torment because he slid forward in the seat, his face softening a little. "Look, everyone knows how you feel about her."

I squeezed my eyes shut. "You don't know shit."

"I don't want to see you mess up a good thing," Jonas continued, as if he hadn't heard the bullshit coming out of my mouth. "Stop being a dick. Lucia loves you, too. We can all see it. Don't push her away out of fear."

Anger rose up in me, blinding me with its ferocity. Did they think I didn't want to be the kind of man that deserved a woman like Lucia? I would give my left nut and probably the right one, too, for even a shot at making her happy. But wanting something didn't make it possible, and there was no amount of redemption that could ever clean my slate. There was nothing I could do to come back from where I'd been, and I would never expose the purest, brightest thing in my life to that kind of darkness.

I owed her that, at least.

"Let's be real here. She is...perfect. I'm not going to pretend I don't want her. A dead man would rise up from the grave for a chance to be with her. But you know who I am, Jonas."

I held the other man's gaze until my friend dropped his eyes with a defeated sigh. After a moment, Jonas put a hand on my shoulder. The touch would have pissed me off coming from anyone else, but the warm weight that only a decades-long friendship could bring was much appreciated right then.

"You feel like you don't deserve her. I get it. But you are the only one she has left, too. Are you really going to trust her safety to someone else?"

After he was gone, I dropped my head to the back of my chair. Jonas could give me all the pep talks in the world and feed me a bunch of kumbaya bullshit all day. But in the end, we both knew what kind of depravity lurked beneath the surface of my skin. We'd both witnessed what it was like when I lost my veneer of civility and returned to my roots. What was in me was not pretty. It was not civilized.

Would Lucia look at me with those trusting eyes if she knew how many lives I'd taken? Could she hold me close at night knowing she was nurturing a man who could torture another without losing a wink of sleep? As a young boy, I had learned that the parents I adored had died, and since then I hadn't had the luxury of emotions or weakness. I'd never even wanted them because in my world, staying alive was the difference between caring too much or not at all.

All this self-reflection wasn't changing a thing. I'd fucked up by getting involved with Lucia. She'd be angry with me for a while, rightfully so, but that didn't change my conviction to protect her. All I could hope was that I hadn't hurt her too much.

The look of trust in her eyes flashed through my mind again. Then I sat straight up as something occurred to me. Something I hadn't thought of this entire time and should have.

Lucia was a sweet girl. Shy. Quiet. For years, she'd lived under her grandmother's roof, and for years after that I'd scared off any guy who tried to get close to her. I prided myself on my attention to detail, so the fact that I could have missed something so monumental was unbelievable. But all the signs were there, plain as day.

"She is never going to forgive this." I dropped my head into my hands.

How the hell had I missed the fact that she was a virgin?

CHAPTER THIRTEEN

Noah

Yeah okay, I knew I had fucked up.

After Jonas had read me the riot act, I'd had hours for regret to come crashing down on me. How the hell had I not known? *Because it felt too good.* My brain ever-so-helpfully offered up images of Lucia, head thrown back in ecstasy. Her perfect tits on display for me. With amazing clarity of detail, I recalled everything from her scent, to her taste, to the softest patch of skin just behind her knee.

You took advantage.

Had I? Fuck, had I hurt her? She'd been tight. *So damn tight.* She'd stiffened as I sank into her. In my defense though, she had begged me to keep going. She'd dug her fingernails into my flesh and raised her hips and—yeah—I'd kept going. I'd lost track of the number of times she'd come around my fingers, my tongue, my cock.

My dick twitched inside my jeans. *Down soldier.* No more of that. I had to figure out how the hell to apologize. That shit was never supposed to happen. One moment, she'd been so sad, hurting. The next, I'd been kissing her. And once I had my lips on hers, there was no going back. She'd given me everything, and like an asshole, I'd taken.

And then left her.

Shit, even Dylan gave me major side-eye when I showed up to

Lucia's apartment. There was no doubt in my mind I'd have a lot of groveling to do later. I cleared my throat.

"Any movement?"

Dylan shook his head. "I relieved Oskar a few hours ago. Right now, she's got her best friend in there." He shifted on his feet and slid his gaze away. "Honestly, dude, if I were you, I'd maybe leave me in my post for a while. Send Jonas, send anyone. But don't go in there alone."

Yeah, okay, I deserved that. I'd been a prick. She had every right to be pissed at me. And my men had a right to give me dirty looks.

I took her virginity, and then I walked out on her. Who the hell did that? Something cold and slithery curled up in my gut. The real question was how the hell had I not known? All the signs were there. She'd looked worried, asked if she was doing things right.

And fuck, if I was being honest, I had pretty much ruined any chance she'd ever had at a real relationship. Usually before the guys got anywhere close enough to her to get her naked. And instead of some nice guy who was all gentle and kind, she'd gotten me for her first time.

Helpfully my brain supplied images of last night. Lucia arching her body into mine. Lucia calling my name. Lucia with her hands in my hair as I licked her. I wanted her again. Hell, I'd wanted her before I woke up this morning, with her body pressed tightly to mine.

I wanted her now. Only difference was now, she very likely wasn't going to want me. Which was fine, because I didn't deserve to touch her anyway.

The way I'd touched her? How demanding I'd been? Yeah, I should kick my own ass.

"Thanks for the advice, but I got this." I nodded at Dylan then drew in a deep breath and pushed open the door to find JJ and Lucia on the couch, empty tubs of ice cream in front of them, and liquor.

Empty bottles of liquor.

Oh shit. Things were going to get ugly, fast. I needed to diffuse as quickly as I could.

"Hey JJ, can I talk to Lucia for a minute?"

From the couch, JJ raised a brow. Then she said something to Lucia, who wouldn't even look at me. When JJ pushed herself up to full height and strode over to the door, I had no choice but to consider my weapon options. She was small, but I knew the look of murder in someone's eyes.

When she reached me, she placed her hands on her hips, legs akimbo. "You are a grade-A asshole. You know that? For years, I have encouraged her. Because like a fool, I believed you cared about her. But now? You've proven you're just like the other douchebags in the world. You hurt my best friend. You only live right now because I *allow* it. And I only allow it because she won't *let* me kill you. And that's only because she's afraid I'll go to jail." She chuckled. "Little does she know I'd be running the joint within a week."

My lips twitched. I wanted to smile. But I knew that was not the right response. JJ was taller than Lucia. All blond hair and big blue eyes. She was cute. I also completely believed that she could run any prison in this country. She radiated Valley girl cheerleader but was tough as nails. She didn't fuck around. Especially not when it came to her best friend and her feelings.

"JJ, if you just let me speak to Lucia —"

"No, asswipe. You do not get to speak to Lucia. Because not only did you abandon her after you two fucked like rabbits— my term, not hers—you put a goddamned armed guard at her door who won't let her leave. Asshole is calling it *detaining*. I call it kidnapping. Not sure, but it doesn't matter because all of this is against her will. Which means I'm about to call every lawyer in the city, and you are going to have your license for security, or whatever the hell it is that you do, revoked. Do I make myself clear?"

I was losing patience quickly. I needed to get Lucia on the same page right the fuck now. I didn't have time to explain to JJ how this was none of her goddamn business.

See, right there? That's what makes you an asshole. Remember what Jonas said?

I forced myself to take a deep breath and to use a gentle tone of voice. This wasn't JJ's fault. This was *my* fault.

"What I'm trying to tell you is that I'd like to apologize to Lucia. An apology works better if I can be sincere and private."

JJ's brows popped up. And her lips formed a small *oh*. "Okay, fine. You can apologize or whatever. But I'll be waiting right here when you're done. If she finds it lacking in any way, your ass is mine."

She punctuated that last statement with a pointy-fingered jab to my chest. And while I knew I was bigger than her, I had a sudden fear for my balls.

"Lucia, can I see you in the bedroom please?" I didn't even wait for her, instead marching ahead straight to her room. I hoped she'd follow, because if not, I'd go out there and make her follow.

No. Remember, finesse. The way I'd been doing things had gotten me where I was now.

The problem with meeting in the bedroom was that it still smelled faintly of sex. And of Lucia. Her perfume, her body oil, her shampoo. There was still evidence of all the things I'd done to her last night, including the twisted, tangled sheets and comforter on the floor. She'd left the bedroom untouched from the morning, which was unusual. This wasn't her.

When she walked into the bedroom, her face was a placid mask showing zero emotion. "What do you want, Noah?"

I started to speak but then couldn't find the words, and my shoulders sagged. "Lucia, I would never have left you if I could've helped it. You have to know that."

She crossed her arms. "What I know is that I woke up and you were gone. That's not your fault. It's my fault. I don't know why, but somehow I trusted that you would be there when I woke up. I trusted that I wasn't just anyone in the legion of women you've slept with. You see, I'd convinced myself that last night was *something.* And that is my fault. Instead of waking up with me to pick up where we left off, or hell, just to do the grown-up, mature thing, you sent Dylan. Which caused all kinds of feelings I can't even explain, but demoralizing comes to the top of my mind."

I strode right up to her. But she held her ground and tilted her chin up at me.

"Lucia, I'm sorry. That is not how I wanted everything to go down. Especially not for your first time." I frowned. "Why didn't you tell me?"

Lucia winced as if she'd been slapped. "You could tell?"

Fuck. And now she felt like shit because she thought I'd known all along she was a novice. I ran my hands through my hair.

"No. I couldn't tell. Which is why I wasn't more —" I searched for the right words and finally settled on, "Gentle. If I'd known—That's something you should tell a guy. I would've taken more time. Or *some-thing*. Shit, I wasn't supposed to be your first, Lucia."

She glared at me. "Well, it's too late for that now, isn't it?"

"Why didn't you tell me?"

She rocked back on her heels, allowing her anger to give way to hurt for the first time. "Because you would have stopped. And I, like an idiot, thought you were what I wanted. But you're not."

I stared at her. She was lying. She may be pissed at me, but her pupils were dilated and her nipples were tight. I could see them clearly through her thin T-shirt. I forced my eyes to hers. "No, sweetheart. You *do* want me. At least your body does. But I'm inclined to agree with you. Last night never should have happened."

"Oh that would be convenient for you wouldn't it, Noah? You were as much a part of last night as I was. You need to deal with me now. I'm not just Rafe's little sister anymore. You slept with me. You don't get to pretend it never happened."

"You think that's what I want? You're wrong." I leaned close, careful not to touch her. I kept my voice low and guttural. "What I want is to drag you back into that bed and rip that T-shirt off of your body because you should never be covered. I also want to bury myself so deep inside you that you don't walk again for a month." I forced myself to pull back. "But that's not what I'm going to do. Because right now there are bigger things at play. Your life is in danger. And not just some unknown, ephemeral danger either. I got a call from an old associate last night. Someone is trying to kill you. So until I can figure out who that is or what they want, you're keeping your armed guard. Sometimes two or three. I will put the whole damn firm on you if I have to, but I *will* keep you safe."

"You know, I'm so sick of you saying things like that to me. Rafe used to do that, too. Keep me safe from whom? Who is this old associate that you know? How do you know him? How is it that a guy who owns a security firm knows when someone's trying to kill me?"

"I can't answer those questions for you. You have to trust me."

"Trust you? After you walked out on me? Yeah, good luck with that."

Her scent filled my nostrils and made me dizzy. "You don't like me very much right now. I understand why. Shit, *I* don't like myself right now. Considering I didn't have the pertinent information that I needed, I didn't know how badly this morning would affect you. All you need to know is that I didn't do it to reject you. I didn't do it because I didn't want you. I did it because I needed to get working on keeping you safe. If you don't like it, I get it. But the truth still stands. Someone's trying to hurt you, and I'm the only thing standing in their way. No way am I letting anything happen to you. Not on my watch. So for the time being, my guys stay on you like glue."

She was having none of it. "Oh yeah? Does that mean you, too?"

"Of course. I'll be sticking closer than any of the others. I shouldn't have touched you. But it's too late for that now, because now that I have, I'm not stopping. So I'm going to stay close until you realize you want me to *keep* touching you. While we're at it, you're not going to that fashion show thing."

Lucia gave me a wide smile and my balls shrank up inside of me. "That's super cute, Noah. But I'm going. If you try to stop me, I will become the biggest pain in the ass you've ever met in your life. My job, my life, is important to me. You want to be the one who protects me. I might not be able to do anything about that, but I can make your life hell. So work fast to figure out who wants to hurt me, and follow me if you have to, but if you think I'm letting you come anywhere near me —"

I shouldn't have done it. I really shouldn't. But there was something about fighting with Lucia that made my blood burn. I dragged her to me and kissed her soundly on the mouth, letting all the frustration of this morning and the revelation that last night had been her first time pour into that kiss.

When I released her, she staggered backwards. "You make my life difficult—I can do the same. If your fashion show is so important, fine, you'll go. But with all of us in tow. I'll be back tonight. I'm on watch duty."

"Send Matthias," she called after me.

As I turned the doorknob, I turned to look at her and gave her an evil grin. "Matthias isn't getting anywhere near you in your T-shirt and panties. I'm the only one who's going to be that close to you."

With that, I stormed out, leaving JJ on the couch with a confused look on her face. I barely grumbled a goodbye to Dylan as I left.

———

Lucia

Noah hadn't been kidding about the extra detail. This morning, it was Jonas and Dylan. At noon, that had switched over to Ryan and Oskar. I had a feeling that tonight when I left the office, Matthias would be joining me in a private car. With this small team, there was no way he could keep this up forever.

So far they'd been discreet. They only stopped me from taking the subway like I usually did and insisted on driving me to work instead. To my chagrin, somehow each of them had managed to get a shift as a security guard at my building. So there was one guy upstairs on my floor by the main entrance. How Noah had gotten that approved by Adriana, I'd never know. And there was one guy guarding the front. I didn't know how they managed to pull that off either, and I wasn't going to ask.

One day, if I ever decided I was talking to Noah again, I'd ask him. But for right now I was too irritated.

Luckily, I had FedEx parcels to be taken downstairs. That gave me something mindless to do. With fashion week so close, much of my work was frantic and repetitive, and I felt like I was running in circles. I hated always feeling like I was behind, or would forget something. But this, taking packages down to messenger out, this I could do. Simple, mindless. And I didn't have to think about people trying to hurt me, or Noah, or the fact that I freaking missed him. Which was just wrong and unfair.

I nodded at Ryan when I passed the security barrier and made a left toward the FedEx window in the building. I wondered if I could even make it out the door without Ryan seeing me and notifying his partner. But there was no way. The front doors could easily be seen, and no one was getting upstairs without a pass. They'd probably tapped into the building's cameras, as well. Which was just damn perfect.

I dropped off the packages and turned back toward the stairs when I gasped. Someone was waiting just to the left, in the doorway.

"Brent?" I shifted my glance over to the guard desk. While I had a clear view of Ryan, he couldn't necessarily see me that well. Or who I was talking to. "What are you doing here?"

Brent ran a hand through his hair. "Look, I've— I've been wanting to call."

I sagged. "I meant to call too. I'm so sorry about what happened with Noah. Just look at him like an over protective adopted brother or something. He's pretty much always an asshole. Even to me."

He nervously shifted on his feet. "Lucia look, I know when you came by the office and asked for information, you said you were looking for something to help someone in your family. And I wanted to help you. I did."

I frowned. "But you did help me." Not that I was going to use that information any more.

"That's just the thing. I gave you enough information that was true, but there's some falsified material in there, as well." He pulled an envelope from his coat. "This is the real information."

I glanced at the manila envelope. "I don't understand."

"I shouldn't be here giving this to you. But look, when I moved to the city, I was desperate. When I got that job at the records office, some guy offered to pay me a shit ton of money just to make sure that no one ever got their hands on these particular records, and I didn't think anything of it. Well, I did, but it seemed harmless at the time. And then you came looking. I did what I was supposed to do; give you the wrong information and send you on your way. But I made the mistake of asking you out. You were just so pretty."

"What are you saying?"

He sighed. "I'm saying that I was paid to notify them if anyone ever came looking. The day you first came and asked, I notified them. But once I got to know you a little and we went out, I liked you. I can't lie to you anymore. You seemed really sincere about why you wanted the information. I'm not sure what you're looking for, but a couple of days ago I noticed some guys following me. So, this information must be important. I'm going to head out of town, but I didn't feel good about you not having what you needed."

"You're being followed?"

I wondered if that was Noah's guys. But with such a small team, how could they possibly do their jobs, watch me, *and* follow Brent? Besides, it made no sense.

"Brent, if you'll just come with me...Noah— he's an asshole, but he'll help. This is important."

He glanced over his shoulder. "No. I got myself into this mess, and I'm going to get myself out. Maybe head back home until things die down. I suggest you do the same thing. But I'm getting the hell out of here."

My fingers traced over the lip of the envelope. I wanted to open it. I wanted answers. That part of me that was always searching, lingering at the edges of my nightmares I couldn't see, that was the part of me that needed to know the truth. *It's not safe. You need to stay safe.* Yeah, but what good was staying safe if I couldn't really live?

"Thank you for bringing me this."

Brent hesitated. "Look, I know you really need that information, but this whole thing is bigger than I knew. Just promise me one thing?"

I met his gaze and nodded. "Of course."

"Be careful. These are not the best guys to get tangled up with, so please, promise me. Even if you need to go to that Noah guy for help, I'll feel better leaving if I know you're safe." He hesitated then added, "I'm sorry."

I watched as he hurried out the front doors. All the answers I wanted were right here in my hands. I just had to be brave enough to take that next step. *Are you ready to accept the danger?* I didn't care. I was done with letting Noah protect me. I wanted resolution, and I was starting with this.

CHAPTER FOURTEEN

Noah

I took everything out of my pockets, including my wallet, keys and phone and placed them in the small plastic basin provided for valuables. Then after walking through the metal detectors, I claimed my things and waited for Matthias.

"Please be careful with that," Matthias protested as the security guard put his headset in the basin.

The guard, an older woman with her dark hair pulled back into a tight bun, waved me through impatiently. Matthias walked through the metal detectors and then had to double back when the alarms blared.

I rolled my eyes as Matthias was subjected to a pat down and then scanned with the handheld metal scanner. A few chirps erupted from the device as she passed over the front of his body. As she brought the scanner right in front of his crotch, it chirped again.

Matthias turned bright red. "Um, sorry?"

The guard pulled her hand back quickly but I caught the faint smile on her face as she turned away. Matthias gathered his stuff hurriedly and then jogged to catch up with me.

It wasn't nice to tease the man who held my entire electronic footprint in the palm of his hand but I couldn't resist.

"I never thought you'd turn out to be the security risk getting in here."

Matthias flushed again but laughed. "Sorry about that. It's a new... um...piercing."

"*Right.* It's always you nerdy types who turn out to be the real kinky bastards."

We were escorted to a small waiting room, and I sat gingerly in a hard blue chair facing a coffee table filled with magazines. The celebrity face staring back from the magazine cover wasn't familiar, although all the recent celebrities looked the same to me. I sighed.

When had I gotten this old?

Matthias walked over to one of the windows and looked out. After a few minutes, he paced back to where I was sitting. It was only when I could see the other man's face that I figured out the weird tension I'd picked up on.

Matthias was nervous.

"Hey, are you okay? If you don't want to do this then we can leave right now and I'll tell the Deputy Director of Whatever to fuck off."

Although this was potentially the most lucrative contract I'd ever been offered, I had more than a few reservations about getting in bed with the federal government myself.

Matthias shrugged. "It's fine. Just feels weird to be voluntarily meeting with law enforcement, you know?"

"Yeah. Believe me, I understand." I chuckled at the thought. I shared Matthias's distrust of all people in power, but for the first time, at least *I* was in control.

Despite my knee-jerk instinct to avoid all law enforcement, I wasn't really worried. There was nothing to worry *about*. When Rafe had taken me on as an apprentice, he'd assured me there would never be any way to tie 'Steven Noah Williams' to my new identity of 'Noah Adam Blake.' My time working for ORUS had screwed me up in the head, maybe more so than I'd already been, but they took care of their people.

Their assets, I corrected myself. The shadows behind the ORUS curtain didn't care about any of us as people. We were tools to be used until we weren't useful anymore. Or until one of us gained the leverage needed to negotiate escape the way I had. The way I'd negotiated for Matthias.

It wasn't something that happened often.

A young woman appeared at my elbow. "Gentlemen? He's ready for you now."

Matthias glanced at me and nodded his head. The woman looked between us in confusion at the delay so I stood. We followed her down a long hallway and when we reached the last door, she stood aside to let us enter.

The man behind the desk stood and came around with his hand outstretched.

"Thank you for coming on such short notice. John Calhoun. I'm the Deputy Director of the FBI's Cyber Division."

I shook his hand. "Noah Blake. This is my associate Matthias Weller. We understand you've had a few threats you can't trace recently."

While we chatted, Matthias remained standing, only nodding his head when appropriate. With every minute that passed he got more agitated, and I decided that we could do without the revenue from this contract. From the day I'd pulled Matthias out of ORUS, I'd vowed to do for the kid the same thing Rafe had done for me. Teach him. Protect him. Show him that there was a better way. I hadn't come this far only to send him back into the lion's den before he was ready.

I glanced over at Matthias again. A fine sheen of sweat glistened on his forehead, and his fingers clenched the strap of his computer bag so tightly the skin was pulled white over the knuckles.

"Thank you for the meeting. I'll take everything back to my team and we'll devise a plan to see if we can tackle this."

Calhoun looked shocked, and I had to smother a laugh. I was willing to bet not too many people cut him off or interrupted his long-winded bullshit. Being the Deputy Director of anything in the FBI tended to gain people's respect. Most people's. Just not mine.

"Of course. Of course. Let me know what resources you need."

I tuned him out again, focused on getting Matthias out of there. When I leaned over to shake hands with Calhoun again, my eyes were drawn to a picture on the desk. Before I had a chance to look closer, Matthias suddenly turned and walked out.

"We'll be in touch," I assured the director before following.

I found Matthias in the waiting room pacing back and forth in front of the receptionist's desk. Wild-eyed, Matthias turned to me, his jaw set like he was daring me to say anything. The kid should have known better because no one understood catching a case of the vapors around the cops like I did. After years on the streets trying to avoid detection, it was ingrained to avoid all law enforcement like you avoided STDs.

Something in my face must have broadcast my understanding because the tension left Matthias's shoulders. In that moment, he wasn't the brilliant killing machine I knew him to be. Instead he looked his age, young and vulnerable, and I didn't care if we lost the contract or not.

Matthias hadn't had an easy life either, although I didn't know many details other than he'd escaped from England right before Scotland Yard could catch him with a rap sheet longer than an escort's contact list. But since the moment we'd met, I'd seen something in Matthias that reminded me of myself. Something worth saving. I would do whatever was necessary to get the kid the hell away from his personal bogeyman.

"Let's go."

Matthias didn't ask any questions, just followed me while muttering hasty goodbyes over his shoulder. Once we were out on the sidewalk, we moved quickly to the second level of the parking deck where we'd left the car. When we were on the road, Matthias looked over at me.

"Do you ever worry that your past will circle around and come back for you one day? That the stuff you did for ORUS will have consequences down the line?"

I sighed. "Every day."

———

Lucia

I was distracted all day and found myself making simple mistakes. Hopefully I hadn't screwed up anything Adriana would notice. But constantly looking over my shoulder had made it impossible to focus on the myriad ridiculous demands I normally handled with aplomb.

Ordinarily, I had a great sense of humor about my job. At least I was doing something I loved, right? But lately I'd started to wonder about the direction of my life. Brent's visit had only hammered the point home. He'd taken a great risk to do the right thing and let me know what was going on before he'd left town. There were a lot of people who wouldn't have bothered in his position.

Who was I to him, really? Just some girl he'd gone on a terrible date with once. He didn't owe me anything at all.

At two o'clock, I gathered my things and stuck my head into JJ's cubicle to say goodbye. Even though I'd gotten approval to take off early from HR weeks ago, I was always strategic when I had plans to leave before my normal quitting time. It wouldn't be unheard of for Adriana to invent some task she wanted taken care of at the last minute.

"I'm off. Hopefully Adriana doesn't need anything while I'm gone but can you cover for me just in case?"

"Sure, no problem. Nonna's okay, right?"

"Yeah, she just has a doctor's appointment today. I like to take her to make sure I hear the doctor's instructions. Now that she's having all these problems with her blood pressure, I want to make sure she's doing what she's supposed to do. She's so stubborn sometimes."

"Wonder who that reminds me of," JJ muttered.

"Hey, I'm not stubborn. I just know what I want." I left JJ with a wave and took the stairs down to the first floor instead of waiting for the elevator.

It was nice to be out in the sunshine in the middle of the day but there was no time to waste. Nonna had an appointment at three thirty so I had made sure to allow enough time to get to Queens even if the trains were running slowly.

As always I had a shadow. Ryan this time. As annoying as it was, he gave me space so it was easy enough to forget he was there. Luckily the subway wasn't experiencing any delays for once, and I arrived roughly thirty minutes later. I knocked once and then opened the door with my key. To my surprise, Nonna was in the living room working on the big book of crossword puzzles that she'd had forever. She was wearing the floral housecoat that she normally wore to bed.

"Hi, Nonna." I offered my cheek for a quick kiss. "Did you forget you have a doctor's appointment today?"

My grandmother blinked. "I had my doctor's appointment last week. Everything is fine."

I let my handbag drop to the floor with a thud. "Nonna! I took off work to take you."

"I'm sorry. I thought I'd mentioned to you that I'd already gone. I didn't want to worry you with my troubles. You're a busy career woman now."

Instantly I felt terrible. I was having a crisis but I shouldn't take it out on Nonna. All these years I'd complained that my grandmother didn't take my career ambitions seriously, and now that she finally was trying, I should appreciate it. I followed as Nonna got up and went into the kitchen. I watched as she put on the kettle for tea.

"You probably did. I've been distracted lately but that doesn't mean I'm ever too busy for you. Well, what about the bill? I can still take care of that."

Nonna didn't look at me and suddenly got very busy cleaning a spot on the countertop. "It's fine, *amore mia*. You don't need to worry about any of that."

I narrowed my eyes. Nonna slipped into Italian when she was nervous or agitated. So that behavior, along with her uncharacteristic reluctance to talk about her doctor's visit, something she'd normally love to complain about, only made my suspicions grow.

Nonna was hiding something.

"Where's the invoice? I'm sure the insurance didn't cover every- thing. I'll pay the balance for you. It's really no problem."

Nonna looked up at me with a hesitant expression. "It's already paid for. I told you I save money for a rainy day."

The sound of the door opening drew both of our attention. My grandmother bustled around the counter, strangely eager to investi- gate. I followed her and we both stopped when we saw Noah standing in the entryway.

"Noah, what a nice surprise!" Nonna welcomed him with open arms and he leaned down obligingly to kiss her cheek.

"Sorry to interrupt, Nonna." Noah glanced over at me. His eyes scanned me from head to toe as if looking for damage.

For a moment, I forgot how angry I was as I took in his appear- ance. His eyes were wild and kept darting around like he expected something to pop out at him. Finally our eyes met, and the energy that crackled between us was palpable. My heart flipped at the anguish I saw in his eyes.

Something was very wrong.

I took a step toward him before I stopped myself. This was how he always drew me back in. He did something unacceptable, but then I'd look into those deep brown eyes and forget all about it. But that wasn't going to work this time. He'd crossed the line, and I was done making excuses for him.

I turned around, hoping my grandmother wouldn't pick up on the tension between us. Ever since Rafe's death, Nonna had accepted Noah as his surrogate in our family. She was from the old school, and while there were a million rules I was expected to live by, Noah had carte blanche to pretty much do whatever he wanted. In Nonna's way of thinking he was the "head" of our family so she'd always turned a blind eye to his faults.

As much as I liked to believe I was a modern woman, I had to admit I'd been guilty of doing the same. All these years, I'd accepted Noah's interference in my life. But those days were over.

"I'm going to go. There's so much work I need to catch up on. I'll see you later Nonna." I kissed my grandmother quickly and then gathered my purse from where I'd dropped it near the couch.

I could hear Noah making his excuses and then his footsteps on the concrete behind me as I walked down the sidewalk toward the subway. Normally I'd engage, start a fight, maybe even scream at him, but no more. He could follow me but he couldn't make me talk to him. It was time to stop entertaining his nonsense.

CHAPTER FIFTEEN

Lucia

I shivered in the cool air of the church, the dimly lit interior forcing my eyes to adjust. Stopping right in front of the holy water font, I gently dipped my finger in and crossed my forehead. I blanketed all of my emotions and feelings in a thick layer of numbness.

I did not want to feel this way. I didn't want to feel anything. I didn't want my pain to rise to the surface and bubble over, spilling on everyone I loved. I didn't want it to affect Nonna, JJ, or even Noah. Despite how angry I was with him, if I didn't do something soon, I was going to combust.

Last night, I'd slept fitfully and agonized over the day to come. It was the anniversary of my brother's death, six long years since his murder. How fitting that last night I'd remembered more of that ill-fated day than ever before.

I could recall being happy at Coney Island, eating hot dogs and riding fair rides. I had consumed more funnel cake than any human being should. My brother had teased me, laughed with me, and won prizes for me. It was a perfect day until everything changed.

I'd gone to the bathroom, and in the span of time it took to wash the powdered sugar from my fingertips, I had washed away weeks of a happy and lighthearted mood. From the moment I'd returned to his side, Rafe's demeanor had gone dark, dour, and desperate. He'd been frantic to leave, frantic to get somewhere else. He'd begun to talk so quickly that I couldn't understand him.

He'd been full of anger and what looked a lot like fear. The whole time in the car, he'd apologized. Kept saying how sorry he was. I knew his worried look, firm brow, the restless tapping of his fingers on the steering wheel.

Rafe only fidgeted that way when he was nervous. He'd been worried about something and I didn't like it. Something had been wrong. I remembered Rafe giving me a gun. The gunshots. My brother going down. The weight of the gun in my hand as I pulled the trigger.

But when I tried to remember the face of the man I shot...nothing.

Nothing but a dark, empty hole in my heart and memory. It haunted me. From the moment I'd fired that gun, my next clearest memory was of being wrapped in blankets the next morning.

I'd woken on the couch in excruciating pain, my muscles so cramped that I hadn't been able to move them. Then Nonna told me Rafe had died the day before.

My grandmother hadn't told me what had happened or how I'd gotten home though. Months later, based on what others had asked me and what the Feds had told my family, I'd realized that my brother had taken me somewhere that warm summer afternoon and had then been shot.

The police had found me in the Hamptons, several miles from the location, huddled under a payphone that I had used to call for help. They'd found me frightened, shaken, and in shock, and they had taken me home. I'd been covered in blood.

I crossed over to the vestibule where the lit candles were. All lit in prayer for the sick, the lost, for those not yet born. I automatically put my stick in the flames and picked a non-burning candle to light. I whispered a quick prayer to a God I wasn't sure I believed in anymore. At the very least, a God I could no longer trust. After all, he had taken my brother.

In my peripheral vision, I caught a glimpse of Noah hovering in the doorway, shadows covering his face, as if he were afraid to step forward.

Yeah, he better be afraid.

I was still angry with him because of the things he'd kept from me and the interference in my life. I could tell he was hiding something even now. The way he had been so frantic when he picked me up from Nonna's yesterday. Normally, I would have poked, prodded, and teased him until his mood improved. This time, our relationship hung in the balance. It was time for him to apologize, and I wasn't going to let it go until he did.

Nonna brushed her hand on my shoulder. I could see her lips moving in silent prayer. I looked at my grandmother and knew I had been wrong. Wrong to let Rafe go, wrong to stop digging.

I had been trying to do what was right, to do what everyone had encouraged me to do daily. Nonna, Rafe, even the guys at Blake Security were always pestering me about my job, my love life, and my future. What did I want to do next? As if they were attempting to fill my life with so many things that I had no time to dig into Rafe's or what had happened to him. It would be wrong to let it go. It would haunt me forever until I found out the truth.

With my grandmother's hand on my shoulder, I turned my attention back to the candles.

"Go on, tell me, Lucia. What did he do now?"

I turned to Nonna. "What do you mean?"

She rolled her eyes. "I have been watching the two of you bicker and squabble since you were a kid. Normally, you argue, work it out, then minutes later you two are laughing like loons. This looks serious. Yesterday, today, the look in your eyes...it's not annoyance or irritation, it's hurt. You look hurt, baby."

I didn't want to get into it. Not here anyway. Not when my heart should be filled with questions about my brother, not when I should be focused on my fury at what happened.

"Just the usual, overprotective nonsense," I replied.

For a moment my grandmother was still. "You could do worse than him, Lucia. I know I've been pushing you to find a nice Italian boy. One who would take you on trips far from New York. One that would give you other things to think about like babies and travel. Take you to a vacation house in Hawaii. I've been wrong about that. Maybe Noah Blake is the kind of man you need."

I turned to face her. "What are you talking about? I don't need Noah. I'm almost twenty-one years old. I don't need a man. I'm not trying to find love or settle down. This is my life; I'll figure it out."

Nonna nodded and squeezed my hand, "Well in that case, there are worse men to figure things out with. Besides, he's the kind of man who'll protect you." Nonna shook her head. "I used to think he had too many shadows, that he was too much like your brother. Now I realize he's exactly the kind of man you need. Nice Italian boys like Antonio won't know what to do when the real trouble comes calling. Noah is the thing that trouble fears. He's the kind of man that would give his life to protect yours. He's good for you, and the two of you need to work out whatever you've got going on."

I turned back to the candles. "It's not that easy. You can't trust someone who does nothing but lie to you all the time."

Her voice was soft when she spoke. "You can't always see it, but sometimes those lies are really there to protect you."

———

Noah

I stayed on the periphery of the entryway. I was neither inside, nor outside. Today being Sunday, usually most of the guys would be off. But I had asked for a little extra help, just in case. Ryan was posted at the front door. Dylan stayed in the car, watching the entrance, acting as surveillance.

Jonas was inside, sitting in the front corner, observing everyone that came in. Oskar was standing near the middle pew, his shrewd eyes watching everything, especially Lucia.

I was no stranger to Catholic mass. When Rafe was still alive, he'd occasionally dragged me along to Sunday mass with Lucia and Nonna. I hadn't minded so much back then, especially since a big Sunday dinner always followed, and I'd been a growing boy with no family. So I'd figured I could survive church for a morning or two.

Even before then, I hadn't been completely unfamiliar with Catholic practices. A few of my foster parents had tried to incorporate the church into my life. The problem was just that I was bad to the core. None of the teachings had stuck.

As I shifted, standing just to the right of the holy water font, my eyes pinned on the one woman I shouldn't want.

Father Patrick Haney slid up to me. "Noah."

"Hey, Padre." I nodded.

"It's been a while since I've seen you here. You came more often when you were younger."

I rolled my shoulders. "The Padre" made me nervous. I worried that given his profession, the old man could see straight to my soul.

"Yes, well, that was before Rafe," I responded.

The Padre nodded silently. "Yes, but just remember, with or without Rafe here, your soul is up to you."

"There you go again, assuming I have one to save."

The father smiled, his cheeks pushing his eyes up until they crinkled at the corners. "Even the darkest of us have some good. Just like the best of us have some dark."

I watched as patron after patron walked up to the holy water and crossed themselves. One little boy pushed both his hands inside, then shook the water off. I swore that I felt a droplet hit my hand and it had warmed my skin. As if holy water knew who it was dealing with.

"Hey Padre, what does it mean when holy water burns your skin?" I stared down at my hand. "I'm, uh, asking for a friend."

I was only half-kidding, but the old priest turned his knowing eyes onto me. "It means you're being healed."

I could only watch in disbelief as the padre marched away from me to speak with Lucia and Nonna. *That old priest must be crazy*, I thought. Nothing was capable of healing me. I knew what I was.

What had happened at the FBI office yesterday had shaken me. I'd put Matthias in that situation, and it didn't sit well with me. I was supposed to be protecting the kid, not exposing him to threats.

Last night, I had tossed and turned on Lucia's couch as I dreaded today, the guilt eating at what was left of my conscience.

And of course the tension with Lucia was killing me. She still wasn't talking to me, and it made for sleepless nights and nightmares I couldn't shake.

Nightmares of an idealistic kid and the family that I had torn apart forever. No one knew the padre was 100% wrong. There was no healing for me. There was no redemption, only duty.

Once Lucia was safe, I had to stay the hell away from her because everything I touched turned to ash.

CHAPTER SIXTEEN

Noah

The tension swirled around me and Lucia in the silence. What was I supposed to say? There was no answer that would work. Because at the end of the day I *was* lying to her. Had been for years.

What are you going to do when she finds out what you did?

I couldn't worry about that now. All I could do was keep her safe. Keep her protected. That was my job after all. What I'd vowed to do. Like I hadn't been able to do for Rafe.

Lighting candles for my friend seemed like the most hypocritical thing I'd ever done. *You are not the good guy.* Despite what the padre said, God didn't hear my prayers.

"You're really going to sit there and not say a word to me?" Lucia's voice was low, but had a razor sharp edge.

I deftly navigated the Manhattan streets heading back to her apartment. "Lucia, I don't know what you want me to say. There is nothing to say. I'm doing my job. I'm keeping you safe."

She turned to me. "You see, that's the problem. I never asked for your help. I never asked you to keep me safe. I never asked for any of this. All I ever wanted was a normal life. But no, my brother was gunned down, and I had to see that. Had to *watch* that. I see it in my dreams every night. And there is nothing I can do about it, just like there was nothing I could do about it then. When you say things like you're *protecting* me, that's a joke. Because you can't protect me from the real horror." She tapped her temple. "It lives in *here*. The nightmare of my own making."

My gut twisted. "I can protect you. And I will. But I need you to stop. Stop asking questions. Stop poking. Stop digging. I need you to start listening because shit is about to get real."

"You think I don't know that? You have your goons following me everywhere I go. My grandmother is lying to me. *You* are lying to me. When do I get my life back?"

That was one lie I couldn't tell. Because if I lied to her now, the consequences would be dire later. "I don't know."

"You see? That answer isn't good enough. Your lies are not going to cut it anymore. You think I don't notice that Nonna has all that unexplained money. Seriously, you think I'm dumb enough to believe she's been squirreling that away all this time?"

"No one thinks you're dumb."

She continued as if I hadn't spoken. "I've been working so hard to give back because I knew there were times she went without to get me what I needed. Meanwhile, she had all that cash. She could've afforded a better place. But she stayed there. It's always been her dream to see Italy. I thought she didn't have the money. $5000 in a tin can and I'm supposed to believe she's saving it for a rainy day? That is a lie. It's been nothing but rainy days a long damn time."

"Lucia —"

"No. Don't you sit there and lie to me. I know something is going on. Noah, you had *cameras* in my apartment. That explains so much now. How you always seem to know when I'm on a date. How you always come in just in time to keep me from doing things. You realize that's sick, right? You're like some crazy big brother stalker. You're worse than my grandmother. You think I don't know that you pay half my rent?"

I whipped my head around to stare at her. "What?"

"Yes, the super stopped me last week, and he said to tell you that the owners are upping the rent next month. At first I assumed he was telling you because he thought you were my big brother or something, since you're the one always asking about security and making changes to the apartment. Now I realize it's because you pay my rent. Damn it, Noah, I'm not a child. It's time everyone stopped treating me like one."

"I'm not treating you like a child. I'm just trying to do what's right. If Rafe were here —"

"But he's not. And he hasn't been for a long time. Any obligation you had to my brother ended a long time ago. At some point, you have to let me live my life."

"You don't understand. Damn it, your life is in danger and you don't even know how much. And instead of helping me keep you safe, you're throwing a tantrum because I pay your rent. You want to put my balls in a vice because there are things that I don't tell you?"

"Noah, this is my life. Much as you would love to live it for me, you can't. How do you know my life is in danger? What's the plan? What are you going to do about it? This is usually the point when people call, I don't know, professionals like the police. I have a right to know."

As much as I wanted to, I couldn't tell her everything. As angry as she was with me right now, she would never speak to me again. It would forever change the way she looked at me. So I did what I did best; I deflected.

"You know, I find it funny how you're all over me about keeping secrets when one of the most important secrets has been held by *you*. You used my stud services, and you left out one very important detail. The secrets I keep from you aren't selfish. The secret you kept...you held on to it for yourself. Because you knew I would have stopped."

Lucia

I stared at him. "Are you being serious right now? You somehow think this compares?"

He'd relieved Ryan of duty and taken over my watch after mass. He was still just as tense as he was yesterday. I watched as his grip tightened on the steering wheel. I could always tell when a point hit too close to home.

"Lucia, this isn't a comparison, but this is a conversation we *can* have. One that doesn't put your life in more danger."

When we reached my apartment, he parked the car. He and Oskar pulled their typical watch pattern, one in front, one in back.

Eyes open, always aware. Oskar took his post outside my door as Noah ushered me in. The placement of his hand on my lower back made me tingle. It also made me fume.

I turned on him. "Would you get your hands off of me?"

"Would you stop being so damn touchy? I was being polite."

"Polite? Like how you walked out on me? Was that polite?"

Noah threw up his hands. "Jesus fucking Christ. You seriously are never going to understand. I woke up, ready and willing to go another round. And then I got that goddamn call. The one that told me that the woman I spent half my life protecting was in danger. So I'm sorry if I couldn't crawl back in bed for a cuddle and a poke, but I had bigger things to deal with, like keeping you safe. I had to scramble to get someone here to watch you. Then I had to get back to the office so I could comb through your life and figure out who has the means and opportunity to hurt you. And then I had to start combing through *my* past, and Rafe's past. Because you've never done anything to anybody, so why anyone would want to hurt you is beyond me. I'm sorry that I couldn't be the kind of guy who brought you breakfast in bed, but you would think I could get some fucking credit for trying to do the right thing."

"You jackass. I wasn't asking for breakfast in bed. Shit, a text would've done. Something...anything so that I didn't have to wake up alone not knowing where you were or what happened. Or wondering if that was the worst sex you'd ever had in your life. But no, you let me wake up alone with Dylan at my door."

My breath heaved out of my chest, and a flush crept up my neck as I remembered the loneliness. The embarrassment.

Noah blinked. His lips parted and his brows furrowed in confusion. "Is that what you thought? Seriously?" He shook his head. "You saw me. I could barely move. I'm pretty sure you almost killed me. I have never felt like that before."

His words didn't compute because the emotion choked all blood flow to my synapses. Before I knew it, I was spilling my guts, emotion charging every word.

"You promised you would always be here for me. Do you know what that's like? When the one person you're supposed to count on is gone after something like that? You've always been my constant, and then you ran like a coward."

"I didn't run. You have to know that it was not my choice to leave you. How can you not know how I feel?"

———

Noah

She felt that way? *Because you're an idiot.* Like a moron, I didn't even think to talk to her. To tell her. Give her any indication. *Instead you walked out. Shit.* Yes, I'd been reeling. I had never felt anything like that in my life. The fact that I felt that with Lucia, that shook me. I'd been her protector for so long.

Who was I kidding? She'd always been more than someone to protect. Even when she was just a kid, I'd always gravitated toward being around her. She was smart, and sassy, and there was something so good about her. Something that I wished would rub off on me.

Even then, I'd hoped for some kind of redemption. I was good at what I did, too good. Someone like Lucia, a part of me had hoped that being near her could save me. And she had.

"You have to know, everything I've done, I've done to protect you. I know you don't believe me, but it's the truth."

I shoved my hands in my pockets and rocked back on my heels. I sucked at this. I didn't do feelings. Feelings got you hurt. Feelings got you killed. *Like Rafe.*

"Noah, when are you going to see I'm not a kid anymore? I don't need protecting."

The fury and self-hatred simmered under my skin. I stormed over to her, deliberately crowding her. I needed her to see what I was. "Do you know where I come from, Lucia? The things I've done? I can't even tell you. You would be so horrified it'd change how you look at me."

She blinked up at me and shook her head. "Noah, why do you think I was a virgin at twenty-one? Why do you think that I never managed to make it work with anyone?"

She wanted answers? Fine, I'd give them to her. "Because I've been interfering. I run off anyone who even gets close to you. What's worse, I lie to myself, and I tell myself that I'm protecting you. But really, I can't stand the idea of someone else with their hands on you."

She held my gaze. "Maybe some of that was you. But if any of those guys ever had a shot, they wouldn't have been easily run off. They would've stuck. They would've stayed. Risked an ass beating. But they *all* ran. And to be truthful, they were all your stand-in. For me, it's you. It's always been you."

I shook my head, but I couldn't bring myself to move away from her. "I don't deserve you."

"Let me decide that for myself."

I stared down into her gray eyes. *You're not good enough for her. You are going to get her killed. She deserves better. She deserves someone good.*

Despite all the things I knew about what was good for her and all the things I knew about that were dangerous for her, I couldn't stop.

"Fuck it." My arms snapped around her and drew her up close and I crashed my lips to hers.

CHAPTER SEVENTEEN

Lucia

I held on to Noah's broad shoulders, trying desperately to keep pace with the kiss. Something seemed to have snapped inside of him, and the barrier that kept him so controlled was gone. His hands ran down my back and cupped my ass, kneading my soft flesh until I moaned into his mouth.

He wasn't being gentle, and heat flashed through me as he took what he wanted, bending my body to his will. When he lifted me off my feet, I wrapped my legs around his waist melting into him.

"You're the only one who has ever loved me," he whispered against my neck and I stilled.

Was he even aware of what he'd just admitted?

Afraid to ask any questions and knock him out of the moment, I squeezed him tighter, hoping I could send my love through my skin to his. For all of his faults, he'd always wanted to take care of me. It had felt like being smothered at first, but maybe it was just because he didn't know how to love. By his own words he'd never had that kind of relationship before.

But I could show him. I could be his light in the darkness, his soft place to land, and the one he opened his heart to. That was everything I'd ever dreamed.

"I do love you, Noah. So much."

At my words, he shuddered and held me tighter. I pulled back slightly so I could see his face, and if my heart hadn't already been his, it would have been right then and there. There was such naked longing and hope reflected in his dark eyes. Had any man ever looked at me like I was as vital as oxygen? Noah stared at me like some fantastical thing that he couldn't believe was real.

"I love you, Noah." I said it again because he seemed to need to hear it.

His eyes closed and then he was kissing me again, gentler this time, like I was the most precious thing he'd ever held.

"I'm the worst man you could have fallen for, but selfish bastard that I am, I'm not turning it down. You're mine now, Lucia. Do you understand that?"

His words would have sounded ominous coming from anyone else, but everything inside of me thrilled at the idea of belonging to Noah.

"You're mine, too. And nothing will ever change the way I feel about you."

His eyes darkened then, and he pressed a gentle kiss to my throat. "I'll be better. For you, I can be better."

Suddenly, he set me gently on my feet and then unbuttoned his shirt. I watched with greedy eyes as he unbuckled his belt and pushed his slacks down leaving him in just his boxer briefs. Oh wow. I'd already been with him, but I couldn't get over how big he was.

Biting my bottom lip, I bent my arm under and pulled down the zipper of my dress, shimmying my hips until it pooled at my feet. Underneath I wore a plain black bra and panties, nothing special, but the way Noah sucked in his breath at the sight made me feel like a goddess.

"Make love to me, Noah. Just us, no secrets, no lies."

He knelt and picked me up, holding me against his chest as he strode down the hallway to my room. I giggled when he dropped me on the bed, spreading my arms to keep from bouncing all over the place. Noah smiled and then crawled over the bedspread toward me.

"I love that sound. All I ever want is to see you this happy, Lucia."

I ran a finger down his muscular chest and then circled his erection with my palm gently. His lashes drifted down on a strangled groan, and then he shot me a look that told me his erotic retribution would be swift.

"You have everything you need to keep me happy."

I stroked him gently and he groaned. "Fuck, princess, that feels so good."

Feeling bold, I slid my hand down his boxers and Noah cursed low even as his erection twitched in my hand. His hips pushed into my hand and he squeezed his eyes shut as he bit his bottom lip. I liked this kind of power. Liked how it felt to make him lose control.

When my fingertip found the bead of liquid and spread it over the tip of his erection, he shuddered but then quickly stilled my hands.

"Princess, you have to stop. My control is already thin."

I frowned. "But I was exploring."

"I promise, you can explore later. Right now, I want my mouth all over you."

He pressed his body firmly against mine, each movement sending a lightning bolt of pleasure straight through me. His lips moved over me, a soft caress that pushed me to the edge of oblivion. His hands cupped my breasts, lightly pinching my nipples as he pulled and tugged on them. I melted into his touch as tingles of pleasure rocketed through me, until I begged for more.

I writhed and twisted beneath Noah's kisses as they trailed down my neck, and he murmured his appreciation against my skin. "You taste so sweet, princess." His hand made its way slowly down my body, over my ribs, around my hips and to the apex of my thighs. He flicked aside the fabric before plunging two fingers deep inside of me, and I threw my head back in pleasure.

With a savage growl, he wrenched my panties down my trembling legs. I gasped in anticipation as my desperate fingers tried to unhook my bra. There was nothing I craved more than the searing heat of his flesh against mine. Noah grabbed my bra in one swift motion and cast it aside with a feral smirk.

His lips danced over my collarbone and then brushed the stiff peaks of my nipples. I arched my back as the tingle of electricity shot straight to my core. While he wrapped his lips around my left nipple and tugged, his free hand teased the other one, drawing it into a tight bud.

I arched and bucked into each caress even as Noah slid his hand down to the juncture of my thighs. I arched up trying to pull his fingers inside where I wanted them again. Noah was happy to oblige, thrusting two fingers deep.

He looked down to where my legs had fallen open and his lips curled up briefly before he slid down and kissed the top of my mound. His tongue found my clit and I moaned at the dual sensations of being licked and penetrated.

"Always so wet for me," Noah murmured appreciatively.

I didn't have time to be mortified by the comment because he added his thumb to the equation, circling and rubbing until all the energy in my body shattered into a million fragments of light and heat. He stayed with me as I bucked beneath him, his tongue lashing over and over, drawing every bit of sensation from me.

"Noah, please!"

All I could do was cling to his shoulders as waves of pleasure rolled through me, spreading from the top of my head down to the very tips of my toes. When I could finally open my eyes again, Noah was watching me with a look of dark satisfaction.

"Look at me, princess. I want to see your eyes."

As soon as our eyes met again, he climbed up my body and arranged my legs over his shoulders. I gulped in air, trying to brace myself for him to take what he wanted. When Noah made love, he didn't hold anything back and I was so ready for it. He didn't seem to think that I could handle his deepest secrets, but I knew that no one else could ever accept him the way I could.

His hands settled on either side of my face. "I love you, Lucia."

I gasped at hearing those words for the first time and then again when he thrust deep. The position allowed me no room to hide and I felt tears well in the back of my eyes. Not from pain but from the stark intimacy of taking him this way, looking deeply in his eyes, accepting everything he had to give.

"I love you. I love you. I love you." He whispered it over and over as he took me hard, like he was afraid that if he didn't say it enough that it wasn't real.

But that had been Noah's only exposure to love, hadn't it? Something that didn't last, something that could be taken away from you at any moment. Tenderness swelled inside for this gentle giant of a man who was so afraid to love but had so much of it to give. My orgasm broke and I sobbed against his shoulder at the intensity of it.

Noah stilled and I felt him shuddering as his own pleasure took over. I wrapped my arms around him, never wanting to let go of what we'd found together.

For years, I had dreamed about this, making love to him with no reservations. Now it was here and I could hardly believe this was my life. That I could touch him, kiss him, and hold him whenever I wanted, seemed too good to be true. But maybe the universe was done torturing me and I was finally going to get my happy ending.

———

A shot rang out.

I moaned and tossed my head back and forth. I didn't want to see what happened next. For the first time, I was aware I was dreaming but could do nothing to stop the horrible images from unfolding before me. I sobbed silently as I watched Rafe rummage through the glove compartment of his car, knowing what was coming next.

"Stay here. No matter what, okay?"

In my dream, I smiled. I remembered thinking that my brother was always so worried about everything and that he really needed to learn to relax.

"Okay, fine. But really, where am I going to go?"

"I'm serious, Lulu."

Rafe pressed a gun into my palm and I gasped. I'd never held a gun before, and the cold metal seemed so heavy in my hand.

"Take this. If something happens...you drive out of here as fast as you can."

"Rafe, I can't drive yet."

"I've taught you enough. Just drive, Lu. As fast as you can."

A shot rang out.

I tossed my head and whimpered.

"Rafe!"

I wanted to protect him, to hold him close but where his body was supposed to be, there was nothing but blood. It flowed around me in rivers that threatened to sweep me away. I raised the gun and fired.

"I love you. Come back," I sobbed, looking around desperately for my brother's body but it was too late. He was gone.

A shot rang out.

Suddenly, I saw the events happen with crystal clear precision, something that had never happened before. The man who'd shot my brother stood right in front of me, and I could see his profile clearly. Tall, dark hair, and so handsome. I'd come to love him over the past few years as much as I loved Rafe. Suddenly, his face morphed from a blur into Noah's face.

I trembled in my dream, watching as the shot rang out and Noah jerked. I'd shot him. The shock of it was so horrifying that I woke up with a scream on my lips.

I turned my face into my pillow and sucked in a desperate breath. Noah slept next to me unaware, and I calmed myself by concentrating on the idea that dreams were just my mind's way of coping with the tragedy. It was just so strange for my mind to torment me by replacing the things I couldn't remember with Noah's face. Was it because of the recent changes in our relationship?

Was I feeling guilty for moving on with Noah instead of searching for my brother's killer?

The explanation actually made sense and helped to slow my racing heart. Maybe it was time to listen to Nonna for once and go back to the therapist I'd seen right after Rafe's death. If I was ever going to move on and live my life, I had to come to terms with things. It wasn't abandoning my brother to want a normal relationship with a man who loved me. I was finally on the verge of getting everything I'd ever wanted, and I didn't want to let fear hold me back.

Noah shifted slightly, and I could tell when he woke up because he stiffened, probably unused to having someone in bed with him. He'd confessed once, after I'd teased him about being a ladies man, that he'd never shared a bed overnight with anyone.

"What's wrong?" he whispered.

"Nothing. Just a bad dream. Sorry I woke you."

"Come here, princess." He held out his arm.

Determined to move past the horror of the nightmare, I curled up against him, resting my head on his chest. The solid beat of his heart lulled me until I could breathe easily again.

"Better?"

"Yeah. I'm glad you're here, Noah." I knew he didn't relax easily and knew what a big deal it was for him to spend the night with me.

"I'll always be here for you, Lucia. No matter what."

Completely content, I closed my eyes and ran my hand over the muscular planes of his chest. He was so beautifully made, and I took my time tracing the dips and curves of his abs, working up over the flat muscles of his pecs and the sharp points of his collarbone. My fingers skimmed over a mass of rough flesh on his shoulder. My brow furrowed as my fingers dipped into the hard knot of skin. It almost felt like...a bullet wound.

I swallowed the sudden sense of unease. Noah was always chasing bad guys; of course he'd probably have bullet wounds. But my fingers kept tracing the skin over and over, and suddenly I was slammed with another image from my dream.

My own hand holding the gun and then the kick of the weapon as I'd pulled the trigger. I watched as Noah jerked and his hand flew up to cover the wound on his shoulder. Our eyes met, and I'd seen the fear, shame, and guilt in his eyes.

I sat up slowly, horror turning my blood to ice as I stared down at Noah's chest, fully illuminated by the moonlight coming through the window. I touched the scar again, and then Noah turned to look at me.

"It was you."

PART 2

CHAPTER EIGHTEEN

Lucia

The well of fury I had been holding on to for weeks bubbled to the surface when I caught a whiff of the brunette in front of me. I tried to stay calm. Tried to push it all down. Tried to keep myself sane. But then I caught sight of Noah at the craft services table, and I lost it.

"For the love of Jesus, Mary and Joseph, Annabelle, I've told you a dozen times not to smoke before you come to a fitting," I all but screamed at the seventeen-year-old leggy giraffe.

Annabelle's eyes went wide as she teared up. "I'm so sorry. I had a rough day. I was really stressed out. I found my boyfriend in bed with my roommate after I got home last night. The asshole tried to pretend like it was somehow my fault."

I ground my teeth. "I'm sorry your boyfriend is a roommate-screwing ass. I really am. But it is both of our jobs to keep these clothes in pristine condition."

"I know. I know. I'll try to keep it together," Annabelle sobbed.

I ignored the twinge of guilt. Normally I could deal with models just fine. I didn't usually fly off the handle. When everything was going well, I was affable and nice. Funny even. The models liked me. But nothing was normal anymore.

After three weeks, two days and eight hours of dealing with *Noah I'm-A-frickin-liar Blake*, everyone was terrified of me.

If I was being completely honest, I sort of liked the power. I liked the way people would scurry away when I walked into a room. But this simply couldn't continue. This wasn't me. I loved my job, what I did, and the people. As a kid, I'd poured over fashion magazines, wishing I could be part of this world. It had been my dream to work somewhere like this. I couldn't let Noah take that away from me, too.

He'd already taken far too much.

With a deep breath and a silent prayer to the patron saint of would-be-murderers, I sent Annabelle to scrub herself down with a washcloth. That skintight A-line dress would trap in the smoke emanating from her skin. The models knew better, and at this level they were professionals. They generally made more money than I would ever see in my lifetime, *if* they took care not to piss off the bosses.

"Don't you think you were kind of hard on the kid? I mean you heard her. She had boyfriend trouble."

I turned around with a start and bumped directly into Noah's chest. "Damn it, Noah. Don't you have somewhere better to be right now? And mind your own damn business."

If this were the old Noah, he would've teased me, prodded me, and bugged me into talking to him. The old Noah was gone.

He'd killed him, just like he'd killed my brother.

I had once been so sure he cared about me and that he would always take care of me. But that wasn't the real Noah at all. *This* Noah was a monster, a monster I'd had the misfortune of sleeping with.

Okay fine. Sleeping with him wasn't the problem. His lies, and deceit, and cruelty were. The misfortune didn't come from sleeping with him, because that had been— I flushed, softened, and warmed at the thought of Noah touching me. *So not going to go there.*

I wasn't going to think about that part. What I was going to think about was the scar on his shoulder. The scar I knew *I'd* given him when I shot him.

My stomach cramped when I thought about discovering Noah's secret. The night we both finally admitted our feelings for each other and made love. I'd lain on his shoulder after a nightmare, secure in the safety of his arms.

And then I'd felt it, the rough, bumpy edge of a scar on his shoulder. I had never seen it before, because the first time we'd made love, it had been dark. I'd been so focused on the intensity and the swirl of emotions, I hadn't noticed. He hadn't taken his shirt off until it was pitch black in the room.

But with one touch my memories had come crashing back. The chaos of that day, the chaos of that afternoon. A man with a gun, pointed at my brother. The sound of my own screaming. As the bullets rained holes in my brother's body, I'd been forced to make a decision. So I'd raised the gun my brother had given me for protection at the man who'd killed Rafe.

I wasn't a very good shot, but I'd managed to hit him in the shoulder. For years, these memories had stayed buried in my mind. But now it had all come back. Before he tumbled down, I'd seen the profile of the killer's face. *Noah.* All along, it was Noah. The man I loved had been responsible for ending my whole world.

The man I'd loved for so long was the same one who had ruined my life.

Now, I was stuck with him because my life was supposedly in danger. From who or what, no one seemed to know. I didn't have all the answers and I didn't know the whole story, because no one would tell me. I'd even gone to my grandmother in the hopes of getting some help.

I wanted to go to the police, to get justice for Rafe, but Nonna had sided with Noah. All she'd told me was that there were things I didn't understand. What the hell was that supposed to mean? I understood perfectly well.

The man I thought I loved had betrayed me and then lied about it for years.

I was surrounded by betrayal. Now there was no shaking Noah. I knew my life was in danger. It was true, but my grandmother refused to go to the FBI with me. And as I had no proof, there wasn't anything that could be done. I was stuck with Noah. A man I didn't trust. A man who'd lied to me for years. The man I'd thought I loved.

"You can give me that sourpuss expression all you want, I'm not leaving you."

I whipped around to glare at him. "You have a whole team. You can't send one of the others?"

He shrugged, "Sorry, princess. My guys have actual work to do. Looping you into protection detail actually puts strain on them."

"Oh, I have an idea. Why don't you stop?"

Noah took a step forward, crowding me. I had no choice but to take a step back. When he didn't stop, I backed straight into a wall. With Noah looming over me, his heat enveloped me. I made the mistake of inhaling deep. The scent of sandalwood and something spicy injected my bloodstream with lust.

Bad idea.

I immediately started remembering everything about him that I was trying to forget. The tenderness of how I felt in his arms. The way he whispered my name softly when we made love. The way he held me tight, his hands tracing over every inch of my skin. I whimpered.

He leaned close and whispered, "Because I'm not going to let anything happen to you." He straightened and took a deliberate step away from me before adding, "You can be rid of me when we get back to your apartment."

"I can't wait," I ground out.

Every cell in my body hated him. Loathed him even. *Liar.* I should hate him. But I didn't. I loved him. Still. Even knowing what he had done. That he'd betrayed Rafe, betrayed me, and betrayed my whole family. God, the lies he'd fed me over the years. So many lies.

But despite that, I still freaking loved him. And I missed him with a bone-deep ache. The kind that had me crying myself to sleep every night. I wished I could pretend it was the sex I missed. The comfort of his body. No. It was his laugh and his teasing. The way he always made me feel safe.

Before that night, I'd never had any reason to fear him. But once I'd touched that scar, pulled the layers back on his secrets, I knew the truth. *He* was my worst nightmare. And there was no coming back from that knowledge.

Noah tossed his hands up in the air. "Lucia, I hope you know we can do this forever as far as I'm concerned. No way am I letting anything happen to you. So, I know you're mad and you have a right to be, but you need to understand your safety supersedes everything else. You don't like it? Tough. But I'm here to stay."

I glared up at him. There had to be another way because if I spent another day in Noah Blake's company, *I* was going to turn into a murderer.

Noah

I led the way into Lucia's apartment building. As she scowled at me, I bit back irritation and pushed down my guilt. After all, she had a point. She had every reason to hate me. I just wished it didn't hurt so much.

Anytime she glared at me or purposely avoided my touch, I was reminded of what I was. *Who* I was. There was no changing that now. All I could do was try and keep her safe. I'd been foolish to wish for more. Completely insane to think that she could love me.

Immediately the hair on the back of my neck stood up. Something was off. The camera I had placed directly in front of the elevator was turned to the side as if someone had very deliberately pointed it that way. I put a hand on Lucia's elbow to stop her. She glared down at it.

"Can you relax? Stay behind me, be quiet, and take off those damn shoes."

"Why would I take off my shoes?" she hissed.

I shot her a glance as I pulled my gun out of my holster. "Because you can't run in those heels."

Her eyes widened, but she did what she was told. She shoved them into her purse and then cleverly slung her purse across her body.

Smart girl. She'd be able to move quicker that way.

I had to fight the urge to run, the urgency to get her to the safety of her apartment. Instead, I deliberately slowed the pace. As we turned the corner, I noted the other camera next to the stairwell. It was also turned up.

Why the hell hadn't Ryan reported that?

It wasn't until we rounded the next corner to the right that I saw why. Ryan was slumped forward in his seat next to Lucia's door. Either asleep—or worse. And from the looks of it, it seemed much, much worse. Like he'd been bent and broken and put like that.

Lucia took one look at Ryan and ignored my warnings. She tried to sprint ahead but I reached out and grabbed her wrist, halting her.

"But he's hurt!"

"Look at him, Lucia. Can you see his face?"

"No."

"So, how do you know it's him?"

Her beautiful face twisted with worry, then she did exactly as I wanted and shifted behind me. I approached cautiously. As we got closer, I saw the ring that Ryan wore on his middle finger. It was simple and silver. I was one of the few people who knew the ring's significance. Ryan never took it off.

I crouched beside the kid, checking his pulse. There was one, but weak. He'd been knocked out. I lifted his plain black shades and saw the contusions around Ryan's eye. To top it all off, blood was running out of Ryan's nose onto his dark suit. Lucia handed me several napkins and I did what I could to plug the leak. Then I noticed Lucia's door was ajar.

"I need you to stay here." I bent to my ankle holster and gave Lucia a gun. "Can you use this?"

She tilted her head and glared up at me. "You have a scar on your shoulder that proves I can."

I gritted my teeth. "Point-and-shoot at anyone that comes out of that door that isn't me. Hell, if you have to, shoot me too. Just make sure you put holes in whoever it is. While you're waiting, call Matthias and send out an S.O.S. We're going to need some transport. I won't be able to carry Ryan all the way back to my car. They're better off picking us up out front. Watch your back. Do you understand?"

She nodded. Even as she swallowed hard, I saw her lift her jaw and square her shoulders. She was scared but she wasn't crumbling. She didn't ask inane questions, scream, or worse, cry. My respect for her shot through the roof. But I didn't have time to think about that. Without sparing her a second glance, I slipped into her apartment.

It was dark, but there was someone here. I could *feel* him. I couldn't explain it, but I knew I wasn't alone in the apartment. The real question was, where was this asshole?

I didn't have to wait long for an answer, because the moment I stepped into Lucia's living room, something shifted on my left. I narrowly missed being hit before the intruder crashed into the left wall of the kitchen, leaving a dent in the drywall.

I wasted no time, rotating on the ball of my foot and throwing a punch that landed with satisfying efficiency. *Crunch.* Instead of crouching, howling, or even muttering a curse word, the fucker remained silent. His head snapped backward then slid back into place as if I hadn't even landed one.

This was no average burglar; this guy was a pro.

We circled each other in the living room like caged lions seeking a time advantage. Then it was on. My assailant applied a series of roundhouse kicks, and I caught one to the ribs.

Shit. That hurt, though they were probably not broken. I kept my vision on the guy.

The intruder was nearly my height. Being several inches over six feet, I was used to towering over most people, but this guy was just as big so the advantage of my reach was nullified. For anything truly worthwhile, I had to get up close and way too personal for comfort.

Throwing a series of combination kicks and punches and having only one or two land, I ducked the kicks and throws sent my way. I fought for Lucia. No way was I letting this guy hurt her.

I took one step in and came up with my right elbow, hitting the guy's chin. This one was the hardest punch of all, landing the unwelcome guest on Lucia's end tables, covering him in shards of broken wood.

I pressed my advantage as my assailant lay on the floor. Even as I approached, the guy had his head up, swiveling, following my movements. As I approached, the guy shoved out a kick that landed high on my thigh. The move was familiar as if the other fighter wanted to injure me, but not kill me.

The move was practiced and skilled enough that I knew I would be sporting a bruise for the next week or so. Although, the guy hadn't hit me in the knee. I would have never recovered from something like that.

I didn't have the same compulsion to preserve the other guy's life. He was here to hurt Lucia, which meant I had no qualms about killing him. I grabbed his foot, and the assailant kicked with the foot in my hand while sweeping me off my feet with the other one. I had no choice; I landed on my ass but was back up in a second, as was my assailant.

We were like mirror images of each other. As one pushed his hands to the left, the other pushed his hands to the right.

This guy seemed to have had karate or jujitsu training. Given his kicks, tae kwon do, too. For what felt like another hour but was most likely mere minutes, we exchanged elbows and fists as we grappled, both trying to get the other to the ground to submit.

Hell, this is almost fun. All I wanted in the end was to pull the mask off.

If this guy was ORUS, that explained why he was trying to preserve my life.

"You don't have to do this. Just leave."

The guy landed an elbow that jarred me so hard I could hear my teeth rattling in my mouth. That was all that was needed to roll me onto my back with an arm bar across my neck. I turned my head to alleviate the pressure on my trachea, but all the while, he threw punches. Planting my heels, I tried to use my hips to buck the jackhole off of me.

But suddenly there was a crash, and the guy was no longer raining fists on my face. He was trying to shake something off of the back of his neck. I risked injury to my trachea and turned my head. And sheer horror slashed through me.

Lucia.

Why the hell can't she ever listen?

Even though I was pissed at her, I still used her distraction to my advantage. As she tried to wrap her arm around the other guy's neck, I used the opportunity to land hard fists in his face. That was all the advantage I needed. With Lucia choking the guy from behind and me using the leverage to push the dude off and jump back to my feet, we had him dead to rights. But then the guy twisted, shoving Lucia backward onto the couch. She landed with a hard bounce and a curse.

The guy turned his attention back to me and pulled me in with two hands around the back of my neck. I knew he intended to hit me straight in the gut. I knew where that knee was going. But instead of using his knee, the guy extended his foot, and sent it straight for the family jewels.

Mother. Fucker.

Brutal, sharp, electrifying pain took over my world. Bright lights shone behind my eyes, and I struggled to keep it together. Scrambling for my discarded weapon on the floor, I fired, grateful I'd thought to put on the silencer.

The guy darted glances between me and Lucia, attempted to go for her, but I wasn't having that and I raised the gun again. Instead of going out the front door as I would've assumed, the guy jumped directly out of the open living room window.

What the—

I scrambled to my knees, my balls screaming at me to stop whatever the fuck I was doing and just lie down.

I was used to pain. What I was feeling now was nothing in comparison to what I would feel if I lost her. I forced myself to stand and staggered to the window. I looked around first but saw nothing. It was only when I looked straight down that I saw the guy clinging to a rope, rappelling down. So he'd had a plan for escape. He had likely been here earlier setting up that hook, planning this.

But why mess with the cameras? And when? Fuck, unless he'd been there before scouting. It was probably because he knew he would have to take out whoever was outside. There's no way the security alarm wouldn't have gone off and no way Ryan wouldn't have heard him rumbling around in here.

Ian was right. Someone was trying to hurt her.

Lucia ran to me. "Noah, oh my God. Are you okay?"

I wanted to lean into her caress, wanted to wrap her in my arms and hold her there, never letting her go, but I couldn't. It was too dangerous.

"What part of stay outside and guard Ryan did you not understand? Everyone has a job. I gave you yours. Next time, don't come in."

She stared up at me, bottom lip quivering. "I just saved your ass."

"You had a job. You failed it. What if he had a second guy out there and Ryan's dead now?"

Horror crossed her expression and she glanced toward the door. "Oh my God. I just heard the fight in here. And I wanted to—"

"You have three minutes. Grab anything you think you'll need for at least the next two weeks. It's time to go. We're going to my place. We've already been here too long."

I didn't want to hear her apologize. I didn't want to hear her say that she worried about me, because those words would soften my stance. Being soft, caring about her too much, would get us both killed.

CHAPTER NINETEEN

Lucia

Exhaustion warred with nerves as I threw clothes hurriedly into a duffel bag. Later, I'd no doubt be annoyed by the jumble of clothes but at the moment the only thing I cared about was getting out of there. Even with Noah watching me from the hallway, I felt exposed. Vulnerable.

Someone had been inside my home. Touching my stuff. Waiting for me. Waiting to kill me. For what? What had I ever done to anyone?

My breath caught as I imagined this nameless, faceless man walking around my room, touching my things. Would he have waited in here until I was going to bed? Perhaps stayed hidden until I undressed? Or even waited until I was asleep?

The possibilities were endless and each more terrifying than the last. If it hadn't been for Noah's dogged insistence on not leaving me alone, I would have been completely at this unknown man's mercy.

That was also something I'd have to contemplate later. All this time I'd been annoyed by Noah's overprotectiveness and had assumed it was just because he enjoyed tormenting me. But clearly he knew something I didn't.

"Lucia, you have to move. Come on, baby."

I blinked in surprise. I stood frozen in place holding a damn T-shirt. What the hell was wrong with me? I couldn't move. Before I knew it, my body was shaking and tears were streaming down my face.

Noah dragged me to him. "Lulu, baby, I'm sorry. I am. This sucks. The whole thing is shitty. But I am going to protect you. I know you don't believe me right now, but you're safe with me. I will die before I let anything happen to you. Do you believe me?"

Dragging in the wracking sobs, I lifted my gaze to meet his. I must be losing my mind, because in that moment, I believed him. He would give his life to keep me safe.

"I believe you."

"Good. Now, that's all we have time for. Let's go." Noah zipped up the bag and threw it over his shoulder. "Come on."

I didn't argue, just dropped the handful of T-shirts I hadn't had the chance to pack on the bed and followed him out. Noah's eyes never stopped moving as we walked back through the living room and I had no doubt that he was completely on guard for anything that might happen.

I didn't have to know a lot about security to be aware that staying here any longer than necessary was a bad idea. Not to mention that we needed to get help for Ryan.

My heart squeezed as I remembered how he'd looked, all bruised and bent. Poor Ryan. I didn't know him well but he'd always been nice to me. He wasn't much older than I was and had a gentle smile.

Like the others, he moved like a guy who was comfortable in his body and very likely was a badass. He didn't deserve what had happened to him. He'd just been looking out for me. Hopefully his wounds looked worse than they were. I swallowed, knowing that was unlikely. He'd looked pretty bad.

When we emerged from the apartment, I immediately saw Jonas talking to the EMTs who had already lifted Ryan onto a stretcher. Noah held up a hand and I halted. He whispered something to Jonas and then clapped him on the shoulder.

"I got this, man. I'll see you at the loft later." Jonas nodded to me gravely as we passed. "You all right, Lucia?"

"Yep. You know, just a normal day. A homicidal maniac tries to kill me and my friends."

He winced imperceptibly. "We'll get him, Lucia. And then me

and the guys will take turns holding him down while Noah makes him less of a man."

I gave him a wan smile then followed blindly as Noah led me downstairs. I vaguely catalogued the heavy weight of his arm around my shoulders and the gentle squeeze of his hand as he helped me into the Range Rover. It was like I was moving through quicksand; all my limbs felt awkward and too heavy to lift. Seeing my trouble, Noah grasped me by the waist and lifted me into the seat. He glanced at me tentatively, probably expecting me to be annoyed that he hadn't asked permission.

Under any other circumstances, I would have found it amusing. Today, however, I was just grateful he was there. For once, his overbearing attitude was actually comforting. It was a relief not to be responsible for anything and to allow him to handle it all. When I didn't say anything his frown deepened but he didn't speak until after we were on the road.

"You're very quiet." Noah slid his gaze over to me.

"I've never had anyone try to kill me before. I popped my almost-killed cherry, so there's that."

Noah glanced over sharply and I bit my lip. It wasn't his fault, but I wished there was someone to blame. I needed a scapegoat right about now. Anything to avoid thinking about how my own actions had led to this moment.

"I'm sorry. I shouldn't—"

Noah shook his head. "You don't have to apologize."

"Yes, I do. I'm being so bitchy, and for the first time ever, you don't deserve that. You risked your life to protect me and I don't know what to do with that."

His smile made me feel a little better but he didn't offer any other reassurances. Probably because there were none to be had. We had no idea who had broken into my place and until Jonas reported back, we couldn't be sure that Ryan would recover. I kept my eyes on the road, watching all the streets speed by, until we took yet another turn and I realized we weren't going to his office after all.

"So where are we going?"

Noah glanced over at me briefly. "The office. But I have to make sure we don't have a tail first."

I glanced behind us. "I don't see anyone."

"If they're good, you won't see them."

It wasn't that late yet so there were still plenty of other cars on the road. How could he even tell if someone was following us? What about when I had to go to work tomorrow? There was no way I could miss it. It was Adriana's first show and we'd been working on this all year. But was I going to be safe? Was I endangering everyone else there by attending?

"What do I do, Noah? I have to go to work. I have a life." I turned to watch his profile as he drove, struck as always by how fierce he looked.

Then something occurred to me and I gasped.

"Oh my God. *Nonna*. You have to check on Nonna. P-p-put her in protective custody or something. That psycho could be after her too."

Noah reached over and grabbed my hand. "She's fine. I've had a friend watching her for years. I texted him while you were packing and there's been nothing out of the ordinary tonight."

"Thank God." I sagged against the seat, the relief so overwhelming it brought tears to my eyes.

I didn't bother trying to stem the flow of tears as I imagined how differently things could have ended tonight. I was too exhausted to interrogate him about just who he had watching my grandmother. That was a fight for another day.

Everything was crazy and I had no idea what I was going to do tomorrow, but I was safe right now. That was all I had to hang on to at the moment. And I knew that was all due to Noah.

When Noah finally pulled into the underground parking garage in his building, I was exhausted and wrung out from crying. He pulled around to his usual parking space and turned the car off. His face betrayed no surprise when he looked over and saw me in tears.

"We're going to get this son of a bitch. I promise you that I will not rest until you are safe."

"I know. You've always protected me."

I didn't bring up the one day that he hadn't. It was confusing to love and hate him at the same time but it was simply too ingrained in me to think of him as a protector to turn it off now. I just wished I could turn the clock back three weeks to when life had been simple.

I tried to smile but figured by the look on his face that I'd failed miserably. He grimaced and I knew he was thinking of that beautiful and awful night when I'd discovered his secret.

"I know this doesn't mean much to you right now, especially in light of everything that's happened. But I will die before I let anyone ever hurt you."

I knew he meant it. Anyone who wanted to hurt me was going to have to go through him first.

———

Noah

I helped Lucia down from the Range Rover and my heart melted a little when she clung to me. My heart wasn't the only thing feeling heated. This was the closest she'd let me get to her in weeks.

I didn't fool myself that she'd forgiven me. More than likely, she was in shock. I could barely remember the first time I'd truly feared for my life, but the emotions released when fighting were intense and Lucia had been sheltered all her life. She had no idea how to deal with something like this. The horror of having someone try to hurt her. I knew the terror she'd felt at seeing Ryan hurt because I felt the same way.

I kept her close as we walked quickly to get inside the building and onto the elevator. It would be a lot easier to deal with things once I wasn't on edge worried about Lucia's safety. With all the guys there and the amount of security wired into the place, there was literally no safer place for her in the city.

The inside of the loft was already busy. Matthias looked up from his computer when we entered, his eyes immediately going to Lucia. I shook my head slightly, hoping that the other man wouldn't say anything about the attack. Lucia looked like she was about to break into a million pieces as it was.

"Let's get you settled," I whispered to her.

I held out my arm to indicate that she should precede me. I kept my gaze on the long fall of her hair so my eyes wouldn't be tempted to stray any lower. Lucia was staying with me out of necessity only, not because she'd forgiven me or wanted to be with me. But a guy could hope.

For the first time in my life I really loved someone. And someone loved me back. Just having even a taste of that, I wasn't ready to let go of it. Deserving or not, I needed her. Needed her love.

Maybe this was my penance for my sins, having the woman I loved right under my nose but still out of reach. She hadn't spoken to me since that tense conversation in the car. I wanted to ask her more about the things she'd been digging into but this wasn't the time. I'd wait until she'd had time to gain her equilibrium back before I asked the hard questions. That was not going to be an easy conversation.

When we reached my room, Lucia shook her head slightly, finally seeming to notice her surroundings.

"Um, Noah? Where am I going to stay?"

I set her bag down on the floor next to my bed. "You can have my room. I don't sleep much anyway, and when I need to crash I'll take one of the spare bedrooms downstairs."

She sat down on the edge of the bed and ran her hands gently over the tangled sheets that I hadn't bothered to straighten that morning. I shivered, watching her fingers tracing over the fabric. Why did that affect me as if she'd touched my bare skin?

"I'll get you some clean sheets."

She waved her hand impatiently. "I don't care about that. You know I'm practical, and there's no sense pretending I haven't shared sheets with you before."

I watched as she stood and walked into the en suite bathroom. When she came out, she'd shed the oversized shirt she'd been wearing and was wearing only a tight camisole and panties.

I swallowed hard. Oh Jesus fuck. My dick turned to steel. I fucking missed her. But she didn't need that right now. Right now she needed me to protect her. Right now, I had to earn her trust and her love again. If that was even possible.

She climbed on the bed and pulled the sheets over her, pulling them up until they reached her chin. In that position she looked like a child. *A terrified child.*

"Make yourself comfortable. I have to go brief the team on every-thing that happened so we can figure out a plan to get this guy." The guy was a fucking ghost and finding him wouldn't be easy, but there was no way I was telling Lucia that.

Lucia nodded. "Okay. I'm just going to read and try to relax a little."

"Good. Text me if you need anything."

She hesitated for a moment. "Uh, Noah?"

"Yeah, Lulu?"

"Thank you. For today. I don't know what I would have done if you weren't there."

I nodded. "You don't have to thank me. Or any of the guys. And nothing's going to happen to you. We're going to see to that."

She burrowed deeper beneath the sheets until only the top of her head was visible. I backed out of the room, pulling the door closed behind me.

Matthias looked up when I came back downstairs. "Is she okay?"

"Not really but she will be. The sooner we figure out who's behind this, the better. Have you heard from Jonas yet?"

Matthias jerked his head in the direction of the conference room. "Yeah, he's here."

"What?"

I pushed past him and into the conference room. Jonas stood next to an exhausted Ryan, who was struggling to remain upright while a man wrapped gauze around his arm.

"Seriously, Ry? You should be in the hospital."

Jonas rolled his eyes. "Already told him that. But Superman here thinks that all he needs is a Band-Aid and an aspirin before going back on the job. He woke up before they could get him in the ambulance and refused all further treatment."

Ryan pointed at the man working on his arm. "You joking? This is a flesh wound. You should see the other guy. Besides, I knew that Doctor Breckner does house calls. Tell 'em I'm fine Doc."

Doctor Breckner didn't look amused. "He's *not* fine. He needs stitches and is slightly concussed. And his ribs are bruised. He's lucky he didn't need surgery."

Ryan shrugged. "I've had worse. Doesn't sound that bad to me." When he saw our faces, he sighed. "Seriously, I'm fine. Is Lucia okay? I feel like shit Noah. I heard a noise, went in and motherfucker got the jump on me. I fucked that shit right up."

"No, you didn't. You did your job. Anything you remember about him?"

"Tall, like you, and *fast*. Well fucking trained. That was no run of the mill burglar. I cannot wait until we find that asshole. I have all kinds of payback in mind for him."

"You're crazy man. And yes, Lucia is fine. We're all fine. Do you remember anything else that might help us find the son of a bitch?"

Ryan grumbled and cursed. "No. Which fucking pisses me off. Like I said, we fought. I got a few hits in, there was nothing else. Fuck, I'm not even sure how he got in the building. Next thing I know, I'm waking up on a gurney and this fool is telling me I'm on my way to the hospital." Ryan pointed his thumb toward Jonas.

I exchanged glances with Jonas. "Ryan is right. The guy was good. Better than good. We fought, no holds barred, and it was like he wasn't even breaking a sweat."

"So I'm right? He's a pro?" Ryan added.

"Yeah, and if he could hold me off with my training and motivation, I guarantee he's been trained by the best. And I promise you, he's not done. He will be back, and we need to fucking be ready because I'm not losing Lucia."

A gasp from the doorway grabbed all of our attention. I turned and standing right behind Matthias was ... Lucia.

Shit.

"Lucia, are you okay? Do you need anything?" I approached her slowly, happy when she allowed me to pull her into my arms. But when I tried to lead her from the room, she shook off my hold. Damn it. The last thing I had wanted was for her to hear any of that.

"Why don't we get you back to the room? You've had a hell of a day. Come on."

But she wasn't having it. "The guy who was in my apartment was a pro? What does that mean? A professional killer?" Her voice rose slightly at the end. "So that hit out on me. It's for real? It isn't some kind of mistake?"

The other guys all glanced at me.

I sighed. "We believe that to be the case, yes. But until we catch him, this is all just speculation. But best guess is yes."

She swallowed hard. "Then he isn't going to stop just because he was unsuccessful. He'll be back. And there will be others."

As much as I wanted to, I couldn't lie to her. I never wanted to lie to her again.

"Yes. He'll be back. But this time I'll be ready."

CHAPTER TWENTY

Lucia

I screamed for my brother. Staring down the man who had shot him, I lifted the gun Rafe had given me and fired. The crack of gunfire startled me awake.

Trying to calm myself, I greedily sucked in deep breaths as I tried to remember all the things the therapist had taught me.

Deep breaths. Nice and easy. Do not panic. I was losing it. That nightmare would be the end of my sanity.

Once I steadied my breathing, I reached over to the lamp on my bedside table, trying to turn it on. It was never this dark in my room. Thin slivers of silver moonlight usually peeked through my blinds. I fought the momentary weight of panic and forced my mind to clear. It was only then that I remembered I wasn't at home.

I shuddered at the thought of the man in my apartment. He was intent on killing me, intent on killing Noah. He'd already given Ryan a concussion. God only knew what he would have done to me.

What if he'd hurt Noah? What if he'd *killed* Noah? Would I have minded?

The answer surprised me, because I *would*. Not just because I wanted the pleasure of doing it myself, but also because I cared about him. That reason was more frustrating than anything else. After everything he'd put me through, everything he had done. I worried about him. Because I cared. It was impossible to stop loving him even though I knew what he was.

You are a damn glutton for punishment.

I wished I could set fire to my feelings and watch them burn in a pyre down to ashes with no regrets. But I couldn't. Despite his lies, he'd taken care of me, even when I didn't want him to. He took care of Nonna and looked out for me.

He was *still* looking out for me.

With a growl, I yanked back my covers. I fumbled around for my phone, finally finding it on the opposite nightstand and checking the time. Damn. Only a little after 4 in the morning. *Far too early to get up.*

After that nightmare, I was neither tired nor was I in a hurry to return to the clutches of the shadow dreams. With bare feet I padded over to the door, slowly creeping it open. Surprisingly it was dark, save for the iridescent nightlights lining the walls.

Okay, just a drink of water then back to bed.

Somehow, a part of me had imagined Noah's office was always open. That somehow he and the men who worked for him were superheroes like the Justice League or something. But apparently even superheroes needed sleep. Besides, I knew better. These guys were no heroes.

Well, maybe the others were, but *Noah* certainly wasn't.

When I reached the kitchen, I dragged a glass out of the cabinet. Suddenly, all of the lights flickered on and I squeaked and jumped, whipping around.

"Oh shit. Sorry. I didn't realize anyone was in here. I just came for—"

I put up a hand. "No, it's fine. I was the one skulking around in the dark."

Matthias nodded. His eyes went wide, and he somehow managed to look every which way but directly at me. Oh no. He was pissed. I'd had him lie to Noah. And now Noah was undoubtedly pissed. That was my fault.

"Matthias, listen—"

He started talking at the same time that I did. "Lucia, look I never meant to—"

And then he gestured to me. "Ladies first," he said with a smile.

He still wouldn't look directly at me, nor did he come any further into the kitchen. Instead, he hung by the wall. But he'd certainly come in here for a reason.

"Look, Matthias. I'm so sorry. I never should have dragged you into this and had you looking for information for me. I certainly never should've asked you to keep it from Noah, your boss. I know how he is and I know you were trying to help me, but I was wrong to ask you to do that."

His eyes flickered to me and quickly looked away again. "Lucia, it's fine. It was my choice to comply or not. I chose not to tell him, but I'm sorry I broke your confidence and told him anyway. I was worried you were in danger and, as it turns out, you *were*. If it had been simple information, I never would've told him."

I rounded the giant island in the kitchen and approached him. He immediately took a step back. Looking even further away from me if that was possible.

Damn, he was so mad at me. "Matthias, I consider you a friend. And I used that. That makes me a bad person and I'm really sorry. I hope that you can find a way to forgive me."

He frowned but still didn't look at me. "Forgive you? Honestly, it's fine. I would do anything to help you. You're family. I'm not mad."

I stared up at him. Then I planted my hands on my hips. "Oh yeah, then why is it that you can't look at me?" I opened my arms. "Can we hug this out, start fresh? I won't take advantage of our friendship again. I promise."

Matthias flushed and hugged the wall like I had cooties. Like the last thing on earth he wanted to do was hug me.

Maybe he *wasn't* a hugger? No, we had hugged dozens of times. *Fine.*

If Matthias wouldn't come to the mountain then I would bring the mountain to Matthias. I closed the distance between us, my bare feet barely making a sound on the concrete. And then I wrapped my arms around him tight.

Go ahead and escape this hug, I thought.

But Matthias didn't escape. It took a second, but then he wrapped his arms around me. I had never noticed how tall he was, and he was nearly as solid as Noah.

Geez, did Matthias have muscle? Why hadn't I ever paid attention before?

I'd always taken the mildly geeky exterior, with the glasses and superhero T-shirts, and categorized him as a nerd. Which to me usually meant soft. How had I never noticed that my friend had muscles?

Granted, they weren't like Noah's. No one had muscles like Noah. I knew I was probably biased, but still.

"I'm really sorry, Matthias."

"You have nothing to be sorry about."

I didn't know how long we stood there, but then Noah's voice came from behind us, cold and furious. "What the fuck do you think you're doing running around here naked?"

Matthias immediately released me, but I took longer to step back. When I turned to face Noah, I took in the sight of his boxers and his completely bare chest, and damn it, I salivated. That didn't mean I didn't still hate him. It didn't mean I wasn't still furious with him, and it didn't mean that I trusted him. All it meant was that I was human. The man looked good.

Good enough to lick, honestly. And I had.

There was still so much I wanted to try with him, so much we hadn't had a chance to do. All the things I'd heard JJ talk about, I wanted to try with Noah. *Well, now you're not going to because, hello, we hate him.*

Yes, I hated him. But that didn't mean I didn't want to lick him. And somehow, simultaneously, I wanted to murder him, too.

"I am not naked." I slid a glance down at myself, slightly flushing. Shit. I hadn't put on shorts. I slid a glance to Matthias, who was looking anywhere but at me *or* Noah. "Sorry. I'm not used to having to cover up." I turned to Noah. "Besides, you're the one who told me to make myself at home."

Through gritted teeth, he ground out, "That doesn't mean run around here naked. Matthias is here. Or did you forget?"

"I was just coming for some water. No one was supposed to be awake. The lights were freaking off. Bite me."

From behind me, Matthias scoffed. Noah's eyes glinted and his smile went menacing and predatory. "Anytime. You just tell me where."

And then something happened to my body. It was like my lady parts had softened, readying my body for him to have me against any flat surface. Hell, screw a flat surface. The wall would do if necessary.

Why did he do that to me? I didn't like him. *You don't have to like him to want him.* Wasn't that the truth? But the last thing on earth I was ever going to do was let him know that.

"Sorry, Noah. Not interested. What's that thing that guys say sometimes? I'm just not that into you?"

And with that, I turned and headed back for the bedroom. I could feel Noah's eyes on my ass. Let him look all he wanted, because he was never going to touch it again.

———

Noah

*Did she just—*she just walked away from—*what* the hell? I glared at Matthias. She'd had her hands all over the kid. I had to work hard at not killing him right now out of pure jealousy.

"Keep it shut."

Matthias put up his hands, but the kid's lips twitched as if he was fighting back a laugh. "You got it boss. Keeping it shut."

But I wasn't in the mood. I never slept well anyway, but the moment I'd heard Lucia's voice I'd snapped awake and I'd gone looking for her. The image of her wrapped around another man was enough to make my trigger finger itch.

I didn't want her wrapped around Matthias. What I wanted was the two of us in my bed, her underneath me, over me, in front of me.

Never going to happen again. Stop living in your fairy tale. Deal with the problem at hand.

But since I'd lived that fairy tale, it was impossible to let it go. Especially as my dick kept coming up with elaborate schemes to get her back in bed. Most of which sounded totally doable in the moment.

"You want to tell me what you were doing with your hands on her considering she's not wearing any clothes?"

Matthias swallowed hard. "Noah, I didn't touch her. She came over here and hugged *me*. I think she could tell I was deliberately not looking at her."

"Damn straight you weren't looking at her. Not if you want to keep your goddamned eyeballs."

There was that lip twitch thing from the kid again. "I like my eyeballs where they are, thanks."

"You seemed to be hugging her back." I narrowed my gaze.

Matthias rolled his eyes. "Mate, Lucia is family. Of course I hugged her back. I'm not mad at her, and *I'm* not the one she's mad at. If she's handing out free hugs, I'm taking them. If you want some hugs of your own, you might want to talk to her."

I stared at him. He wasn't usually so defiant. I knew the kid looked up to me. Granted he could use some better idols. I also knew the kid knew enough to fear me a little.

"Yeah, you might be right about that."

Except so far no amount of talking or apologizing was working. But as I watched her ass stroll down the hall, I knew I had to keep trying.

I followed after Lucia, knowing it was probably a bad idea. But lately I was full of all kinds of bad ideas. I grabbed the door before she could slam it behind her. "Lucia, wait."

She pushed against the door. "Noah, what am I waiting for? We don't have anything to say to each other. You were right. Someone is trying to kill me. They broke into my apartment, and one of your men is injured because of me. So I'll listen to you. I'll do what you want, shut up, and go where I'm told. The only thing I ask is to be able to work. And for you to not talk to me, touch me, or even look at me."

"Sorry, I can't do that last part."

She opened the door and I nearly tumbled in. "Why? Why can't you? Because you had no problem lying to me for years, watching me struggle and suffer. Now, when I ask you to do something that would actually help me recover from that, you refuse to do it?"

"You don't understand." I lowered my voice so only she could hear me. "Ever since I touched you, I can't help but think about it. So if it's more convenient for you, if it makes things easier for you, I will try. But I have to look out for you. I just can't help it."

"You're telling me you can't help it? Try, or better yet, *talk* to me. Tell me what the hell is going on. Tell me who that man in my apartment was, or at least who you think he was. Something tells me you weren't surprised to see him there. Something tells me you *expected* him to be there. And you keep saying my life is in danger. I think you know who's after me."

I sighed. I couldn't tell her. She knew that I was the one who'd hurt Rafe, but she didn't know the rest. The rest would shatter any possibility she ever had of trusting me again. I knew how she felt about me. Hate was a strong word, but right now she was so far past hate. She wanted to completely annihilate me for life. Not that I blamed her.

"You know I can't tell you that."

She crossed her arms and stared me down. "So far, my experience is when you say things like *can't*, you mean *won't*. I don't want to hear about how it's for my own good or how you're protecting me. I'm done unless you are going to start talking to me, treating me like I'm someone who deserves to know the truth. Otherwise, I have no interest in saying anything to you."

"Lucia, this is in your best interest."

"You keep saying that. You've broken into my place, you've chased off boyfriends that might've liked me. You've interfered in my life by paying for my apartment and paying for Nonna's house. You have interjected yourself in every aspect of my life, so much so that I'm not even allowed to live it for myself. Then I find out you killed my brother. I ask you for answers, anything, and you think that taciturn bullshit is going to work?" She sneered at me. "Get the hell out of my room. I don't want to see you. I don't want to talk to you. I'm done. As a matter of fact, you might want to transfer my case to some other security firm or something, because I don't want to be anywhere near you."

"It's nice to want things, princess. Trust me, I wish you didn't have to know. I wish we could just go back to being Noah and Lucia, and I could tease you and you not be mad at me anymore. But we can't. This is real life now, real brass tacks. I'll do my job and stay out of your way, but I'm not going to hurt you anymore than I have to."

I turned and walked out, very gently closing the door behind me. The anger simmered just under my skin. I hated the way she looked at me now. Contempt, distrust— it was all there. She was right. I had interjected myself into her life. At the time, I had told myself I was protecting her, keeping an eye on things, making sure she didn't need anything.

She was right. It was selfish.

I was just trying to assuage my guilt over Rafe. Now, I'd hurt the only woman I was even capable of loving.

I stormed back toward my room, catching Matthias in the kitchen as he scarfed down the remnants of a key lime pie. "You're on Lucia duty tomorrow. She's got some fitting for the show, I think."

Matthias stopped, fork midway to mouth. "Okay, who am I going with?"

I sighed. "We're stretched thin. I think I can send Dylan. We'll put him in the audience while you're back stage with Lucia. There's a lot of security already there. The event has security to protect the models, so we'll use the set up to help protect her."

Matthias nodded. "We'll make it happen."

I rolled the tension out of my shoulders. I hadn't been able to sleep because I kept picturing how she would look at me all day tomorrow. Plus, I was needed on another job. I hated not being there to protect her, but I would make sure there was someone there who could. She trusted Matthias, as evidenced by the way she'd wrapped her little body around him. I suppressed the twinge of jealousy. Matthias was a kid. I'd worked hard to save the kid's life so killing him now would be counterproductive.

"Good. Call me if there are any issues."

"Will do, boss."

I stomped back to bed, as if I were going to get any sleep anyway. I might as well just get in a workout, because every time I was around Lucia, my thoughts kept me up.

Because you want more.

More of what happened that night three weeks ago when I had altered her world. Well, just like I'd told Lucia, it *was* nice to want things. Unfortunately in this case, I was never going to get what I wanted again.

CHAPTER TWENTY-ONE

Lucia

"Okay, Hettie, put this on. No, we don't have time to alter it. Just suck in and make it work."

I grabbed my head between my hands and squeezed. We had less than thirty minutes until show time and somehow I'd managed to lose a belt that had been right in my hand, one of the girls had accidentally spilled a drink on herself and was all sticky, and another somehow didn't fit into a garment that had fit perfectly just the prior week. It was as if the fashion show gods were displeased with me and decided to make everything go wrong simultaneously. With everything else going on in my life lately, I didn't need this.

Please just let me pull this off, I thought.

Matthias appeared at the door to the dressing area. When he took in my expression and the sheepish model standing behind me, he raised his eyebrows slightly. "Everything okay?"

"Yes, I just need about five extra pairs of arms. That's all."

Once Noah understood how important this show was, he'd stopped trying to convince me to stay home, so that was a win. However, he'd insisted on keeping Matthias with me backstage while Dylan was in the audience. I'd been trying to think of good excuses to explain his presence, but so far everyone had just accepted that he was a friend. The fact that he was cute went a long way toward their acceptance.

The model behind me eyed Matthias with interest. I snorted. They were probably all assuming I'd brought my boyfriend along. The fact that this hadn't stopped anyone from flirting with him was pretty sad in my opinion. It was a good thing he wasn't actually my boyfriend or I would have been annoyed.

"Hettie, my friend Matthias is helping me out today. I hope you don't mind."

Hettie tossed her mile long blond hair extensions over her shoulder. "I don't mind at all. He's a cutie. Why are all the cutest guys batting for the other team? So unfair."

I froze.

Matthias blinked. The smile on his face faded slightly. "Batting for the other team? No, I'm on our—"

"Yeah, we don't mind," Annie chirped before he could finish. "He's *soooo* cute."

"Really cute." Another one of the models stroked a hand gently over his hair.

Matthias turned red and mumbled something about making a phone call. I couldn't help laughing. They were going to give the poor guy a heart attack.

While I was inspecting Annie to make sure I'd cleaned all the spilled soda off her skin, Adriana walked by and quirked an eyebrow.

"Let's go!"

I jumped up and grabbed my phone. The models all fell in line and stood still while Adriana inspected them. For the next hour, I tried my best to keep up and stay out of the way when appropriate. But this was probably the only thing that could take my mind off the events of the past twenty-four hours. I'd been dreaming about being backstage at a major fashion show since I was a teenager and now I was here. I peeked around the curtain and watched as the next to last model strutted down the runway. As many times as I'd watched fashion shows online, nothing captured the pure electricity like being there. A million camera flashes lit up the space like a fireworks display.

Then there was a sudden hum, and the entire room was plunged into darkness. The cameras kept flashing, which made the sudden darkness even more jarring. At first the crowd was quiet, and then the murmur of voices got louder as people started to panic. Someone screamed.

I went still as my brain tried to make sense of what was happening. There was a brush of movement behind me, and a shiver stole down my back. *Stop, that's Matthias.*

But then someone moved again and wrapped an arm around my waist, their other hand snaking around my face. Every cell in my body said run, scream, fight. I opened my mouth to scream but opted to bite down instead. Whoever it was grunted, and I took three steps forward.

Then someone grabbed my arm. And this time I screamed.

"It's okay, it's just me."

I sagged with relief at the sound of Matthias' voice. "Oh, God, I thought—" I couldn't finish the thought. Had I imagined that hand snaking around me? "What's going on?"

"I don't know, but we need to get the hell out of here. Follow me."

When he grabbed my hand, I allowed him to lead me. My sense of direction was usually pretty good, but before long I had no idea where we were in the building. It felt like an endless stream of twists and turns. Finally, there was a soft, slow whine. The sound of a door closing.

Something was wrong. Matthias, who would normally have put me at ease, wasn't saying anything. I was scared to say anything since I wasn't sure who was near us and might overhear, so I bit my lip and counted down from one hundred in my head. After a few minutes, Matthias pulled out his phone and started typing a text.

"Dylan didn't see anything before the power outage, so maybe this has nothing to do with us." He didn't sound convinced, though, and I wasn't either.

Seriously, what were the odds of there being a power outage randomly the day after someone broke into my apartment? I shivered. This was the perfect opportunity for someone to grab me. If Matthias hadn't gotten to me first, someone could have knocked me out the same way they'd gotten to Ryan.

"How are we going to get out of here?" I whispered.

"We aren't. If someone is looking for you, I'm not going to put you in their path. We'll be safe here while Dylan investigates. I scouted this closet as a possible safe spot when I did my rounds earlier."

There was another sudden hum, and the lights came on. I blinked in the bright lights as my eyes adjusted. I gasped when I saw Matthias crouched next to me with an intense look on his face and a surprisingly large gun in his hand.

"Where did that come from?"

Matthias gave me a strange look. "My holster. Did you think I was protecting you with a water gun or something?"

I laughed nervously. He was right, it was a stupid question. But I didn't know how to say that I'd been unprepared to see him looking like a real bodyguard because that wasn't how I saw him. He'd already had to deal with models treating him like a cute mascot today. Although if those girls had seen him like this, all fierce and determined, they might not have been so quick to treat him like a little boy.

"Of course not. I just couldn't tell where you'd hidden it before. That's a ... really big gun."

Luckily Matthias didn't pause to analyze my silly statement. He pulled me to my feet gently. "Once Dylan gives us the okay, we'll go back to grab your things and then get out of here. No need to stick around, right?"

"Yeah, the show was basically over." I'd get shit for leaving early but I was hoping that all the confusion would cover my early departure.

Seeing Matthias in full bodyguard mode had snapped me out of the confused state I'd been in since yesterday. This was serious and it was happening, and I wasn't just going to sit back and do nothing.

If some asshole was going to come for me, I wasn't going to just let him.

———

Noah

I was running on the treadmill when I saw Matthias's name show up on my phone. I'd been out on a job that morning and had only gotten back a short while ago. That Lucia was exposed at that damn fashion show had been in the back of my mind the whole time. I'd agreed not to interfere in her life more than necessary, but it didn't mean I had to like it.

Since I knew Matthias was with Lucia, I hit the emergency stop button and grabbed the phone.

"What's going on? Is Lucia okay?"

"Everything is fine. But there was an incident at the show. A power outage."

As I listened, my heart rate slowly went back to normal. I clapped a hand over my chest. If I reacted this way to just the idea of Lucia being hurt, I didn't want to think about the future if I failed to keep her safe.

Hell no. Not a possibility.

"We're almost at the loft now. Just wanted to let you know what was going on. Dylan stayed behind to talk to some of the people in the audience."

"Great. Just get in here."

I hung up and then took a quick shower. Then I walked back to the main area of the loft to fill in Jonas. This was the second incident we'd had while protecting Lucia. Everyone on the team needed to be briefed because her situation was now considered high risk. If it had been a random break in at her place, the likelihood that she'd be attacked again would be very low. But clearly, nothing about this was random. Someone was determined to get to her and they'd just proven they weren't going to give up until they got what they wanted.

I clenched my fists at the thought. What they wanted was Lucia. So whoever these assholes were that were targeting her, they'd just become number one on my shit list. I didn't care how many resources I had to dedicate, they weren't getting anywhere near Lucia.

Jonas and I were still standing there talking when Matthias and a very shaken Lucia walked in. My first instinct was to grab her and hold her. I'd already taken a few steps in her direction before it all came back to me. We weren't together anymore.

She hates you now, remember? You're the source of all her nightmares. The last thing she's going to want is comfort from you.

Before I could say anything, Matthias started talking. "It appears to have been a false alarm. But the show was basically over anyway, so I figured it was better to get the hell out of there."

I took my eyes away from Lucia long enough to clap a hand on Matthias's back. The kid had done well even though this wasn't his usual thing.

"You made the right call. After you fill the others in, why don't you check with the power company and find out which areas were affected by the outage. That might help us pinpoint whether it was truly random or part of a targeted attack."

Matthias nodded, and I could tell he was happy to have something tangible to do.

I turned to Lucia. "Don't worry. We're going to figure out who is behind this. They won't touch you. I promise."

She nodded but looked like she was on the verge of crying. I cursed myself internally. I wanted nothing more than to be able to pull her into my arms and wipe away those tears but that wasn't what she wanted from me anymore. I'd lied to her too many times. Even though it was for her own good, there was just too much deceit between us now for her to ever trust me again. Even knowing how things would end between us, I wouldn't go back and change things. I'd done what I had to do in order to protect her and even if that meant we couldn't be together, I'd take her safety over my own happiness any day.

After standing there awkwardly for a few seconds, Lucia surprised us both when she pushed past me to envelope Matthias in a hug. "Thanks for coming with me today, Matthias. I really appreciate it."

Matthias wore an expression that was a cross between elation at the hug and fear at what my response would be. He kept glancing over as if expecting me to pull out a weapon and ice him right then and there.

I gritted my teeth. I wasn't that bad, was I?

Okay, maybe I was, but not in this case. I was happy Lucia trusted the others enough to follow their directions in the heat of a situation.

Matthias walked in the direction of his room, and I followed Lucia. She dropped her handbag on the floor next to the bed before slipping out of her shoes. After glancing at me worriedly, she took her jeans off, too. I had never been jealous of an inanimate object before, but in that moment, watching as she slipped beneath the sheets with a sigh, I would have gladly traded places with my bed. Lucia let out a long sigh that told me better than any words could have just how scary and exhausting the day had been.

"Matthias was amazing back there," she murmured. "He grabbed me and led me to a closet to hide. When the lights came on and I saw him holding that huge gun, I don't know, it brought it all home for me.

This isn't just about me. If we don't figure this thing out then so many people could potentially be hurt and that's not what I want."

"That's not what I want either. I swear we're doing everything we can to figure this out."

She rolled over until she was facing me directly. "But we haven't done the most obvious thing. This entire time we've been tiptoeing around each other, but we can't ignore the elephant in the room forever. This whole thing started because I was asking the wrong questions. Or I guess they were the right questions."

I ran my hands over my head. It shouldn't be this hard to talk about everything, considering what she'd already discovered. But if we were going to get to the bottom of this, Lucia was right. We needed to get it all out in the open. Which meant telling her things I'd always hoped I could take to my grave.

"You're right."

"I am?" Lucia sat up, looking shocked.

I would have laughed at her astonishment but truly it was a sad commentary on how often I'd kept her on the outside. There was very little that she knew of my life before I'd met Rafe. I still wasn't ready to spill that whole story and honestly, it wasn't relevant. What we needed to talk about was *that day*. That horrible day when I'd made a mistake and her brother had paid the price.

"It's time we had a talk."

CHAPTER TWENTY-TWO

Noah

"Before we do that, I have to ask. You're sure you're okay?" My voice was soft.

She shook her head. Her body was still tense, arms wrapped around herself as if they were the only things holding her together. "The lights went dark. Someone tried to put a hand over my mouth. The next thing I knew, Matthias had me in a closet. It was pandemonium and we couldn't get out, so he locked us in with his gun trained on the door."

I cursed low under my breath. "The kid did good."

She glared up at him. "He's no kid, Noah. I mean, you should have seen the look in his eyes. He was ready to kill whoever tried to hurt me. I've never seen him like that. That guy out there," she pointed in the direction of the door. "He is not at all the guy I thought he was. What happened to sweet, affable Matthias? Computer nerd. You know the guy who can't say no to me? At the show, he was lethal. Deadly. I didn't even recognize him."

I sighed and spoke quietly. "That's kind of the point of having a bodyguard. It's better when they seem unassuming. But don't mistake Matthias for your favorite plush toy. The kid is dangerous." I slid my glance away from her. "We all are."

Matthias more than some, I thought. I would have to talk to him.

I worked hard to keep Matthias away from violence usually. The kid went to the dark and scary places too easily. I always worried I'd pulled Matthias out too late. That ORUS had already broken him. Tainted him. Turned him into the kind of killer that didn't even think. But we'd have that conversation another time. Right now, Matthias had done his job. He'd protected Lucia. Put himself between her and a bullet ... or worse. That was all that mattered. Or at least that was all that mattered to me.

Lucia, on the other hand, was furious.

"Noah, you didn't see what I saw. I swear to God, he would've shot me somewhere nonlethal if he thought that would shut me up and get me to comply. I've never seen him like that before."

I knew she had to come around on her own. She and Matthias would have to talk about it.

"He did his job. Right now, all I am is grateful."

A shudder tore through her body, and all I wanted to do was pull her close, take her against me, tell her everything would be all right. But that was a lie. Because nothing was all right, and it wasn't going to be until I found a way to stop this hit.

"Noah, I just want some answers. And then I want to sleep. Sleep for a very long time."

I didn't know when I decided to do it. Tell her the truth. All I knew was in that moment she held herself together by sheer will and arms that were too thin. So I told her everything.

"Lucia, I know how much you loved Rafe. I wish to God every day that he was here. But there was a side to Rafe you didn't know. He's the one who trained me. The one who was my mentor. He taught me everything I know. How to be the *best* assassin. How to be the *quietest* assassin. He taught me how to talk my way into and out of places. He taught me how to sneak in silently and never leave a trace of myself behind."

When I finally glanced over at her face, she stared at me, mouth agape.

"So what are you saying? That *Rafe* was some kind of killer?"

I paused. I wanted to be honest with her. Tell her as much as I could, but I had to find a way to keep her safe. To not compromise her.

"Yes. I will tell you as much as I can. I won't tell you the organization we worked for. I'm probably telling you way too much as it is. Do you understand the stakes now? This isn't a matter of me playing games with you, or keeping you in the dark. It's a matter of me trying my damnedest to keep you alive. I'm doing anything it takes to manage that."

She stared at him. "Rafe killed people?"

I swallowed hard. Then gave her a brusque nod. "And so do I. At least I used to. I left the organization shortly after Rafe's death. We were supposed to be doing things for a good cause. Taking out the worst of the worst. But after my friend, my mentor, was gone, I just couldn't anymore. As part of my negotiation for release in my contract, I took Matthias with me. In so many ways, the kid is just like me. Too good at killing. Too good at being dark."

Lucia shook her head. "I don't understand any of this."

I shoved my hands in my pockets and started pacing. I couldn't stand still and wait, watching for the hatred and derision to cross her face. So I walked the length of the room.

"When I was sixteen, I was mostly on my own. Technically I was still considered a ward of the state. They had me listed as being in a foster home but about that point, I discovered that the foster homes were more likely to kill me than being on the street. So as often as I could, I made my escape."

She frowned. "Where were the people that were supposed to protect you?"

I shrugged. "Unfortunately in the foster care system, those people are few and far between. They're so overwhelmed with their case-loads, paying attention when one sixteen-year-old spends more time on the streets than he does with the family that's supposed to be feeding him is hard."

She shook her head.

"Anyway, I was what you would call a petty thief. I was real good with sleight-of-hand. Real good with distractions. And women. I recognized young that women got a little hung up on my face. It made them easy marks. All I had to do was dress nice, show the lady a little attention and I'd have the contents of her purse in no time. Sleight-of-hand here, a little misdirection there, and I was usually in and out without anyone being the wiser. I stayed away from things like burglary and other things that could go wrong, but I was still nothing but a common thief."

I kept walking; I didn't dare stop to watch her face. I didn't dare stop to see what she thought of me now. I just kept moving.

"One night I was supposed to be doing a job with some friends in the theater district, but they hadn't showed. They probably got a bigger score and didn't want to cut me in. So I was going to do the job on my own, but in the back of this alleyway next to this Chinese restaurant, I heard a groan. It sounded like someone was in a world of hurt. Normally you learn quick and early to avoid those kinds of sounds, and honestly, I don't know what made me stop that night. But I did. And I found Ian."

Lucia frowned. "Who's Ian?"

"He's the one who told me you're in danger. He's also the man responsible for turning me into a killer. Sure, it wasn't by his hand directly. But saving him that night put me on a particular path. One I didn't quite know how to get off of. One I didn't *want* to get off of."

"He was an assassin, too?"

I nodded. "He got hurt on the job. I won't bore you with the details but I dragged him to a safe place to lie low. My friends and I would use it to stash the stolen goods we usually grabbed. It was an abandoned studio no one ever went to. The building was pretty much condemned. I don't even know how I managed it because he was in a bad way.

"But I managed to half-carry, half-drag him over there. I kept an eye on him. He had some nasty knife wounds. But he walked me through the whole first-aid thing. It was my first battle triage." I shrugged. "It wouldn't be my last. Anyway, I brought him food and water for the next couple of days. Once he was on the mend, he asked for my help to get him to a safe house. From there, my life completely changed. Rafe was assigned as my partner. Assigned to teach me, to look out for me. Honestly, I don't think your brother was too enthusiastic about that at first. But then he sort of took to it. I guess he already had practice being a big brother to you."

She shook her head. "I still can't believe you and my brother were assassins."

"I don't want to tell you any of this. I know how you already look at me. I know how you'll look at me when I finish telling you everything. I'm doing that with eyes wide open because right now, if I don't tell you, you won't be able to protect yourself if you need to."

She stared at me. "So what happened to Rafe? I know you were the one who shot him. But why? If he was like your brother, why would you kill him? Why do that to me? To Nonna?"

I stopped directly in front of her. I sat on the edge of the bed so I could meet her gaze. "That day I had a target. And so you know, I won't be using names right now. I'm trying to keep you as shielded from this as I can. The target was a major player in a drug cartel. Until then, no one had been able to get close enough to take either him or his boss out. The word was that the head of the cartel was no longer the man in charge, but rather a puppet. Word was that our target was the real man in charge.

"The way my former employers used to work, when a government organization couldn't do the legal thing, they'd call us to do the shadow thing. All I knew was that I had my orders. For years, everyone had been trying to get in with the cartel leader. And I finally found an easy way in. His daughter. That part was easier than I thought. She was young. About my age when I started. Seventeen, barely. I managed to talk my way into her school when they were having a sports day. Hundreds of students from other schools were there. It was easy to get past the security. I chatted her up, and the next thing she knew, we were dating. Just a few weeks, all very innocent. But she wanted me to meet her father, and that was my in. It was a risk, sending me in with a gun. So, we managed it with a 3-D one. For several days, I sent her presents with parts of the gun hidden in the boxes and the wrappings. When I finally went to her house, I asked her to bring me everything I had sent her, including the specially made bullets. None of it was metal, so even if the security guards used the wand metal detector on me, they wouldn't have found it. It was brilliant."

The horror froze on Lucia's face. "But Noah, you could've been killed."

"I am very well aware of that. In truth, I had no business being there. I'd done more than a few jobs with Rafe. That's how we worked, two-man teams. When one fell, there was a backup built-in."

I tried not to take her shuddering too personally. It was a wonder she wasn't running away from me with her hair on fire.

"I begged the higher-ups in the organization for solo jobs. I wanted to prove myself. Everyone kept talking about how much of a natural I was. How good I was at all of it. You needed someone to run a deception plan; I was your guy. You wanted someone to run surveillance; I was good at not being seen. You name it, I could be that guy. And I wanted to prove myself. In our organization, failure was not tolerated. I wanted to show my worth outside of Rafe. So I volunteered. In truth it was too big a job for just one of us. It should have been a two-man job. I was no doubt going to get myself killed. But I didn't see it that way. Get in, take out the target, and get out. All I had to do was finish the job." I hung my head in shame. "I was cocky. That's what got your brother killed."

"Why did you shoot him?" Her voice quivered.

Before I knew what was happening, the sorrow and grief I'd been holding back all this time bubbled to the surface. My eyes stung and I worked to hold back the tears. But they wouldn't be dammed. I had to get it all out. I had to tell her the truth.

"I honestly don't know what happened. It was simple. The plan was go in with the girl, which I managed. Meet her father. Stick around. It was his birthday celebration. Take out the target, egress through to the south side where there was a boat waiting. Simple. But that's not how it worked out."

"What went wrong?"

"I made it in the house. I met her father. While everyone was drinking and laughing at his 70th birthday party, I had my target in sight. He'd slipped away from the party. I followed him. I'd already taken care of the cameras, so no one would see me in the security feed. What I didn't count on was Rafe. I didn't count on him coming into the courtyard and stepping in front of my bullet. He didn't want me to do it. I can still hear him screaming, '*No. Noah don't.*'"

I shook my head. "I hear that over and over and over again. I never understood why. But I was in such a hurry to prove myself. No, in a hurry to prove that I could do the job. That I deserved every chance to come my way. Our targets were the scum of the earth. I was doing my job. I was being the good soldier." I sighed. "Or so I thought. I never expected Rafe to jump in front of that gun. I never expected that bullet to hit him. It's a nightmare I live with every single day. Seeing my best friend go down. Seeing the man who trained me, the man who loved me like a brother or father would. Knowing I was the one responsible."

Lucia sat forward. "What happened from there? All I know is that I shot you. I don't remember anything else."

"After I shot Rafe, my target was on the run. He immediately started to bolt, and I should've gone after him but I couldn't. I couldn't leave my best friend lying there. Before I could even move there was the crack of another gunshot, but this one came from the wrong direction. A direction I didn't expect. That one came from you."

"I'd followed him. I heard the gunshots," she whispered.

"With the pain of the bullet, I knew that I absolutely deserved what was happening. But then in my peripheral vision, I saw that it was you. I knew there was no way Rafe would've wanted you to see what you'd seen. He wouldn't have wanted you anywhere near that mess. By that time, the gunshots had alerted the guards and they were coming toward us. I couldn't let them find you." I glanced at her and then dropped my head into my hands. "I saw you collapse. I knew your brother was gone, so I went directly for you. I had to keep you safe. It's what he would have wanted. He wouldn't want those monsters with their hands on you."

Lucia shuddered again, her eyes going vacant while her mind tried to put the pieces together. "Oh my God. You made sure I got home?"

I nodded solemnly. "I failed my mission. And Rafe was down. I'd hit him dead center mass with three bullets. I'd fucked up. But I could get to you. So I made the choice; I chose you instead of Rafe. I took you to the south side, to my exit. I knew my people would be looking for me. You were so out of it. Complete and total shock. I wasn't sure if you knew what was happening. You were practically catatonic at that point. I didn't know what else to do, so I took you to the safest place I could think of. The ice cream place at the Wingate Hotel. That was where one of the island's only payphones was. I called the police, and I called the Feds for you. As soon as you were safe I went back for him. But the place was already crawling with cops. From that point on, all I could do was follow the usual protocol— get back on my egress route, and have my people get me out of there. But I made sure you were safe first."

Lucia dragged in shallow breaths. "I couldn't remember any of it. I blocked it all out. For years, I asked you what happened."

I swiped at my eyes. "I'm so sorry I had to lie to you. I was terrified you'd wake up one day and remember everything. Remember that I was there. That I was the one who shot Rafe. That I was the one who took you away. But you didn't. Even after your time with the therapist. I tried to stay away from you, I did. I swear to God. I tried to just look out for you the best that I could but every time I turned around, you were there, insisting I speak to you. You were calling me, asking for advice, telling me when Nonna needed something, and inviting me to dinner. And the guilt turned. I could do for you what I had failed to do for Rafe. I could protect you. I could step in as big brother. I could keep you from harm. It was the least I could do for him."

"All that time? Why did you even save me?"

"Isn't that obvious by now? I have loved you since long before I knew it was hazardous to my health. Deviating from the plan was necessary to keep you out of the crosshairs of the people I worked for. At the time, no one seemed to notice the delay from me making my egress route to calling back to home base. The only person who noticed was Matthias. He didn't say a word. He protected you, too. It was one of the reasons I pulled him out of there. I knew he could be trusted."

I watched her closely, worried. She looked a little green around the gills, like she might throw up.

"Lucia, that's everything. I'm not lying to you. I know you don't believe me, and I have no right to ask for your forgiveness. I tore this rift between us, and I have no idea how to rectify it. Not that I can. All I can do is what Rafe would want. Which is to keep you out of harm's way."

"Were you ever going to tell me any of this?"

She spoke so softly I wasn't sure I'd heard her correctly.

"I wish I didn't have to tell you now. The people I used to work for, they're ruthless. I don't want you anywhere near that part of my life. But things are out of my hands now. That guy they sent to your apartment, they aren't fucking around. I've managed to avoid a war with them for a long time. But that truce was broken the moment they started coming after you. If they want war, I'll take one to them."

"Why did you start staying with me? Wouldn't it have been better for you to stay away?" She didn't sound upset about it, merely perplexed.

I cleared my throat. "It would have been so much safer to stay in the periphery of your life. But I couldn't. Because I cared too much. That was my mistake. And now it will probably cost you your life."

"Noah Blake, you could have had any woman. Why me? Was that part of the plan? To keep me from remembering? To keep me so distracted with your general assholery and eventually so weak with good sex that my brain never worked?"

My head snapped up. "I wanted you long before I even knew what to do with you. What's been happening over the last couple of months —I haven't been able to fight that any more than I could *not* protect you. To me, this is real. But I never wanted *this*, who I am, to touch you. This was never supposed to be part of your world. I know I'm not good enough for you. Now you know it, too."

We sat like that for a long moment— me with my hands covering my face. Lucia watching me. When she finally spoke again, her voice was mellow.

"I always felt there was something with us. Even when I couldn't recognize it. Back then, after he died, I knew there was something about the way you protected me. And that nothing bad was ever going to happen when you were looking out for me."

"You should feel that way. Because it's true."

She licked her lips nervously. "I don't know what to do with my feelings about you and my brother. Knowing what you've just told me, I have so many more questions. Why would Rafe stop you from killing that man if the guy was really so bad? Was he some kind of traitor?"

"I have no answers. I wish I could take back that day. I wish I could take back my ego, my determination, my ambition. I wish I had listened to your brother. I wish you'd gotten there just a second earlier or a second too late. I wish all kinds of things. But if you asked me to do it all over again, to protect you, or to ask Rafe those questions, I would always choose to protect you." I ducked my head. "But I know it doesn't matter how I feel about you. I could never deserve you. I promise that I'll continue to keep you safe until this threat is gone. Then you can have that life that you've always wanted. With no inter-ference from me."

"Noah." She waited until I lifted my head. "I don't know what the circumstances with Rafe really were. But I know you." The tears streamed down her cheeks. "I know you wouldn't have hurt him on purpose. Especially not after what you've told me now."

She reached for my face. With the delicate touch of her fingertips along my cheekbone, I had no choice but to look at her.

God, she was so fucking beautiful.

"Lucia, I'm not Prince Charming. I'm not some nice Italian boy who's going to marry you and give you lots of babies. I'm not."

"I'm glad you're not that guy. I don't want little Italian babies. All I want is you." She leaned forward, brushing her lips over mine.

CHAPTER TWENTY-THREE

Noah

I never knew you could taste love.

We'd kissed before but it hadn't been like this. Kissing Lucia was every dream I'd ever had made real. If it hadn't made me feel like a complete pussy I would have cried at the overwhelming waves of affection and acceptance I could feel emanating from her every caress. She was holding me in her arms and stroking my skin gently like I was something precious. Something that she treasured.

How long had it been since anyone made me feel my existence made their life worth living? So long ago that I couldn't remember.

Maybe never.

"I love you so much, Noah. There were so many times I wished I could tell you how I felt."

I kept my face buried in the curve of her neck. She allowed me to stay there, her fingers stroking through my hair gently. I closed my eyes and inhaled the unique scent of Lucia. The scent of home.

"Why didn't you?" I finally asked.

"I was scared. You always treated me like a kid. If you'd rejected me, I think I would have died."

Her softly whispered words shook me. Although I wasn't the most demonstrative guy in the world, surely she'd been able to tell how she affected me.

Could she not see how jealous I was when she gave those sweet smiles to anyone else?

Maybe she hadn't noticed that I went on a rampage when her safety was threatened. It seemed insane that I could feel the things I did for Lucia and she would have no idea the entire time. There had been times I'd been sure my obsession with her was tattooed on my forehead for all to see.

"The only reason I tried to treat you like a little sister is because you're so young, Lucia. You needed time to grow up without some guy sniffing around your heels."

"I'm not that much younger than you," Lucia protested.

Although it was factually true, I snorted. Then I winced when she tugged my hair.

"I'm a grown woman, Noah. Even if you still see me as that stupid teenage girl who has no idea what's going on."

I pulled back slightly so I could see her eyes. "I've never thought you were stupid. What you are is ... sheltered."

"Whose fault is that?" Her voice had softened slightly though.

"Mine. I acknowledge that with pride. Some things in this world should be sheltered because they're too precious to risk. You are too precious to risk, Lucia. A bright shining light in a world of darkness."

She let out a soft sigh and pressed a kiss to my forehead. "So are you. I know that you've had such a hard life, Noah. The things you've had to do to survive." Her voice wavered slightly. "But I understand. You've never wanted to hurt anyone. I know that with everything inside of me. And you deserve to be protected, too."

Then she was kissing me again and not with the gentle hesitancy I'd expected. She gripped my hair in both hands and devoured, sucking on my bottom lip with a carnal growl that sent most of my blood racing south. I groaned as I hardened instantly and Lucia purred when she felt my arousal. The little vixen had the nerve to slide her legs up and around my waist, squeezing tight and rocking against my length.

"Lucia," I breathed warningly.

"Yes. Did you need something?" She batted her eyelashes innocently. It was supposed to be innocent anyway but everything she did was sexy.

"Everything. I need everything from you."

Something snapped in me and I was suddenly intensely grateful we were already on the bed. We fell back onto the covers in a tangle of arms and legs. I couldn't get my mouth everywhere I wanted to at once and the urgency drove my need higher. Lucia bucked under me when I took a big mouthful of her breast, sucking hard through the fabric of her T-shirt.

"Need more," I growled and then pushed her shirt up and pulled the lacy cup of her bra down so I could get at what I wanted.

"Yes, that feels so good," Lucia whispered.

Her mouth fell open as my tongue swirled around the delicate point. I couldn't have stopped if I'd tried. I couldn't get enough of the taste of her skin. She whimpered my name several times before I gave her a break. When I pulled back, her nipple was hard and red as a cherry. Lucia's eyes followed the movement when I licked my lips.

"Noah! Take this off," she demanded.

I loved hearing the need in her voice, and her eyes glittered when I helped her sit up and pull the shirt off. At my first sight of her in nothing but panties and the lacy black bra, the swells of her generous breasts overflowing the cups, I almost broke down and begged right then and there. She was a goddess walking amongst mortals. Oblivious to my internal thoughts, Lucia pulled at the hem of my shirt.

"I'm the only one undressed. I'm feeling a little lonely over here."

"We can't have that." I yanked my T-shirt over my head and threw it on the floor.

Lucia sighed and wrapped her arms around my neck, pulling me down into her embrace.

"I really was lonely, you know. For so long all I've wanted was for you to see me. For you to let me love you and give you the family you've never had. I'll be your family, Noah. Me and, hopefully one day, our children. You'll never feel alone again."

My world stopped spinning and I pulled back to see her face. "Our kids?"

It shouldn't have been a surprise. I knew Lucia wanted children and a traditional family. Wasn't that why I'd hated watching her date so much? Because I'd known that one day she'd find some guy, marry him and pop out a few adorable babies. It had torn me up to imagine my Lucia round with another man's baby.

But the idea of fathering her children hit me like a ton of bricks. I came from the streets and had very few memories of my own father. What the hell did I know about any of that? I'd seen so few functional relationships that it was almost laughable to think I could suddenly be husband and father material. Lucia needed a man who could do both. I looked down at her all flushed and glowing with love in my bed. What had I ever done to deserve the love of a woman like this?

You don't deserve it, the insidious voice in the back of my mind whispered. *She has no idea what you are truly capable of.*

"Noah? What's wrong?"

I hadn't even realized I'd pulled away until she spoke. Lucia crossed her arms, covering her breasts. My mind raced as I was assaulted with images of what the future might hold— Lucia holding a beautiful baby with my dark hair and her gray eyes. Lucia happy for a while until she figured out that I would never be the man she needed.

Lucia leaving me.

"Nothing. I need to check on things. Stay here." I kissed her forehead softly when she started to speak. "I'll be back."

I could feel her eyes on my back as I knelt to grab my shirt off the floor. It felt like a laser drilling a hole through me and it only made me move faster. I needed to get away. Away from expectations and the love shining in her eyes. I had a job to do. I would never be the man Lucia truly deserved but I could be the protector she needed. All this emotion was enough to make me forget what was truly important, keeping her safe. Emotion made you soft and I couldn't afford that.

Not with Lucia's life on the line.

———

Lucia

I watched with mounting fear as Noah dressed quickly and left the room. He'd moved stiffly while yanking his shirt back on, like he couldn't wait to get away from me.

I sighed.

With Noah the dance never ended. Anytime I thought I was making progress with him, something would happen to remind me that he wasn't just a guy. He was a complicated man with an extremely dark past.

Despite everything we'd talked about today, I didn't fool myself into believing that he'd been completely honest. There were so many things about his past, especially his childhood, that he never discussed. I'd tried over the years to cajole information out of him.

Where had he lived up until his parents died?

Did he remember his life before then?

How had he survived being shuttled from foster home to foster home?

So many questions. The only reason I even knew he'd been in foster care or that he was an orphan was because Rafe had told me once. Looking back, it was surprising that my secretive brother had shared even that much, but he'd been trying to make me understand why Noah was different from the boys I knew, despite being closer to me in age than he was to Rafe. No doubt my brother had thought it would turn me off and keep me away from Noah, but it had done the exact opposite.

Ever since I'd found out about his tragic beginnings, it had fostered a deep well of affection for the lost boy who'd become such a serious, brooding but protective man.

A man who was going to need more than a few *I love yous* to trust me. I slid off the bed and found my shirt. After putting it on, I went into the en suite bathroom. My hair was wild around my head but my eyes shined with a secret knowledge. I looked ... happy.

It was true, I realized. Even though Noah had walked out, I'd gotten through to him. I'd shown him how I felt and received his love in return. Things weren't perfect but this was the happiest I'd ever been. Because now I knew Noah truly loved me, too.

After splashing water on my face, I patted my skin dry and secured my hair in a bun on top of my head. I walked back into the bedroom and then out to the hallway. The loft was always busy, so the sounds of voices didn't alarm me, not even when the voices turned into shouts. The guys who worked for Noah communicated the same way he did— loud and proud.

When I descended the stairs, Jonas stepped out of the kitchen. Just who I wanted to see. I didn't know the whole story with Jonas but he definitely seemed to understand Noah. If anyone could shed some light on his behavior it was Jonas. My second choice was Matthias, but

I knew Noah thought of him as a kid. Plus I couldn't be sure he wouldn't go blabbing to Noah.

"Hey, can I talk to you for a minute?"

Jonas eyed me warily but followed me to the other side of the loft. There was a seldom-used sitting area with two couches separated by a glass-topped table. I walked over to the tall windows looking out over the city. The view up here was simply breathtaking. The city looked like a maze of concrete and buildings. Jonas joined me at the window and took a sip from the mug of coffee he held.

"You've known Noah a long time, haven't you?"

Jonas nodded but didn't speak. I smiled. These guys were all cut from the same cloth— suspicious, hesitant but loyal to the core. Jonas liked me, but he wouldn't do anything to betray his friend. It made me like him even more.

"Don't look so worried. I'm not asking you to tell me anything. I'm just happy that he has you as a friend. He deserves to have good people around him."

Jonas glanced back at the window. "He's hard to get to know, but it's worth it. There have been so many times that guy has saved my ass."

"I'm sure you've done your share of saving, too."

He chuckled. "That I have. That is one crazy dude. You know I used to be a cop?"

"Sure I did." I shook my head back and forth while I said it which made Jonas laugh.

Considering how closemouthed all these guys were, I was lucky just to know their names. Although, I could see Jonas as a cop. He was the type of guy who liked to follow the rules. He would have been one of the good ones, the kind in it for the right reasons, to serve and protect their community. The kind we needed.

"Well, there was a lot of corruption behind the scenes in my precinct. Noah got me out of a seriously fucked up situation and I never forgot it. When he offered me a job years later, it was a lifeline. I know you get frustrated with him but he's only trying to protect you. Funny thing is, I think you might be the one who can save *him*."

I gulped, wishing with everything I had that it was true. "It's hard to hold someone close who doesn't know how to stay in one place. Noah isn't used to being loved."

Jonas was quiet for a minute and I resisted the urge to beg him for more information. Although I did want his help, I'd never want to make him feel that he was compromising his loyalty to his friend. Sometimes that was the only thing you could count on. Now that I knew more about Noah's background, it was apparent why his friends were so important to him. I was glad he had a whole team of people he could count on in his life. I loved him, and that was all I wanted for him. Even if I wished with all my heart that I could be one of those people he trusted implicitly.

"Don't give up on him. Be patient with him. He's only going to let you go so deep. Hell, he'll probably try to get away just because he thinks he's not good enough for you. Don't let him," Jonas finally said.

"I won't. I promise."

I squeezed his arm before he walked away. In a way, I felt like I'd passed a test. Jonas had trusted me enough to tell me that and these guys, they didn't trust easily. But hopefully I'd shown them that I was trustworthy and, most importantly, that I loved them all. I would never do anything to hurt or compromise them.

CHAPTER TWENTY-FOUR

Lucia

The whole drive to Nonna's house, Jonas and I sat in relatively companionable silence. Our earlier conversation had given me a lot to think about, and for that matter, so had Noah. When we reached my grandmother's house, Jonas parked then immediately busied himself with the football game on television. While he screamed about the Giants losing, I took the time to question my grandmother.

Too bad Nonna was having none of that.

"Lucia, I've told you once if I've told you a hundred times, you sometimes have to let these things go."

My grandmother stood at the stove stirring the sauce. The entire room smelled like rich tomatoes and spices. My stomach growled just from breathing the scent. Usually spending time in the kitchen with Nonna was one of my favorite things to do. It was so relaxing to work side by side creating all of my favorite comfort foods. But today I got no joy from watching Nonna work. Because I *knew* she was keeping things from me.

"I refuse to believe that, Nonna. This is my life, too. I've got these large, missing gaps that I think you can help me fill in. I want to be able to mourn Rafe properly."

Why did everyone always meet me with resistance? Was it so

wrong to want to know what had happened? To want to know the truth?

"He's gone, Lucia. You have to accept that."

I threw up my hands. "I know he's gone, Nonna. I know nothing is going to bring him back, but these answers will help me put him to rest once and for all. I love Noah, but there is so much he hides from me. So much he's unwilling to show me."

My grandmother sighed. "Sweetheart, maybe you weren't meant to see everything. You're only frustrating yourself. Men like to keep their secrets."

"I'm sorry, but I feel like that's a cop out, that notion that I just wasn't meant to know. I'm strong enough. Sooner or later everyone is going to have to see that." I lifted my gaze to meet my grandmother's while she was at the stove. "I know you are hiding things from me. And don't tell me that you've been squirreling money away for a rainy day. Don't tell me that over the years you've set something aside. That was a lot of money I found that day, Nonna. I know something is going on and I want to know what."

At first, I was convinced that my grandmother wasn't going to tell me. That once again she'd lie or evade. But then Nonna sighed and stopped stirring the sauce on the stove. She turned it down to a simmer then took a seat at the table.

"Ever since your parents died, you and Rafe lived with me. I'd always known that he was different. Sure he got in trouble, but there was a fierceness about him. A protectiveness. He wanted to do the right things. He wanted to look after you, look after me. He just didn't always choose the best roads to get there. Hit a little trouble here and there. Mostly kid stuff."

"Boys will be boys," I offered helpfully. I hated that excuse. But my grandmother was old school.

Nonna nodded. "Yes. But your brother also had his own code of justice. When Bobby Nederlander down the street was bullying Jimmy Oates next door, calling him all kinds of horrid names, Rafe found the one way to make Bobby pay. He wanted to make sure he never did it again. It was public and harsh. But it got the point across."

I frowned. I vaguely remembered, but it had been right after we came to live with Nonna. I was seven, maybe eight? But I remembered

Bobby Nederlander. He'd been tied to a telephone post out front in just his boxers with 'Coward' written on him in lipstick.

The interesting thing was nobody had been in a rush to cut him down. He stayed like that for two and half hours until old Mr. Jamison down the street was heading for work. Everyone else was too scared to do it. It was as if there was some kind of code that everyone understood.

All I knew was that after that day, Bobby had never bothered Jimmy again. Hell, Bobby kept the lowest profile ever. He'd never said who tied him to the pole. It became this crazy urban legend, that there was some kind of bullying vigilante.

"I remember. That was Rafe?"

Thinking about it, I remembered how after that day, somehow Jimmy had suddenly become all buddy-buddy with the jocks. Like he was under their protection or something. No doubt my brother's doing, though I didn't know it at the time.

Nonna smiled. "I know I shouldn't condone violence or vigilantism, but it made me feel proud. That even though your brother saw Jimmy next door as the annoying little kid, even though they had no friends in common, even though Jimmy was scrawny and not pleasant to be around, Rafe wanted justice and he fixed it the best way he knew how. Then he took care of him afterward like he was his. I'm still not entirely sure what he did to Bobby, but whatever it was put the kid back on the straight and narrow. He now works as a parole officer or something. Never had a spot of trouble after that."

I wasn't entirely sure giving a kid like Bobby power was a good thing, but Nonna seemed to think it was. "I didn't know Rafe did that."

What else didn't I know about my brother? How much of himself had he kept hidden from me, from Nonna, from everyone?

My grandmother nodded. "Noah is the same kind of person. From the moment Rafe brought him home and said he was the boy's mentor, I knew something was up. Noah was too edgy. The kind of look you get from a lifetime on the run, a lifetime of never being able to relax. Poor kid had no family. I'm not even entirely sure he was old enough to work at the security firm, but every other night or so Rafe would drag him home for dinner. What was I gonna do, not feed the kid? And then, he was always there, glued to your brother's hip. I finally started dragging the lot of you to Sunday Mass, trying to give all of you as much family time as I could."

I sniffed back tears. "I needed that, Nonna. Noah knows what you did for him, too. He loves you."

"And just like your brother, he has a firm idea of justice and what's right. When that money started to turn up six years ago, I knew it was him, seeing that we were taken care of. He knew if he tried to give it to me outright, I wouldn't take it. So he gave it to me in a way that I couldn't deny it. Pure hard cash. He's been sending it to me for years. Once a month, on the first, a few thousand dollars. It helped with the extras, especially when you were younger. I wouldn't have been able to afford the Catholic school that I sent you to in high school on my own. The money helped a lot."

I blinked back my shock. "I had no idea. Nonna, if you need money—"

My grandmother waved me off. "No, no, no. It's not that I needed money. Because we would've figured something out. You would've gone to that school on a scholarship, no doubt. But it was about the extras. So that I could get you a nice prom dress instead of having to make it for you. So that when your school took an international trip, I could afford to send you. That money made all the difference. Noah saw to it. I don't want to know where the money came from or how he went about it. But I know I can count on it. He does it because he loves us, although he can't always find the words."

I hugged myself tight, rocking back and forth. For six years, Noah had helped look after my grandmother. Something I'd been trying to do but had been unsuccessful at thus far. He'd looked after me and made sure I hadn't wanted for anything. Even when I wanted to dislike him. Like with my rent. Like now. My heart squeezed. How could he not see how good he was?

"Nonna, has Noah ever said where the money comes from? He only started Blake Security four years ago. What was he doing for money before then?"

My grandmother lowered her lashes. "I have learned over the years, when people do good, sometimes it's best not to ask how or why. Just accept it and be grateful."

I wished I could do that. Turn the other cheek and not ask questions. But I couldn't. All I wanted to do was understand Noah.

———

I wished the afternoon with Nonna had given me more insight. Well, I'd gotten a few answers to my brother's past. And I knew how long Noah had been looking out for us. Nonna hadn't said it directly, but my grandmother was likely assuming he hadn't gotten the money legitimately. Thankfully she'd never guess the truth. I knew what he was capable of but I didn't want him hiding anymore. I didn't care who he'd been or what he'd done, I knew who Noah *really* was.

Despite all that, I was still not completely ready to accept this new version of Rafe. I couldn't bring myself to believe that part. It was difficult after having one image of him my whole life to suddenly realign all those facts into a new picture.

When Jonas brought me back to the office, I gave him a tight hug and told him I was sorry about the Giants. Of course that made him moan and grumble as he walked toward the kitchen to rustle up some food. As it was Sunday, it was really only me, Matthias, and Jonas around.

Matthias had been making himself scarce. Noah was God knew where. As I headed back to my room, I passed Noah's office and hesitated.

No. You can't go in there. Snooping is not going to get you anything you want.

Yeah, that and Noah would be *pissed.* But seeing as he refused to tell me anything, this might be the only way. At least that was the lie I told myself. Justifications were a funny thing.

Looking around, I noted that Matthias and Jonas were still hanging around the kitchen. That meant they wouldn't see me on the cameras. At least not yet.

Quickly, I tiptoed into Noah's office, closing the glass door behind me. I had no idea what I was looking for. The office was stark at best. Massive glass table. Modern leather chairs, steel, chrome, glass. Eggshell walls. No pictures. A stark, bleak canvas. That was Noah. I always wondered how he could possibly work in here. It just felt so empty.

Maybe that was how he felt all the time. I had no idea.

My only option was to check the bookshelves. I did it meticulously, putting each book back exactly as I found them. *What do you think you're going to find?* I had no idea. Hell, I had no idea what I was even looking for. Just some kind of clue. Something labeled 'Rafe and Noah's secret redacted file' here, but I doubted I'd get that lucky. I just had a feeling that finding answers about Noah would help me find some answers about Rafe.

In the end it didn't matter what I searched, since Noah's office was as impenetrable as the man himself. His laptop was password protected, and most of the drawers in his desk were locked. Except for one. The top one. Inside, I found a picture of him and me, at the beach. It was taken maybe last year. There was no frame. Just the picture. He'd picked me up and had me tossed over his shoulder. I was kicking frantically, trying to get him to let go of me. Of course, we were both laughing like loons. *I* didn't even know he had a picture of that day.

And underneath the picture, I found a friendship bracelet. The strings were pink and green, purple and yellow. I remembered exactly when I'd made it. Summer camp when I was thirteen. When I returned home, everyone still treated me like I was a kid, but not Noah. He talked to me, asked me questions. Wanted to really know about me. I had given it to him, because for a thirteen-year-old girl, that was the height of friendship. Someone who would actually listen to you and didn't overlook you because you were a child. He'd kept this all these years? I fingered the cotton delicately when a voice startled me out of my reverie.

"I must've lost my shit when you gave it to me."

I dropped the bracelet and the photo. "Noah, I —"

He crossed his arms and leaned in the doorframe. "You were just what? Doing a little light snooping?"

"Sorry. I should never have—" I looked down at my hands. "I shouldn't have invaded your privacy. I know. But, since that's what you do to me ..." I shrugged. "Turnabout's fair play."

Noah stayed in the doorframe. Arms crossed, gorgeous face turned down into a scowl. "No one had ever given me anything before. Not really. Not anything meaningful. And you were just a kid. Thirteen, fourteen? You gave me that bracelet. I still remember asking you what it was for, and you said it was for friendship."

I smiled at the memory. "I don't think I ever saw you without it after that."

Noah licked his lips even as he shifted his gaze downward. "I didn't take it off. If you look at it closely, you'll see there's blood on it. I stopped wearing it after that day."

My bottom lip quivered. "Noah. I'm sorry."

He left the doorway then and strode toward me. Anyone else would have been scared. He moved like an animal on the prowl. But I wasn't going to run. He didn't scare me. I shoved the drawer closed and came around the desk to meet him halfway.

"You shouldn't be sticking your nose where it doesn't belong," he growled low.

"I know. I'm sorry, but after we talked you shut down on me. I'm just trying to know you. Know something about you that's real and not an illusion, not a charade, and not a lie. Since you won't talk to me, I'm—No. I shouldn't have snooped. It was invasive. Sorry."

I lifted my head and met his gaze. His eyes were stormy as he looked at me. "Lucia. God, what are you doing to me?"

Then his lips crashed over mine. Automatically my arms wrapped around his neck and with a low growl, Noah lifted me and placed me on the edge of the desk. His tongue stroked against mine, teasing, drawing a response out of me. He tasted like coffee, and mint, and something spicy. And I loved it. I wanted more.

He tried to pull back, but I locked my legs around him and tightened my arms. Logically, I knew I couldn't hold him if he wanted to go. But it didn't stop me from trying.

Noah whispered against my lips. "I couldn't stay away from you if I tried."

"Then why are you trying?" I whispered.

"Because I know the fire will consume us." He delved back in with his tongue, licking into my mouth, making me shudder. My body wanted the things that he silently promised; things dark and delicious that made me feel desperate.

When he ran his fingers up underneath my shirt, tracing along the edge of my ribcage with his thumbs, I gasped and rose up to meet his skillful touch. He dragged wet kisses across my jaw and down my neck while his hands ghosted over my ribs, and eventually just below the swell of my breasts.

I knew precisely what I wanted. Noah. I had to make him realize he wanted me too.

He pulled back, a glint in his eyes. "Be sure, Lucia," he said gruffly, "because if I have you, I'm never letting you go."

I met his gaze and said in a sultry tone, "I'm sure, Noah. I love you."

A satisfied smile curved his lips as he kissed me so passionately that I was consumed by the heat of it.

"Good" he growled against my lips, "because I love you, too."

CHAPTER TWENTY-FIVE

Noah

I picked her up, my control gone. When our lips met, it was a hard mesh of lips and teeth and hot panting breaths. There was something in the back of my head screaming at me to treat her gently. Not to unleash the animalistic urge to take, bite, and ravage. But Lucia didn't shrink away as I kissed my way across her neck to take the lobe of her ear between my teeth. No, she moaned and dug her delicate fingers into my shoulders, the sharp bites of pain sending my already crazed desire through the roof.

"You weren't supposed to know," I rasped in between hot, suctioning kisses down her collarbone.

"Know what?" She squeaked when I set her down on top of the desk. Her eyes were slightly unfocused and her lips were red and swollen.

I grunted, pleased by the evidence of her desire. I wanted to see it all over her. She should always look this way, flushed and satisfied.

"You weren't supposed to know how long I've wanted you. I was supposed to be your protector, and I tried so hard to stay away. Not to want you."

My words seemed to please her because her lips curled into a devious smile. "You didn't have to stay away."

"I did, hell, I probably still should. But I've tried that and it doesn't work. I'm drawn to you and nothing is keeping me away now. You're mine."

I loved how she clung to me, like she couldn't get enough of the feel of my skin. Her touch made me feel primal, like I'd kill anything that ever threatened her. I picked her up, enjoying the feel of her curvy little ass in my hands. Lucia was petite but lush in all the right places. I could spend an entire night just worshipping the perfect globes of her ass.

She moaned as I squeezed the soft flesh, hefting her higher so I didn't have to break the kiss. If it were possible, I'd have my hands and lips all over every inch of her skin simultaneously. Desire rode me hard, making me crazed to do it all, touch it all, have it all at once.

"You make me so fucking crazy," I growled, charmed when she giggled and clamped her legs around my waist.

"I haven't even done anything." Lucia pulled my head down and peppered kisses all over my face.

Goddamn, she was so sweet. She touched me gently and each one of those delicate little touches made me hard as stone. I clenched my teeth, trying to keep myself in check. As much as I wanted to just throw her down on this desk and fuck her hard, I needed to be gentle with her. Careful.

Lucia seemed to have different ideas because she bit my bottom lip before soothing the hurt with her tongue. My eyes flew open and our gazes locked and held. In that moment I saw everything in her eyes. This woman was the one I'd never dared hope to wish for, the other half of my broken soul and the one person who would love me despite my past.

She seemed to sense the importance of the moment also because her hands tightened around my neck.

"Noah, I need you. Right now." Her words were strangled before her mouth was on mine and she yanked at the front of my shirt.

Dimly, I heard the soft clatter of buttons hitting the floor but it was swallowed by the roaring in my ears. *She needs me.* There was nothing she could have said that would have aroused me more than that.

We were a blur of movements as we wrestled to get out of our clothes. I moaned aloud when her teeth sank into the bare skin of my shoulder. Shocked that she would actually bite me, I growled and shoved everything on the desk to the floor.

"Noah, your laptop!"

Lucia looked up at me in surprise as I stretched her out over the surface of the desk. Most of her clothes had been shed and littered the floor at my feet except for a pair of sheer black panties. Her nipples tightened under my gaze, the perfect rose points drawing my attention like beacons. My mouth watered just looking at her.

"I'll buy another fucking laptop."

Then I leaned over her and used my teeth to nip at those damn candy-colored nipples. How could any woman be this sweet? I'd been with a lot of women, probably way too many, and no one had ever made me feel like this. Crazed to touch, taste and stroke every inch. It wasn't just for my own pleasure either but I wanted to drive her crazy and treat her the way she deserved. I *needed* to hear Lucia scream my name. Needed it like I needed my next breath.

When I moved to kiss her belly button she giggled, her torso twisting away from me. She gripped my hair as if to stop me, but of course that only made the game more fun.

"Noah, stop teasing."

"Never, princess. I plan on teasing you until you barely know your own name."

Her sigh hit my ears just as I buried my face between her thighs. The sigh turned into a moan as I nuzzled the soft curls on her mound. I liked the fact that she didn't shave or wax it bare completely. All the women I'd been with before had been like smooth, plastic Barbies between their legs. They'd made noises calculated to sound sexy, moved their gym-toned bodies to pose in perfect positions and said what they thought I wanted to hear.

But none of that shit had ever mattered.

Lucia was real. She didn't know how to be anything but who she was and I never wanted her to learn. Nothing about her was calculated or fake. She was the one person who'd always loved me for absolutely no reason at all.

"You are perfect, Lucia. Absolutely fucking perfect." I punctuated each word with a kiss, licking deeper and harder until she was moaning wildly. "That's it, just let go for me, beautiful."

Lucia's fingers tangled in my hair until I was sure I'd have a bald spot. Not that I cared. It was a small price to pay for the honor of having my tongue deep in the sweetest pussy I'd ever had.

When she came, her grip tightened and she let out a soft, keening cry. Her thighs clenched around my face and I had to restrain myself from beating my chest. When I finally lifted my head, she was flushed and dazed, watching me with sleepy gray eyes.

"Don't check out on me yet, baby."

That seemed to spark something in her because the sassy look I loved came back to her eyes.

"Check out? Can't a girl take a breath?"

She sat up then and put her arms around my neck. I kissed her, allowing her to taste herself on my lips. Lucia moaned and then wrapped her legs around my waist.

"Are you sure you aren't checking out, old man?"

I chuckled at the familiar joke. I'd never known sex could be this much fun. But then again, Lucia made everything fun.

"You've almost worn this old man out. But not quite. Hold on to me."

She squealed when I lifted her and carried her to the wall behind my desk. With her legs locked around my waist, she was at the perfect height for—

"Oh my god," Lucia moaned as I slid inside in one smooth stroke. Her head fell back against the wall with a thump. The look on her face was pure ecstasy.

I would have taken more time to appreciate the view if I wasn't so consumed by the sensation of being wrapped up in her. It was like having my dick encased in heaven and I didn't want to miss a moment. I clenched my teeth against the urge to come immediately. Lucia was moaning and gyrating in my arms, making my job even harder. Then she clamped her arms around my neck and pulled my mouth to hers.

And the battle was lost.

I thrust harder and harder, ignoring the voice in the back of my head screaming for me to be gentle. She was so open, her soft wet flesh enveloping me over and over until she tensed and smacked my shoulder, tears streaming down her face.

"Fuck, I can't take it," I growled.

Lucia lifted her head. "Yes, come with me."

I gave up the fight then and succumbed to the most intense pleasure I'd ever experienced. Having her eyes on me the whole time made it even more intense because I felt like I was inside her in every way, body and soul. When the last shudder of pleasure left me, I wasn't sure how I managed to remain upright. The wall behind us was the only reason we weren't both flat on our asses right then because my legs felt like jelly.

Suddenly I heard the muted sound of clapping. My head whipped around and I saw Oskar right outside my office wearing a big grin and clapping like a madman. I cursed. I hadn't remembered to frost the windows in my office so we were still visible to everyone.

"Thanks for the free show!" Oskar yelled and then gave us both a big thumbs-up.

Lucia groaned and then buried her head in my shoulder. When her shoulders started shaking I saw red. I would pound Oskar for embarrassing her later.

"Don't cry, sweetheart. I'm sorry about the windows. I forgot—" I stopped abruptly when she lifted her head and I saw that she wasn't crying. The little brat had the nerve to be laughing.

"Noah, I'm not the one who gave the show. Your naked ass is what everyone has been looking at the whole time!" She broke off into another fit of giggles that instantly made everything right in the world again.

Lucia

I woke while he was carrying me up the stairs. I smiled and turned my head into Noah's chest. It was fascinating to observe him when he wasn't aware. My warrior. That was what it felt like. Maybe it was shallow but I couldn't deny it was insanely sexy the way he insisted on picking me up all the time. How was I supposed to resist a guy who treated me like the most precious thing in the world? I imagined this was what the queens of old had felt like being protected by knights who'd pledged their lives.

I sobered slightly at the thought that Noah truly would sacrifice his life for me. That was the last thing I wanted. In a perfect world, I imagined our future, growing old and cranky together. He'd annoy me with his overbearing nature and I'd drive him crazy by defying him at every turn.

And I'd love him until the day I died.

"Sleep, princess." Noah tucked me under the covers and smoothed the hair back from my face.

I scooted over and held the covers open. "Not unless you come, too?"

He hesitated, glancing over his shoulder at the open door. The muted hum of voices floated up from the floor below. I sighed. Having me around was probably putting a huge strain on Noah's workload because he obviously wasn't used to taking meals or retiring at a decent hour. But I couldn't help myself. I wanted more of him, *needed* more of him. It felt like nothing too bad could happen if he was there. I didn't mean to use him as the human equivalent of a blankie, but there was no denying that his presence comforted me.

"Okay, let me just check on a few things."

He leaned down and pressed a kiss to my forehead before walking back out, pulling the door closed behind him.

I rolled over to face the window. He was probably hoping that I'd fall asleep in the meantime so he could get back to work. Tears pricked at the corners of my eyes. I didn't know what to do with all these new feelings. Noah had always been there as a part of my life, but he'd never been the center of it. Our new relationship had thrown me completely off balance, and it was scary to be out here on the limb dangling all alone. Noah said that he loved me, but I didn't know if it meant the same thing to him as it did to me. I hated to feel so needy, but truthfully, I had to acknowledge that I'd always needed Noah. It was only recently that I'd been able to openly admit it and embrace the way he made me feel.

It was probably way too much to hope that he felt the same way.

I wasn't sure how much time passed before the door opened, the hum of voices getting louder and then cutting off again when the door closed. I squeezed my eyes shut, as if it would keep Noah from seeing how upset I was. The bed dipped slightly under his weight, and I squeaked when he grabbed me and dragged me against him.

"You've never been able to fake sleep, Lu. Not even when you were a kid."

I huffed out a breath and rolled over to face him. His eyes traced over my face, taking in the tear trails and my no doubt puffy eyes, but he didn't say anything. Not that he needed to. All I needed was what I had right now—Noah holding me close and making everything better.

"I'm glad you're here." I rested my head on his chest, lulled by the steady thump of his heart under my cheek. I counted the beats, imagining that each one beat to the rhythm of his love for me.

"Me too. I love having you in my bed. This is where you belong."

I wrapped an arm around his waist and hugged him tighter. Every inch of him was covered in muscle, but somehow he still made a very comfortable pillow. I had to smother a laugh at the thought of his reaction to being called cuddly. Noah was totally the alpha male, aggressive, hear-me-roar type. He'd probably hate being considered sensitive in any way.

"What are you giggling about down there?"

"Nothing," I lied. "Just thinking about everything. We've known each other so long that it feels like you've always been in my life."

He shrugged, the movement displacing me from his chest slightly. I sat up and looked at him in the darkness. Even in the dark room, his eyes glowed with intensity. I had no doubt that even now, when he appeared to be relaxing, he was on alert for anything that might pose a threat. He'd been taking care of me and Nonna for years now. But who took care of him? When did he get to relax?

It was a telling thought that I'd never considered that before. I'd been more than content to live life unaware, happy in the world Noah made safe for me without ever thinking of the things he must have sacrificed to keep me that way. It shamed me that I'd been so oblivious for so many years. Despite being the ultra-capable, alpha-male, badass type, I liked to think that someone was looking out for Noah, too.

"I was just thinking about how you've been so amazing, always being there for me and Nonna over the years."

"That's no hardship, Lu. I want to be there for you two. You're my family."

"I know. But I'm just grateful that you feel that way. Nonna doesn't let people help her easily, but she told me about the money you've been sending every month. Nonna's too stubborn to thank you so I'll do it. Thank you for taking such good care of us."

I leaned down and hugged him again. He was stiff against me for a long moment before he slowly relaxed. I knew it was hard for him to show affection; it just wasn't something he was used to. Everything I'd learned about his past made me want to shower him in love and show him that he was worthy of it. He might not be used to this kind of attention, but I would continue to show him with my actions how much he meant to me.

"Nonna is stubborn. So ... what has she been doing with the money?"

I shrugged. "She says she's saving it for a rainy day. But it's not like she'll ever need it. I saw that you paid her hospital bill, too. You're so good to us, Noah."

He pulled me tighter and kissed the top of my head. "You deserve everything in the world. Now go to sleep. I know you're tired."

"No, I'm not," I protested but the words were broken by a huge yawn. My eyes closed involuntarily and once they were closed, it was hard to open them again.

Noah's husky chuckle warmed me. It was so nice to hear him laughing instead of being so serious for a change. After everything we'd gone through together, all the tragedy, I decided then and there that I would bring laughter back into his life.

"Goodnight, princess."

It was the last thing I heard before I dropped off into sleep.

CHAPTER TWENTY-SIX

Noah

I didn't want to leave Lucia's bed again. Not after the last time. But I couldn't sleep. However, if I stayed I'd only wake her, and then neither one of us would get any sleep. Not that I minded, but she needed rest. It had been a long few days, and she was running on nothing but adrenaline.

She hadn't been sleeping well lately, but given that last orgasm, I hoped she'd be out for hours. Unless I was losing my touch. Though given her cries of "Oh my God, I ...There, right there ... Please oh God, yeah," I doubted it. With a smirk, I dragged on pajama bottoms that I found in the back of my drawer. When was the last time I put on pajama bottoms?

Quietly, I padded out of my room, gently closing the door behind me. My first stop was the tech room. I doubted Matthias was asleep. The kid barely ever slept. Too many nightmares, I guessed. What I wasn't sure of was whether it was stuff from his life before or the things that ORUS asked him to do that kept the kid up. Anyway, if I didn't live with him I would have never known he barely got more than three or four hours a night. Occasionally he'd take a catnap, but somehow the kid was always alert, hyperaware, ready to run.

As expected, I found Matthias in front of a couple dozen monitors. Most of the computer screens were security feeds. Places that needed watching. Our building. Lucia's building. A couple of clients' locations. The other monitors displayed code. Lines and lines of code. I learned from experience, that it was never a good idea to ask exactly what Matthias was working on. He would either go into extreme detail, boring you with the nuances of every one and zero, or he'd tell you exactly what he was doing, which occasionally would make your hair stand on end. Especially when it dealt with nuclear codes. I shuddered.

I hated to think of just how many governments Matthias could fuck with just because he felt like it. Good thing he was one of the good guys. *Good thing you saved him.*

"Kid, need any help?"

Matthias spun around, dragging an earbud out of his ear, the other hand in his lap, wrapped around the muzzle of a gun. "Fuck, Noah. You startled the shit out of me."

I held my hands up. "Easy does it, kid. You could hurt someone with that."

For a long moment, the guy gave me a flat stare. Completely dead eyes, as if he were running through the scenarios. That was the shit that scared me. For a moment in time, I thought I had lost my friend. And then Matthias blinked. He was coming back to himself.

His hand gently eased off of the gun. "Sorry. I thought you guys were asleep. I'm just edgy after the fashion show."

I nodded and gently eased my hands down. "You know, we didn't talk about it. After you brought her back, we didn't —"

Matthias grimaced. "I'm fine."

I sighed. "I know you're fine, but I need to know if you're tight. That day probably triggered a whole bunch of bad shit for you. I'm sorry I put you in that position."

Matthias looked down at the gun in his lap. "I had a job to do. I didn't even think twice. That's the shit that scares me. It was like an instinct. Every goddamn move, pure instinct. I was ready and willing and wanting to rip the head off of whoever walked through the door. I was *disappointed* that there wasn't something bad on the other side. I *wanted* to kill something." He picked up the gun and put it on his desk. "So yeah, I'm fine. But maybe not tight."

Shit. I had to get the shrink. "Okay. I hear you. I'm feeling like I shouldn't have given you that assignment so soon after we talked to the FBI."

"No. We're running ourselves ragged here. I need to pull my weight. Besides, it was Lucia. Maybe that's why I didn't blink. I knew I had to protect her."

My gut curled. I knew the kid had a crush but didn't that sound vaguely like love? "Listen, kid, I know how you feel about—"

He shook his head. "I'm good. You love her. And she loves you. Besides, she and I were only ever going to be friends. I know it's not like that."

Damn straight it wasn't. Every one of my territorial instincts had already been triggered having her around all the guys. Probably why I was just about ready to fuck her on every flat surface of my office as much as I could. But I didn't say that out loud. "Good," I managed.

Matthias smirked and began turning the chair around. "Besides, given how loud she is, the whole office heard she's pretty much yours."

Motherfucker. They'd heard her. Every damn word. "You guys need to learn to shut your fucking ears off."

Matthias lifted his brow. "Can't. You pay me to watch and listen to everything. Eyes and ears, bruv. And unfortunately I got more than an eyeful. And earful."

We'd been in my office. Sure Oskar had gotten a view, but how had Matthias? "You didn't see shit."

Matthias glanced over his shoulder and winced. "Next time, boss, you might want to use the privacy glass and remember I've got cameras in every corridor. Everyone pretty much stayed in the conference room until you guys, uh, finished. Except Oskar of course. I was unlucky enough to come in after you two uh ... commenced."

I cursed. "You're saying all of you guys got a good look at Lucia's ass?"

Matthias shook his head quickly. "No, unfortunately, we all got a good view of *your* ass." He shuddered. "I'd rather not have to see it again."

I dropped my head and laughed. "Sorry. Privacy glass. Got it."

"Thanks. I know the only reason you're not waking up half of this building with her screams is because you need something."

Damn. This was going to be tricky. With her here, my whole crew was going to get an eyeful of her at some point. *You have to figure out how to mitigate that.* But that was another problem for another day. Right now I had a very specific problem.

"Okay, so according to Lucia, Nonna's been getting money for years. Since Rafe died. Not just a little money, either."

Matthias frowned. "How much?"

"Thousands every month. The kicker is she thinks I've been sending her that money."

"You're shitting me right?"

I shook my head. "We need to find out where the fuck that money is coming from."

Matthias tapped away on one of his keyboards. "And it started showing up after Rafe was gone?"

"According to what she told Lucia, as soon as Rafe died, the money started coming. Now, if it was an electronic transfer or something, I would say that was what Rafe had set up. That when he died, all of his money would go straight to Nonna and Lucia. Hell, that's my set up. But this is something else. It's coming in cash to her door."

Matthias shrugged. "Maybe Rafe had someone set up to bring it to her."

I didn't buy it. "Yeah, but if he did, it would have been me. Nonna practically raised me to adulthood. Hell, I already give her money. Not as much as that, but still every month. I take it over when we do Sunday dinner. She never says a word." I ran my hand through my hair. "I need you to find out where the money's coming from. While you're at it, find out what happened to Rafe's accounts. I knew that man better than I would know my own brother. He would've wanted Nonna and Lucia taken care of. Why hasn't his money from ORUS been coming back? That's a good place to start."

Matthias nodded as he started typing frantically. "If there's a trail to be found, I'll find it. If worse comes to worst, we put a man on her house, round-the-clock, and find out how that money is being delivered, and by whom."

I heard Lucia softly calling for me. I turned my attention briefly to Matthias. "Let me know when you find something."

I didn't wait for Matthias to answer before I was already heading back to the bedroom. Apparently Lucia's nightmares were too much for her to sleep, too. Good thing I knew exactly how to help get her back to sleep.

———

Lucia

I stretched gloriously. Noah Blake knew how to deliver one hell of a wake-up call. I may not be able to move my legs ever. I was certain they didn't work properly.

After he'd stretched over me that morning, intent on giving me the wake-up call to end all wake-up calls, he'd told me to join him in the shower. Lord knew I would have, but I could barely sit up, let alone stand.

And if I knew Noah, no way would he have me in there *just* to shower. Oh, it might start innocently enough. A little harmless soaping of my back here, a little rinsing of my breasts there.

It was a slippery slope with Noah. He really was shameless.

The things that man could do with his hands. And his mouth. *Wow.* I'd never even known it could be like this with someone. Sure, I'd had a feeling we could be explosive, but there was no anticipating Noah Blake. The problem was now that I knew he wanted me, would I ever be able to stop?

More than once I'd been sure he was trying to kill me with sex. There were worse ways to go than death by orgasm.

Truth be told, I was tempted to throw the covers off and join him as he suggested. I wanted to run the soap all over his body. It didn't take much before my imagination was running away with me. If I could move, I *would* join him. I would help soap his back and his abs. Because *obviously* he would need help washing his abs. There were so many of them, after all.

And of course I'd wash other things too. I'd never admit it to him, but I loved being able to snap his control. It always gave me a rush of feminine power that I could bring a man like Noah to his knees. I wanted to learn all the ways to do just that. It made me wish I'd brought along the box of lingerie, toys, and videos I'd gotten from that bachelorette party.

While I was mulling the possibility of Noah allowing me back into my apartment to retrieve it, my phone rang. Unwilling to get out of bed into the chilly morning air, I wiggled sideways and leaned over the side of the bed to pick up my purse and drag my phone out. The number was unknown so I didn't answer at first but then wondered if it might be important.

"Hello?"

"Lucia?"

It took a moment before I could place the slightly familiar voice. "*Brent*? Where are you?"

"It's better that I don't tell you." His voice was garbled for a moment, and I strained to hear. "Lucia, listen to me. You're in danger."

Wait, how did he know that? Did he know about the attack? "Brent, what do you mean? How did you know? It only just happened. Besides, I thought that you were out of this whole thing. I thought you had managed to run."

He coughed. "I didn't run far enough. Listen. Maybe I did something stupid, but after I saw you I started to poke around some more. I think I asked the wrong kind of questions. Because there's been a team following me since I left New York. I should keep moving, but I needed to tell you."

Why would he do that? Why would he risk his life, his freedom, for mine? That was madness. "Tell me what?"

"Listen, not over the phone. It's too dangerous. But there are people trying to hurt you. You need to get out of town, too."

I sat up, wrapping my arms around myself. "What mistakes did you make? You have to give me more to go on. You can't just tell me to leave town. You don't understand. My whole life is here."

"Lucia, this is serious!"

"I know, please don't think I'm not taking it seriously. I know that someone is after me, but Noah and his team have told me they'll look into it. I trust him to keep me safe. I don't want to run away. You shouldn't have to run away either."

There was a long pause on the phone. Then he spoke, his voice low. "Lucia, you don't get it. This isn't just some guy with a grudge. It's too big. It's too organized."

I gasped. "What do you mean, like the mafia?"

Brent shushed me. "I don't know if they can tap the line you're on, but we can't talk about this openly. Look, I'm coming back to the city. Can you meet me?"

Was he insane? There was no way in hell Noah was letting me out of his sight. Unfortunately, Noah also wasn't going to tell me a damn thing about who was after me. If I wanted some information, I was going to have to dig it out on my own. And Brent obviously knew something I didn't.

But the real trick would be getting away. One of the guys was always with me. Maybe it was time to call JJ. She'd have a way.

"Okay look. I'll meet you. You name the place, we'll come and you have to let Noah help you. This is what his team does. He can keep you safe. He can hide you a damn sight better than you're hiding yourself right now."

"No. He can't. And as a matter-of-fact, I think your boyfriend knows more about this than he's telling you. Look, we can't talk on the phone. I'll give you all the information when I see you. Come alone. I'll text you the location."

I bit my bottom lip. I'd promised Noah that I was going to let him and his guys deal with this. But if Brent would only talk to me, that's just the way it was. Besides, I would be cautious. I wasn't going to lose this opportunity to get more information.

"Fine. Text me the address. I'll be there."

"Okay but remember—Come alone. I don't trust that guy. You may think he's on the up and up but you need to be careful. We all do."

CHAPTER TWENTY-SEVEN

Lucia

Noah was going to kill me. Kill me dead. But only after giving me that disappointed *you don't trust me* look.

He's going to great lengths to protect you and this is how you betray him? I tried to shove that thought to the back of my mind.

I battled back the guilt that kept trying to surface as I patted down the blond wig that hid my dark hair. In the next stall, I could hear JJ changing into the clothes that I had been wearing. If all went according to plan, I would leave the restroom dressed like JJ and no one would be the wiser.

Except you. You will be the wiser. You will know that you're lying.

Oskar was going to be pissed if he figured out what I was up to, but I honestly couldn't think of anything else to do. I was all out of options and Brent was offering me a lifeline. I had to take it.

I pulled out my phone and looked at the text message I'd received from Brent earlier in the day. Considering how much he'd already done for me, I figured it was worth my while to see him.

Even if that meant ditching my bodyguard. Oskar was family now. I felt terrible ... except I didn't. As bad as I felt, I knew what was at stake.

"Are you ready?" JJ whispered. There was no one else in the

restroom so her voice was audible almost as if we were in the same stall.

I yanked up the skinny jeans that didn't want to cover my ass. JJ was a lot taller so I'd had to roll up the bottoms slightly. Hopefully once I put on JJ's hat over the wig and the huge handbag, it wouldn't be as noticeable that I'd lost a few inches in height. Or that I didn't have my best friend's characteristic swagger and flair.

It wasn't too late. I could still stop this. I could go back and let Noah handle this. *But can you really?* I knew Noah would protect me from everything that he could. But I had to do this. This was for Rafe.

"As ready as I'll ever be."

I opened the stall and walked out and instantly laughed at the sight of JJ in my blouse and too-big jeans. My friend wasn't as busty so the blouse gaped quite a bit while the jeans were baggy and way too short.

"Don't you dare laugh!"

I clamped my lips shut. "Thank you for this. Just walk fast and then go in the bathroom of the coffee shop. I'll tell Oskar later that I had diarrhea or something."

JJ's eyes went wide. "Okay that's way TMI. But it will definitely work. If not, tell him you have your period. No guy is going to ask for details at that point."

She handed over her large purse and waited while I took out my phone from my own bag. Once I had a chance to see Brent, we'd meet back up at the coffee shop and switch our clothes back.

"Okay let's go. Hopefully He-Man out there won't get too close otherwise the jig is up."

I blew out a breath and waited while JJ went out first. We were hoping Oskar would follow JJ for a while, giving me time to slip out. And lovely as he was, he did just as expected. After all, I was the target, I was the one who someone wanted to hurt. Of course Oskar followed Noah's orders. I almost felt bad for how much shit he'd catch if anything happened to me today, but I couldn't think about that now.

After two minutes, I opened the door and walked quickly with my head down. I didn't see any sign of Oskar, so I rushed out onto the sidewalk. It wasn't easy to navigate all the people rushing by with my head down but I didn't want to chance being seen in case Oskar was still hanging around. All I needed was a ten-minute window to get the information I needed. My breath came fast as I approached where Brent had asked to meet.

I opened the door to the small restaurant and looked around the dim interior. There was a table free near the window so I slid into the seat and put JJ's oversized bag on my lap. After a few minutes, I started to wonder if I'd made a mistake. Noah was going to be pissed if he found out and really, how had I thought I'd be able to pull this off? I was hardly a super-spy.

Just when I was contemplating getting up and leaving, someone pulled out the chair across from me and sat down. Brent looked up from under the hoodie he was wearing.

"Hey." I didn't know what else to say considering how bad he looked.

Brent was usually a pretty good-looking guy but now he had large bags under his eyes and his skin was sallow. He hadn't shaved in days, if not more. And he'd lost weight. If I hadn't just seen him a few weeks ago, I wouldn't believe it was the same person.

"I'm glad you came," he finally said.

"Thank you for meeting me. I understand that you didn't have to call to warn me. I really appreciate it."

He nodded but then looked around apprehensively. I glanced around, too. There were only a few other people in the restaurant. No one was paying us any attention.

"I can't be here for long. The only way I've stayed ahead of them this long is by moving around a lot. There's less chance they'll find me if I just keep crashing on a different friend's couch every night."

"They?" I repeated. "Who are we talking about?"

Brent fidgeted with the strings dangling from his hood. He glanced around again. "I'm still not sure I want to say. Maybe it's better if you don't know. But then when I heard about what happened at your place—"

I looked up sharply. "How did you find out about that?"

"I was worried after I realized someone was following me. My friend works at the police station and told me there'd been a robbery report at your address."

"Yeah, some guy broke in. But he got away."

Brent sighed. "If it's the same people who've been following me, he'll be back."

I leaned across the table. "Brent, please. If you know something, tell me. I can't protect myself if I don't know who I'm supposed to be afraid of."

His eyes met mine. "I'm pretty sure it's the Del Tinos. The crime family."

"Yes, I know who they are," I whispered hollowly. I didn't even pay that close of attention to the news and I knew who they were. Racketeering, human trafficking, etc. Thus far all the government agencies had been trying to pin something on them. The Del Tinos were smart. Only Nico Del Tino had seen prison time. And that was for failure to pay back child support. As far as I knew, all the Del Tinos had legitimate jobs.

But the rumors were abundant. Their family business was import/export, which just sounded shady. But every time their books were subpoenaed, they came up clean. One of the big evening news programs did a story on them last year, but that was all I knew about them. I had no personal connection to them.

"Do you know them or something?" Brent asked

"No. I've never met a Del Tino, never seen a Del Tino and I have nothing in common with them other than being Italian."

Why would the Del Tinos be coming after me? My mind raced as I mentally sifted through all the information Noah had given me. He'd mentioned that his target was part of a drug cartel. Could that have a connection? Maybe if I could peel back the layers on what had happened that fateful day, I could finally have some real answers. Hopefully figure out a way to stay safe at the same time.

Brent leaned closer, keeping the hood of his jacket over his face. "I just wanted to warn you not to let your guard down. You have that scary guy hanging around so maybe you'll be okay. But once I gather enough cash, I'm leaving the city for good. It's harder to disappear than I thought."

"If you need anything ..."

He shrugged. "Just stay safe, okay? If I could go back in time, I would have never made that call. But I didn't know you then. And they'd already paid me a lot of money. It seemed like a lot of money at the time anyway. Wasn't nearly enough for selling my soul."

"Thank you."

He nodded and then left the restaurant. I waited a few minutes then followed him out. By the time I hit the sidewalk, he was nowhere in sight. I walked quickly back to the coffee shop where JJ should be in the restroom. I spied Oskar in the corner at a small table but ducked my head quickly and hustled toward the bathroom. I ran into the end stall since the middle one was occupied.

"JJ? I'm here."

"Thank God. He already opened the door once and asked if I was okay. Well, asked if *you* were okay. You know what I mean."

I quickly stripped off the borrowed outfit and held it under the stall. A moment later, JJ held out my clothes. Once I was redressed, we both came out of the stalls. I pulled the hat and blond wig off and JJ put them both in her bag.

"That was a lot of stress. Hopefully it was worth it?"

"Honestly, I'm not sure."

I must have looked as dejected as I felt because JJ pulled me into a spontaneous hug. "Come on. Let's go get a coffee before He-man out there starts to get suspicious. Then you can tell me all about it."

Noah

I put my phone back in my pocket, determined not to bother Oskar with another message. When I gave an assignment, I trusted my men to do it without hovering over their shoulders. Plus, Lucia was just hanging out with a friend, nothing that Oskar couldn't handle alone.

So why was I so distracted?

Okay truth be told, when Lucia wasn't with me, when I wasn't the one protecting her myself, it scared me. Right down to my core. Trusting someone else with her life made me edgy. But I had to remember that I'd trained these men myself. They all cared about her. Besides, if I continued to smother her, she'd fight against that and I'd lose her. I would rather die than let that happen. I needed to get my head back in the game and trust my team.

The comm unit in my ear crackled to life. "Boss, we've got a disturbance at the back elevator."

Matthias was back at the office but monitoring the hotel security feeds remotely. It had been a real challenge to keep men available to cover all our open client cases, but luckily Matthias and his magical hacker fingers were skilled at doing the work of three people simultaneously.

"I'll go check it out."

I motioned for Dylan to stay with the client while I walked down the private hallway and swiped my keycard for the penthouse elevator. We were on a new detail today protecting a YouTube star named Sherrie Sweets who'd been receiving death threats. I shook my head. I wasn't even entirely sure how someone made money with online videos, but our client was the head of a makeup channel with millions of subscribers. The shit women did in the name of beauty made no sense to me, but I figured it didn't have to. All that had to make sense to me was the best way to protect her.

She had millions of fans, which meant millions of potential suspects that could be trying to kill her.

The elevator arrived and I rode down to the basement level. My team had worked in conjunction with hotel security to close off as many access points as possible. The main lobby and the back service entrance were now the only two ways to gain entrance to the hotel. The elevator doors opened to a team of caterers all wearing white uniforms. I scanned over each face, looking for anyone who looked out of place. At first glance, everything passed muster. The head of hotel security had provided a list of events taking place in the hotel that day and the catering company logo on their uniforms matched the name listed for the first event of the day.

I stepped aside to allow them to pass. The woman in the front smiled flirtatiously while eyeing me up and down. That's when I noticed the man in the back. I glanced down and noticed that his uniform didn't have the same insignia over the breast pocket as the others.

I drew my weapon. "Sir, I need for you to step aside," I said calmly. The last thing we needed was a panic.

The man looked up and then shoved the girl in front of him into me. She screamed and latched her arms around my neck, forcing me to take precious seconds to get free before I could give chase.

Fuck.

"Matthias, I need eyes. Where is he?"

"He went down the service corridor to the laundry room. There's a blind spot there as soon as you turn the corner. I've already alerted hotel security, and their guys are on the way."

I raced to the end of the hallway and paused. I should wait until the others arrived but what if there was some way out that we'd missed? This could end today, and my client could resume her life without worry that this asshole would track her down again. I raised my weapon higher and then charged around the corner.

The hallway leading into the laundry area was empty. I took a breath and then ducked into the main laundry room. It was bright and well-lit, but there was still something ominous about the huge rolling carts of sheets and the metal baskets wired to the walls holding supplies. Somewhere in the distance I heard water running.

Something shifted behind me and I swung around. "Son of a b—" Pain exploded behind my eye as something heavy banged into the side of my head. I backed up, waiting for my vision to clear. The shithead had gotten the jump on me.

"Ahhhhhh!" The man swung at me again and again, his movements slowing as he struggled to heave the large bottle of detergent he was using as a weapon.

I almost laughed at the absurdity of it all but didn't have time as one of the blows knocked me into the metal supply racks. I easily sidestepped the next attempted blow then countered with a punch to the sternum that dropped the guy to his knees.

"You must be hard of hearing. I feel like I told you to step aside," I growled. "Come quietly and you won't get hurt."

The asshole slanted me a glace filled with pure malevolence. "I have to save Sherrie! She doesn't know what she's doing, tempting men with that harlot's paint."

Ooookay then. This dude clearly was past the point of reasoning if he thought the bubblegum cutesy makeup videos our client was known for was the devil's work. But then again, I wasn't sure why I'd bothered trying to reason with him in the first place. Reasonable people didn't stalk someone they only knew from online videos.

"Okay, well it looks like you're going to save Sherrie from prison. Come on."

I hauled the guy to his feet, grabbing him by the arm. But I miscalculated. With a swift flick of a wrist, the guy had a knife out of his sleeve and was arching his opposite arm upward.

Pain, sharp and biting, slashed through me. I let out a low grunt as burning fire lanced my gut. I was going to kill that little shit. Just as soon as I could convince my body of mind over matter.

My breath seized in my lungs as adrenaline raced through my veins. Years of training was the only thing that saved me from serious injury as I instinctively twisted in the opposite direction. The pocketknife clattered to the floor at my feet.

Pain quickly gave way to fury. I could thank my ORUS training for that. Every operative was well versed in acknowledging pain then compartmentalizing it. If it was life threatening, the directive was to get to safety. If the injury wasn't life threatening, the directive was to kill the source of the pain then resume the mission. So unfortunately for this guy, I was going to complete the mission which was to protect my client.

Pissed now, I kicked the knife across the room and then punched the guy straight in the nose. He collapsed in a heap.

I tore my shirt off and pressed the fabric against my side. The sound of footsteps had me raising my weapon until I recognized the head of hotel security.

"What happened?" His eyes fell to the guy on the ground and then on the blood-soaked shirt pressed to my side. "You okay?"

"Yeah. That's what I get for trying to be reasonable." I waved away offers of help and stood back as the others dragged the guy on the floor to his feet. Suddenly all I wanted was Lucia. Visions of her danced in front of my eyes and I blinked several times to clear my vision.

"Sir, I really think you should get that looked at."

I ignored them and pushed forward into the hallway. I held the shirt to my side with firm pressure and focused on making it down the hallway.

I had to get to Lucia.

CHAPTER TWENTY-EIGHT

Noah

I was screwed. I knew that. I was bleeding like a goddamned stuck pig and as I eyed the road ahead of me, I was suddenly aware that walking out without medical attention may not have been the smartest idea I'd ever had.

I shook my head hard, trying to clear the gray fog threatening the edge of my vision. It wasn't as if I hadn't taken any precautions. I wasn't just running around letting myself bleed to death. I'd dressed the wound myself and I knew what the hell I was doing.

The problem was the damn dressing wouldn't hold. That's what I got for doing my own field dressing in the car. But now I had the added problem that all the guys were out on jobs and Lucia was at home. I could have gotten Oskar to come and help me, but that would have left Lucia unguarded. And that was never going to happen. I could have called Dylan to come for me, but he had to stay with the client.

So I was on my own.

Damn it, we were spread too thin. I knew it. We all freaking knew it. Something had to let up. But there was no way I was leaving Lucia unprotected and there was no way I was giving up on the people who counted on me. Who counted on *us*. There had to be a way. I'd have to bring on more men, or outsource, or something.

Because I couldn't keep doing this. I had been too distracted today with my attention too divided. Now I was leaking all over the place because some punk had gotten a lucky swipe. A lucky swipe that was definitely going to need stitches. I might even need a tetanus booster shot or something. That piece of shit. I'd gotten off lucky. If I hadn't evolved from the old days, I might have taken a little bit of extra time with him.

But you're not that guy anymore, are you?

No, I wasn't. Though it scared the shit out of me when I had flashes of wanting to return to that place. All I had to do was get to Lucia. I'd be happy if I just could see her.

I pulled into the basement garage and swiped my keycard to bypass the security gate. My usual spot was concealed in the shadows, just how I liked it, but it still had easy enough access to the elevator. Just because I was stuck and bleeding didn't mean I'd ignore security procedures. I put a hand on my belly and frowned when I drew back and saw that some blood had seeped through the bandage and my dark T-shirt. Damn it. Before climbing out of the car, I placed a 911 text to the team's on-call doctor.

Maybe if I just made it into the medical bay, Lucia might not see me. *Yeah, good luck with that.* To get to the medical bay I'd have to walk straight through the kitchen. From the kitchen, you could see everything. So one way or another, she was going to see that I was hurt. I sucked in a deep breath.

Now that we were trying, the last thing I wanted was for her to see me like this. I didn't want to put out a neon beacon that said, 'Look over here, I'm a killer.'

Yeah, some assassin you are. Getting nicked by some two-bit punk. So stupid.

If my head had just been in the game, this wouldn't have happened.

Between looking for information on the Del Tinos (anything to give us leverage), trying to handle our current client caseload, and then figuring out how to stop ORUS from carrying out their contract on Lucia, I was doing too much. But was there really any other choice?

Mustering enough energy to open the door to the Range Rover, I slumped out, praying my legs would carry me at least to the elevator. It was a private elevator that went straight up to Blake Security. Once in there, all I had to do was push a button and then I could lie down. Lie down and sleep.

Oh God how badly I wanted to sleep.

No. No sleeping. That was the blood loss talking. With a hand pressed over my wound, I lumbered over to the elevator, stopping once because I needed a damn break.

Five more steps.

God, I wanted to see Lucia. She had been so twitchy this morning. I hadn't been able to get to the bottom of it. But that's what I'd been thinking about all day. That's what had me distracted. Because *she* was twitchy. Fuck, I was so pussy-whipped. I had to get a handle on that shit.

Three more steps.

My mind, seeking a refuge from the pain, went to the one source of comfort I could conjure up. *Love.* I'd had women want to sleep with me, want to use me, want to claim me. I'd never had one want to love me before. I had no idea what to do with that. All I knew was I wasn't letting her take it back. No way. She was mine now.

I still couldn't believe it. She loved me. No one had ever loved me. *Besides Rafe.* And now Lucia. I wanted to be in her arms.

One more step.

As soon as the doors opened, I fell in with a sigh. Almost home. Almost to Lucia. Damn I was tired. I just wanted to—

The elevator doors opened. I forced myself to a standing position. All I had to do was make it to the med bay, and then I could pass out in peace. The doctor would get here soon. They'd patch me up and I would be fine. But fuck, why was I so tired? I could barely keep my damn eyes open. But luck was on my side. There was no sign of Lucia. Because while I wanted her and her comfort, I also wanted to shield her. So it was a good thing she wasn't back yet. That was great. All I wanted to do was make it into the—

"Noah. Did you just get back?" Lucia's voice, soft and melodic, floated down like a song from heaven.

Then she appeared, her sharp eyes running over me, no doubt taking in my disheveled appearance. I was still holding the bloody shirt, but had thrown my jacket over it. My fingers tightened, holding the edges of the jacket closed.

I managed to grind out, "Yeah. I'm just going to my—office." Fine.

The office wasn't where I wanted to go, but it would do until the doctor got here. *Damn.* I'd been so close.

She frowned. "What's wrong? You look pale."

"I'm fine, sweetheart. I'm just gonna go to the office for a minute." I kept my back straight and forced my legs to move in the correct direction. With every step, I warned them not to shake, not to crumple. I also warned my brain that nobody was passing out. Not yet. I wasn't having any of that shit. If she saw, she'd be terrified. And she'd had enough fear to last a lifetime.

"You are not fine, Noah Blake. Look at you. Something is—" And her gaze went to the floor, and then back to the elevator and then to me. "Oh my God, you're bleeding." The horror and terror were apparent in her gray eyes.

I frowned at her. How did she know? I was doing an excellent job of hiding this. I had protected her from myself, from the kind of life I led. She couldn't know I was bleeding.

"I'm fine." Shit, was I slurring?

The room started to spin too. Damn thing was tilting upside down. I felt drunk with the worst headache known to mankind.

It's blood loss. Stay on your feet.

If I could just keep it together, she wouldn't have to see me like this. I'd hoped to always protect her from this kind of shit.

How's that working out for you?

I went down on my knees. The gray started to encroach on my vision, just in the periphery. It shadowed out the light, creating a pinhole effect. The last thing I registered before I went down was Lucia screaming for help.

———

Lucia

This was it. I was going to kill Noah. Okay, first I was going to make sure he was absolutely better. Then I was going to kill him.

Four damn days. Four days that I had been watching Noah sleep. Four days I'd been watching the doctor change and dress his wounds. Four days he'd been going in and out of consciousness. The knife he was cut with had been rusty as hell, and he'd needed a tetanus booster.

He'd had a fever yesterday that fortunately had broken quickly. He grumbled at Ryan for fucking up his breakfast this morning so he was definitely feeling more like himself. Meanwhile, I'd never been so scared in my whole damn life. Noah kept insisting it was fine.

Yeah, well he should have seen the blood. How he'd missed the fact that he was leaking was beyond me. The slash in his abdomen was nasty. At least nothing major had been punctured. With most of the infection gone, he had less to worry about. But he wasn't out of the woods yet.

How dare he try and hide something that serious from me? From what I could gather, his intention had been to go to his office, either patch himself up, kind of like he attempted to do in the car, or call Matthias to do it. He wouldn't have let me help, because even when he was hurt, he was trying to protect or shield me from himself. Who he was.

I was not down for that.

He had to get it through his thick skull that we were in this together. That he mattered to me. I didn't just love the Noah who irritated me, then teased me into watching bad action movies. I loved this other side of him. The one that was edgy and dark. The one that needed my love the most.

He never wanted to show me that.

Well, too bad for him. That morning, after the doctor had left, I offered to take his dressing duties over. I knew how to apply a bandage thanks to Nonna, who'd been a nurse back in her day. She'd taught me the basics.

I hesitated outside his bedroom for just a moment. What if he didn't want to see me? Well tough shit for him. I loved him and he'd scared me, so I didn't bother to knock. Hell, I'd been sleeping in here every night anyway. On the couch in the corner, ready to wake up if Noah needed me. Who was I kidding? There hadn't been much sleeping happening. I'd sat in there and stared at his sleeping form. And the moment any of the guys had come in to try and relieve me, I'd threatened their balls.

For some reason that made them all smile. What the hell was wrong with them? They might not fear me, but they would if they understood how much I loved him.

My chest squeezed just thinking about how much blood he'd lost. How much worse it could have all been.

So, no, there'd been no sleep for me. Not when the man I loved was in pain. I was too terrified something would happen to him if I closed my eyes.

With a smile firmly in place, I pushed the door open. "Hey, I need to change your dressing."

He shifted his laptop and pinned his intense green gaze on me. "I —you don't have to do that."

I ignored him. "Funny, you don't seem to know the difference between have to and want to. *And* you don't seem to understand how love works."

He sighed. "I —"

I put up a hand to halt him. "No. I don't want to hear about how you were protecting me. Blah, blah, blah. The same old song and dance. We established that I love you, and you love me. That means no secrets. And after everything you've told me, I thought we were done with that. So you don't get to hide this part of yourself. The parts that need bandaging. The parts that need help. I'm just here to change the dressing so I can help you get better faster. The moment you're better again, I'm going to kill you."

His green eyes sparked with fire, and I saw that my threat to harm him had the exact opposite effect. Instead of him looking scared for his life or even remotely docile, his gaze turned predatory.

"Just how do you plan to kill me? With your mouth? With that sweet tight p—"

"Noah Blake. Stop that now." His brows popped and his eyes widened to form a mock innocent face. "I know what you're doing. You will not deflect."

"Lucia, I'm fine. I wasn't trying to hide. I just didn't want you to do what you ended up doing; sitting by my bedside all night worrying. Freaking out."

"I will have you know that I did not freak out. I had to lug your injured carcass into the med room. Granted, Matthias helped with some of that. But I was extremely calm."

He shook his head. "I know you're strong. That still doesn't stop me from wanting to shield you from these things. Wanting to shield you from *me*. I never wanted this side of me to touch you."

"Newsflash— It's already touched me. And it wasn't necessarily from you. I need to be prepared. I can't be surprised by things. I love that you want to shield me and keep me safe, but you can't have it both ways. Either I'm a child who needs protection, or a woman you see as your equal who deserves your love."

His gaze snapped to mine and held. "I'm the one who doesn't deserve your love."

"Well, that's too bad then because you've already got it." I leaned over and kissed his shoulder. Right over the scar I'd given him. "Please stop hiding from me. So that we can both get started really loving each other."

"Okay, I promise you. No more hiding. From now on, you get the raw truth. Every time."

"This means, no more shielding me from things that you think would be painful. Either I'm an equal or not. If I'm not, then I probably don't need to be in your bed."

His gaze narrowed on me. Yes, I was bluffing. Because I knew well enough by now, that I would be in Noah's bed. But I needed to stand my ground. So I met his gaze directly.

Even as he worked his jaw, he nodded. "I'll tell you everything."

I nodded. "Good. Now, I need to figure out just how to get you naked without disturbing your bandage."

Noah laughed. "I swear woman, you just want me for my body."

CHAPTER TWENTY-NINE

Lucia

I brushed the hair back from his face, taking in the sharp features and the strong jaw that I loved so much. Watching him struggle to recover the past few days had been as painful as being hurt myself. The crazy man had no idea how much he meant to me, did he? Apparently not if he thought he could hide an injury or that I wouldn't want to be here taking care of him.

This was where I was meant to be.

"I definitely want you for your body. But that's not what I want the most."

At his questioning look, I pressed my hand over his heart. I would never forget the gentle, awed look that passed over his face. For just a moment, Noah looked ... vulnerable. I knew how hard it was for him to let me in and I'd always assumed it was because of his past. But now I was starting to think he just had trouble believing good fortune was real. He looked at me like I was too good to be true.

So I'd just have to show him.

"I want you to hold still and let me do all the work." I gave him a stern look before pressing a gentle kiss to his bare chest.

"Yes ma'am." Noah grinned, happy to play the role of the obedient patient for now.

His eyes followed the movement of my lips as I explored the

incredible chest that I never got tired of looking at. He was just so damn sexy and had muscles on top of muscles. *But even he isn't invincible*, I thought as I skipped over the bandages covering his wound. I nuzzled my face into his lower belly so he wouldn't see my expression as I struggled to get my emotions under control. I'd been a basket case for the past few days and he had to be tired of seeing that. Now was the time to show him how happy I was to be with him. To make him feel good.

"And where exactly are you going, Miss Nurse?"

I laughed at his attempt to play the role. Even when I was supposed to be 'in charge' Noah had a way of taking over and directing things. It was something he did unconsciously but this time I wasn't going to allow it.

"Quiet, young man. You're supposed to be resting."

His pupils dilated slightly as I continued down his belly, following the trail of hair that led beneath the pajama pants he was wearing. I gripped the edges and tugged them down until his cock popped free. Noah let out a strangled groan when I bumped it with my nose.

"I'm resting, I am."

I gripped him firmly, tugging slightly on the soft skin, enjoying how he fit in my hand. "You seem to be recovering quite quickly. Maybe you don't need me anymore."

He shook his head frantically. "You are definitely needed here. Things have been so *hard* lately."

"Really hard, huh?"

I gripped him tighter before taking the head between my lips. I loved his slightly salty taste and the way he got even harder in my mouth. It was intoxicating to pleasure him this way and know that I held him completely within my thrall.

"Lucia. *God* you don't even know what it's like to watch you do that."

I glanced up to see Noah watching me, his face twisted in pleasure-pain. His eyes were fixed on where my mouth surrounded him. It normally would have made me self-conscious to have him watch, but there was no way to interpret the wild, animalistic look in his eye as anything other than pure lust.

I pulled back and licked the head, drawing a husky moan from Noah. "I like watching you, too."

I deliberately kept my eyes on his as I took him deeper this time, trying to relax my throat so I wouldn't gag. The women he was used to could probably do this without any trouble, I thought bitterly. But then I pushed the thought aside. He wasn't with those women. He was with me.

He only wanted me.

When he hit the back of my throat I choked a little, but it seemed to turn Noah on even more.

"You trying to take all of me, baby?" There was a warning in his voice that I couldn't decipher. But my body responded to the dark eroticism in his voice, my nipples pebbling as I clenched between my thighs against a stab of desire.

He didn't wait for my answer, just circled my throat with his hand. But he must have seen something in my eyes because he cursed viciously and pulsed in my mouth.

"Lucia, I need to be inside you."

I pulled back and then climbed on top of him carefully. He'd recovered quickly over the past few days but I didn't want to take any chances of him hurting himself. He rested one hand lightly on my hip while using the other to guide his erection in place. I moaned softly as I sank down on him, going slowly to give myself time to adjust. No matter how many times I was with him, I wasn't sure I'd ever get used to being filled so completely.

Noah's fingers flexed on my hip when I finally took him all the way. I rocked forward slightly and then gasped at the entirely new sensation. In this position, everything was stimulated simultaneously as his pelvic bone rubbed up against my clit.

Noah's low, sexy chuckle rumbled through me. "Looks like my princess likes being on top."

I clenched around him, making him groan. "I do. You might not be able to get me off you after this."

"Well then, by all means take the reins."

He let his hands fall away and raised his eyebrows as if to say, "Game on." I was more than ready to take the challenge. I rested my hands on his chest and then lifted up slightly before dropping down. We cried out together at the jolt of pleasure.

"Again," Noah ground out.

I lifted my hips and then ground down on him again, crying out as my orgasm started, rolling over me in waves. I clenched around him, my hair flopping into my face as I struggled to keep the rhythm. Noah's arms came up to support me and I gladly let his hands guide my hips until I felt him stiffen beneath me.

I fell forward, careful not to rest my weight directly on him. We rested together until Noah pushed my hair back so he could see my face. I grinned at him and then kissed the tip of his nose.

"You are a very bossy patient," I muttered even as I settled into his embrace. I never wanted to leave his arms.

His soft smile made him look years younger. "Clearly I need a lot of help. You have your work cut out for you. You sure you're up for that job?"

Although the question was asked in a joking manner, I understood the deeper meaning immediately. My arms tightened around his neck.

"Just try and get rid of me."

———

Noah

I ignored the aching pain in my side as Lucia flitted around me, straightening this and plumping that. It seemed to calm her to fuss over me. She'd endured so much over the past few weeks and if our newfound relationship was going to have any chance of survival, we needed to find solid ground.

"I'm fine, Lucia. Come back to bed."

She stood next to me wringing her hands. "Are you sure? I saw that face you made when you turned over. We shouldn't have done that while you're still hurt!"

I chuckled, ignoring her chastising look. "By that, you mean climbing that sexy little body on top of me and rocking my world? We definitely should have done that. And we should definitely do it again as soon as possible."

Matter of fact, if she just gave me a couple of minutes, we *could* do that again.

After all, sex with the woman who loved you was really the best medicine. I wondered if I might be able to get the doc to write me a prescription for it. Would she go for that?

"Noah, be serious. I hate seeing you like this. It scares the living hell out of me."

"I've had way worse than this." It was true, though I wasn't going to go into any details right now. I didn't want her scared any more than she already was. She had been through enough.

Her face fell and I wanted to kick myself for reminding her just what type of man she was climbing in bed with again and again. Not that Lucia would ever forget the things I'd done—how could she—but I didn't need to remind her I was a stone-cold killer at every opportunity either. I lived in fear that one day instead of curling into me, she'd turn away from me. No way was I hastening that moment in any way if I could help it.

A knock at the door broke the tense silence. Lucia knelt and picked up my shirt from the floor. "Just a minute." Once she'd helped me put my shirt back on and smoothed her hair, she walked over to the bedroom door and opened it a crack. "Yes?"

Matthias's voice floated through the small sliver of space. "Hey Lucia, I need to talk to Noah." When she hesitated, he continued, "You know I wouldn't bother him unless it was urgent."

With pursed lips, Lucia pulled the door open all the way and allowed Matthias to come in. I barely smothered a laugh at the blush working its way over her cheeks. Knowing her as well as I did I could tell what she was thinking; that the room smelled like sex, her lips were swollen and that her wild hair looked like she'd just been thoroughly fucked by her man six ways to Sunday.

It probably made me a caveman, but I grinned harder at the thought that everyone who saw her today would know what we'd been up to. Granted, everyone in here pretty much always knew what we were up to.

It wasn't my fault I couldn't keep my hands off of her. She was just too damn sexy.

Besides, I wanted everyone to know she was taken by a man who wouldn't hesitate to kill for her. She'd had enough fear in her lifetime and she deserved to know that she would be protected and cared for. I might not be white picket fence material but protection, now that I could handle.

Maybe Lucia being with a killer had its advantages.

Matthias stood next to the side of the bed. "Hey, boss. Feeling better?"

I shrugged. "You know how it is. I'm not dead. What more can I ask for?"

"I hear that." Matthias glanced over his shoulder at Lucia hesitantly. Although he would never say it aloud, I could tell that whatever he wanted to talk about probably wasn't fit for sensitive ears.

"Lucia, would you mind getting me some water? I think maybe I'm getting a little dehydrated."

She came off the wall so fast I was surprised she didn't leave scorch marks. She looked horrified at the idea that she might have missed something vital to my health. "Of course! I should have thought of that. I'll be right back."

"Maybe some food, too? I can come down and help you carry it." I moved to get up, knowing that she'd protest and then flopped back down when a bolt of pain lanced through my side. I'd only been playing around about needing help but apparently I wasn't as healed as I'd thought.

"Absolutely not. Stay right where you are." Lucia rushed to my side and placed another pillow behind my head. Then she aimed her glare at Matthias. "Don't let him get too riled up."

"Roger that," Matthias said with a nod. Then he waited until she left the room before he turned back to me. "The Feds want another meeting."

"Shit. Already?" I didn't have to ask why this had Matthias so freaked out. Anything that put the kid in the vicinity of law enforcement was bound to make him twitchy. With me laid up, that made it even more likely that Matthias would have to deal with the Feds directly since no one else was up to speed on that particular case.

"I'll be on my feet in twenty-four hours. Don't worry about it."

Matthias gave me a skeptical look. "Even if you are, do you think Lucia is going to let you get out of bed?"

My brows snapped down. "Let me? The woman is no bigger than an ant. How exactly is she going to stop me?"

Matthias made a face and suddenly I felt like shit for indirectly pointing out the elephant in the room. Clearly Lucia had her ways of keeping me in bed. Uncomfortable silence fell between us, and I tried to think of anything to take his mind off the obvious.

"I'll take care of the Feds. You just keep working your magic behind the scenes. Maybe if Jonas has time, he can take over for me. He speaks that government language from his time as a cop."

Matthias gave me a mock salute but looked noticeably lighter as I left. I gritted my teeth and slowly sat up. I was healing pretty quickly but it wasn't fast enough for my taste. There was someone out there putting a target on Lucia's back, and I wanted to be right on the front lines tracking them down. Now with all this extra shit with the Feds, the last thing I wanted was to be confined to a sick bed.

The door swung open and Lucia appeared carrying a tray. When she saw me sitting up, she hurried to place the tray on the dresser.

"Noah, what are you doing?" She rushed to my side and placed a warm hand on the center of my back.

"Getting up. I've been in this damn bed too long."

"Well, you're going right back in this bed if I have anything to do with it. No matter what I have to do to keep you there!"

The little smile on her face told me she wasn't unaware of the dirtier implications of her words. I grinned.

"Well, I guess if I have no choice." I rested back against the pillows and patted my thighs. "Come on up here and keep me company, Nurse Lucia."

CHAPTER THIRTY

Noah

For the second time in the same number of weeks, I traversed the hallways of the FBI. This time, I left the kid at home. I still wasn't sure this was the right thing to do. After all we had a lot going on right now. But with everything happening and ORUS still an unknown, it wouldn't hurt having an ally with government resources. If Blake Security scratched their back, they'd be forced to scratch back when I came calling.

When I was led into the Assistant Director's office, I stiffened my spine, wincing only slightly as my knife wound pinched. Yeah, maybe I shouldn't have gone that extra round with Lucia this morning, but well, I was a bit of an addict. So what? I had gone for years without her. I had a lot of lost time to make up for.

Assistant Director Calhoun looked up with a smile. "Mr. Blake. Where is your associate?"

"He will not be joining us today."

The other man frowned. "You're not a tech expert. You can't decipher these encrypted codes. We need him here."

Once again, I was glad I hadn't brought Matthias. The kid was right to be twitchy about the Feds. They wanted their claws in him. And like hell was I going to let that happen. I hadn't helped the kid escape from one prison only to be put into another.

"We agreed to do the job. And we're doing it. I came here to give you a status update."

The Assistant Director sputtered. "B—b—but for access to all our files, he'll need to be on site."

I smiled. It wasn't a particularly nice smile. It was more of a shit eating one.

"*Sir,* you want to use Matthias because he is the best hacker in the world, depending on who you ask. You think you have something here in the FBI office that he doesn't have access to?"

"But we need—"

"You need status updates. Which he'll provide through me. You don't ever need to see him in person. If he needs access to your FBI database, you can either give it to him, *or* he can take it. Let's not fool ourselves and think that he can't. He'd probably enjoy breaking in more to get the information he needs but considering you're paying us to do a job, it's probably easier if you just give it to us."

I didn't even flinch as Calhoun blustered and yelled something about classified information for another thirty seconds. Then when he finally realized I wasn't going to back down, he sat.

"If he's going to access our servers, I need one of our people on location to make sure he doesn't access anything he's not supposed to."

"You guys are hilarious." I shook my head. "You think I'm going to let an FBI trained hacker into my systems under the guise of showing my guy what he needs? You need Matthias. He knows not to trust you, which is why he's not here. Look, if you want our help, you'll follow our lead. Otherwise, we'll leave you to your own devices. How far was that getting you on your own again?"

Calhoun looked like he might blow a fuse. And I waited for that. Finally the man calmed down and sat back.

"You're never going to let us near him, are you?"

I shrugged. "You have access to him. You just don't have it the way that you want."

"Fine. We'll do it this way. But sooner or later, your hacker kid is going to have to answer some questions."

The hell he will. I forced a smile. "That's a conversation for another day. In the meantime, you want your status update or not?"

Calhoun nodded his acquiescence and I gave him the information I had come to deliver. Shipping routes. Known associates. Current location of merchandise or last known port. The only thing Matthias had yet to crack was finding the head of the organization. But knowing the kid, he only needed time.

When I was done, I sat back. "That's all we've got for now. Matthias should have the rest of the information in a few days. Worst case scenario, a week. We'll let you know if he runs into any roadblocks or problems. But, knowing Matthias, he won't."

Calhoun sat back. "You mean to tell me, in the span of a week, he's done what my guys couldn't do in the months we have been searching for these assholes?"

I shrugged. "I don't know how the kid does it. I just know that he does."

Calhoun shook his head. "He could do a lot of good here. Make a difference, help people. Wouldn't you like to give him a chance to do that?"

My gut twisted. Yeah, I would love to give Matthias that opportunity. The opportunity to do nothing but pure good, but the kid made his own choices. Right now, it was my job to protect him. At least as much as I could.

"Matthias makes his own decisions. If he doesn't want anything to do with the FBI, then I support that. Just so you know, he helps a lot of people. He just does it in his own way."

"You mean outside of the law?"

"I mean by any means necessary, and we are a legitimate security firm. You wouldn't have called us in here if you didn't think we were the good guys."

Calhoun scoffed. "Since taking on this job, I've learned to work in the gray areas. And you, Mr. Blake, you and your men are one big patch of foggy gray sky."

I stood. "Sometimes you need the gray before the sun comes out. I'll take my patchy, foggy sky." As I turned, a picture on his desk caught my attention. There next to John was a man that I recognized.

I knew that face.

"Is this your family?" With a shaking hand, I picked up the frame.

The other man beamed in the self-satisfied way that only men who had it all could. He pointed to the woman. "Yes, that's my wife Diana. We've been married for almost forty years. Hard to believe!"

"And this is your son."

Calhoun puffed out his chest. "It is. He's with the Bureau as well, has been ever since he graduated."

Bile rose in my throat as I set the picture down and turned to leave.

Through clenched teeth I murmured, "You'll get another update as soon as we have a location."

I muttered a hasty goodbye, bumping into the doorframe on the way out. The pain that ran through my shoulder and abdomen anchored me. All my training was the only reason I got out of the building without drawing any further suspicion.

Outside on the sidewalk, I moved quickly to the second level of the parking deck. All the while, memories realigned and my mind raced over every bit of information from that day long ago. I'd never forget that assignment, of course. It had been the single worst day of my life. That case had stolen my best friend from me and changed my life forever. But now I couldn't be sure if I'd ever truly known what was going on.

That face. I knew that face. I'd studied it from every angle. Then I'd stared it down over the barrel of my gun before firing the shots that changed everything.

If my target was alive and well and not affiliated with the cartel, then what the fuck did that mean for me?

Had ORUS known they were targeting an undercover FBI agent?

———

Lucia

I tripped into the penthouse loaded down with bags. All samples for an event. I'd been closer to Noah's than to my office, and I needed to pee so bad I might burst, so I'd stopped off quickly.

I hadn't wanted to leave the ten thousand dollar dresses and accessories in the car downstairs no matter how secure it was supposed to be, so I'd had Oskar help me carry them up. I popped one of the hats on top of his head.

"You look very dashing," I said.

As I handed him the dress bags, I ran quickly to the bathroom and back to Oskar, but before we could start the trek back down, Noah came up the elevator.

I turned with a smile. "I was just going to have Oskar help me with this. But I think that you make an even better —" When I got my first good look at him, I paused. He didn't look well. "What's wrong?"

Even Oskar, who liked to pretend he was above it all, frowned with worry. "Boss, everything okay?"

Noah swallowed hard and nodded. "Oskar, get Matthias and Jonas. I need all the information you can dig up on Assistant Director John Calhoun. And I mean everything. Even if his wife has a hobby that she writes off as legitimate business, I want to know. Anything and everything. Financial statements. Anyone with a grudge. All of it."

Oskar nodded and even though he gave Noah an ominous glare, he went to do as he was told.

I grabbed ahold of his arm. "Noah? Are you okay? You look like you've seen a ghost. What happened? Are you hurt?"

He didn't say a word, just stood there, his handsome face stricken with worry. I'd never seen him like this.

Noah shook his head. "No. I'm not okay. I think I was sent to kill an innocent man."

I dropped the bags where we stood. "Come on." I dragged him through the office, into his bedroom then shut the door gently. "Tell me what's going on. You're scaring me. Was it your meeting today? I thought that was at the FBI office?"

Noah shook as I tugged him down onto the bed.

"Talk to me, Noah."

Noah dragged in a shuddering breath. "I don't know. I'm going over it. It's all like this hazy blank space my conscience refuses to let me see."

"Tell me what you think you know."

He filled his lungs with air. "Okay, the day I told you about. The day Rafe died. I told you what I thought was important. How I got there. My assignment. All true. All accurate. I didn't leave anything out." He shook his head. "But I think there is something I wasn't seeing. Something I didn't know."

I rubbed my hand over the strong muscles in his back. "Okay, we'll figure it out together."

"The man I was sent to kill. I was told that he was a lieutenant for the Del Tino family."

I froze. The Del Tinos. So Brent had been right to warn me about them. My heart sank, knowing I couldn't tell Noah about my secret meeting with Brent now. If he ever found out about that, he'd lose it. Although, I didn't have to, I reasoned. If Noah already knew about the Del Tino connection then telling him wouldn't accomplish anything.

I turned my attention back to him just in time to catch the rest of what he was saying.

"I was told that although this guy was officially the second in command, he was actually the real brains behind the organization. The real reason the Feds could never get anything on them. Because the Del Tinos were clean. The old man was only a puppet figurehead. So my target that day was the lieutenant, Sanders."

I nodded. "Okay, he must have been a bad guy."

Noah rocked forward, placing his elbows on his knees. "If he was a bad guy, then why was his picture on the desk of the Assistant Director of the FBI's Cyber Division? That guy I was sent to kill is Director Calhoun's son."

I frowned. "That doesn't make any sense." Then it hit me. "Oh my God, he was undercover."

Noah ran his hands through his hair in frustration. "Probably. Now I have to keep playing that day in my head. That moment I raised my gun and Rafe stood in front of it. Did he know? And if he did, how? Because we worked for the same people. Sure, Rafe was higher up than I was, but we were teamed together for a reason. Failsafes. He would have given me that information."

"Maybe it was new information that just came in? Maybe they realized they had it wrong?"

Noah shook his head. "ORUS never had it wrong. It was their job to have it right. We were supposed to take out the worst of the worst. Not undercover FBI agents. How many innocent people have I killed? *How many?*"

His moss green eyes were anguished, terrified, and haunted. I had no idea how to help.

"Noah, if Rafe stood between that guy and a bullet, and he knew the guy was FBI, then he would never have let you kill any of those other people. So there has to be another explanation."

He frowned, his brows knitting tight, his brain clearly working it through. "But how did he know? He was determined to stop me, and he had never attempted to stop me before. More often than not, he acted as my spotter, my guide. What made that any different?"

"That's the real question, Noah. Why was Rafe determined to save *that* life? But yet determined that all those others had to go?"

He nodded slowly. "I need to start from the beginning. That whole day. What do you remember? From the time you woke up to the time —" His eyes shifted down to his knees. "The time that I shot Rafe. Tell me everything."

CHAPTER THIRTY-ONE

Lucia

I tucked my hands under my arms, suddenly cold. Even though I'd told Noah we'd figure it out together, what if I couldn't do it? Talking about the day Rafe died wasn't something I knew how to do.

"I hate that I'm even asking you to do this. I'm supposed to protect you from harm, not ask you to walk straight into it."

Noah's dull voice broke through my thoughts. As soon as I saw his face it was obvious this was taking just as great a toll on him as it was on me. He looked like he was staring straight into the pit of hell or perhaps reliving every horrible thing he'd ever done. That probably wasn't far from the truth if he was thinking about his time working for that horrible organization. I shuddered and wrapped my arms around myself trying to ward off the chill.

I still couldn't believe my brother had been a part of something like that. Then again my memories of Rafe had always been faulty, hadn't they? All I'd seen was the doting, protective, maddening big brother. That was all he'd wanted me to see. That's probably what hurt worst of all--that I hadn't known the brother I'd adored as well as I thought I had.

I closed my eyes. *God, Rafe what were you doing?*

If someone had told me that anything could hurt worse than losing my brother, I wouldn't have believed it. But this, learning that every memory I had of our time together was faulty, was agony. It was like losing him all over again.

"You aren't asking me to do anything that I haven't tried before. I spent years in therapy trying to remember. It's just ... useless. The things I remember aren't helpful at all."

Noah looked up, his forehead pinched. "Maybe that's not true. Because the things Rafe was doing beforehand might be the missing piece to explain this whole thing."

"Okay. I'll try. It's all such a blur sometimes."

I sat on the edge of the bed next to him, my hand moving over his back in a circular motion. I wasn't entirely sure who I was trying to comfort, him or myself. Although I doubted there was any comfort to be had when trying to remember my brother's final moments.

"We'd had such a good day. It was nice weather, one of the last nice days of the fall and I'd absolutely stuffed myself on funnel cake. Rafe always thought it was funny that I loved them so much I'd eat until I was almost sick."

The emotion of remembering caught me off guard and I crumpled. Noah wrapped his arms around me and pulled me into his lap. I buried my face in his shoulder and breathed in the comforting smell of Noah.

"I'm so sorry. What I wouldn't give to be able to go back and change what happened that day," he whispered.

I wiped at my cheeks. "I know. Me too. It's just hard, you know? It hits me at the weirdest times, remembering how much fun he was. He was so serious with everyone else, but with me he was a bit of a goofball. He was the best big brother."

Noah sighed. "He was an amazing big brother and he took that seriously. Which tells me there's no way he would have brought you to the site of a takedown without a very good reason. Did he say anything before you arrived? Maybe on the way there?"

I tried to remember. "We'd finished eating when he got a phone call. I'm not sure who it was, but suddenly he said we had to go. I kept asking what was going on but he wouldn't listen, just pulled me to the car. The whole way there he was on the phone and kept telling me that when we got there, I needed to stay hidden. I'd never seen him like that before. So I promised that I'd stay in the car no matter what."

Noah pursed his lips. "That's it? All he said was for you to stay in the car and then he left?"

"Well, actually no. He went to the trunk and he was doing something back there for a minute. I'm not sure what."

"Probably getting his weapon."

"But he gave me his gun from the glove compartment."

Noah got really quiet and I realized he was trying not to point out the obvious. Rafe had been an assassin, so he would have had more than one weapon. Just another reminder that I hadn't really known my brother at all.

"Okay, so he was probably getting another gun. But that shouldn't have taken that long."

"No, it shouldn't have. Maybe he was calling someone."

I shook my head. "I really don't know. I told you. My memories are pretty useless."

Noah brushed my hair back from my face. "I'm sorry to make you relive all this. Part of me thought if we went over it something would stand out. Something that would make this whole thing make sense."

"I don't think anything is going to make sense of this."

He didn't answer but then again, I hadn't expected him to. There was no end to the shadowy paths that Noah and Rafe had traveled before his death. Suddenly I was exhausted, and so incredibly furious at it all. The rage inside had nowhere to go and I practically vibrated with it. It was all so unfair that I wanted someone to blame but no matter how I went round and round in my head, it all came down to a disastrous series of events. The universe had caught us all up in an unfortunate spiral that led to death, pain and a lifetime of regret.

Each of us had been doing the best we could with the hand we'd been dealt. Noah had spent his life in service to an organization that was more evil than good, my brother had been in the wrong place at the wrong time, and I had just been there to be witness to it all.

Not that any of it mattered anymore. Rafe was gone and nothing was going to bring him back. Heartbroken, all the rage left in a rush, leaving behind an emptiness that made me incredibly tired.

"I miss him."

Noah kissed the top of my head. "Me too. I'm sorry for dragging all this stuff up."

"I'm tired, Noah. So tired of worrying and missing him. So tired of being afraid. I just want it to be over."

"And it will be. I am going to finish it. I promise."

Something about the way he said it sent alarm skittering through my nerves. Despite my fatigue, I raised my head and regarded him warily.

"What does that mean?"

But his mask was back in place, the placid expression he always wore hiding whatever I thought I'd heard. He lifted me, placing me on the bed. After pulling the covers up, he stood.

"Nothing princess. Go to sleep."

Noah

I stared down at Lucia as she slept, peaceful at last. It had taken her a lot longer than usual to fall asleep, agitated no doubt by my questions. I hated to see her like this and it was even worse that I'd driven her to this state. It was everything I most feared about our relationship, that I'd hurt her just by nature of who I was. Even though it was unintentional, I'd hurt her today.

Never again.

I ducked into my closet and changed quickly into black jeans and a navy blue T-shirt. From a box on the top shelf, I pulled down a black skullcap to cover my hair. Considering how warm it was, too many layers would only draw attention but a hat always helped to obscure the details. Not that I expected there to be any questions about this meeting. If all went according to plan, no one would even see me arrive. However, it was ingrained to plan for every contingency.

If I needed to be invisible, I would be invisible.

After dressing, I put in the combination for my gun safe. It wouldn't do to let down my guard around Ian, even though we'd once been friends.

I almost laughed out loud at the thought. There were no friends inside of ORUS. Men I'd worked beside, slept beside, killed beside would have taken me out without a second thought if given the order. It was the way we were trained. I wouldn't have expected anything else. When I'd gotten out, it had been a chance for a new life. A life where I could form attachments, come to rely on others for more than just back up and have something for myself. Something worth protecting.

Someone worth protecting.

Armed to the teeth, I emerged from the closet and took one last look at Lucia sleeping between my sheets. She'd twisted in the linens so they wrapped around her torso and one arm was flung up, like she was bracing herself for a blow. Even in sleep she didn't look restful anymore, and that was just one more thing that was my fault. I turned away.

"Where are you going?"

Startled, I looked back to see that Lucia was awake. Her eyes roamed over me, taking in the dark attire and the bulge of the weapon in my holster that even my leather jacket couldn't hide.

Without a word, she opened her arms and I was powerless to resist. I sat on the edge of the bed and leaned down into her embrace. The soft caress of her fingers against my cheek made my heart skip a beat. *God, the way she made me feel.* She didn't even know the power she held over me.

"I don't know what you're about to do and I probably don't want to know. But I don't want you to go. Stay with me." Lucia's fingers brushed over my lips like a kiss.

I inhaled, wanting to pull the smell of her scent into my lungs, maybe into my very soul. If I could carry it with me, maybe it would cover the stain of all the horrors I'd endured. Horrors that I didn't want to touch her. The thought reminded me of what I was about to do.

"I can't. Lucia, there are things that are happening. Things I can't tell you."

She squeezed my arms. "Aren't we past this? The secrets and the lies? I thought we were starting over?"

"We are but until I close out the past, it'll just keep coming back to haunt us. This is something that I have to do."

"Can I come with you?"

I winced. Just the idea of Lucia anywhere near Ian with his cold eyes and even colder soul sent shivers through me. I didn't want any part of my past to ever touch her. She belonged in a castle surrounded by adoring knights not in the dirt with the commoners. Men like Ian, hell, men like me, didn't deserve to even breathe the same air as Lucia.

"Hell no. You aren't going anywhere. The guys are all here and this place is locked down. This is the safest place for you."

"Then that means it's the safest place for you, too. Stay with me, Noah. I don't want anything to happen to you, either."

I opened my mouth to say something, anything to dissuade her from the completely impossible idea of her coming with me but she stopped me with a kiss. It was like a drink of cool water on a hot day, her love flowing over me and healing everything that hurt. My arms tightened around her and I speared my hand into the midst of her wild curls. Lucia sighed as I peppered soft kisses over her face.

"I love you so much, Lucia. Everything I do is for you."

Her face fell, recognizing that there was nothing she could do to change my mind. She threw herself into my arms, almost strangling me. For a moment, I allowed myself the indulgence of feeling her soft weight against me and the silk of her hair pressed against my cheek. Then I did what I knew had to be done.

Pushed her away.

"I have to go."

She turned her face away, refusing another kiss. I laughed at the petulant look on her face. Then my laugh dissolved when I saw the sheen of tears in her eyes.

"Hey, don't cry. Lucia, nothing is going to happen to me. I'm not leaving this earth before my time now that I have something to live for."

"Stupid, stubborn man." She muttered it angrily but all the while her fingers curled around my arm. Reluctant to let go.

"Take a bath. Watch a movie. I'll be back before you know it."

She rolled her eyes. "Don't worry your pretty little head, is that it? This is not the Middle Ages, Noah."

"I know it isn't. Because my princess has a soaker tub with jets. Unless you'd like me to call your handmaidens to bring up water and pour it in a bucket for you. I'm sure Jonas wouldn't mind."

Her lips twitched. "I'm telling Jonas you called him a 'handmaiden' just for that."

"I'm sure he won't mind. As long as I tell him he's pretty he'll forgive me for anything."

That got a genuine laugh. I was glad I didn't have to leave her angry with me. Things had to be done; there was no getting around it. But I didn't want Lucia worrying about it.

She pulled me close and kissed me thoroughly. Just before my brain completely scrambled, she turned over and curled up with my pillow.

"Wake me up when you get home. I don't care how late it is."

"Oh I'll definitely wake you up."

By the time I got to the parking deck, I was already wishing this meeting with Ian was over. As it turned out, my princess was pretty good at negotiating. She may not have convinced me not to go but she'd made damn sure that I would hurry back.

CHAPTER THIRTY-TWO

Noah

The sound of gravel crunching under the weight of my tires was the only company I had as I drove past the warehouses that lined the Hudson River.

Yeah, the meet was cliché, but I knew the spot. Had multiple exits just in case something went wrong. I wasn't taking any chances. There had been a point long ago when I would've trusted Ian with my life. The problem now was that I didn't trust *anyone* except my own men and Lucia.

Ian was already there when I arrived, and that fact made me chuckle, as it had been *my* intention to be early. It also made me twitchy, as I had no idea how long Ian had been here. My old friend could've scoped out places to attack.

So much for old friendships.

When I exited the car, Ian smirked as he lounged back against the Audi sports car he drove. "I see you like to come early."

I shrugged. "Well, since you're already here, that makes me late."

Ian chuckled. "Good to see you, kid."

I smiled hearing the term. How long had it been since I'd heard that? It shouldn't be a surprise. Ian had always called me a kid. But I had lived ten lifetimes since then.

"I'm hardly the kid anymore, right?"

Ian only inclined his head. Ian hadn't been much older than I was now when he had first joined ORUS. And he'd been in for at least a decade before I had ever shown up.

"That's true." Ian pushed himself to standing with crossed arms. "So you wanted to talk. Talk."

I met his gaze straight on. "You have answers I want."

"And you know I can't give you much."

I rolled my shoulders. "So, us working side-by-side doesn't count for anything? Me saving your life doesn't count for anything?"

A muscle in Ian's jaw ticked. "It counts for enough. I called to warn you. You should've gotten the girl the fuck out of town. New cover. New identity. You should've put her on the run. But instead you kept her around. Not my fault if someone comes knocking on your door because of it."

"Trust me, if I could have I would've handed her a passport and sent her on her way. But this is Rafe's little sister. No way was she going to run and I couldn't leave her unprotected. If I had tried that, she would've found her way back. Besides, didn't you train me to take care of the threats and not spend my life watching my back?" I stared at my former friend. "You regret teaching me that now, right?"

"You weren't supposed to use it to get the fuck out of the organization," Ian said, the hint of emotion in his voice surprising.

I shrugged. "I did what I had to do. And I found a way to get it done. Sorry if that blindsided you but I couldn't stay. I'm glad I didn't. Considering what I know now."

Ian tossed up his hands. "Come on, kid, were you really that naïve? We are assassins. We kill people. How did that fact escape you? Sometimes you don't like the name that's called up. But that's the job. You do the recon, you take out the target. Unseen, undetected, and you live to fight another day."

"Except this time, the target is the woman I love."

Ian flinched. "You went and fell in love with her? Man, oh man, you are the dumbest smart dude I know. You know how risky it is to partner up. To care about someone. To attempt to have a family and shit. That is a disaster. It gives enemies the chance to hurt you."

"Look, it wasn't the plan. For years I've been protecting her. She's Rafe's sister. I was doing right by her. Then things changed. What was I supposed to do? Stand by and let you kill her?"

Ian shrugged and shook his head. "I told you, I didn't take the job. But someone else did."

I inclined my head. "Who is it? I recognized the moves in her apartment when I fought the guy. He wasn't big enough to be you. Tall, but not over my height. Nasty son of a bitch, too. I have the bruise on my thigh to prove it. But he tried like hell not to kill me, so it must not be one of your new guys."

Ian frowned. "What are you talking about? No one was sent yet. Roland, one of our newer guys, just took the job. Most of the rest of us were feeling too nostalgic to pick off Rafe's sister."

I shook my head. "Happened a little over a week ago. After we talked. Some guy broke into her apartment. The guy was a pro. I got some shots in but we were evenly matched. You know if it was anyone else other than ORUS, it wouldn't have been a draw."

"You're out of practice, my man." The thought seemed to amuse Ian.

"No. I'm not. *He was that good.* Never seen anyone like that. You got any new guys that are fast? Like you used to be?" I hid my smile at Ian's reaction to the dig. Nothing like hearing about how fast you 'used' to be. We were badasses, but we had egos just like everyone.

Ian put out a hand. "No man. I already told you. Roland just took the job. Today, in fact. He's going to make an attempt soon, very likely tonight. I assume you have your guys on her. The kid is eager to please, so I hope you make his life difficult. Never did like that kid if I'm being honest. We didn't send anyone to you before."

My whole fucking world turned upside down. One, somebody was coming for Lucia. Two, ORUS hadn't sent someone before. That meant all kinds of crazy shit, and I was in no mood to deal with that yet. Right now, I had to see Lucia.

"You're sure he'll try tonight?"

"I would. So probably. I thought you'd be smart and get the fuck out of town. Not sit there playing house with ORUS agents about to crawl up your ass."

Oh shit. I'd left her alone. Not alone, the guys were there. All of them. And the penthouse was a fortress. Thank fuck, but I should be there. Protecting her. I spun and hopped back in my Range Rover, gunning the engine.

Right now one thing really scared me. If ORUS was only coming after her today, then who was the other player trying to kill her?

———

Lucia

"Okay, one of you needs to explain the timeline of these movies to me. So did the series reboot and go back in time to show progression? Or is this a brand-new timeline because they sent Logan back to stop Mystique? Now they can do whatever the hell they want? I'm confused."

From the opposite couch and the massive lounge area, Oskar groaned and rolled his eyes before hitting pause on the remote.

"Jonas, please explain to her again how the X-Men movies work. Because if I have to try and explain the back-in-time thing, and the Logan thing, and the Phoenix thing, my head is gonna explode."

Jonas chuckled. "Lucia, you know you're driving him insane, right? He loves all things X-men."

I bit back a laugh. "Yes, I know. But I'm just trying to figure out how everything works together. And then what does this mean for the whole Marvel universe? The whole Avengers situation and Jessica Jones, Daredevil, and Luke Cage? Because I'm confused. It's like they don't even know about each other, but they sort of do."

I gave Oskar my best wide-eyed innocent look. The dude looked like he was going to pop a vein on his forehead.

"Lucia," Jonas warned, "You keep this up and he will eat all the chocolate in this house just to spite you."

I narrowed my gaze on Oskar. "You wouldn't."

The big German nodded and gave me an evil smile. "You better believe it sweetheart."

I could only blink. He was gorgeous enough when he was all stoic and stern. But when he smiled ... He should do that more. Not that he in any way compared to Noah. Though, I was probably biased.

I squared my shoulders and called his bluff. "The guy that's super fast on the X-Men, isn't that the exact same character who was one of the twins who died in Sokovia?"

He threw himself back on the couch and cursed under his breath in German. His accent was almost unintelligible most of the time unless he was irritated like now. I knew I was driving Oskar crazy. For someone who was so buttoned up, whenever he was watching one of these movies, he became a total comic book geek.

I smothered a laugh. "So, you're not going to hold my chocolate hostage?"

"You and I both know that would make you a raving lunatic who would make Noah pay. Then Noah would make all of us pay," he grumbled.

On the other couch, Matthias said nothing. The two of us still hadn't gotten back on an even keel. When he headed to the kitchen for popcorn, I waved at Oskar to turn the movie back on and followed him.

"Hey, Matthias?"

He didn't turn as he pulled a beer from the fridge. "What do you need?" His voice was arctic. Not a hint of warmth.

Okay, so he wasn't going to make this easy.

"Can we talk?"

Now he did turn. Gone was the affable, always smiling Matthias. This guy was harder. Sure, I'd seen him smile since that day at the fashion show. But it was as though those smiles never reached his eyes.

"We don't need to talk. We're cool." He moved to brush past me, and I reached for his arm. He immediately flinched away, and I held my hands up.

"I'm sorry. I just thought—we were friends. And then everything changed. I didn't say it that day, I was way too freaked out, but thank you. What you did. I don't know where I'd be or if I'd even still be alive."

He shook his head. "I was doing my job, Lucia. That's the end of that."

"Yes. You were. And I'm sorry if I've been distant. We were friends before that day. We've both sort of tried to pretend like everything is fine. But I saw a part of you I have never seen before, and I have to tell you it scared me. Then you shut down. I'm trying to figure out how we get back to being friends again."

He sucked in a deep breath and then set his beer on the counter. "It's fine, Lucia. It's because I care about you that I dug into the part of myself I never look at. Cold, calculating. That other guy was a mask I used to put on like a suit every day. I don't have to do that now. The job was to look after you. There was no way in hell anyone was going to hurt you on my watch. Even if it meant letting out a part of me that's hard to shut back in the bottle."

I studied him closely. "I'm sorry you had to dig into that part of yourself for me. Sorry any of you—" Before I could even get the thought out, his arms wound around me like a vice and he dragged me to the ground. Something ricocheted off of the granite countertop, sending shards everywhere.

From the living room, Jonas and Oskar cursed and there were more loud pops of gunfire.

Matthias reached above us and grabbed a gun that was stored underneath the countertop, pulling me with him to the other side of the island. Shots rang around us and all I could do was curl myself into a ball.

Matthias tucked me firmly in front of him where the bullets wouldn't hit me, and he stood firing off two rounds. The loud *bang bang pop pop* sounds echoed in my ears.

From the other room, Jonas shouted, "*Motherfucker. Oskar!*"

Then there was silence. Wait, not entirely silent. I kept hearing the *pffft, pfft* sound, but couldn't identify it.

Usually the sound was quickly followed by what sounded like things breaking or being hit, or shattering. And then I heard the real gunshots, their booming noise echoing all around the penthouse.

There was a moment of silence then I heard a whistle. Somewhere to the left of the kitchen. Two short whistles, then Matthias whistled back.

When he turned his attention to me, he whispered, "Listen, we're going to get you to the panic room okay? I need you to do exactly what I tell you. I'm trying to keep you safe."

I nodded then took the hand that he proffered. And then we were running. My feet were bare, and the shards of glass and marble shredded my soles but I didn't even stop to think.

Suddenly there was a loud *oomph*, and Matthias was flying forward. I was forced to let go of his hand, and I stumbled backward. Gunfire rained around me, and all I could do was duck and tuck my head.

In front of me they were fighting; Matthias, Jonas, Oskar. All of them fought a man in all black, complete with black mask. But Oskar only seemed to be able to use one arm. I watched in horror as the man in black grabbed Oskar by the hair then aggressively assisted him to the ground ... headfirst. The resounding crack made my stomach lurch.

Fear and anguish took hold. All this was for me. *They're all going to get hurt.* I had to do something.

Anything.

Matthias and Jonas traded shots with the guy. Somehow Matthias was better at blocking the blows but Jonas took a hard kick to the head.

I wanted to scream, "Leave Matthias alone. Take me. Do whatever you want with me." I didn't want to see Matthias hurt.

But Matthias wasn't getting hurt. He was on his feet and going hand-to-hand with the guy. Trading punches and elbows and kicks in a flurry of moving arms and legs. And then I saw it. This wasn't my friend Matthias. He wasn't affable and lovable. That was his Matthias suit like he'd said. Matthias, like Noah, was a killer.

I'd seen a hint of it at the fashion show. But this ... this was the real him. The guy procured a knife, and instead of showing fear, I was pretty sure Matthias smiled. It wasn't a nice smile. It was a smile that said he was going to enjoy killing him.

Behind them, Jonas shoved himself to standing and went after the guy, then it was two-on-one again. Jonas and Matthias, bearing down on the guy. Backing him off.

The guy in black reached into his pocket, pulled something out, and threw it straight into Jonas's face. The next thing I knew, Jonas was wheezing and coughing, clutching at his throat. I ran over, trying to help. Trying to do something. My movements must've distracted the attacker because his attention drifted for just a split-second.

Just long enough for Matthias to get a good hit. The attacker's head snapped to the side, and Matthias kept hitting him, his handsome features a mask of rage and ... joy. He was enjoying himself. The man in black started to go down.

I tried to grab Jonas by the shoulders and drag him back into the kitchen. To get something that could wash whatever it was that was hurting him off his face.

Matthias was going for the guy, sitting over him. *Pop. Pop.* He got him twice before the assailant managed to deflect one of the punches. In a split second they rolled and fought over the knife.

Shit. Oh shit. Oh shit. Matthias was going to die. They all were. Because of me. No way was I letting that happen. I searched for a weapon. *Anything.*

And then I noted the recycling that hadn't been taken out. There were some wine bottles in there. I left Jonas where he was and ran into the kitchen, well aware now of the cuts I was getting on the bottom of my feet.

My first stop was for a towel. I wet it and then snagged one of the wine bottles out of the recycling bin. Running back to Jonas, I wiped his face. He was able to blink up at me. At least that was something. What the hell was he mouthing? Oh. Run. He was saying run. My gaze slid to the door and then flickered back. Oskar was down, unconscious. Jonas was also incapacitated. And Matthias, if I didn't do something, he'd die. Hell no. I wasn't leaving my friends.

I wiped Jonas's face again and shook my head. "I'm not running."

And then I went straight for Matthias and the asshole in black. As they tumbled and fought for the knife, I raised the wine bottle. Matthias shook his head. I ignored him, trying to bring the bottle cracking down on the guy's head, but it was as if he sensed the movement and deftly rolled out of the way. Putting him on top of Matthias and giving him the leverage with the knife. Hell no.

I ran right up to him and wrapped an arm around his neck, trying to drag him off Matthias and remember all the things Noah had taught me.

Eyes, nose, throat.

I tightened my arm around his trachea. But I didn't have enough strength to pull him off Matthias. Switching tactics, I took my thumbs and pushed them straight to the guy's eyeballs and he howled and threw me off, but he still didn't let go of Matthias.

Instead, he delivered a straight shot to Matthias's nose. I could hear his head hit the wood floor before he groaned. The man in black turned and looked straight at me. I scrambled for the wine bottle again, raising it like a weapon. All he did was shrug his shoulders, rolling them back. Preparing to attack.

Jonas pushed to standing as he blinked rapidly. He held his hands out in front of himself. He couldn't see. *Shit.* Now was a good time to run. Spinning around, I bolted, my bare feet crunching on the glass and the shards of marble. I just needed to get to the stairs and scream bloody murder. Someone would come to help me. Right? What if this guy had brought friends?

I could hear his heavy footfalls behind me. And then the blood on my feet must have made me slip because next thing I knew I was ass over teakettle, and I had barely made it around the foyer.

But I didn't hit the ground with a crack. Instead he threw me over his shoulder. As he positioned me, he wrapped something around my waist, like a belt. I used the wine bottle to hit him in the side over and over again. No way in hell I'd go quietly. But his grip was too tight.

"Relax. You only hurt yourself doing this." He was carrying me back toward the bedrooms.

Oh fuck no. No way in hell.

We passed Jonas who was now on his knees as he blindly tried to get to Matthias. Matthias was also getting back up. But Oskar didn't move. *Fuck.* I fought as hard as I could.

Because no one was coming for me. Noah wouldn't be back for God knew how long. I couldn't let him take me in there.

"Lulu, I told you to stop it."

And then it filtered in. That voice. The way he said my name.

Oh my God.

"Rafe?"

His hands stilled. But he didn't say anything. Nor did he remove his mask.

My voice was hoarse as I asked again, "Rafe?"

The crack of gunfire hit the doorjamb just as we passed through it. The guy tossed me to the bed and looked around, and then pulled a knife and threw it toward the door. All I heard was a grunt of pain and then another crack of gunfire. I scrambled away from him. The guy looked from me, to the door, then back to me again, cursed, and went for the window. He took something from his hip and attached it to the edge of the windowsill. Then he hopped up and was out the window.

Shock still flooding my body, I eyed the window. We were in the freaking penthouse, where was he going to go? Then I saw what was on the windowsill. A grappling hook. I raced to the open window and looked out. The man rappelled down the building to the wide balcony several floors down then he dashed inside.

Oh God. That voice. Could it be? Behind me, I heard the one voice that could break through my terror and anguish.

"Lucia. Oh my God. You're okay?"

I turned to find Noah in the doorway. He stumbled and reached for me as though I were his lifeline. I limped and met him halfway. He grabbed me and the cocoon of his warmth calmed me as I sank into him.

"Where is he? Did he hurt you?"

All I could do was shake my head and point to the window and the grappling hook still attached to the sill. "He went out the window." It was on the tip of my tongue to tell him I thought it was Rafe, but I knew how that would sound. My brother was gone.

So then who the hell was it that just used my nickname?

PART 3

CHAPTER THIRTY-THREE

Noah

The best snipers knew the secret to the perfect shot was all mental. Great marksmanship required mastery of your own senses. Even in the middle of a firefight, you learned to shut out everything but the sound of your own heartbeat. There was a moment when everything was quiet, all was still and you had complete and total focus.

As I surveyed the remnants of my destroyed office, my mind blocked out everything but the task at hand. I couldn't think about the fact that Matthias had been beaten almost to a pulp. I had to temporarily forget about Oskar's dislocated shoulder and that Jonas had been gassed and could possibly lose his sight.

I definitely couldn't remember the image of Lucia sobbing on the bed after almost being kidnapped or the fact that if I'd been sixty seconds later, she'd have been lost to me. I pushed that mental image into a closet and locked the door.

Not going there.

"Jonas, keep rinsing your eyes. The doctor is on his way."

He gave a thumbs up and splashed more water in his eyes as he stood over the sink in the kitchen. Oskar sat at the counter, resting his arm on the surface while holding an ice pack to his shoulder. He'd probably be back to normal before any of the others.

I'd already popped the arm back in the socket but it would be sore as hell for a few days. The doctor was going to give us hell for doing it ourselves, but Oskar had been suffering and we'd all dislocated something at some point. I wasn't going to leave my friend in agony when I could fix the problem.

Too bad I couldn't do something to help the others. I hated feeling so helpless.

I knelt next to where Matthias was stretched out on the floor and placed another ice pack against his jaw. His face had already swollen beyond belief, the eyelids so puffy his face was unrecognizable. It was a miracle the kid was still conscious. I suspected it was pure force of will because Matthias would hate the idea of being unconscious and at the mercy of others.

"I wish you weren't so fucking stubborn, kid. You need to be in the hospital."

"No way. Not putting you at risk."

His words were muffled and slurred, but I could easily understand him. Mainly because I'd known what Matthias would say even before he spoke.

With how paranoid the kid was about his information being in the system, he'd have to be literally kissing the Grim Reaper before he'd consent to being hospitalized. Looking at his swollen, distorted features, I honestly thought he wasn't too far from that scenario.

He looked bad. *Really* bad.

"Fuck putting us at risk. This is your life, Matthias. We can find a way to keep the heat off of us. We'll say you were mugged or something. Shit."

"No hospital. Please."

It was the please that did me in. I could feel the waves of panic coming off the other man. Nothing short of knocking him out completely would get Matthias through the doors of a hospital, and I didn't have the heart to put him through any more trauma.

"Doctor is here."

I looked up with relief at the sound of Ryan's voice. The only stroke of luck so far had been that Dylan and Ryan hadn't been in the office when we'd been hit so they were available to help out.

Well, maybe it wasn't luck.

The asshole who'd taken out half my team had probably known damn well exactly how many people were in the building. He seemed to have planned it all out. The only thing he hadn't counted on was Lucia.

I glanced over to the couch where she'd been sitting for the past ten minutes. She'd been inconsolable at first, clinging to me with all her strength, but now she was disturbingly silent. I'd tried to talk to her but was met with a blank stare each time. I wasn't sure if she was going into shock but in the midst of all the other physical injuries, I'd had no choice but to just keep her in my eyesight while trying to take care of everyone else.

Jonas had told me that she'd refused to run. It enraged me that she'd put her life in danger, but I couldn't deny being proud as hell that she was so courageous.

Not that I wasn't going to paddle her ass later for that stunt.

"Where should I start?" Dr. Breckner's eyes flared slightly when he took in Matthias's appearance. He moved forward without waiting for an answer.

I stood back so the doctor could examine him. The doctor had been our on-call physician for years, but we'd never had to call him for anything this severe. It was usually stab wounds, cracked ribs, or the rare graze of a bullet.

Matthias looked like he was sporting all of the above and then some.

A young woman, probably only a little older than Lucia, approached her. "Hi, my name is Robin. I'm a nurse with Dr. Breckner. Are you injured?"

Lucia shook her head. The nurse glanced over at me uncertainly. I really wanted to argue, but something about the set of Lucia's mouth made me rethink trying to force her just then. I motioned for Robin to assist Jonas.

"Jonas, there's a nurse here to take a look at your eyes."

He blinked rapidly but nodded to show that he'd heard. Apparently he still couldn't see anything.

Fuck.

The nurse approached, speaking in low tones. Satisfied that the medical professionals had things in hand, I approached the couch where Lucia sat staring at the wall.

"Lucia, you really should let the doctor examine you."

She didn't move or acknowledge my words in any way. I put my arm around her shoulders and she flinched. My heart sank. God, she looked so small and vulnerable sitting here all alone, but it seemed she didn't want my comfort. Not that I blamed her. If I hadn't been so damned insistent on going to see Ian tonight then I would have been here to protect her. It was the same thing over and over again.

I just kept letting her down.

Then my mind flashed to Lucia curled up on the bed sobbing her heart out and my blood chilled for a totally new reason. I had no idea what that bastard had done to her before I'd gotten there.

Had he ... touched her?

She was showing some of the signs of sexual assault, especially not wanting to be touched.

Dylan waved, trying to get my attention. I thrust my hands through my hair roughly, taking out my frustration on the strands. The pain centered me, bringing me back to the present. There was a team of people counting on me to get them through the storm and to safety. A team that included Lucia.

Their safety was paramount so I had to get my head out of my ass.

"I'll be right back, princess." I murmured the words to her without expecting a response so I was shocked as hell when she nodded.

"Please tell me you have some good news," I growled as I approached Dylan.

The other man blew out a breath. "I found a place that's big enough. It's not exactly up to our usual standards but maybe that's a good thing in this case. It's underground."

I looked around at the marvel of glass and steel that had been my pride and joy. A symbol of everything I'd overcome. In the end, it had been a weakness because of all the glass and how open it was. When we rebuilt, I was going for bulletproof glass for sure.

In the meantime, going underground was perfect. It wasn't going to look like much but it would be a rock solid hideout while the team recovered and I spent some time in the trenches to smoke out the bastard targeting us.

Lucia. Targeting Lucia.

Because I couldn't forget for one moment what this was really about.

"Then underground we go."

Lucia

My eyes followed the movement of the light the doctor flashed in them. I blinked to clear the halos from my vision before allowing him to listen to my heart. The nurse had already taken my blood pressure. All the while Noah watched from the background like a silent sentinel, looking like he would slaughter anything that so much as startled me.

For once, his watchfulness wasn't annoying. It was actually comforting to have someone else taking charge because I was operating strictly on autopilot.

Oxygen in. Oxygen out.

Blink. Swallow. Smile.

I could only hope my expressions and reactions were appropriate because inside I was spinning out. The whole world as I knew it had been scrambled and then put in a blender.

How could I care about anything when it was possible I'd lost hold on reality?

I'd heard him. I'd heard my brother's voice in that room and nothing would ever be the same again.

I glanced around frantically, afraid that the others could hear my thoughts or somehow read the truth on my face. I took a deep breath, but nothing could stop the slew of memories. A fun-filled day at Coney Island. Rafe smiling over funnel cake. My beloved brother on the ground covered with blood. Years of pain missing half of my heart.

Then a voice in the dark that I'd thought never to hear again.

It took everything within me not to start screaming at the top of my lungs. I couldn't show that I was freaking out because Noah wouldn't understand. My breath started to come faster despite trying to control it. It was all too much and I couldn't hold it in. The voices were too loud; the slide of fabric over my skin was too rough. Even the air smelled strange.

Everything was all wrong, and I feared if I made one wrong move I'd crack into a million pieces.

Being in a new place didn't help. The past three hours were a blur, but somehow Noah had gotten us all moved to a new location; some dark lair underground with bare walls and no furniture. Someone with a truck must have come as we were leaving because the couch in the middle of the room was the same one I'd been sitting on at the old place. How that was possible I wasn't sure, although apparently anything was possible with enough money.

"You don't have a concussion, Miss DeMarco and your vitals are strong. If you need something to help you sleep, I can give you a shot. Is there any chance that you could be pregnant?"

My eyes shot over to Noah in surprise. His stance didn't change but there was no hiding the slight tension around his eyes. Even under these strange circumstances, I could still feel something, it seemed. After everything we'd done to and with each other, it was ridiculous that *this* could make me blush.

"No, I'm on the pill."

"Excellent. I can give you—"

I held up my hand. "I don't need anything." Although I knew I wasn't going to sleep now or anytime soon, the last thing I wanted was something that would mess with my mind. I needed to keep my mind sharp. It was hard enough already to determine what was real.

The doctor smiled in that detached way all medical professionals must learn in school. "Okay. Just keep the lacerations on your feet clean and dry. The stitches in your right foot will start to dissolve within a week."

I had already forgotten about my feet. The memory of running across glass was muted by everything that had come afterward. What were a few cuts compared to what the others had gone through? I climbed down carefully from the makeshift examining table Noah had set up in one of the spare rooms. Out in the hallway, I paused at the door of the room where Matthias rested while the same nurse who'd tried to help me, Robin or something like that, monitored the equipment hooked up to him.

"He should be in the hospital," I muttered, feeling guilty as hell.

I'd truly thought Matthias was dead after watching that brutal fight. That he'd managed to hold his own was a miracle. Although it had been a shock to see him in that full-on, aggressive mode. It had made his behavior at the fashion show seem like child's play in comparison. To think, I'd been shocked then just to see him handle a gun.

Noah followed as I turned away and walked back toward the main room. "Are you sure you don't want the sedative, Lucia? You've been through a lot tonight. You were almost kidnapped."

"I'm aware, Noah. I was there, remember?" I immediately regretted the sharp words, especially when I saw his wince.

The silence between us was fraught with all the things I couldn't say aloud. So many questions.

Why did you leave me alone?

Who keeps trying to kill me?

Am I losing my mind?

He was trying so hard to be considerate and I was being so bitchy. But my mind was a mass of feelings and some of them weren't fair to Noah. Part of me was angry with him because he hadn't kept me safe even as I realized that was unfair. He wasn't infallible and if he'd been there, he'd likely be hurt just like the others.

"Sorry, I'm just wound up from everything."

"No, I'm sorry," Noah mumbled. "I just don't want you to suffer needlessly. You've already suffered enough. All I've ever wanted was to protect you. But I can't even do that."

He walked past me toward the kitchen. The new place was laid out completely differently than the old one. It was only one level with exposed brick walls and no windows. It was dark and cold and ugly. Fitting for how I felt. I sat on the couch, happy to have this little bit of familiarity in the middle of everything. I watched as Noah waved two men through carrying a mattress. It was mind boggling to think of all the details he'd had to handle in order to get us set up in a new place so fast.

Thankful that he had it all under control, I burrowed deeper into the cushions of the couch, resolved to ignore it all. I didn't want to think about Matthias fighting for his life in one of the spare bedrooms or Jonas with his head wrapped in gauze, looking like a mummy.

Seeing the physical evidence of tonight was just one more thing to make me feel guilty. My friends, my family, were in various stages of injury because of me. Whoever was targeting us was fixated on *me*. I'd started digging into the past and sifting through secrets that were apparently more dangerous than I could have imagined. Now we were paying the price.

An hour later, I lifted my head and listened. It was noticeably quieter. Ryan came out of one of the rooms and nodded a silent greeting. I waved and then walked in the other direction. When Noah had been in full on alpha wolf mode earlier, I'd heard him barking out orders, specifically telling Ryan and Dylan that they needed to stay on site until further notice.

When I passed Matthias's room, the steady beep of the machines followed me down the hall. Behind the last door on the end, Noah sat on the bed with his head in his hands. He looked up when I entered the room.

"Your things are in the bathroom. I had them bring everything on the counter."

"Luckily I didn't have much at your place. What happens to the rest of your stuff?"

He shook his head slightly. "I have someone working through the night to box up everything. We'll have it all within twenty-four hours."

That was good. I hadn't wanted to think about him losing everything he owned just because he'd had the misfortune of helping me.

"Lucia, if something happened..." He stopped and wiped a hand over his face. "You can tell me anything. I'm not sure how long he had you in there before I found you—"

His voice cracked slightly and I rushed forward and wrapped my arms around him.

"Noah, I'm fine. He didn't do anything. I mean, not what you're thinking. You got there in time." I repeated it several times because it seemed to soothe him.

Guilty that my silence had fostered his fears, I continued to stroke his hair gently. I suspected that Noah hadn't enjoyed a lot of softness in his life, and he seemed to drink up my affection like a thirsty plant. I would never want him to suffer any longer than necessary worrying that I'd been assaulted.

A huge yawn broke the silence and took me by surprise. Despite everything that had happened, I didn't actually feel tired. The adrenaline in my system kept me on edge, making me cranky and fidgety. However my body seemed to be on a completely different schedule than my mind because I was suddenly so exhausted I wasn't sure I had the energy to even undress for bed.

Noah, as always, seemed to know what I needed before I did.

"Raise your hands, princess. Let's get you out of these clothes and into bed."

I let him undress me, quiet and docile as a child. When he'd finally stripped off the shirt and jeans, I climbed between the sheets, letting out a deep sigh when my face met the pillow. It smelled like him, like Noah, and I realized they must have moved the mattress and pillow with all of the original bedding still on it. I wasn't sure why that struck me as so funny but suddenly I was laughing so hard I couldn't breathe.

The laughter went on and on until I was spent. When I glanced over at Noah, I braced myself for him to be annoyed or disgusted. Our friends were injured, his home was destroyed and I was laughing. Except when I saw his face it wasn't disgusted. He watched me with an expression that could only be pity. He brushed my cheek with his thumb and when I saw the moisture there it shocked the hell out of me.

I was crying.

CHAPTER THIRTY-FOUR

Noah

A few days later, I sat carefully on the edge of the bed and watched Lucia sleep. I was exhausted but finally everyone was settled for the night and I was the only one still awake. She shifted slightly, her lips parting as she let out a small sigh.

God, she is so beautiful just like this.

Her dark hair spilled over the pillowcase like a riot of satin ribbons. I touched her cheek gently, unable to resist the urge to touch her when she wasn't awake. When I couldn't see the look of disappointment in her eyes. Problem was, she wouldn't talk to me.

The doctor had said she'd recover physically. The lacerations on her feet and hands would heal. The bruises would fade. But she wasn't talking. What's more, she wasn't yelling. I was used to Lucia giving me hell. But lately, it was an accomplishment to get any kind of reaction out of her. Most of the time, if she was awake, her eyes were blank and vacant.

I ran a hand through my hair in frustration. It was killing me to see her like this, so cut off from everything and everyone. She'd retreated into her own world and there wasn't anything I could do about it. Or at least nothing I'd tried so far had worked. It was like the lights were on but whoever was in there refused to answer the door for fear of solicitors.

What the hell had happened? She said she hadn't been assaulted, but *something* was happening with her. I closed my eyes and tried to focus, to remember exactly what I'd seen. My memories were a jumble of fear, horror and then pure rage. I didn't even like remembering. I'd walked into what looked like the set of a horror movie with bodies strewn all over the place and broken glass glittering on the floor like diamonds.

Then I'd heard Lucia screaming.

By the time I'd followed the sound, all I'd seen was that walking corpse—because the guy was as good as dead as far as I was concerned—holding her way too tightly as Lucia struggled in his arms. He hadn't assaulted her, but there were a million ways to hurt someone. And I knew them all. What had that piece of shit done to her before I got there?

Had he tortured her by telling her what he was planning to do? I had no idea. So of course I couldn't fix it, because for once in our lives, Lucia wasn't giving me hell.

"Lucia, wake up princess." I repeated it softly over and over until she stirred.

She let out a soft sigh and then rolled over. Her eyes blinked open and she stilled when she saw me sitting next to her. I touched the hand resting on top of the comforter, buoyed when she didn't move it away. Her fingers curled around mine trustingly. The vulnerability in the action was a shot to the heart. Even if she was angry with me, there was a part of her that trusted me instinctively to protect her.

And I'll always protect you, princess.

It was a vow I'd carried since the day Rafe died and one I'd carry with me to the grave. But first I had to get her to eat.

"Baby, I brought you a tray. You need to eat something."

She immediately shook her head. "I'm not hungry."

I knelt next to the bed so she wouldn't have to crane her neck to see me. "Look, I know after the craziness of the last few days, you're coming down off that adrenaline high and aren't particularly hungry at the moment. And I know with the moving around you're having a hard time feeling safe. But I need you to keep your strength up. Try some of the fruit or maybe a piece of toast. Anything. Soup, you want soup? Can you do that for me?"

She slid me a glance that at least gave me some hope. It was a flicker of annoyance, but she sat up and scooted to the edge of the bed where I'd placed the tray. Lifting the spoon, she took exactly three sips of soup. Then she put the spoon down, gave me a pointed look, and scooted back to curl into a ball on the bed.

If I weren't so worried, I'd have laughed. That was the first hint I'd seen in a couple of days that my Lucia was in there somewhere. But I still needed her to eat, dammit. And more than three bites. But I knew how Lucia operated, and I couldn't force her to do anything she didn't want to. She'd only dig in her heels and hold out to spite me. People always thought I was the hardass, but they had no idea how stubborn one tiny little woman could be.

"Okay, fine. We'll try eating a little bit later."

This whole thing was completely fucked up. I'd almost lost the woman I loved, but even now that she was physically safe, she was gone. Or at least she was hiding and it didn't look like she had any intention of coming back soon. Luckily I had one more ace in the hole. I just hoped that Nonna would be able to get through to her. If this didn't work, I'd call in JJ. But JJ was a lot more difficult to control with all her questions and her suspicious nature.

"Lucia, I'm gonna need you to talk to me eventually. Tell me what's going on with you. We don't have to talk about it right now. But sooner or later we need to. You just take your time and rest for now."

At the door to the bedroom, Dylan gave a nod indicating that my surprise was here. I just hoped this was a good idea. I'd called Nonna and told her that there'd been a break in at the firm and while Lucia was fine, she could use a visit from her grandmother. It was all I'd really been able to tell her.

What the fuck was I supposed to say?

A homicidal maniac tried to kill Lucia the other day?

It wasn't an easy situation to explain.

Right now, I was down to a three-man crew. Me, Ryan and Dylan. Everyone else was still recovering. Oskar had a hell of a concussion. Jonas could still barely see. And Matthias, well, he was all kinds of fucked up. His pretty boy face would heal soon enough, but I owed the kid a debt I could never repay. He'd stopped that sonofabitch from taking Lucia at great personal cost. He'd always carry the scars from fending off that guy.

Considering the kind of hits he'd taken, he should be dead, but the kid would recover physically. He'd only ended up such a mess because he'd fought someone better trained, which was damn near impossible since Matthias had been trained by some of the best. I hated to think of the kind of monster he had been forced to let out of the cage in order to protect Lucia.

Was the killer here to stay now? I couldn't ask him, because unfortunately, the kid was another one who wasn't talking.

Granted, a temporarily wired jaw would do that to you.

I strode out into the living room and nodded thanks to Ryan for picking up Nonna before I turned to the woman who was the only other person besides Lucia that I considered family.

"Nonna, good to see you."

She gave me a brief hug, and then pulled back. Her dark eyes searched mine. "Where is Lucia? What on earth happened?"

I patted her shoulders. "Come with me. Lucia is in the bedroom. She's fine, just resting. I think it would be good for her to see you."

Nonna followed, hesitating before she spoke. "You know I don't ask questions. But was Lucia ... hurt?"

I knew what she meant immediately. "No, not like that."

Her shoulders dropped in relief. "Oh thank heavens. I didn't know what to think when you called."

I sighed, mentally working through what I could tell her. "There was a break in. My men were there. Someone tried to abduct her."

Nonna gasped and clutched her hand to her chest as she muttered a prayer. When she opened her eyes, I squeezed her hand to reassure her.

"She wasn't hurt physically, except for some scrapes and cuts. She's fine. I just think it would be good for her to see you."

Lucia was the only person the older woman had left of her family, so I felt like even more of an asshole to drop this kind of news on her so suddenly.

"She's in there."

I hung back as Nonna tiptoed into the bedroom. Lucia turned her head, then her eyebrows rose when she saw who it was. She pushed herself to a sitting position and her grandmother wrapped her arms around her, all the while whispering softly to her. Lucia started sobbing immediately, clinging to her grandmother like she was the only thing keeping her afloat. Seeing her so undone almost broke me completely. I should have called her grandmother immediately; she'd obviously needed the kind of comfort that only the woman who'd raised her could give.

But it was what Lucia said next that tore through me. "Nonna, I saw him. It was Rafe. He was here."

———

What the hell?

I left Lucia with her grandmother and staggered out into the hallway. I took a moment to lean against the wall, trying to make sense of what she'd just said. Did she really think the man who'd been here was Rafe?

The anguish in her voice made it even worse. No wonder Lucia wasn't talking to me. She'd hardly talk about her beloved brother with the man responsible for his death. I was suddenly overwhelmed by everything that had happened and all of the emotions tangled up in it. I pressed my hands over my eyes, as if I could hold in the guilt and my own grief by pure force.

"I did this to her," I whispered out loud.

The guilt of it hit me so hard I almost dropped to my knees. I'd made the mistake of thinking Lucia was fine after the trauma of seeing her brother shot in front of her. Nonna always said Lucia was her rock during that time. We'd commended her on being so strong and moving past it when clearly she'd been struggling this whole time. We'd been happy to assume she was fine because it meant we didn't have to worry about her anymore. We'd failed her.

Especially me.

Because I knew more than anyone just how traumatic the experience had actually been.

I contemplated getting my things and leaving. The other guys could protect her, and she wouldn't have to see me again. It couldn't be good for her having to look at the man responsible for the single most traumatic event in her life every day. I was the cause and root of the very thing haunting her. Even as I had the thought, I knew I couldn't leave. Even with a houseful of guys watching her, she'd still almost been taken. It wasn't hubris to think I was the best man to protect her. I'd been a top operative with ORUS for a reason, and it wasn't because the big bosses had wanted to throw me a bone. I was one of the best because I'd been trained by one of the best.

I might be the last person Lucia wanted to see, but I was still her best shot at survival.

No matter what, she needed to talk to someone. Blake Security didn't have a shrink on call, but I'd find the best. After all, it was only money. I had more than I would ever need of that. She was mine and always had been. The love of my life. I had to protect her no matter what.

I knew the anniversary of her brother's death had messed with her for years. But this?

She seriously thought she had seen Rafe?

Maybe I should have been more up-front with her. Or maybe I'd been *too* honest? Maybe she hadn't been ready to hear the truth about her brother and what we'd done.

My Lucia was in there somewhere. I just had to help her find a way out.

With a deep inhale, I pushed away from the wall and strode down the hall to check on the rest of my men. We'd turned the master bedroom into a temporary sick bay with three smaller beds. Dr. Breckner was checking Jonas's sight.

"How are we doing, Doc?"

"He's improving every day. But whatever that substance was, I think I have a hit." The doctor left Jonas's side and went over to his computer. "When I tested the sample of what was in his eyes, I found traces of what appears to be a synthetic toxin. I've never seen anything like it, especially in aerosol form. The properties of this particular compound attack the optic nerve. But he seems to be recovering, which is remarkable. It's as though the effects are only meant to be temporary. I plan on spending the rest of the afternoon digging through literature to see if I can find anything like it."

Fucking hell. I sighed.

"Don't bother. I know what that stuff is. There's an antidote. I have a contact; I can get you some." And Ian had better fucking come through for me.

The doctor blinked at me. "You know what this is? Where does it come from?"

I shifted on my feet under the scrutiny of the doctor. I didn't want to tell the guy too much and get him killed. But then again, he was an on-call doctor for plenty of shady types. He probably did other things worthy of getting killed.

"It comes from the Himalayas. The aerosol is derived from a plant. Once I get my hands on the antidote, I'll let you know. I need Jonas back on his feet as soon as possible."

"But that's impossible. His vision is getting better, but healing takes time. Even a month is an optimistic estimate, and two is more likely."

I squared my shoulders. We didn't have a month. Jonas was one of my best. Hell, we needed all hands on deck. We were going after that asshole.

"Trust me, Doc. I'll get it to you later today."

That was the least Ian could do. Yeah, my old friend had alerted me, but he'd still done nothing to stop it.

You know that's not how it works.

I ground my teeth. Yeah, I understood how ORUS worked. Once a hit went out, there was no way to stop it. And any interference by any agent would result in immediate termination—the hard way. But still, I hated it. Hated that I'd almost lost. Hated that it was my past that almost cost me the woman I loved.

Ian at least owed me that antidote. And when this was over, we were having a conversation about exactly how ORUS was run and who was steering the boat. Because if I had to, I would dismantle the whole organization brick by brick, man by man. It wouldn't be easy, but if anything happened to Lucia, that would be my new life's goal.

The doctor looked skeptical, but nodded. "I know better than to ask questions. But your man, he's still my patient. I want to run some tests on whatever you bring me before I use it."

I sighed. "Fine. But you'll find out just what I told you. It'll work. And it'll put Jonas back on his feet in a couple of days, not months. What about Matthias and Oskar?"

Dr. Breckner consulted another chart. "Matthias is healing well. He won't need reconstructive surgery and will probably only have minimal scarring. But emotionally, like your girlfriend, he's not responsive. Answers questions when asked, but otherwise he's not talking."

I felt like a hand was squeezing around my heart. Matthias needed me, but I couldn't take the time out to deal with that right now. We were under attack.

"And Oskar?"

"He'll need another few days. His concussion was more severe than Matthias's. The arm was dislocated, but nothing was broken, so give him a couple weeks and he'll be back to one hundred percent."

"Thanks, doc. I appreciate you coming on short notice."

Dr. Breckner nodded. "Of course. We go way back, Noah. You call, I come."

I nodded my thanks again and went to find Dylan for a status update on the penthouse. I found him messing with the security monitors.

"Everything look okay?"

Dylan grunted. "I'm decent with these things but I'm no Matthias."

"I hear you. The kid's gonna be on his feet soon enough, so you'll only have to play tech-support for a while. What's the status on the old penthouse?"

"I got to the place before the police showed up. There was a body on the fourteenth floor. Dressed in all black, ski mask. Dead. Looked like he'd been that way for a while. Thing was, there was no blood on him. Cause of death was probably a pinprick found in the base of his neck. Poison of some sort, I think. But it clearly wasn't the guy the rest of the team fought."

I frowned. "They sent two of them? What the hell? Did one of them kill the other?"

It made no sense.

Dylan shrugged and continued. "I took care of the body. Took it to the incinerator down at the morgue. I wasn't seen."

I nodded. "Thanks."

Dylan shifted on his feet. "Boss, there was something else."

I lifted a brow. "Yeah?"

"He had tattoos on him. On each of his wrists, on his back, and his feet. At first, they looked like random freckles or dots. But when I looked closer, they looked like stars. I took a picture and then plugged it into a search engine. I was right. It was a tattoo of the constellation Aries."

"Aries?" I hoped my voice was even. I'd known the body would have the signature markings. What I didn't anticipate was Dylan finding out.

"Yeah. I noticed it looks similar to the ones you and Matthias have. Yours is Leo. Matthias's, I'm not sure."

I pinned an intense stare on Dylan. "You don't want to open that particular Pandora's box."

He backed off. "Yep. I know better. Just saying. Whatever you guys are into, or whatever's coming back to bite you in the ass, we're a team. I just want to know, are they coming for you, or are they coming for her?"

I crossed my arms and met the other man's dark stare. "They're coming for all of us."

CHAPTER THIRTY-FIVE

Lucia

I woke up with the beginnings of a scream in my throat. I panted for a few seconds as the tendrils of the dream slid from my mind. I rolled over, confused when my eyes landed on bare brick walls. Then I blinked and it all came back. The attack. Moving to a new place.

Rafe.

I'd been dreaming about that day in the car with Rafe. It was bothering me that I couldn't remember what he'd done right before leaving. What had he been doing at the back of the car for so long?

Lulu.

That voice was going to haunt me until I figured it out. There were so many different explanations for what I'd heard. Maybe it was someone I'd known as a child. My nickname had been used more then. Although I couldn't imagine someone holding a grudge that long. Why come back and hurt me now? It could have been the result of all this stress, causing me to imagine things. But then why had the guy tensed when I'd said Rafe's name?

I hadn't imagined that part, I was sure of it.

The futility of it all was maddening. But this wasn't going to paralyze me. I was determined to do something productive.

After pulling on a tank top and shorts, I walked out to the main area. Oskar sat on the couch watching TV, the sling on his arm not detracting from his incredibly ripped bare chest.

Sweet Lord.

These guys were enough to give a woman a heart attack. I'd always been Noah's through and through, but I wasn't dead. Any woman with a pulse would take a second look at a man like Oskar when he was shirtless. I giggled. Even Nonna would probably take a second look, although she'd no doubt say a Hail Mary afterward.

"Morning, Oskar. Have you seen Noah?"

He inclined his head toward the hallway. "He's been in there with Matthias for a while. You need something?"

My heart flipped over. I really was the luckiest girl in the world. These guys would do anything for me, including give their lives to protect me. I walked closer and put a gentle hand on his shoulder right above where the sling started.

"I should be asking you that. How is your arm?"

He shrugged. "It's still attached. What more can I ask for?"

I couldn't resist a grin. He really was too much sometimes. Big, brutal and aggressive, but then he'd turn around and do something sweet out of the blue. Whatever girl caught his eye was going to have her hands full not falling head over heels for the big lug.

"Do you want breakfast? Although I just realized we probably don't have any food here."

"You're cooking? Oh thank you, thank you. I'll be a good boy Mommy if you just make me pancakes." Oskar leaned his head against my arm and softened his gorgeous face into a pitiful mask. It was all the more amusing since he was such a huge, aggressive-looking guy.

"Pancakes? I'm thinking we'll be lucky to find cold cereal in this place."

"Noah had a huge order of groceries delivered earlier. So there's hopefully something decent in there. I'm ready to eat cardboard at this point."

I stroked his hair affectionately, unable to resist a little tenderness. "That won't be necessary. I'll find something."

I walked into the kitchen and discovered that Oskar hadn't exaggerated when he said the order was huge. The pantry was filled until there was almost no space left and the refrigerator looked just as packed. Since all the guys were hanging around it made sense though. This food would no doubt be gone in just a few days.

My phone vibrated in my pocket, and I answered it absently while sifting through the contents in the pantry.

"Lucia! Thank God. I just heard what happened. Are you okay?" JJ's voice was just shy of hysterical.

When I finally found the pancake mix, I put it on the counter and then started looking through the refrigerator for milk and eggs. It took a while since I had to shift stuff around to see what was in the back.

"Sorry, I was going to call you today. Things have just been so crazy. Wait, how did you find out?"

"Adriana told us that your boyfriend called in for you. Said your apartment had been vandalized and you'd need a few days off."

"Noah called. Of course he did. That's not exactly what happened though."

As I filled JJ in on everything that had happened, I mixed the pancakes and started frying them in a pan I found in one of the lower cabinets. I ended with, "So Noah showed up just in time before the guy could get me out the window. I think that thing he put around my waist was some kind of harness. Otherwise, I'm not sure how he planned to get down the side of the building carrying me but I guess kidnappers aren't that smart."

JJ huffed out a laugh. "Either that or he was planning to tie you to his back first. Maybe he's not used to stealing people. He's probably used to snatching laptops or something."

I thought back to how the man in black had held off Oskar, Jonas and Matthias simultaneously. I shivered. This was no garden-variety purse snatcher. He was more like Superman.

Just my luck to attract a near-invincible psycho stalker.

Once I had a nice stack of pancakes, I made a plate for Oskar and brought it to him in the main area along with an unopened container of pancake syrup and a fork. The look of adulation on his face made me laugh all over again.

"The moment Noah fucks up, I'm taking his place. I don't need much. Just keep feeding me like this." Oskar speared a huge hunk of pancake with the fork and took an obnoxiously large bite.

"Be a good boy and I'll make you some bacon, too."

"I love you. Please leave Noah's cranky ass and marry me. I may not be as pretty but baby I've got everything else you need."

"Whose sexy voice is that?" JJ demanded. "And why do you have all the hotties breathing on you lately? Share the love, please!"

I laughed. "It's just Oskar being silly." I turned to Oskar. "Don't let Noah hear you say that or he'll dislocate the other arm."

Oskar rolled his eyes but then turned his concentration to working the fork left-handed. I left him with his exaggerated moans and groans of enjoyment and went back to the counter to eat my own food.

"Well, I'm glad that you're okay."

I was quiet, unsure if I wanted to tell JJ the whole truth. But as usual my best friend could sense when I was holding out.

"Are you really okay, Lucia? Things have been pretty intense lately. Anybody would be freaked out."

"I *am* freaked out. Especially since the guy who was here ... JJ, he had my brother's voice. I swear, it sounded just like Rafe."

JJ didn't respond and I could practically feel my friend's concern coming through the phone. "Lucia ..."

"I know what you're going to say. It sounds crazy, believe me I know. But when I said his name he froze, like he wasn't sure what to do. And he called me Lulu. No one really calls me that anymore, not even Nonna."

"That's ... okay I'm not going to pretend I can explain it, but that doesn't mean it's Rafe. People don't just disappear for years with no trace. Why would he even want to do that?"

"People fake their deaths," I protested.

"Yeah, in the *movies*. Or people with shitty lives they want to escape. Or tax evaders. None of which applies to Rafe. Your brother would have never left you and Nonna to fend for yourselves. He adored you."

I hung my head. It made me feel disloyal to have even thought it when I knew that JJ was right. My brother would have never just disappeared with no word no matter how bad things were in his life. Rafe had been many things but never a coward. He would have faced bullets head on before leaving me and Nonna alone in the world.

But that voice...

I couldn't just let this go when the sound of my brother's voice was still echoing in my ear.

"It sounded just like him. Don't I owe it to him to at least investigate?"

"How? There really isn't anything you can do. I hate to point out the obvious sweetie but we have no resources to handle something like this."

I smiled. "Actually that's not true. I have the best resource of all. My memories. I know Rafe. What he liked, what was important to him. If he really is alive, then he's still the same person and as much as he might try to disguise himself, there are some things you can't change."

JJ sighed. I knew my friend was trying to be supportive but didn't really believe me.

"Just say it. You think this is crazy."

"I think you're distraught and grasping onto anything that can bring you comfort. I understand that. What worries me is that you seem convinced already that he's alive. I don't want you to get hurt, that's all."

"You're worried about me, I know. But I'll be careful, I promise."

After talking about a few random things happening in the office, we hung up with me promising to keep JJ in the loop about what was going on. The whole time in the back of my mind I was turning over ideas.

How did you smoke out a person who was hiding from everyone?

By the time I finished cleaning the kitchen, I had a plan.

———

I didn't have the opportunity to put my plan into action until the next week. It had taken that long to figure out how to get Noah's help. I couldn't just ask him for it straight out because he'd think it was weird and probably just keep pushing me to talk to a shrink. It was so irritating the way he assumed he always knew best.

I rolled my eyes. I'd long ago learned that the best way to handle these alpha-male types of guys was to let them think everything was their idea. Rafe had been the same way and I'd been a master at handling him before I even hit my teen years.

Thinking about Rafe brought my mind back to what I was doing. I looked out the window at the scenery flashing by as we raced over the highway.

It was a beautiful day for an adventure. At least that was how I had posed the idea of visiting the clock tower at the state library in Connecticut. It had been my mother's favorite place in the world, and she'd taken Rafe and me there often before she died.

After our mother's death, Rafe would bring me there whenever I was sad or lonely. When the girls at school picked on me for wearing secondhand clothes or for my wild bushy hair, he'd pick me up from school early and we'd go sit in the courtyard behind the library and look up at the clock tower. I used to pretend that if I stared hard enough I could make the hands of the clock turn faster or even go backward. That I was in control of all the bad things that happened and could fix them whenever I wanted. Even after I was old enough to recognize just how powerless I was in the world, it had brought me comfort to see it.

Rafe had never had much imagination, so he'd sit and eat sunflower seeds while I hummed to myself, lost in my daydreams. He'd been patient that way, not needing to say or do anything, content to just let me dream. I'd often wondered how he could do that, just sit and wait without moving a muscle, but he'd never rushed me or made me feel like he'd rather be somewhere else.

My brother had always made me feel like I was the most important person in his life. Maybe that was why none of my boyfriends had ever had a chance, even if they'd been able to get past Noah. Rafe had taught me early how I should be treated by a man and I wasn't willing to settle for less. Even in death, my brother's shoes were hard to fill. I'd always known it would take a hell of a man to even come close.

And I did come pretty close, I thought as I looked over at Noah.

His fingers were sure on the steering wheel and his profile was tight with tension but he hadn't tried to talk me out of coming here. When I'd explained that I needed to go somewhere familiar, somewhere I could remember the good times with my family, he just nodded and got to work making it happen.

Was it any wonder I loved him so completely? Even when he made me crazy, I couldn't deny he did it all because he thought it was for my own good.

We pulled off the highway and Noah finally spoke. "Ryan is following us and will observe from a distance. I'd like to keep our visit to less than an hour if possible. I want you to have your time, you know that, but I can't put you at risk." He glanced at me warily as if worried I'd be pissed about the restrictions.

"I understand. Thanks for making this happen for me. I'm sure you'd rather keep me at home under lock and key."

Noah snorted but at least there was a smile on his face now. "I'd bubble wrap you and put you behind glass if I could."

I didn't doubt it. "Let's pass on that. It'd be hard to cuddle if I was in bubble wrap. And other things." I leaned over and cupped him between his legs, insanely turned on by his deep groan.

"*Christ*, are you trying to make me crash this car?" He gently removed my hand but kissed my fingers before releasing them. "What happened to my innocent little princess?"

"You corrupted me and I decided I liked being bad."

I was teasing but even as I said it, I realized it was true. Being with Noah had opened me up in so many ways and I loved feeling so confident and safe to explore with him.

I was quiet the rest of the way and didn't even notice how much time had passed until Noah turned the car off. The parking lot was mainly empty since it was the middle of a weekday. Noah got out first, looking around the car with a shrewd eye and a harsh expression. Anyone who wanted to screw with us would be crazy to try anything while he looked like that. Later, I'd be sure to tell him just how arousing I found that harsh, unyielding expression. Maybe I'd whisper it while he was inside me just to drive him crazy.

I smiled at the thought.

When he opened my door, I accepted his hand to get down and then followed as he led me toward the library. We walked inside and I looked around, anxious to see if it looked different after so many years away. The far left wall had been converted to a row of computer stations which was new; it had previously been the periodical section. The carpet was a different color and I didn't recognize the librarians behind the counter. Other than that, it looked much the same. Warmth flowed through me at the familiar sights that used to represent family and comfort.

Access to the courtyard and the clock tower was through the back door, so we walked across the main floor. I grinned at a small group of toddlers huddled around a librarian reading in an animated voice. When I was younger, I'd imagined that one day when I grew up and got married I'd bring my own children here for story time. It had been so long since I'd thought of that. Of course, that was before everything in my life changed so dramatically. After Rafe's death, I no longer dreamed of weddings and princes to sweep me off my feet.

Not when I'd gotten the most definitive proof of all that fairy tales were just that, tales. Real life was never so neat.

We stepped onto the back patio and followed the path leading to the clock tower. I gazed up at it, still awed by how majestic it seemed. I turned in a slow circle, noting the neat landscaping of small shrubs and flowers around the base of the tower. The color of the red brick had faded slightly over the years, but it was obvious that it was clean and well cared for.

"It looks the same," I whispered.

I wasn't sure what I'd expected. For it to look as weathered and tired as I felt on the inside, perhaps? But no, it looked solid and strong, exactly as it had always been. The only thing that had changed was me. While my world had been shattered, the rest of the world had kept on spinning.

"What's wrong, Lulu?"

His use of my nickname just made it worse somehow, reminding me of days long gone and a time that I could never recapture. I'd never again be that girl who believed in the impossible and only had to look to my brother leaning against the tower to feel centered again.

What had I really hoped to accomplish coming here? Had I thought that Rafe would coincidentally be there and pop out saying 'Surprise' or something? It was ridiculous that I'd allowed myself to get excited about yet another fairy tale that couldn't come true.

"Let's go. I've seen enough."

"Okay, whatever you want." Noah watched me with a worried look on his face. No doubt he wanted to ask why I'd wanted him to drive me all the way out here only to then leave after two minutes. I was glad he didn't ask because I had no answers to give him.

I walked to the base of the tower and put one hand on the cool brick. The rough texture under my hands made it real somehow. This was the last time I'd ever come here. It was too painful to look back at the past knowing what I'd lost.

"Goodbye Rafe," I whispered.

Then I saw it. At the base of the clock tower.

Sunflower seeds.

CHAPTER THIRTY-SIX

Noah

I watched as Lucia moved to the base of the clock tower and leaned against it. I never should have brought her here. This was bringing up bad memories, obviously, since she was already crying. I moved closer, intending to pull her away when she suddenly smiled.

It was the first time I had seen Lucia smile in ages. Her *real* smile, not the strained version she'd had pasted on for the last week. What the hell was going on?

"You okay, sweetheart?"

She grinned up at me. "I'm perfect. Thank you for bringing me up here. I missed this. Missed that sense of home."

She shivered a little. The hot and sticky July had given way to an even hotter and stickier August for the most part. But from up here, the breeze coming in from over the ocean hit just right, making it much cooler up here at the clock tower.

Lucia wrapped her arms around my neck. "I love you, Noah."

Automatically, my arms wrapped around her, holding her in the shelter of my embrace. Jesus, I'd missed this. I'd missed *her*. Her smile, her laugh and even her shouting.

"I love you, too."

She rose on her tiptoes to press a soft kiss against my lips. But this was different from the brief, chaste kisses she'd been giving me for the last week or so. This kiss lingered. Just like in the car, I was taken off guard. I wanted her so badly, but I didn't want to push her too fast or pressure her. I needed to let her drive.

Waiting to see what it was that she needed, I kissed her gently, letting her take the lead. It went against every fiber in my body to do so, but I could do it. *Do it for her.*

She pulled back with a frown. "Noah, why aren't you kissing me?"

"I thought that's what we were just doing, princess."

She shook her head. "No, that's not how you kiss me. When you kiss me, it drowns everything out. And all I can think about is you, and me, and us, and getting naked as quickly as possible."

Oh, yeah. Real helpful. She just had to go and say the naked word. One word from her and my dick was ready to play. The blood rushed to my cock like the damn thing was on fire.

"Sweetheart, you've been through a lot. So maybe we should take it slow?"

Lucia gave me a coquettish smile that told me she knew exactly what she was doing. "And if I don't want to take it slow?"

I licked my lips. What was she playing at? What the hell was going on with her? At the same time, all I wanted to do was nuzzle her, inhale her scent, and see if I could get her to make that sound at the back of her throat that she always did when she was about to come. I was desperate to hear it again. But I knew something was off.

"Sweetheart, you know how much I love you. And you know how much I miss you."

Lucia pressed against me and we both moaned.

"You can feel how much I've missed you. But I want to make sure you're doing okay before we move forward. I don't want you to retreat again. It scared the shit out of me."

"I'm not retreating. I just know what I want. I've missed you. Everything was a shock and I didn't know how to deal, but now I've sorted it all out. Coming here, coming home in essence, it's making me better. I just want you to help me feel better. Feel more alive, more like myself." She rocked her hips slightly, and I swore I saw stars.

"Lucia —"

She nuzzled into my throat, her lips softly teasing and playing over my Adam's apple. "Noah—" she mimicked my tone.

"Sweetheart, this is not the best —"

She cut me off effectively by delving into my jeans and wrapping her delicate hand around my erection.

Oh shit. It was as if all higher brain processing had been turned off, all functioning ceased. Lucia snapped open the top button of my jeans, and the *zick-zick-zick* as the zipper went down only ratcheted my arousal even higher. She had me out of the confines of my jeans and boxers in seconds.

"Lucia. This isn't a good idea. Anyone could see us up here."

"So what if anyone sees us? I need the man I love inside of me right now. I don't want to wait. I don't want to go back home. I want to enjoy the view. I want to dig my nails into your back as you slide into me. I want to feel alive, Noah. Help me feel alive."

Her words tore through me. I knew what I should do. I knew what would probably be better for her. The problem was, that knowledge was somewhere way in the recesses of my mind. Because, well, I was a guy, and she had her hand on my dick. So that meant I didn't have two brain cells to rub together at the moment, let alone the cognitive willpower to stop this.

"Sweetheart. I love the way you do that."

Fuck, did I love it. Her hands were so soft and warm. And they certainly felt better than me making good use of my right hand in the shower every morning. But I had to at least try to be the reasonable one.

"Let's at least go back—"

She squeezed me and my knees buckled. "I told you, I don't want to go to the car. I'm ready here. I'm wet, Noah. You want to feel how much?"

All thinking stopped. All I knew at that moment was I needed to be inside her. Needed to feel her warmth and her slick heat as she wrapped around my dick, squeezing, pulsing, and milking me. Her dress rode up. And my hands slid up her knees, widening her thighs the farther I went. With my thumbs, I traced the edge of her panties, and Lucia threw her head back.

"Oh God, Noah."

Hearing her moaning my name, all low and sultry like that, made me jerk. The only thoughts my brain offered were, *Inside. Now. Need.*

Yeah, full sentences were so not my thing at the moment. She was wet. So fucking wet. Both thumbs snuck past the edge of her panties, one went straight to her clit, gently smoothing over it, as I dipped my head and took her mouth. As I kissed her deep, licking into the warmth between her lips, my other thumb found her wet center and slid in easily. She rocked her hips into my hands, questing, searching.

God, I needed this. *We* needed this. Maybe we could find our way back to each other if I could just wrap myself around her, hold her tight and keep her safe. And keep her loved. If I kept her loved, we'd both be able to stop worrying.

Lucia was impatient. She shoved at my jeans, pushing them down over my hips and my ass.

With a curse, I drew back, hooked my whole hand into her soaking panties, and tugged. The ripping sound barely registered as it mixed with the sound of her panting and my groan. In seconds, my cock was nudging her slick entrance. I held the base tightly and gently rubbed against her. Covered myself with her slick juices. Shit. So fucking good. She was so wet. So ready.

"Noah. Please. I need—"

She didn't have to ask twice. I slammed home.

Lucia tossed her head back, exposing her throat. I leaned over to brush my lips along the column of her neck and sucked gently. Even as one hand scooped under her ass to keep her stationary as I made love to her, the cold of the unyielding stone against my arms made me flinch but I didn't care. All I wanted was to drive home. To keep feeling her slick heat tightening around me. Fuck, how had I lasted for more than a few hours, let alone days without this?

Lucia shoved her hands in my hair and held me to her. With a frustrated groan, she yanked at her clothes, struggling to tug down the strap of her sundress.

Against her neck I whispered, "You want my mouth on you? You want me to suck your nipples?"

"Yes, Noah. God, yes."

I shifted her up and back until her head and shoulders were just off of the stone platform, giving me the angle I needed to dip my head and take her into my mouth. The moment I did, she moaned low and her inner walls tightened around me. I switched to her other breast, sucking her through the thin material and fabric, while my thumb teased her other nipple, pinching lightly. All the while, I drove deep, claiming her once again as mine. My cock sliding and retreating, sliding and retreating. Every time I bottomed out, she made this low keening sound at the back of her throat like she'd just discovered bliss.

And then I felt it. Her hands tightened in my hair, and she held me to her breasts as she screamed out, "Oh, my God, Noah. Yes, right there. Right there. Right—" Her climax crashed into her, and her whole body locked around me like a vise. She was never letting me go.

"Oh shit. *Fuuuck, Lucia.*" With three quick jerks, I was following her. Our climaxes mingled so I couldn't tell where one of us ended and the other one began. Exactly the way it should be.

"I love you," I whispered.

"And I love you, Noah Blake."

Lucia

An hour later, I stood in the shower and let the hot spray pelt my skin. Had we really just done that? The blush on my cheeks mingled with the hot water.

Public sex.

I'd never done anything like that in my life and as reckless as it had been, I couldn't bring myself to regret any of it. I could still feel Noah's hands gripping my hips. The bruising sting of his kiss. He'd been completely out of control, and I'd loved every minute of it.

I'd certainly taken him off guard. Truthfully, I had taken myself off guard. But considering what I'd seen that day, a little uncharacteristic behavior was to be expected. It had been such a shock to see those sunflower seeds there. Despite what I'd told JJ, I hadn't actually thought I'd find any evidence of Rafe just by haunting the places we'd used to go. But this was something I couldn't ignore. Anyone else would think I was insane, but I just *knew* how those seeds had gotten there. And they'd looked fresh.

He'd been there. Recently.

Rafe was alive.

Or you're crazy.

I let the thought slide over me, turning it over in my head. Maybe I was crazy. Maybe I was seeing things that weren't there. My behavior up in that clock tower was reckless at best. Everything I'd done lately was reckless and out of character. The only thing my digging had accomplished so far was to get me nearly killed, more than once. Not to mention the danger all of my friends were in because of me. Matthias, Jonas, and Oskar were going to be suffering for weeks because of me.

All of this was because I was asking questions ... about Rafe.

I didn't want to think I was losing it. I'd heard his voice. *But you didn't see his face.* No, I hadn't. But it was possible.

The memories had been coming back a little more every day. I remembered so much more about what had happened before the gunshot that changed everything. When Rafe had gone around the back of the car, he'd taken his shirt off and put on something else, then put the shirt back on. Was it possible that he'd been putting on a bulletproof vest? There was no way to know for sure, but the fact that it was possible was just one more puzzle piece in a jumble of others that I had to make sense of. But no matter how I spun things, it was possible that he was alive.

But, if he was alive, then what was he doing? Why was he trying to hurt me?

He hasn't actually tried to kill you.

Maybe we had been looking at everything the wrong way. Had he just been trying to take me? Why? And where the hell had he been all this time? I leaned against the wall and tried to drown out the doubt and worry.

Noah knocked on the bathroom door. "Hey, princess? You locked the door. How am I supposed to join you if you lock me out?"

I knew full well if he wanted in, he'd just take the damn door off the hinges. But he was giving me some semblance of privacy. "Sorry, I just needed a few."

And man did I. My shoulders, my hips, and my ass were all abraded thanks to that stone platform Noah had put me on to screw me senseless. *No, that wasn't his fault; that was yours.* I'd just been so happy to find those sunflower seeds. So happy to know that maybe I wasn't crazy, I'd wanted to celebrate. I'd wanted to feel Noah.

"You can come in," I called out.

"Okay, give me a minute. I'm just going to check in with Jonas so we won't be interrupted."

I smiled at that. I figured he was trying to make me laugh by mentioning the other guys' tendency to interrupt or walk in on us accidently.

He was trying so hard, but no matter what I did I couldn't claw myself out from the darkness. I just kept hearing Rafe's voice over and over again. All these years later, clear as day. Calling me Lulu. And of course every time I looked at Noah, I saw Rafe. So that made things worse.

But now that he might be alive? I needed to know everything. Where he'd been, what he had been doing, why he left me, left Nonna. It wasn't going to solve everything, but at least if I could get some proof I wouldn't have to see that look on everyone's faces. The look that said they thought I was losing my mind but were too polite to mention it. Maybe they all thought this was just an overdue break-down that I should have had right after my brother's death.

The only person who was fully in my corner was half-crazy herself. JJ was always ready to run in like a crusader.

But what if you're right? That was the thought that dragged me out of the darkness. If my brother was alive, I was going to find him. Even if I knew everyone else would think it was crazy.

The slap of cold air on my backside brought me out of my thoughts. I hadn't even heard Noah unlock the door.

"Is everything okay? You've been in here for a while." He picked up the loofah sponge that I'd been using and dragged it gently over my arms and then down my back.

I smiled up at him. "Just thinking about everything. Plus the hot water was helping soothe all the muscles I strained while having sex against a brick tower. Remind me not to do that again."

Noah's hands followed the path of the sponge. The gentle touch sent shivers up and down my spine. I closed my eyes and enjoyed the sensation of being warm and naked with him.

"I would point out that I tried to be responsible and stop things. But I was forced by a saucy vixen to do dirty things in public against my better judgment."

I raised an eyebrow. "Against your will, huh?"

"Well, you were saying dirty things like *I need you inside me, Noah* and *I'm so wet for you, Noah.* What red-blooded man could resist that? There is no willpower in the world that could withstand that kind of sorcery."

I chuckled at his disgruntled expression. "Does that mean you don't want me to use my witchy powers on you again? Because I could leave you to shower alone. But that would be a shame because I really wanted to taste this."

He sucked in a hard breath when my hands circled him, tugging on his hard length and playing with the soft skin of the head.

"Oh, you should definitely do what you want to do. I'm already under your spell after all. What's one more thing?"

I nodded my head slowly and then sank to my knees before him. His eyes got dark as he watched greedily. I took him in my mouth, happy to lose myself in bringing pleasure to my man instead of worrying about things I couldn't control.

CHAPTER THIRTY-SEVEN

Noah

I knocked on Nonna's front door. It occurred to me that I probably should have called first but as soon as I'd had the idea, my feet had started moving. Honestly, I wasn't even sure what I was going to say. I was completely winging it here. Lucia would be pissed if she knew where I was, but I needed to talk to Nonna. I was *that* worried, and Lucia's grandmother was quite possibly the only one who could help.

Footsteps sounded inside and a second later the door opened. Nonna was wearing a beautiful rose-colored sweater and had her hair twisted back into a low bun. Although I knew objectively that she'd aged over the years, to me she would always be the same. Elegant. Angelic. One of the only people who'd looked at me and seen more than what was on the outside.

As usual, when she saw me she smiled like she was getting a visit from a celebrity. I grinned back, thinking as I always did how lucky I'd been that day Rafe dragged me here for dinner. Rafe had done more than mentor me; he'd saved me in every way that mattered. When a man got used to having a family that treated him like this, it was no wonder he'd lay down his life for them.

"Noah, come in. Don't just stand outside. I don't know why you don't use your key. You're family." She welcomed me with a hug and I stooped down slightly so she could kiss my cheek.

Her protestations made me smile, although I would never tell her why I didn't use my key. The friend I'd tasked to watch over Nonna had been strangely closemouthed about her activities over recent years, and I had a sneaking suspicion that it was because they were more than just friends. I didn't have any true family anymore. Nonna and Lucia were the closest things to it I had, so I valued them highly.

The last thing I needed was to walk in on my pseudo-grandmother in a compromising position. An unfortunate mental image popped into my mind, and I shut it down immediately. I shuddered.

There were just some things you couldn't unsee.

"I never know where my key is, so it's just easier to knock," I lied, feeling no shame for it. I wasn't sure I believed in God, but surely any benevolent being would forgive me an untruth under these circumstances.

I followed her into the interior of the house and instantly felt at home. It was a talent that Nonna DeMarco had, making visitors feel like family within seconds of entering her home. I glanced around at the old furniture and handmade throw blankets covering the back of the couch. Nonna despised waste of any kind so everything in her home was either handmade or secondhand. It was the most comforting place I'd ever been.

Not sure how to bring up the reason for my visit, I allowed her to fuss over me, making me a cup of coffee even though I'd already had some. By the time the coffee was ready, I'd had a chance to think about how I wanted to bring up Lucia's recent behavior in a way that wasn't going to alarm the older woman.

When we were settled on the couch, Nonna raised her eyebrows at me. If I'd been younger, it was the kind of look that would have made me think I was in trouble for something or other.

"What?"

"Just wondering when you're going to tell me the real reason why you're here. I know it's not just to visit."

Feeling like a little boy caught with my hand in the cookie jar, I smiled. "Maybe I just wanted to check on you."

"Hmm. You know I'm fine."

I sighed. There was no point in trying to ease her into it. Just like when we were young, Nonna had radar for when one of her 'children' needed something. "You're right. I'm not just here to chat. It's Lucia. She isn't doing well."

Immediately Nonna's face lost its teasing smile. "She's been through so much. I think the stress is finally catching up with her."

I didn't want to voice my true thoughts, that this was so much worse than stress. Lucia had lost all grip on reality. After days of wondering what was going on with her, she'd finally confessed why she'd asked to go to the clock tower and what she'd found there. She was convinced her brother was alive, which didn't make any sense considering that she'd watched him get shot. I had shot him point blank. I'd searched for a pulse before taking Lucia away to safety.

There was no one outside of Lucia or Nonna who wanted Rafe to be alive more than I did, but it just wasn't possible. Her insistence on something she *knew* to be impossible worried me more than anything else could have.

"Give her time." Nonna's softly creased face bore the signs of her worry for her granddaughter.

I hated to drop all this in her lap and cause her worry, but I truly didn't know who else to talk to about this. No one else understood our situation, and she was also the only person I believed could get through to Lucia. Nonna could make her see that pursuing this was just asking for more heartbreak. She was the only one on the face of the planet who loved Lucia as much as I did. I knew how much she'd sacrificed to take in Rafe and Lucia after their parents' death.

"I've given her time. Maybe too much time."

Maybe I'd been a fool to think that we could just move past it once she remembered our traumatic shared past. Watching the man you love shoot your brother wasn't the kind of thing one could just get over. Lucia likely needed more therapy. A lot more. Not that I could convince her of that.

The whole thing was a fucking mess.

"There's no such thing as too much time when mourning a lost family member," Nonna murmured. "I'm still not over losing Luca."

I could understand what she meant, but I feared that I'd already done too much of that. The way I felt about Lucia was dangerous. I would forgive her anything, and I was worried that my love for her blinded me to serious issues. If she really needed help, I wanted to make sure she got it. There was a very real danger that I'd bury my head in the sand because I didn't want to admit that she needed help.

For her sake, I had to be stronger than that.

Apparently my thoughts were evident on my face because Nonna reached over and grabbed my hands. I startled but forced myself not to jerk back. I wasn't used to physical contact. Usually when I got this close to someone, it was because I was about to take their life. But when Nonna touched me, all the stress and pain of the last few days hit me at once. Her fingers curled around mine and I had to avert my gaze, afraid I was going to cry like a baby at the show of tenderness.

"Noah, I know you don't understand yet, but women are different. Lucia is like me, strong on the outside but she is *dolce*, sweet and soft, on the inside. There were times right after Rafe's death when I wasn't able to accept that he was gone. I would catch a glimpse of a man on the street and be convinced it was him. I would hear a voice in a crowd and follow it, sure it was Rafe. These things haunted me. I was like a walking ghost searching for what I'd lost. I wasn't ready to let him go yet. Lucia needs time to sort this out on her own."

I lifted her hand to my lips. Her skin was paper thin and soft as tissue. She smiled tremulously when I leaned over and kissed her forehead.

"Thank you, Nonna. I'll try to be patient."

Her smile was slightly smug as she watched me stand. "I had a feeling that you were going to be the one. Ever since Rafe brought you home all skinny and haunted-looking, I knew."

I laughed then. "Well, you knew more than I did. Sometimes I still can't believe I'm this lucky."

Nonna regarded me for a long moment, her shrewd eyes moving over my face. It was tempting to squirm under the scrutiny but I forced myself to hold still. It mattered more than I'd ever thought it would to have her approval. She was the person that Rafe and Lucia had loved more than any other and I desperately wanted to know that she approved of me for her little girl.

"No, you wouldn't believe it, would you? Sweet boy. All you've ever known is disappointment and pain but this is for real. My *bambina* loves you. So this is not luck, this is fate. You are strong in all the ways she needs you to be. When she loses her way, you'll bring her back. Take care of her for me."

I hugged her gently. "Always."

———

Lucia

I moved my stapler to the left and organized the papers on the top of my desk into a neat pile. It should have been strange to be back at work after everything that had happened. Instead it was comforting. For once, all I had to do was focus on whatever ridiculous demands Adriana came up with and drink my coffee. Compared to worrying about killers and conspiracy theories, this was a breeze.

I took a long sip of coffee and savored the witches' brew I couldn't live without. The coffee I made at home was never as good as what I got from a proper barista.

JJ had taken care of everything in my absence so I wasn't even coming back to a bunch of work. Honestly, it might have been better if I had been. That would have kept my mind too busy to focus on everything that had happened lately.

"So you went to the clock tower, and because you saw sunflower seeds, you think it means your brother is alive?" JJ said.

The way our cubicles were angled, I could only see a flash of my friend's blond hair every now and then while I moved around.

"Um, not exactly." I wasn't sure how to respond. Especially since technically that was how it happened, but it sounded much crazier saying it aloud now that I wasn't in the moment.

Things were quiet for a moment before JJ leaned back again. "Sorry. I shouldn't have said it like that."

I shrugged. "It's okay. We've always been honest with each other. Let's not change that now."

"True. But that doesn't mean I want to hurt you. You've been through so much lately. Hell, not just lately. Your mind is just trying to give you the one thing you want more than anything else. No wonder you saw sunflower seeds and came up with *my brother has risen from the dead.*"

I took another sip of my coffee. When put like that, I supposed it did sound a little crazy. All weekend I'd been over the evidence, if you could call it that, and had come up with a million and one scenarios that would explain how Rafe could be alive. I'd gone from the entire thing was an elaborate dream sequence to my brother was actually a mutant that was impervious to bullets.

But the one thing I wasn't willing to consider was that this was all a coincidence. Despite my conscious mind telling me it was ridiculous, there was a part of me that just couldn't let it go. Even if the other things could be explained, I hadn't imagined hearing Rafe's voice.

It might sound crazy to someone else, but I knew what I'd heard and it hadn't been grief or longing or whatever else Noah seemed to think I had going on. It had been in the heat of an extremely scary situation, the last place my mind would have been prone to delusions. After all, I'd adored Rafe, and my mind had no reason to associate him with some scary kidnapper.

But if it was Rafe, why would he have done that? He almost killed your friends.

I brushed the thoughts away. I had no explanations for that part of things, but I'd figure it out.

"It's not just that. It's everything. The voice, the weird kidnapping attempts, and yes, the sunflower seeds. When you put it all together ..." I held out my hands.

"Put it all together and you get a very thin case for something that is not likely to be true," JJ finished with a gentle smile. "This is all just speculation at this point. Let's not get ahead of ourselves."

I reminded myself that she was just looking out for me and trying to keep me from getting hurt. JJ wasn't trying to hurt my feelings by dismissing the idea. Plus, I was objective enough to admit that if the tables were turned, I would be pretty sure that JJ was off her rocker to believe that someone dead and gone for six years was magically alive.

"I agree. It's early days, and there's no need for me to draw any concrete conclusions yet. All I'm doing is reporting to you what I experienced over the weekend. Also, Noah and I had insanely hot sex under that clock tower."

JJ leaned her head out of her cubicle so she could see me. "You should have led with that. Damn girl, that's what I'm talking about! How is my favorite alpha asshole?"

"Cranky. And hot as hell. The usual."

Noah would probably object to the characterization, but it was definitely true. It made me smile. He definitely was a cranky thing. Hot but cranky.

"God, you have all the luck. Ugh. Put in a good word for me with the sexy German, will you? That man looks like he was carved out of concrete." JJ made an exaggerated panting face and fanned herself dramatically.

I laughed at the idea of putting in a good word with Oskar. He was so cantankerous that it was impossible to imagine him with the vivacious JJ. They'd probably kill each other inside of a week. Although knowing JJ, she'd kill him with sex. Oskar might not mind meeting his maker if that was how he got there.

"I'll tell him you said hello," I finally conceded.

JJ scoffed. "Don't tell him I said hello. Tell him I said I want to suck his—"

Adriana appeared at the edge of our cubicles, and JJ went silent. I had just taken a large gulp of coffee and struggled to swallow it without sputtering or spitting it all over myself. Of course, a large portion of it went down the wrong way, and I ended up coughing like I was hacking up a lung. Adriana backed up a step with a look of disgust on her face.

I sucked in a few breaths and then cleared my throat. "Sorry."

Adriana ignored me and instead turned around to speak to someone behind her. "And this is where the real work is done, Mr. Nelson. I pride myself on having the best and brightest in the fashion industry. It takes a great team to create the fashions you saw on the runway."

I refrained from rolling my eyes. Every so often Adriana would bring investors around to see how we operated and to convince them to part with their money to fund her international expansion. That was the only time she seemed to think that what we did was a 'team effort.' On any other occasion, it was all Adriana, all the time.

"Jessica Jones is our extremely talented makeup artist who has been instrumental in creating our signature runway looks. And this is Lucia DeMarco, a design intern who shows great promise."

Adriana widened her eyes at us as if to say, *look alive*, so JJ stood and extended her hand.

"Nice to meet you, Mr. Nelson. I hope you'll be joining the Adriana Fashions family soon."

JJ was smiling so widely that I could tell the guy had to be cute. She only acted like this around the investors she thought were hot. I pasted a smile on my face but couldn't see past JJ since my friend was still hanging on to his hand. I was glad that JJ was so good at the schmoozing stuff because I wasn't. All I'd ever wanted was to hole up and work on my own designs, not convince someone else that it was worthwhile.

"Glad to meet the people on the front lines. Perhaps I could get a tour while I'm here. Miss DeMarco could show me around, perhaps?"

At the sound of my name, I choked slightly on the last sip of coffee. Adriana frowned, and I hurriedly grabbed a napkin to dab at my lips.

"Sure, I mean ... of course. I can give you a tour. There's not much to see though."

"There's plenty to see," Adriana interjected with a sideways look at me that was sharp enough to cut glass. "Show him the samples closet and the design floor at least."

"Yes ma'am. Follow me, Mr. Nelson."

He stepped from behind Adriana, and I immediately noticed the cut of his suit. It fit perfectly and looked like it had been designed and tailored just for him. Then he turned his head and I got my first look at his face and realized why his voice had sounded so familiar.

The coffee cup in my hand fell and would have hit the floor, but his hand shot out and caught it in midair. He placed it gently on the edge of my desk.

"Careful. We don't want to make a mess, do we?" His eyes narrowed meaningfully as I just stared with my mouth open.

It was Rafe.

CHAPTER THIRTY-EIGHT

Lucia

My heart thundered against my ribs. I tried to drag in a deep breath, but my breathing was shallow and thin. I wanted to turn around and ask JJ why she hadn't recognized him. He was wearing what was obviously a wig, since it was threaded liberally with gray hair, and a thin pair of wire-framed glasses obscured his eyes.

But it was him.

It was Rafe.

You're not crazy. He's here.

For the life of me, I couldn't think of one word to say to my brother. After six long years where I'd grieved him, and missed him, and was so desperate to talk to him sometimes I talked to myself, I couldn't think of a single thing to say.

"Miss DeMarco, right after you."

I could only stare at him. He was waiting for me. My boss was waiting for me. Everyone was waiting for me to do something, say something. Somewhere Ryan was in the building. All I had to do was push my panic button and he'd come running, and the whole team would have my immediate GPS location.

Ryan was there to protect me... from Rafe ... *my brother*. I spent several long seconds debating what to do, what to say, and how to say it. But in the end, I just pushed my hair back and forced a smile.

"Of course. Follow me."

At my side, Rafe smiled and nodded at my coworkers, while I tried to get my nerves under control. My hands were sweaty, so I wiped them on my slacks. Once we left the main pen and emerged into the hallway, I turned to face him. It was a shock all over again, to see him here out in the open like this. I repressed the urge to reach over and pinch him to see if he was real.

"Why are you doing this?"

Despite the wig and the glasses, the smile Rafe turned on me was pleasant and familiar. It reminded me of summers at Coney Island, teasing pillow fights, and brotherly hugs. It reminded me of a lifetime ago when his smiling like this would have been no big deal.

It reminded me of a lifetime I'd been robbed of.

Rafe's pleasant smile fell like he could sense my thoughts. "There's plenty of time for asking questions. Just give me a moment."

Shudders racked my body. I tried to keep my hands still by clasping them together tightly. Where was Ryan? Was he going to find us? Was he going to hurt Rafe? Was Rafe going to hurt him? The fear of either of those things happening was the only thing that kept me from pushing my panic button.

Rafe had already hurt Ryan once before, when he'd broken into my apartment. I'd never forget the sight of Ryan slumped over in that chair, looking like a broken doll. The only member of Blake Security that Rafe hadn't yet hurt was Dylan. I didn't want to give him that opportunity. It made me sad to have the thought, but I couldn't trust my brother. An entire lifetime had passed between now and when we'd eaten funnel cake together. This man was capable of anything and I could never forget that.

"I don't even know you anymore," I whispered.

He stiffened, but his expression never altered. "Lulu, I know you're concerned." Anyone watching would think we were having a friendly conversation about the weather, or how I really must try some divine new Italian restaurant. It was a charming smile. It was also the smile of a killer.

He's still your brother.

"Follow me," he said with that false smile. I would never under-stand how he got the smile to reach his eyes as if he meant every word.

And then it hit me. Men like Rafe, men like Noah, men like Matthias —this was what they were trained to do.

Lie, kill, betray.

He directed me, even though it appeared to everyone who passed as if I was giving him the grand tour. He led me down the back stairwell. Down to the next floor where hair and makeup was, and then down to garment repair.

As soon as we hit the third floor, he visibly relaxed. "Okay, through here there's a laundry chute. It'll put you into one of the laundry baskets. Not to worry; that's the one I've got marked to go to my van. I need to walk upstairs and do the whole routine before your security figures out you're missing. We leave in exactly seven minutes. Do you understand?"

He turned me toward the door, but I couldn't move. All I could do was stare at him, bile rising in my throat. My heart hammered behind my ribcage, and my lungs refused to cooperate. This was my brother. *I needed to do something.* But I couldn't move. It was like my legs had gone wooden or become encased in lead.

"Rafe, what is going on?"

"Lulu, I will explain everything as soon as I have you to safety." He took my arm gently and pushed me toward the hallway where the laundry facilities were.

I tugged my arm free of his hold. "You've been trying to hurt me."

His dark gaze focused on me. "Listen to what you just said. My whole life, my one and only goal has been to protect you. Do you think that I would ever hurt you?"

"But you tried to take me. You broke into my place." My legs wobbled and I stumbled backward.

He held his hands up. "I didn't try to hurt you. Think it through, Lulu. I broke into your apartment the first time to try and get you away from Noah's men. I tried to grab you at your fashion show. I underestimated that they'd have an ORUS operative watching you. And I tried to take you again from the penthouse. Take you. *Not hurt you.*"

"You hurt my friends."

"Those men are not your friends. Those men are killers. Every last one of them. I trained Noah myself so I know what he's capable of. He's not your friend."

"And I should trust you?" I laughed bitterly at the thought that he was judging Noah when he'd done something so much worse. He'd lied to me and let me mourn for years. For nothing!

"Yes. I'm your brother."

I tipped my chin up to meet his gaze. "Oh yeah, then where have you been for six years? When I was grieving, when Nonna was grieving, where were you? I buried you. The only person I had to lean on was Noah. *Where were you?*"

He opened his mouth, and then it snapped shut. "Lucia, I'm not going to get another chance like this. Come with me. I'll explain everything. You'll understand."

I wanted to. I wanted to trust him. I wanted to believe in him. But it hurt. The six years of compounded pain and loss, they hurt. Not to mention, I didn't think his plan was going to work. If I didn't show up on the cameras any second, Ryan would be on to us. Then Dylan, Matthias, Noah, Jonas, Oskar, all the people I cared about, they would engage with my brother. And somebody I cared about was going to get hurt again.

I pulled back. "I can't. We can't just leave."

"Yes, you can. It's easy. Walk through that door." He gestured toward the laundry room holding aside the plastic door dividers. "You get in the laundry chute, you land in the basket, you get moved onto my truck, and I take you to safety. That's the plan. Simple. You think I exposed myself because I want to hurt you?"

"I don't know why you're here. I wished and prayed you would be alive. And now you're here. But I love Noah. I can't just leave."

He jerked as if he'd been slapped. "I knew he was watching you. But I didn't think you'd fallen in love with him. You're too young to know what he's capable of."

"I know what he's capable of. I know what *you're* capable of. He told me all about it. You trained him to be a killer."

Rafe winced. "I know. There's a lot to explain. But you can't trust him. He's the reason I've been gone for six years."

I shook my head. "I remember that day. I remember he shot you. Clearly you're still alive. But I remember how it happened. You stepped in front of a target. It wasn't like Noah sought you out and hurt you. You did that."

His dark eyes searched my face. "Lucia, there's so much you don't understand."

"I'm not leaving until I do."

His watch beeped. "Shit. We're out of time. Go. Please, I'm begging you."

I shook my head. "No. It's time for me to go. If I'm not up there in a second, Ryan is going to come looking for me. And I don't want either one of you hurt."

He ran his hand through his hair roughly. "Are you kidding me? You're seriously in love with the enemy?"

"I'm in love with *Noah*. He's a good man. And I can't just walk away."

He checked his watch again. "Out of time. Let's go back."

He took me by the elbow and his touch was gentle, but still dominant. He knew exactly where he needed me to go. Exactly which path would avoid any cameras. And then we were on the main floor again and he eased his hold, put on that smile again, as if we'd had the most pleasant stroll in the world.

"Well, thank you very much for a lovely tour, Miss DeMarco." Then he leaned closer and whispered, "I'll find you again."

Then my brother was gone.

Noah

"Boss, we've got a problem."

I looked up from my computer and rubbed my bleary eyes. Being tired wasn't anything new but the events of the past couple of weeks had taken me to a new level of exhaustion. Not to mention it was an adjustment being in a new place. We'd had all our stuff packed and brought over, but nothing was in the right places and I'd spent a ludicrous amount of time just searching for my mouse the first day I'd tried to use the computer. But in the end, we'd gotten our shit together. Our offices may have been shot up to hell but Blake Security still had work to do. We had open cases and clients who were depending on us.

"What's up, Matthias?"

I put my computer to sleep so I could give the kid my full attention. Matthias had gone back to work a few days ago, over my objections. He seemed fine, but there was something so cold and reserved about him. I had tried a couple of times to get him to talk about that night in the penthouse but he'd said he was fine. Whatever the hell that meant. If he didn't seem to settle in soon, I was going to pull him out of the field permanently. We were short staffed, but having a loose cannon in the field was potentially more dangerous.

"We've got a problem. One of the guests who logged in for Adriana Fashions today was using an alias. There were layers upon layers of background laid so on first glance, everything was fine. But like always, I kept the decryption algorithm running. Just in case. Around lunchtime, it started to pull back the layers. There were five or six. Which is why it took so long to see it, but Andrew Nelson doesn't exist. He's not real."

My heart stopped. "Fuck. *Fuck*."

I pushed myself to standing then dragged my phone out of my pocket. The only thing swirling around my brain was Lucia.

Lucia, Lucia, Lucia.

"Pull the camera footage from the office. All of the goddamn cameras."

"Already done. They've been running on a continuous loop all damn day, since about 9:15 this morning. The bitch of it is I can't even see when he would've inserted that loop. The guy is good. Whoever it is, whoever did this—"

I tried to remember my training. Tried to stay calm and in control. I took a deep breath before I responded. It wasn't the kid's fault that I was about to lose my mind. "Find me some goddamned cameras that can see who went in and out of that building. Pull every camera from the surrounding buildings."

"Already on it. I'll let you know as soon as I have something."

That made me feel a little better. I should have known Matthias would be all over this. He took any breach of security personally. Quickly, I called Ryan's number. And waited not-so-patiently as three rings went by.

When Ryan finally answered, he sounded out of breath. "What's up, Boss?"

"*Where the fuck is Lucia?*"

There was a pause before Ryan said, "She's right here. You want to talk to her?"

The bottom dropped out of my stomach. She was safe? She was okay? My hands shook. I forced myself to drag in a deep breath. "Yes. Please put her on."

"Noah?" Her voice was soft. "What's the matter?"

Shit. Her voice was a soothing balm over the raw frayed ends of my nerves. "Oh, baby, I just needed to hear your voice. Did you have a good day?"

She hesitated for a moment. My internal radar went crazy in those few moments. What was she hiding? Was there someone there with her forcing her to respond a certain way? Well, no. I'd just spoken to Ryan. But could Ryan really be trusted? In the span of five seconds, my mind spun through a loop of worst-case scenarios until Lucia finally sighed.

"Yes. An average day. Are you sure everything's okay?"

Things had been tense between us since she'd made her confession the other day. She'd told me what she thought was going on and I'd reacted badly. She knew I didn't believe her. I cursed. I should have been more supportive and then worked her around to the idea of seeing a professional. Instead I'd been harsh with her and hadn't taken the time to reassure her. The trust we'd worked so hard to earn, the groundwork for our relationship, was rotting at the edges and I wasn't sure what to do about it.

But I knew the truth. Rafe was gone. The longer she clung on to that delusion, the more worried I became. But for right now, I'd settle for her safety.

"Yep. I can't just call to hear my girl's voice?"

"Okay, if you say so. But why didn't you just call me?"

I sighed. She had me there. And then I went back to what I did best. I lied. "I was calling Ryan for a status update, anyway. Figured I'd kill two birds with one stone."

Lucia giggled. "Well, that's going to make the phone sex a lot more awkward. But if Ryan's cool with it, then—"

All I heard next was Ryan's voice. "Sorry, Boss. Not with my phone. You can call her later. I'm not letting you torture me by making me listen to that. It's already bad enough that I walked in on you guys in the gym."

I winced. Yeah, I was going to have to work out a more private arrangement for all of us. This place might be more secure, but it was smaller than the penthouse. And sooner or later, it wasn't going to work anymore. I needed to figure out if we were ever going to go back to the penthouse. I had a *lot* of things to figure out.

I ran a legitimate business, and that business needed a base of operations. Right now this would do, but it wasn't a long-term solution. Nor was it a good home base for me and Lucia. Sooner or later we'd have to look at a good permanent option.

Permanent. For once the word didn't scare me.

Now when I closed my eyes and imagined the future, I could see it clearly. Me and Lucia together, with however many kids she wanted. I would do whatever I had to for Lucia to have everything she deserved.

But for now, our downtown hideout would have to do. I would make it work until I was sure she was safe.

"Ryan, keep this quiet, but it seems one of the visitors to Lucia's building today was using an alias. Were there any anomalies that you were aware of?"

Ryan replied slowly. "No. I would have called it in. Everything looked good. Should I go route number two?"

After what had happened at the penthouse, we'd taken the time to map out various alternate routes from Lucia's job back to our new home base, trying to take into account various scenarios and the possibility of traffic.

"Yes. And Ryan?"

"Yeah Boss?"

"Please bring her home safe."

CHAPTER THIRTY-NINE

Lucia

As soon as I walked in, Noah wrapped me in his arms and lifted me off the ground. I squealed at the sudden motion but alarm quickly morphed into heat when his head nestled into the crook of my neck. I wasn't even sure what he was doing, breathing me in? Whatever he was doing, it felt amazing. I tipped my head to the side to allow him better access to the soft skin of my neck which ignited under his caress.

A throat cleared behind us, and I was reminded of where we were, in the entryway where anyone could see us. I turned slightly and caught Ryan's amused smile as he walked past us to the kitchen. I blushed. I hadn't even taken my coat off. Embarrassment warred with desire as I glanced back at Noah. The man could make me forget my own name sometimes!

I pulled back and adjusted my clothing. "Wow, this is quite a welcome. What's going on with you today?"

He held me tighter, resting his head on top of mine. It was so uncharacteristically tender that for a moment, I wondered if he knew. Could he sense my duplicity? Did betrayal have a scent?

Stop it.

I wasn't betraying Noah by not telling him about Rafe's visit. The situation was complicated and I was only trying to make sure that no one got hurt. There was a long, tense history between the two men and it wouldn't take much to set it off like a powder keg. If I wanted us all to be standing at the end, it was crucial that I handle things properly.

First things first, figuring out just what the hell my brother was up to and where he'd been all these years. It wouldn't be easy to keep a level head in this situation. I'd wanted Rafe back for so long but I couldn't ignore the many ways his death had changed me. I was no longer the innocent, naïve girl who accepted things at face value. Grief and loss had taught me what a bitch life could be, and I wasn't ready to just accept Rafe back into my life without understanding his motives. Because now that I was older and wiser, I understood that everyone had an agenda, even my beloved brother.

He'd come back for a reason. Why now?

And why did I have the horrible feeling that his agenda was to hurt Noah and the rest of my new family?

"Nothing has gotten into me. Just missing my girl." Noah kissed my forehead before setting me on my feet.

The sound of Ryan's gagging behind us made me giggle. Noah just raised both middle fingers before grabbing my arm and leading me down the hallway to our room. As we passed Matthias's room, I paused.

"Is he sleeping?"

Noah nodded. "He's doing better. He's been working every day but gets tired earlier than usual. Hell, I probably should have insisted he take more time but we need him too much."

I placed a hand on the doorjamb, torn between wanting to go in and see my friend and fear that he wouldn't want me there. Not that I didn't deserve his derision, but if I saw that look on Matthias's face it would kill me.

It brought home everything I'd learned today in a whole new way. These men had put their lives on the line for me not knowing the whole truth. Would they still stand for me if they found out that it was my brother who was targeting us? The whole situation was my fault. Matthias wouldn't have been beaten up if my insane brother wasn't playing some sort of game. Whether I'd meant to or not, my curiosity, or stubbornness--whatever you wanted to call it--had brought this whole thing down on us.

"He's going to be fine."

I turned to see Noah's knowing look. As usual he could read my mind. Though I was glad for once that he couldn't *actually* read my mind, otherwise he'd know how much I was hiding from him.

"I know. Still doesn't make it easy to see him like that. Especially since it's because of me."

Noah pulled me gently, steering me toward our room. Once we were inside, he shut the door behind him gently then flicked the lock with a twist of his wrist. My pulse instantly sped up. I couldn't even play it cool, not when my panties got instantly damp at the knowledge that we were now alone.

"Oh, now I see why you missed me."

His lips turned up but he didn't bother to respond. Just spread his fingers through my hair and yanked me toward him until our mouths clashed in a furious erotic clinch.

It was a shock to be treated so roughly, especially coming from Noah. Everyone saw him as such a badass but he'd only ever touched me with tenderness. He held me like spun glass or like a mirage that he was afraid would disappear at any moment.

Like I was a goddess and he was unworthy.

When in truth, I was the one who felt unworthy. Noah had many hidden layers but they were all out of necessity. Everything he'd ever done had been to protect me. I tightened my arms around his neck and savored the slide of his tongue against mine. Would he still want me if he knew that I wasn't as noble? The things I was concealing, was it for his benefit or my own?

Just who was I protecting?

"I've been waiting all day for this. Thinking about what I'd do. How I'd do it." He spoke in jerky tones as he stripped my clothes from my body.

I moaned when his teeth sank into my shoulder. I hadn't even known that I could make these sounds, wild, wanton and completely untamed. Emotions roiled inside and amplified the desire until it was all I could feel. Guilt, lust and shame were a heady combination.

"Show me," I panted. Our eyes met and something dark and dangerous sparked in his eyes. "Show me everything you imagined."

It was obvious when his control finally snapped. Noah growled and hitched my legs around his waist. We'd barely made it onto the bed, pressing and humping against each other while standing before we fell in a heap onto the comforter, desperately undressing each other. I gripped the linen between my fingers as his head dipped and followed the curve of my spine. When his mouth settled between my thighs, I reared up with a hoarse shout.

"Yes. Give it all to me." He pressed me back down with a firm hand on my stomach and the sensation of being restrained sent me straight over the edge.

I came hard as he teased my clit with his tongue, staying with me as I squirmed helplessly against wave after wave of pleasure. When it ended, I was exhausted and wrung out. Then he sat up and slid in with one thrust, bringing me right to the edge again.

"*Fuck.* Nothing in the world will ever be better than this."

I grabbed at his hair, needing something to anchor me as he rode me hard. He was completely absorbed in me, rubbing his nose against my neck like he just needed to be connected from head to toe. I felt the same way, like I would take him into my soul if I could. Nothing should ever come between us and the knowledge that my lies could do just that scared me to death.

"I love you, Noah. No matter what happens." I needed him to know how I felt. Because there was a part of me that was terrified he'd never understand what I'd done.

His head fell back while his face twisted with pleasure. I could tell he was getting close by the low, sexy sounds he was making and the bunch and tense of his muscles beneath my hands.

"Nothing is going to happen. Except you are going to come for me again. *Now.*"

I couldn't deny him anything when he rasped it in that demanding voice. Desire curled through my veins, started low in the pit of my belly and radiating outward until I was crying out with every thrust. Noah tensed and then whispered my name, and that was what sent me over. I clung to him weakly as every one of my muscles seized, clenching around him like they never wanted to let go. Like they were afraid to let go.

As he finally fell to the side next to me, exhausted, I could only hope that I would never have to. Or that he'd forgive me if I did.

———

Noah

As I rested, completely exhausted and sated, I should have been thinking of nothing except how amazing that had been. Instead all I could concentrate on was the nagging sense that Lucia was hiding something from me.

For one, she hadn't looked me in the eye except for when she was reassuring me that she loved me no matter what. Why did she suddenly feel the need to make that distinction?

I pulled her closer, nestling against her back and absorbing the comforting heat of her body. She was always so cuddly after sex and although I wouldn't have thought it possible, so was I. I loved sharing body heat with her and wrapping her in my arms. It was the time when I felt closest to her and after the day I'd had, I needed it.

Lucia apparently wasn't in the same place. After wiggling around to get free, she sat up and stretched, the sheet sliding down to reveal the tips of berry nipples. "I have so much work to catch up on."

My body responded with a predictable clinch. Damn she was perfect. Lucia either didn't notice or care that her nipples had burst free because she was squirming and stretching without a care to the way she was arousing me. My eyes must have given me away because she gathered the sheets to her chest, hiding her breasts from my view. Her cheeks flushed, but I could tell she was pleased by the way her eyes crinkled at the corners. She'd come a long way in recent weeks, going from a shy, hesitant lover to slowly coming into confidence in her sexuality. It was an honor to be witness to her blossoming. It also made me want to drag her back under the covers and not let her up anytime soon. Since I knew she wouldn't go for that, I tried desperately to think of something to distract me from the enticing bounce of her full breasts as she moved.

"Sorry things are a bit cramped here. I know it's hard to find room to think when there are so many people on top of each other."

She tilted her head adorably. "You're apologizing for keeping us all safe?"

Relief that she got it spread through him. "When you put it like that, no, I'm not."

"Good. Because you're doing the best you can, Noah. That's all anyone can do. And for the record, your best is pretty damn good."

She leaned over and kissed me gently. The sweetness of the kiss caught me off guard, sending a bolt of pure longing and awe through me.

Would I ever get used to the idea that she was actually mine?

I watched her dress, my heart flipping over as she kept glancing at me with intimate little looks that made me feel like I was ten feet tall.

I hoped I never got used to her, to us together. I never wanted to forget how fortunate I was to have someone to love and who loved me in return.

"Let me know when you're ready for dinner. I promised Jonas that we'd get burgers tonight. I think he's going through withdrawals."

"Oh, thank you! I thought I was the only one. Home-cooked meals are awesome but if I don't get something greasy and fattening in my system soon I'm going to lose it."

I chuckled. As long as we'd been together, Lucia had been harassing me to eat better and just take better care of myself in general. So I couldn't resist the opportunity to tease her for missing junk food.

"You know, I've been trying to eat better like you said."

Lucia gave me a death glare. "Don't even start. I have been through too much in the past couple of weeks to care about the state of my arteries. I want grease and fat, and I want it *now*."

"Yes, ma'am. Your wish is my command."

Lucia leaned over the bed and kissed me, her lips lingering against mine until I was hard as a rock. I reached under the sheet and grasped my cock firmly, squeezing just below the head until I didn't feel as though I was in danger of coming just from the sound of her voice.

"Say that again," she whispered.

"Anything you want is yours, baby. You know that."

"Good because what I want is the most fattening, delicious burger in the state of New York."

Lucia winked before leaving the room, pulling the door closed behind her.

I was in the middle of dressing when someone knocked on the door. I pulled my shirt over my head hastily before stalking over to the door and yanking it open. Then I blinked when I saw that it was Matthias standing there.

"Can I come in? I have something to show you."

I stepped back and allowed him to enter the room. Although Matthias had been insisting for days that he was fine, he was still slightly pale. The bruises had faded but there were dark shadows under his eyes, making him look gaunt.

"I was finally able to pull camera footage from the bank across the street. Their encryption was pretty decent so it took a little longer than I expected."

He held out his tablet, and I turned it around to see the image displayed. It took a moment to process what I was seeing, but when it finally sank in, my breath left my lungs in a sudden sharp exhalation. The edges of my vision went gray, and I would have fallen if Matthias hadn't clapped me on the shoulder.

"You okay, Boss?" Matthias peered at me with concern.

I pounded on my own chest, trying to jumpstart my heart. "Rafe. This is Rafe," I repeated needlessly.

Matthias brought the tablet closer and stared at the image as if that would somehow make it clearer. The man pictured was in profile, but I would never forget that face. I'd stood by his side and watched that profile for years, after all.

Matthias touched the screen, and it switched to another image. In this one, Rafe faced the camera and the shock of seeing him hit me all over again. He was wearing glasses, no doubt to hide his face since Rafe had always had perfect vision, and a suit that looked expensive. My friend was definitely older, his dark hair threaded through with gray at the temples and above the ears, but it was undeniably Rafe.

"This is not possible." I stared. How was this possible? How was she right?

Matthias frowned and then glanced down at the image. "Wait, when you say that's Rafe, you don't mean–"

"That's Rafael DeMarco. Lucia's brother."

Matthias stared at him blankly. "I thought her brother was dead?"

"I thought he was, too. Especially since I'm the one who killed him." Six long years ago. The grief and the shame had almost killed me.

I turned the tablet off, unable to stomach looking at my old friend's treacherous face any longer. A million thoughts clamored for space in my brain but at the forefront was, *What the hell am I supposed to tell Lucia?*

Except ... she'd tried to tell me, hadn't she? I'd assumed she was losing it. That the pressure had been too much. But she'd been right.

And you didn't believe her.

"What are we going to do?" Matthias finally asked. My face was a blank mask, but that didn't fool him. The kid would have questions, along with all of the others.

The things I'd done in my past were coming back to haunt us all, and it was only fair for them to expect answers since they were the ones paying the price. Matthias had taken a brutal beating and Jonas could have lost his sight, so if their injuries had anything to do with my skeletons falling out of the closet, they had the right to some answers.

But first, I had to ask the right questions. Because with how strange Lucia had been acting all day I couldn't ignore the very real possibility that she had more than an inkling that Rafe was alive. Something that went beyond hearing his voice that night. Something more concrete, like seeing him.

"Nothing. You are not going to do anything. He was in the building with Lucia, but he obviously didn't hurt her. So that's not his end game."

The kid frowned. "Do you really think he'd hurt his own sister?"

"Hell if I know. He's not the same guy I once knew, obviously. I can't pretend to understand what he would or wouldn't do. So I'm going to ask the only person who might know."

"Lucia. Shit, this is going to get ugly." Matthias shook his head. "You really think she knows?"

"God, I hope not." I took the tablet and tucked it under my arm. "She and I are going to have a little talk."

CHAPTER FORTY

Noah

I wasn't sure whether to be furious with Lucia, or thrilled that she was right. Either way, we needed to have it out. She'd made love to me not two hours ago, but when she'd looked at me and told me she loved me, she'd been lying to me.

She didn't lie. She just kept it to herself.

Damn it. Keeping a secret like this was tantamount to lying. How the hell was I supposed to keep her safe, keep us *all* safe if she didn't tell me the most pertinent information of all? As much as I wanted to justify it, I couldn't deny the bitter tang of betrayal on my tongue.

I found her in the living room, cross-legged on the couch, wearing one of my shirts and a pair of my boxer shorts. She had the sleeves rolled up to reveal her slim forearms. Head bent over, she was going through a stack of fashion magazines labeling things and putting Post-its on them. Writing things like, *Pull, Check with Adriana if we have it,* and *Can we partner with this designer?*

She was working. Completely in her zone. Well, too bad for her; I was about to interrupt her. When I stood next to her, she looked up with the sweetest smile I'd ever seen. So sweet it pulled at the places in my heart I'd have sworn didn't exist anymore. She looked so perfect there, the lamp on the table creating soft shadows and halos all over her. She looked like an angel.

"Hi. What's up?" There was an invitation in her smile and, like the traitor it was, my dick swelled. I couldn't seem to keep my mind or my hands off of her. But we needed to talk, so the big guy downstairs would just have to wait.

"I was going to ask you the same thing. Is there anything you want to talk to me about?"

Her brows furrowed even as she continued smiling up at me. "No. I mean, unless when you say *talk*, you mean—" She lifted a brow and her eyes danced mischievously.

Okay, so I could totally understand how even the most hardened spies could fall for the enemy. Because right about now, I wasn't using the brain cells God gave me. I was using the other part of my brain. The one completely responsible for manning the sex train. The one that wanted to yank off her boxers and sink into her, right here in the middle of the living room, where anyone could walk in.

No. Stay strong.

Besides, we'd done enough of that. After one too many close calls, the tracking devices I had everyone wear were now used to track where me and Lucia were, so the team could give us a wide berth.

Not exactly the use I had planned for them, but whatever. We had enough privacy. And maybe if I just sank deep into her, I'd stop riding the razor's edge and focus enough so I could ask her what I needed to ask her. If I slid the boxers off, spread her wide and stroked deep, we'd both feel better. We'd be relaxed enough to have this conversation. It was amazing the things I could come up with when I let my dick do the thinking.

I considered it. For a long moment, I considered it. She'd taste so sweet. Was she sore from earlier? Or, from this morning? I hadn't exactly been gentle. But then again, neither had she. I still had her nail marks on my shoulders. I grinned with purely male satisfaction. I could still feel how those scratches had stung this morning in the shower when the water hit them.

Oh shit. I did not need to think about the shower, or what we did in there.

And I probably shouldn't think about her taste because then I'd think about what we'd just done and—no. Never mind, there it was. In amazing Technicolor and surround sound in my mind. I cleared my throat.

No. We were having this conversation now. Because I was pretty damn certain that after we had this conversation, the last thing on my mind would be sex.

"Nope. Nothing to talk about."

Her gaze searched mine. And I saw pain there. I hated that I'd had a part in the pain there. Because I was pretty damn sure there was one thing she probably wanted to talk about, but she didn't trust me to be open-minded. That hurt more than anything else, that she couldn't talk to me. Didn't she understand that all I wanted was her safety and happiness?

Behind my back, my fingers tightened around the tablet I held. A tablet that held the image of a ghost I'd long since buried. A ghost that was back to haunt us all.

The question was, what did he want?

I took the tablet with the photo on display from behind my back and slapped it on the table. "Explain."

Lucia glanced at the picture, and her breath caught. Her fingers flew to her lips then her gaze flickered to mine. "I don't know what to say."

"Matthias came into my office freaking the fuck out because Nelson came back as a false name. I lost years off of my life in that split second when I was worried about you."

"Noah, I can explain."

I shook my head. "I was terrified that something happened to you. Terrified that once again I was too late. And then I called Ryan and everything was fine. So I need to know what's going on. After everything we've been through, I would have thought honesty was a given. Then Matthias showed me something that should be impossible. Something you already knew."

"I didn't lie to you, Noah."

I crossed my arms. "Oh yeah? Then what do you call it exactly? Omission? You just happened to forget that you saw your brother in your office today?" I kneeled down so our gazes were level. "Or please, tell me you didn't see him. Please fucking tell me he came into your office but you didn't see him. Tell me that so I don't think the woman I love lied to me."

She pushed herself off the couch and shoved at my chest. Not that she could move me, but still. I didn't know what I'd expected. How I'd expected her to respond. All I knew was I hadn't expected this. I'd never seen her like this before.

"How dare you? Don't stand there acting like I knew what was going to happen and deliberately deceived you. No, I didn't tell you I saw him. But why would I? You would have had me fitted for a lovely white jacket with funky straps. *Fuck you*, Noah. I tried to tell you I saw Rafe already, remember? You didn't believe me."

That did make me stagger. I didn't think I'd ever heard her use the word *fuck* before. I'd never seen her this furious. After everything we'd been through over the years, she'd never gone off on me like this before.

"Lucia, I never said I didn't believe you."

"Oh didn't you? You insinuated it. Tried to make me think that my mind was playing tricks on me. That I wanted to think he was back, so I fabricated it all. The damn sunflower seeds, the voice when he tried to take me from the penthouse. I thought I was losing it. I needed you to be in my corner. I needed you to tell me we'd figure it out. Hell, even if you'd said, 'I think someone's deliberately fucking with you,' that would've been far better than, 'Princess, your mind is playing tricks on you.' You might as well have taken out a billboard saying 'This bitch is crazy.'"

We squared off against each other as I stared down at her. "I never called you crazy."

"Did you or did you not think I needed a shrink?"

I opened my mouth then snapped it shut. *Fuck.* "Look, I was worried. I love you and I was watching you drown."

"Well, how was I supposed to feel when I thought my brother was back? And newsflash, turns out he is. Turns out I wasn't losing my shit after all."

"Lu—"

"Don't you dare start with me. I told you. You didn't believe me. That hurt. It hurt so deep."

She started to shake then wrapped her arms around herself and rocked back on her heels. All I wanted to do was hold her. I hated this, what we were doing to each other. Hated that I'd fucked up.

She was right. She'd tried to tell me. But I'd only seen it one way and if I was going to figure out what my old friend was up to, I needed to be able to look at it from all angles. I didn't want this to be our undoing, so I gritted my teeth, knowing she was going to fight me, but I wrapped my arms around her anyway, rocking our bodies together.

"I'm sorry. I'm so fucking sorry. I saw the picture and I lost it. I almost lost you that night. I almost lost three of my friends. I just couldn't see what you were seeing. And that's no excuse because I should've believed you. I love you. You are my entire world and I should've trusted in you."

I kept hold of her until eventually she wrapped her arms around me and I breathed a sigh of relief. We might not be okay right now, but we would be. Because she loved me, too. And she wasn't going to stop no matter how dicey things got.

"Let's try this again. Tell me what happened today."

Against my chest, she whispered everything that happened in her office. Rafe trying to direct her out and away. And how he'd told her not to trust me or anyone that worked for me.

I frowned in confusion. If he was alive and keeping tabs on his sister, Rafe had to know that I had left ORUS by now. Was something else going on? All I knew was my best friend was back from the dead. And had tried to kill me and/or my men on more than one occasion. So right now, I didn't fucking trust Rafe at all. Certainly not with Lucia's life.

I wasn't sure how long I held her, but eventually she started to relax. I pulled her on my lap. "Please forgive me. I was worried. But I should've listened."

She nodded. "I'm sorry. I should've told you. I wanted to; I just wasn't sure how you'd react."

I licked my lips. "Can I ask you a question?"

She nodded.

"Why didn't you go with him? Having him back is all you've ever wanted."

Lucia eyes settled on mine and what I saw there rocked me. Complete love and trust.

"I love you. I couldn't just leave you like that. I knew how much you'd worry and honestly, I'm not sure how much I should trust him. He let me and Nonna grieve for him. He put us through torture. And you too. He's hurt Ryan, Matthias, Jonas, and Oskar. I love Rafe, and part of me is so full of joy that he's alive, but I don't know what's going on. All I know for sure is that you love me and would never let anyone hurt me. So I stayed."

My gaze searched hers. "I would absolutely come for you. I would turn over every corner of this earth to find you if he'd taken you away from me."

She nodded. "That's part of what I'm afraid of. Starting some war with you and Rafe. We're already in the middle of a war. One I don't understand and I don't know how to stop. I didn't want anyone else getting hurt on my behalf. Not you, not me, or anyone here. All of you are my family so I just didn't say anything. Sorry if I compromised anyone's safety."

I nodded. "I get it. I shouldn't have asked you to choose."

"So what do we do now?"

"If I know your brother, he'll try again. But he's certainly not going to talk to me. He's not going to come to us head on. ORUS trained him too well. He wants you."

"So what are we supposed to do?"

"I think I need you to wear a wire."

She stared at me. "Are you kidding me right now? You want me to wear a wire the next time I talk to my brother? Whenever that is."

I sighed. "This is Rafe. He won't wait long before he contacts you again. If you have any other suggestions for the best way to find out what's going on with him, I'm open. Where has he been? And given that he tried to kill several members of my team, I don't think he'll be willing to talk. But if anyone can get through to him, it would be you. We need to call a cease-fire for now and look at the bigger picture. Do you have a better idea?"

She chewed her bottom lip. "I don't, but it doesn't mean I have to like this one."

CHAPTER FORTY-ONE

Lucia

If I thought Noah was relentless when he wanted something, I hadn't seen anything. I'd seriously underestimated my best friend. I'd been dodging JJ's calls ever since leaving work early on Friday. Normally we would have hung out or at least spoken every day but I had no idea what to say to my friend. Even thinking about everything that had happened lately made me tired. Truthfully, all I wanted to do was stay in bed and pull the covers over my head.

I thought my method of dealing was working pretty well until Noah appeared at the door of our room one night holding out his phone and wearing an expression of annoyance.

"JJ is trying to reach you. Also, I have a missed call from Nonna, too. But call JJ first. She's already threatened to cut off various parts of my anatomy if I don't stop hoarding you."

Even as exhausted as I was, it made me smile. Noah was such a badass to everyone else but even he was a little scared of JJ. I made a mental note to mention it to my bestie since she'd definitely get a kick out of knowing she scared grown men. In JJ's mind that would be the ultimate compliment.

I sat up. "Sorry, it's my fault. I've been avoiding her calls because I wasn't sure what to say. Is it safe to tell her what's going on? I'm not putting her in danger if I confide in her, am I?"

"I think that train has already left the station. Call her. Please."

I sighed. I knew he was right. It was way too late to worry about keeping JJ in the dark when I'd told my friend everything previously. Before I could overthink it, I grabbed my phone from the nightstand. Sure enough, I had several missed calls and two from Nonna. I really needed to call her back so she wouldn't worry. But first I hit the speed dial for JJ's number. My friend answered immediately and the familiarity of her voice was like being enveloped in a warm hug. I was startled by the rush of emotion that brought tears to my eyes.

"Hey, it's me."

"So, you finally decided to call me back. You shady bitch!"

I laughed and pressed the back of my hand against my eyelids, holding the tears and the emotion away. "Noah made me. It turns out that he's pretty attached to whatever part of his anatomy you keep threatening to cut off."

JJ snorted. "Aren't they all? Babies, all of them. But that's not why I've been calling. Happy birthday!"

Shock had me pulling back from the phone and hitting the calendar app so I could check the date.

What? It was my birthday.

How could I have forgotten that?

I closed my eyes. That must be why Nonna had called twice already. Every year she insisted on singing to me and baking me a cake. I'd been floating in a fog for days now, sick with worry about Rafe, where he'd been and why he'd come back now. Personal things, even something that I'd been anticipating for ages, could easily slip anyone's mind when under this kind of stress. Which also explained why Noah had forgotten. I almost wished I could hide it from him. He would be so hard on himself for forgetting but I couldn't blame him. We had life or death things to focus on right now.

"I had forgotten, believe it or not."

"You forgot your birthday? But you've been talking about it all year. Hell, I've been talking about it all year." JJ's voice lowered until it was just above a whisper. "What is going on with you?"

"There are so many things I need to tell you. Things have been more than a little crazy around here lately."

"Well, you can tell me tonight after you buy me a margarita. I'm totally excited now that I don't have to get drinks for you anymore. Just kidding."

"No you're not."

JJ laughed. "No, I'm definitely not. Now we just have to figure out how to get your warden on board with the plan. He's keeping you locked up like a prisoner."

My thoughts went to my brother, back from the dead and with questionable motives. If JJ knew that Rafe was not only alive but had been in our office only a few feet from us, she wouldn't make fun of how vigilant Noah was being.

He would never hurt me. Would he?

It was painful to think of my brother as a potential enemy but I couldn't relax my guard. I'd asked him what he was doing and he hadn't been able to give a straight answer. Which no doubt meant he knew I wouldn't approve of whatever his plan was. I was suddenly very afraid that whatever Rafe was planning would tear me away from Noah. Suddenly I wanted to see him. Needed to feel him in my arms one more time to make sure he knew we were real.

"Maybe I should just stay in tonight. With things the way they are, I'm not sure ... "

"Lucia, seriously?" JJ interrupted. "You're really not going to celebrate your birthday. Your *twenty-first* birthday? No way, we are going out and getting you drunk."

"Somehow I don't think that's what I need right now. Noah would hit the roof."

"Contrary to popular opinion, Noah doesn't control the world," JJ muttered.

I hated feeling like this. I'd never been the type of girl who ditched my friends for a guy and didn't want to start now. It probably seemed that way to JJ, like I was changing now that I'd hooked up with Noah finally, and the thought was all I needed to change my mind. Bad things were happening and there was nothing I could do about that. However, I could control how I responded to those things. My response wasn't going to be hiding away and putting my head in the sand.

No doubt I was going to have to argue with Noah to convince him that it was safe but I didn't even care. What was the point of hiding in the house? Rafe had already proven that he wasn't averse to breaking in to get to me. So staying home was probably counterproductive anyway.

"You know what? You're right!"

"I am?" JJ said slowly.

"You are. It's my birthday and I'm going out. We are going to have fun and ... whatever. I'm not entirely sure on the details yet but I can't sit at home on my birthday."

"You're damn right you're not. Yay! Okay, so I'll figure out where we're going and then I'll let you know so you can clear it with the goons. I don't care if they come with us. Hell, I'll get them drunk too. We're going to have so much fun."

Her enthusiasm was contagious and I found myself excited about the prospect of an adventure. I would probably have a whole slew of guards on me like body lotion while I danced, but at least I wouldn't be at home feeling sorry for myself. I could only hope that Rafe wouldn't do anything crazy like try to kidnap me while I was out.

Or maybe he would. I sat up, the idea taking root.

It felt treacherous to even think about it. Noah was so worried about me and working so hard to ensure my safety that I felt like a total Judas secretly wishing to see Rafe again. But now that I'd had the thought, I couldn't deny that I was hoping he would try to make contact. If I could only talk to him again maybe he would see reason. I could convince him to stop working against Noah and instead work with him. Clearly Rafe knew things that we didn't and despite what Noah thought, I couldn't believe my brother would ever actually hurt me.

"We are definitely going to have fun. I'll have Noah send someone to pick you up and we can get ready here." Belatedly, I realized how presumptuous I was being. Maybe JJ would have preferred to get ready at home. "Sorry, I'm just thinking that Noah will want us where he can protect us."

"It's okay. I get it. The big lug is protective of you. I like that, you know? He really loves you, Lucia. I know I give him a lot of shit but the two of you together, it's a good thing."

"Thanks. I like us together too."

"And tonight you are finally going to tell me the real deal about what's going on with you lately. Because I'm your bestie and you know you can't fool me. You haven't been yourself for weeks."

"I know. You'll get the full scoop tonight, I promise. Although once you find out everything you might wish you'd never asked."

JJ was quiet for a minute and then said, "No matter what you tell me, you know I have your back, right? The only thing I care about is making sure you're okay. Whatever it is, we'll deal with it the way we always have. Together."

It made me smile remembering how many scrapes and tight spots JJ had helped me scheme my way out of. But those things had been childish dilemmas, not life or death situations. There was a part of me that wished I didn't have to involve my friend in all these crazy shenanigans but if the tables were turned, I'd want JJ to trust me.

"Yeah, together. And it's probably good that I'm twenty-one now because we are definitely going to need alcohol for this conversation."

———

I walked away from the bar slowly, careful not to spill the drinks. The very first drinks I'd ever bought legally. It had been a weird thing to just walk up to the bar and order something. The times we went out, JJ always got the drinks since I hadn't been old enough. Not that I was much of a drinker anyway. Mainly I'd just gone along to keep JJ company and to get out of the house. I'd always been a bit of a loner, happy to lose myself in a fashion magazine with a hot cup of tea beside me. JJ often teased that she was the only thing keeping me from turning into an old maid.

Thinking about the things Noah had done to me before we left the house, I figured my friend was no longer the only thing keeping me from being old before my time. Noah hadn't even cared that the others were in the living area waiting for us! The man was a menace. He truly had no shame. The only reason he'd stopped was Nonna calling again.

JJ accepted the drink I handed her and then raised it in the air for a toast. "To my sister from another mister. I'll stick with you like a blister. Happy birthday, Lucia!"

I had to laugh at the creative toast. "*Aww*. I love you, too. Cheers!"

JJ took a sip of her drink and then wiggled in delight. "Ooh, that's good."

I took a sip of my own drink and had to agree. I had decided to go for something different in honor of my birthday and ordered us mojitos instead of doing shots. The sugary drink was exactly what I needed. Considering the mood JJ was in, I'd probably need the sugar in order to keep up.

When we'd arrived at the bar, I'd expected Noah to crowd us and hover like he usually did. To my surprise, he'd found a table for us and then retreated to stand against the wall on the other side of the room. Ryan was in the crowd somewhere, but I'd only seen him once. It was comforting and strange at the same time to know that they were out there watching my every move.

My hand went to the delicate necklace resting between my breasts. After my conversation with JJ, I'd teased Noah about forgetting my birthday. It turned out he hadn't forgotten at all but was just planning a special dinner for me. I'd felt bad about ruining his dinner plans but he hadn't seemed to mind. He'd given me a carefully wrapped box instead which held the necklace I was now wearing. Even though he'd given me a lot of birthday gifts over the years, I knew I'd always remember this one. Maybe it was because this was the first gift I'd gotten from him after knowing that he loved me.

"Okay so what's the deal? You've been acting so weird all night. What did He-Man do this time?"

I snorted at JJ's never-ending litany of creative nicknames for Noah. Knowing his ego, he'd probably like the He-Man moniker.

"For the first time ever, it's not about Noah. I've been having a hard time ... remembering things about when my brother died."

JJ paused with her drink halfway to her mouth. We rarely talked about the dark period surrounding Rafe's death. That was one of the benefits of having a longtime friend: you didn't have to explain certain things because they'd been there. JJ knew how lost and inconsolable I'd been for years afterward. She didn't ask questions about that time because she'd been right in the thick of it with me.

"I'm so sorry, Lu. Of course you'd be thinking about your brother right now. You're an adult and it must be so hard to go through all these milestones without him here."

JJ was quiet for a moment and when she glanced over, I was shocked to see tears in my friend's eyes. JJ was the ball buster, the brash, loud, fearless friend that I relied on to push my boundaries and challenge the status quo. I'd only ever seen JJ cry from frustration or anger. Even when her feelings were hurt, she defaulted to rage instead of sorrow. But there was no mistaking that these were genuine tears of sadness.

"You're crying," I finally said, feeling stupid for stating the obvious but still in shock to see my friend so undone. In that moment, I was able to step outside of myself and realize how hard it must have been on JJ to watch me going through all these things over the years. It would be heartbreaking on my end if something horrible happened to JJ and there was nothing I could do to help.

JJ pressed her fingers below her eyes, pressing the skin as if determined to use sheer force of will to stop any tears from actually falling.

"Of course I'm crying. I'm a shitty friend. All you've been saying is that you need time and want to be alone while I'm here dragging you out for drinks. All because I feel like we're drifting apart and that scares me. This whole time I've been worrying about me instead of thinking about what you're going through."

I put my hand over JJ's on top of the table. My friend smiled and flipped her hand over to clasp mine tightly.

"First of all, you are not a shitty friend. You're the best friend I've ever had. The only person in the world that I could tell that—" I stopped before blurting out that Rafe was alive again. You never knew who was listening. "—certain things without you assuming I was crazy. I don't know what I'd do without you."

The relief on her face made me feel incredibly guilty. I hadn't realized how abandoned JJ had felt during this whole thing. If the roles were reversed, I'd probably feel the same way, but I'd never had to experience that because JJ had never put her boyfriends above our friendship.

"And I appreciate that you dragged me out tonight. Don't ever let me get so boring that I sit at home on my birthday, okay?"

By the appreciative way that JJ squeezed my hand, I knew my friend was happy to take our conversation to a lighter place. Neither of us had ever been the overly mushy type and if we kept up this line of conversation we might as well be at home watching sad movies and eating ice cream.

"You got it, babe. Speaking of not being boring, let's dance!"

I tossed back the last of my drink while JJ did the same and then followed my friend to the dance floor. Noah wasn't anywhere around but I knew he still had eyes on me; that was a given. But without seeing him it was easier to close my eyes and get lost in the music.

This is what I need. To forget everything and just be.

JJ danced around me, all loose hips and sinuous arm movements. I would never be able to dance like that; my friend had more sexiness in her pinkie finger than I had in my whole body, but under the influence, I let the rhythm of the music roll through me. For one night, I could forget all my problems and just do what felt good.

Then I opened my eyes and jumped slightly. Rafe danced next to us, looking for all the world like he belonged in a nightclub.

Before I could say anything, he put his finger over his lips. I nodded and then glanced at JJ who was staring at Rafe like he was ... well, like he was a ghost. Without his businessman disguise, there was no doubt as to his identity. He motioned with his head for us to follow him. He moved through the crowd easily, people parting as he walked like he was some kind of messiah. I glanced over my shoulder to find JJ following behind with a dazed expression on her face.

"It's okay. Trust me."

JJ nodded and grabbed my hand. Together we navigated the crowd until we finally reached a set of stairs that led to the rooftop bar. It was usually roped off for VIP guests but strangely, it was completely empty.

As soon as Rafe turned around, I threw myself into his arms. "Where have you been?"

From this position, I could see JJ standing off to the side, watching with wide eyes and a *what-the-fuck* expression.

"It doesn't matter where I've been. What matters is that I'm here now, and I'm never leaving you again." Rafe's words made my heart leap and then crash.

"Easy for you to say it doesn't matter," I mumbled.

His soft chuckle was at once so familiar that my knees buckled slightly. How many times had I heard that laugh, something he seemed to do only for me? It was a sound I'd thought never to hear again in this life. My arms tightened around his neck until I must have been strangling him but he didn't protest, just rested his head on top of mine.

And for that moment, he was right. Nothing else mattered.

CHAPTER FORTY-TWO

Lucia

"Jesus, Lulu, I've missed you."

When I looked up at my brother, all I wanted to do was hold him. "I missed you too." I looked down at my feet, shoving my hands in my back pockets. "My life was never the same after. My whole world fell apart when you were gone."

He reached for me and stroked his thumb over my cheek. "You have to understand. If there was any other way, I never would've left."

I frowned up at him. "Then tell me what happened. Why did you leave? What was so important that you had to go to that house? Do you know that for years I wasn't able to remember what happened?"

"Lulu, that's not something you have to worry about anymore. I'm back."

"All due respect, Rafe, but I do have to worry about it. You've shown back up in my life, and you expect me to just trust you blindly. When I needed you, you weren't here. Now that I'm able to stand on my own, you want to tell me I can't trust the man that I love." I threw my hands up. "You're going to have to give me more than that. I need more to go on."

Rafe ran his hand through his hair and stepped back. "You don't think I want to tell you? You don't think I want to give you every reason to run away from him? The problem is the more you know, the more danger you're in. I've exposed myself coming for you. But there was no way I was going to let them hurt you. The people Noah works for, they're dangerous. They're ruthless. And they wouldn't hesitate to kill you just for knowing that I'm alive. I've stayed hidden a long time just to keep you safe. That's why I need to take you with me, get you to safety."

I shook my head. "You don't need to get me to safety. I'm safe with Noah."

"No, you're not. I don't know what game he's playing considering it's his organization that is hell-bent on killing you. Maybe he wants to hold you for information. Either way, it's not safe for you. I was able to get to you in that penthouse. Imagine what a horde of them could do. This isn't some little security company that plays at doing the right thing. Blake Security is a front. All of those guys in there, killers. That one guy, with the knife. Did you see the way he was enjoying it? He wanted to kill me. But he didn't want to make it quick. He wanted me to hurt. He wanted to enjoy himself. Those are the kind of people you're protecting? Those are the kind of people that you call friends?"

"You don't know anything about it. Because you weren't here."

He stared at me, pain evident in his eyes and the tight set of his lips. "I wanted to be."

"Not good enough. Not good enough by miles. And you just turn up at my office one day, no warning, no nothing. And you expect me to leave with you. Are you insane?"

He tossed his head back. "Clearly. Because if I had my way, I would just sedate you and carry you out of here. But you had to pick somewhere really fucking public. Let me guess: Noah's guys are posted at the exits? There's no safe way to take you out of here unless you can walk on your own. Too many innocent people could get hurt."

"You mean like my friends? Matthias and Jonas? Heads up, you could have permanently blinded him."

My brother shrugged. "If the enemy can't see you, they can't kill you."

"For the love of God, they are not the enemy. They help people."

"Is that what Noah told you?"

I stared at him. That familiar face, but yet, somehow, unfamiliar. "Yes, that's what he told me. But it's also what I see. When some woman walks in there because she has a stalker ex-boyfriend and they make that stalker stop, I see that. I see the good that they're doing."

Rafe stepped into my space, staring down at me. When he spoke, his voice was low, and icy. "Just how do you think they make that stalker boyfriend stop? Do you think they have a stern conversation with him? Do you think they file a restraining order? They take that stalker ex-boyfriend and make him go away. Permanently."

"You're wrong. They don't kill people. Noah doesn't do that anymore. Besides, isn't this a case of the pot calling the kettle black? He told me you trained him. You're as much of a killer as he is. Why would I trust you?"

"Because I'm your goddamned brother."

I stepped back. "You'll have to do better than that."

Rafe scrubbed his hand over his face. "Yes, I did train him. There was a time the organization we worked for did good things. We took out the worst of the worst. The people who trafficked children and drugs and wanted to see whole populations decimated, those were the kinds of people we went after. But somewhere along the line, something changed; we became the people we were trying to stop. I saw it, found a way out. And I took it. Noah, he never left."

"Yes, he did."

"No, he didn't. He's still in touch with them. How do you think he found out about the hit on you? He's still in bed with those people. And I need to get you away from him."

I gasped.

JJ put her arm around my shoulders protectively. "Stop trying to scare her," she growled.

Rafe looked between us in frustration. "She needs to be scared. I'm trying to get her to see reason."

I squeezed my friend's hand. JJ was worried about me, but I didn't want her getting in the middle of all of this. I didn't think Rafe would hurt my friend but that was the thing, I wasn't really sure what he would do now.

"You need me to go willingly, and I'm not leaving him. You need to talk to him. Work out your differences; figure out what the hell is going on. Because there was a time when the two of you were on the same side."

"That time was a long time ago. Noah and I have nothing to say to each other."

"Just talk to him. I can set it up. It'll be okay. At the very least, you can stop trying to hurt each other. You're both my family."

"He's not your family. *I am.*"

"Well, you know what, Rafe? You abandoned me and he took over as family. Who do you think has been looking after me and Nonna all this time? Making sure that Nonna had money to pay for things like my prom. Like college?"

He took me by the shoulders "I did. I sent money every month to make sure that you had what you needed."

My jaw dropped open and I staggered back a step. "What did you say?"

"I sent money. Every damn month. I made sure Nonna was taken care of. I made sure you were taken care of."

"It's not just about money. Noah has been there for the Sunday dinners. He's been there when some idiot broke up with me and hurt me. When Nonna started having health issues, he was there, helping me take her to the hospital and getting her checked up on. Bringing doctors over. Where were you?"

"Lucia, I was always watching from afar, making sure you would be okay. I was never far away."

"What I needed was someone to help me carry the burden."

"You don't understand. He's pretty much got you brainwashed. If you just come with me, you can see things clearly."

"I'm not going with you, Rafe."

A mask slid over my brother's face. Cold and efficient. Suddenly I could see the killer he must've been.

"Yes, you are Lucia. Even if I have to knock you out and drag you out of here. I have one other exit. It's not ideal, but I can take you unconscious."

The next three seconds happened so quickly I didn't understand what was going on at first. It took me a moment to catalog everything. Suddenly, Rafe's hands were off my shoulders and he was fighting with Matthias.

Oh God.

Next to me, on one side stood Ryan, his gun trained on my brother. On my other side stood Dylan, in the same position. His gun was ready and trained on the fighting duo, safety off. Oskar, Jonas and Noah watched as Matthias unleashed on Rafe.

"Stop it," I screamed.

But either they couldn't hear me, or they didn't care. Either way, they were going at it. Elbows crunched noses, arms got dragged behind them. I heard cracking noises that sounded like bones were breaking. I shuddered.

What I saw terrified me.

Dylan, Ryan, Noah, Jonas, and Oskar all just watched calmly as Matthias and my brother fought. And Rafe was right. Matthias looked like this was a good time. The problem was so did Rafe. Their expressions were identical as they fought. With a flurry of kicks, Rafe was pushed back toward me. Ryan and Dylan stepped in front to shield me, and I tried to see around their massive shoulders.

"Stop. Please, you'll hurt him. Rafe, I swear to God if you hurt Matthias..." I felt like a girl watching a schoolyard fight.

The two shifted again, prowling around each other, and finally Noah put up a hand. "Okay, that's enough Matthias. You got it out of your system. Anyone else have anything you need to say to Rafe?"

"I've got a bullet with his name on it," said Oskar.

A bullet?

Hell no.

It was one thing when Noah asked me to convince Rafe to talk to them. It was another thing if Rafe was going to get hurt. I shoved against Dylan, who I must have caught off guard because he actually shifted enough for me to get by. I stepped around him, sprinting to my brother before stepping directly in front of him.

"No. No one else I care about is going to get hurt tonight. So all of you put your guns down. Now!"

"Lucia, get away from him!" Noah reached out, as if he could pull me to safety even from a distance. But before he could move, I saw Rafe's arm come up.

And in the span of a few seconds, I went from peacemaker to hostage.

———

Noah

I stared at the man who had been my mentor. It really was him.

I knew from the surveillance footage that the guy in Lucia's office looked like Rafe. But to see him fight, to see him holding a gun on the woman I loved, I knew it was him, the man I'd once called my brother.

Where the hell had he been? All this time—as the guilt had wracked me and the sorrow had torn Lucia apart—Rafe had been alive. But where? What the hell had happened?

"Rafe, you can understand my surprise in seeing you, you know, alive and shit."

"Sorry to disappoint you."

"Disappoint me?" I shifted on my feet. My eyes tracked the gun pressed to Lucia's side.

Would Rafe really do it? Would he shoot his own sister?

If he thinks he's saving her life. If he thinks he's saving her from you.

Just how fucked-in-the-head was Rafe right now?

"I mean, dude, you did me a favor. I carried a lot of guilt around. But you're alive and well, so now I can feel free to be my usual shameless self."

"Nothing's changed for you Noah, still too cocky. You still think you know everything."

"I will admit I did *not* know this. You can imagine my surprise when the friend I buried walked into his sister's office."

"How did you even know I was here?" Then he let out a dark chuckle. "Let me guess. You've got her wired?"

Lucia winced. "I'm not wearing a wire, Rafe."

His arm tightened against her throat. "Really? He hasn't given you anything new lately?"

Her hand flew to the necklace at her throat before her eyes met mine. "Noah?"

I cursed under my breath at the look of betrayal.

Rafe narrowed his gaze. "Lulu, you really are in way over your head. Which is why I'm getting you out of here."

I looked at my men. All of them with kill shots. None of them moving. Especially not Matthias. He had his killer face on. The one that remained detached and unemotional, and didn't give two shits. At a time like this, that was the face he needed. We'd all pay for it later though.

So I did the one thing that Rafe wouldn't expect. I reached around my waist, and pulled the Velcro for my bulletproof vest off. When I slid my arms through and tugged it over my head, I tossed it to the ground. And then I de-armed myself. Tossed the gun in the holster at my back, tossed my ankle piece, and the one I was holding. I also rid myself of the knives. *Almost* all of them anyway. That was saying something.

Rafe frowned. "What are you doing?"

"What was that thing that pirates used to do? When they wanted to have a conversation to see if it was really necessary to blow each other out of the water? I saw it in the *Pirates of the Caribbean* movie. Parlay?"

Rafe scoffed. "You think that's a real thing?"

I shrugged. "I'm not sure. But considering Lucia has put herself in harm's way to save your life, I figure you're worth having a conversation with before I let my guys kill you for real. And I'd rather you point that gun somewhere other than your sister. You want to shoot something, shoot me."

"My *sister* doesn't seem to know what's best for her. So if I have to convince her, then so be it."

From the periphery of my vision, I saw Jonas's eye twitch. And I prayed that twitch was a result of what the toxin had done and not an emotional response. If Jonas was going to get emotional, that meant trouble. Jonas was usually the coolheaded one. But when he had an emotional response, shit got out of control real quick. And I knew I wasn't the only one who loved Lucia. All the guys did. Any one of them would give their life to protect her. And I didn't need anyone getting all emotional and trigger-happy right now. We'd all come way too close to death lately.

"Even if it's not a real thing, it's got to be worth a shot. No one's dying today, Rafe. You seem to have a problem with me. And I get that."

Rafe shrugged "Well, you *did* shoot me dead."

"Is that how you remember it? I seem to remember you jumped in front of my bullet."

"Oh, Noah. Semantics. Either way, you shot me. Period."

"Yeah, about that, Rafe. We're even. Gotta say, seeing you back like this makes me real paranoid. Care to explain what the hell's going on?"

"What's going on is I'm trying to keep my sister alive."

"Okay, I feel like you're being deliberately obtuse, and you're missing the irony, seeing as you have a gun on her. I'll break it down. Who the hell do you work for?"

There was a long pause. Lucia slowly rotated in her brother's hold, giving her back to me. "It's a fair question, Rafe. One both Noah and I deserve the answer to."

Rafe sighed then clenched his jaw, but he didn't holster his weapon. "I work for the FBI. I've been an undercover agent for the past eleven years."

What the fuck? That was not what I was expecting. "So what, ORUS was doing some sort of exchange program?"

Rafe shook his head. "No. For years, ORUS was the government's dirty little secret. The group to do the kind of wet work even the CIA wasn't going to do. The government sent ORUS into the worst places. Gave them the hardest targets. And we got the job done. But at some point, someone in ORUS started making their own targets. When the Feds got wind of it, they needed a young recruit, someone to go in and infiltrate. A deep, deep cover assignment. At the same time, it offered me the ability to stay close to home. All I had to do was be me."

Lucia shook her head, completely in disbelief. "That's not true. If you had been in the FBI, I would've known about it."

"No. You wouldn't. I was recruited during my junior year of college. My entire training was centered around breaking into cells like these. Exposing the traitors and moving on. I came by my position in ORUS the good old-fashioned way. I worked my way in. A little padding of my mercenary resume, and I was recruited, just like the Feds wanted me to be." He nodded at me. "I'd been there a year when they assigned you to me."

I shook my head. *No.* "There were jobs. We took jobs. No Fed would be able to do that."

"We all do what we need to do to survive. The hits that I took, the hits that I let you take, they were legitimate kills. The one time I stopped you, you were about to kill an undercover FBI agent. Even if you were none the wiser, I didn't want them to come after you."

So it had been deliberate. "You worked with him?"

Rafe nodded. "I was undercover with the Del Tino crime family. We shared a handler. About a year into my assignment, we realized that many of ORUS's assignments coincided with Del Tino hits. We were working both cases together when the job came in to take out a Del Tino lieutenant. Someone blew my cover and they sent you in to kill him."

My stomach churned.

Rafe continued. "When I found out they sent you to make the kill, I couldn't let that happen; for your sake *and* mine. Because if you'd done it, they would've hung you out to dry. It was a set up. So I took the hit."

The pent-up fury, grief, and anger from the last six years spilled forth. "You let us think you were dead. You let *her* think you were dead. Just so you could play undercover. What happened to the man I knew?"

Rafe shook his head. "You didn't know me. Just like I didn't know you. I thought after you murdered your mentor, you would be out of ORUS. But instead you're still doing their bidding."

"No. I left. After what happened to you, I couldn't stomach it. I couldn't sleep at night. So I left." I inclined my head toward Matthias. "Took him with me."

Rafe's brows drew up. "Orion allowed that?"

I shrugged. "He didn't have much of a choice. I don't work for them anymore."

Rafe released the safety of his gun. "And here is where we reach an impasse. Because I know for a fact that you're in touch with Phoenix."

"He called, warning me about the hit on your sister. That's it. As far as Phoenix is concerned, ORUS are still the good guys. He doesn't know what they are. Either that or he thinks it's too late to get out."

Rafe scowled. "No. I know you're still in."

Lucia spoke up. "Rafe, I told you. He isn't lying. He's been out."

For the first time, I saw hints of my former mentor.

"The kind of surveillance you had at Lucia's place, I would have sworn you were still inside. I knew I had to get her away from you."

"I only added that extra security because they were coming for her. What was I supposed to do? Watch them kill the woman I love? Never going to happen."

Rafe stared at him. "You almost sound like you mean that."

I slid a glance to Lucia. "I do mean that."

Lucia reached a hand out for her brother's gun. "Rafe, we have to start trusting each other at some point. We've all lied. All hurt each other. It has to stop. Because we're fighting the wrong people. The enemy of my enemy is my friend, right? These people will keep coming for me. We need to work together."

Rafe squared his shoulders. "I'm your brother. I'll protect you."

I stepped forward. "She's mine. *I* protect her."

Lucia just rolled her eyes. "You two can stop posturing and marking your territory. I'm not having it. Right now we need solutions. If you're down for solutions, great. If not, we need to go."

I slid a glance to Rafe. "Maybe it is time to call a truce. We'll sort everything out as we go." I held out my hand.

For a long moment, I was pretty sure Rafe wouldn't take it. Then my once-mentor looked between me and Lucia and slowly took my hand.

CHAPTER FORTY-THREE

Lucia

I hadn't thought a truce meant we'd all be friends, but I hadn't expected it to feel as dangerous as when we all had guns on each other either. I glanced around the living room of Blake Securities' new office with trepidation. Rafe stood on one side with me and JJ while Noah and the rest of the guys stood on the other. When I caught JJ's eye, she tried to smile but it came out more like a grimace.

I'm sorry, I mouthed. Once we'd decided we would talk, Noah had insisted that everyone be present. Apparently he didn't trust anyone to leave and possibly inform anyone else of our whereabouts. He'd loaded me and JJ in the van with him and Matthias and we'd all rode over in silence. I hadn't seen Rafe get out of a car but he'd ended up in the garage with us when we arrived. Clearly my brother had the silent but deadly ninja thing down pat.

"So maybe we should start with the most important thing," Noah began when no one else seemed inclined to speak. "Someone is trying to kill Lucia and you claim it isn't you."

Rafe glowered. "Of course it's not me. I thought it was you. I've been trying to get her away from you to keep her safe."

"I've spent the last six years trying to keep Lucia safe in your memory. Why would I kill her now?"

"How the hell should I know? Orders. Greed. Because you're a sonofabitch." Rafe crossed his arms.

"I am but she makes me better," Noah countered.

I softened hearing Noah's gruffly muttered declaration of love. With a man like him, this was the equivalent of him taking out a billboard to announce it to the whole city. JJ nudged me in the side with her elbow and I finally let go of the smile I'd been holding back.

"God, this is ridiculous. You've got my baby sister shacked up here with you and smiling like some lovesick airhead."

"Hey, that is unnecessary," JJ cut in.

Jonas glared at her. "Maybe don't antagonize the psycho who could decide to switch sides and kill us all at any moment, hmm?"

"Hey, he wasn't gunning for me, big guy. Maybe Lucia and I should just step aside and let you all fight it out."

Jonas looked like he wanted to say something else but I held up a hand to stop the conversation.

"This isn't helping anything. None of this stuff really matters. I don't believe that my brother was gone for years only to come back to kill me. That doesn't make any sense."

Rafe smiled at me. "Glad to see you haven't completely lost your mind lately."

"Oh no. You don't get off so easily," I jabbed him in the chest with my finger. JJ's gasp would have been funny in any other situation. We were all treating Rafe like a ticking time bomb, but once it had sunk in that it was truly Rafe, my big brother, my defender, I wasn't afraid of him.

How could I be afraid of him when I remembered him holding me after I had a nightmare? Rafe was the one who'd told me not to let mean girls or clueless boys get me down. He'd told me that I was special and that I could be a fashion designer if I wanted. That I could do anything.

And I'd known it was true because I'd have my big brother helping me no matter what.

"You don't get to just show up out of nowhere and pretend like nothing has happened. You died, Rafe." My voice broke slightly on the last word, and for the first time I saw a crack in his stark exterior and a little bit of the brother I remembered peeked through.

With a muffled curse, he grabbed me. Although I heard Noah and the guys shouting, I didn't care. I clung to him just like I had when I was a little girl. And when his hand landed on the back of my head, the heavy weight of it both familiar and foreign, it felt like my world was breaking apart.

"I never should have left you. Should have taken you and Nonna with me, we could have run together." Rafe sounded almost as tortured as I felt.

"Why didn't you? You just left us. How could you do that?"

"I didn't want that life for you, Lulu. Never that. You deserved so much more. I thought I could watch over you from afar and then you could have all the things you'd dreamed about. Going to design school and having your own fashion company. I wanted that for you."

I sobbed against his neck, not even listening at this point. I heard what he was saying, but didn't he know those things hadn't mattered once he'd gone? I'd rather have had my beloved brother a million times over than anything else.

"Don't leave again. Promise me."

When I pulled back, I was shocked as hell to see tears on my brother's face as well. He blew out a breath before glancing over at the others. I turned too and found the whole group staring at us. Noah didn't exactly look happy and I knew there would be a lecture coming later about not trusting Rafe so easily, but I didn't care.

I had my brother back.

"I'm not leaving this time, I promise. I'm going to find a way to end this thing for good. It's the only way you'll be safe."

Noah finally spoke up. "Any ideas about how to do that?"

"A few. Are you going to trust me to execute without slipping a knife in your back?"

I tensed in his arms, and Rafe glanced down with a slightly annoyed look on his face. It was so him, so pre-tragedy Rafe, that despite the seriousness of the situation I laughed.

"Threats of violence make you laugh now? Maybe you have been good for her." Rafe glanced over at Noah, and after the longest, tensest pause ever, extended his hand.

I could almost feel everyone else in the group let out a collective sigh of relief. The men might not like each other or trust each other but they'd work together. For now.

"I don't think there's any doubt that Lucia is the one who has been good for me," Noah said as he accepted the handshake.

Rafe smiled again but this time, it looked predatory. "Finally something we can agree on. Now let's get to work."

Noah

I watched Rafe leave with a sinking feeling. Correction, I watched *Lucia* watch Rafe leave with a sinking feeling. Her eyes followed her brother's form as if she was afraid she'd never see him again. A valid fear, all things considered.

"My brother's really alive," she whispered.

I wasn't sure if she knew she'd spoken aloud, but I'd had just about enough of talking about Rafe. It was so odd to go from thinking of him as a friend and mentor to a potential enemy, but there was no other option to consider when Lucia's life was on the line.

I believed Rafe when he said he hadn't been trying to hurt her. My only concern at this point was whether Rafe might put Lucia in danger inadvertently trying to achieve his goal. Whatever that was. We'd hashed out quite a bit but the one thing Rafe had made sure to avoid was his current status; if he was still undercover with the FBI, what was he working on and did it relate to ORUS in any way? So many questions and Rafe had always been a secretive bastard. We wouldn't get anything out of him unless he wanted us to.

However, there was one thing I knew for sure; Rafe loved Lucia. People changed, sure, but not that much. The old Rafe had structured his entire world around the little sister he loved more than his own heartbeat. Six years wouldn't change that.

"Yes, he is. And we're going to figure this all out. Rafe will work on his contacts and we'll continue to do everything we can to keep you safe. I might be out of ORUS but that doesn't mean we don't still have our ways of keeping tabs on them."

Lucia leaned against my chest, taking me by surprise. She'd been standoffish since we'd gotten home. She was annoyed that I'd made her wear the wire and then even more annoyed that I'd used it to ambush her brother. But this one simple action showed that all was right in our world. Or it would be.

Eventually.

"Promise you'll be careful. I made Rafe promise not to leave again but I need you to do the same thing. Despite what you think, I need you just as much. When Rafe died ... when we thought he'd died, it was the worst pain I could imagine. But I survived."

She stood back and looked me in the eye as she spoke and I had never been more fucking proud of her. This was no scared little girl; my princess was a survivor. Beautiful, strong and stubborn as hell. God, I loved her. She put her hands on my face, bringing my attention back to her words.

"I survived because I had you. You were the one who kept me anchored. That's always been you, my port in the storm. But if anything ever happened to you, I don't think I'd survive it."

Just like that she fucking slayed me, absolutely tore my heart out with her sweet words and those big, beautiful eyes that saw straight through to my soul. This woman was my everything and for her, I'd do the impossible. I, Noah no-name Blake, who'd always been only two steps ahead of a bullet at any time, would live forever. I'd cheat the Reaper; I'd say however many Hail Marys it took; but I wasn't leaving Lucia alone in this world.

There were going to be quite a few things I'd have to accomplish to give her that peace of mind but somehow, I'd make it happen.

"Nothing is going to happen to any of us. I'll make sure of it."

Lucia didn't look convinced but she didn't press the issue. Instead she wrapped her arms around me in a quick hug and then glanced behind her where JJ was making uncomfortable conversation with Jonas.

"Now I need to have a long overdue conversation with my best friend. I think she deserves some explanations after being held against her will for the past hour."

I observed the body language going on between Jonas and JJ. They both looked pissed but ... intrigued. Oh no. The last thing I needed was a member of my team getting freaky with Lucia's best friend. I'd be right in the middle of the drama if anything went wrong, and I had no patience for that. I made a mental note to tell Jonas to sniff elsewhere as soon as I could get him alone.

"Good luck with that," I said finally.

While Lucia walked over to talk to her friend, Matthias approached with a smug look on his face. I had only seen that look a few times, so whatever the kid wanted to tell me was probably going to be good.

"Why do you look like you just got finished creating the perfect computer wife?"

Matthias scowled. "I have good news, actually."

"You put a tracker on Rafe?"

"No. I wish. None of us can get close enough to the bastard to even try that." Matthias touched his jaw absently, probably remembering what happened the first time he'd tried. "I was able to access information from the time period in question."

"Do I even want to know how many laws you broke to do that?"

"Not really. Anyway, everything supports Rafe's story. All signs point to him being an agent, although I can't tell which agency. Maybe CIA?"

Finally something was going our way. I took a deep breath. I'd made promises to Lucia. But even though she'd be pissed if she found out I was investigating her brother, it was necessary. I would rather have her angry than hurt. Besides, hopefully she'd never have to know. As long as Rafe was telling us the truth, I was happy to work with him if it meant Lucia was protected.

"At least he was honest about that," I mumbled.

Matthias laughed. "You know, as weird as this is going to sound, it was kind of nice to actually talk to him when he *wasn't* trying to kill me. The dude is a beast with the hand to hand. I've never seen anyone move so fast."

I laughed, too. After all the tension lately, it was good to have something to smile about again. Only Matthias would think it was fun to talk to a guy who'd beaten him to hell.

"He was a legend in ORUS. Even if I'd been paired with him for twenty years I don't think I could have learned everything he had to teach."

"Well, now you can. Seems like everyone's getting a do-over, huh?" With those words of wisdom, Matthias walked off, leaving me thinking about possibilities.

CHAPTER FORTY-FOUR

Lucia

"Let me guess, you're mad."

I turned to Noah and shrugged. "Oh, you think so?" I unhooked my earrings and slid them into my jewelry box before turning to face him. "First, you had me wired and I didn't know it."

"Lucia, you agreed to wear a wire."

"Yes. I did. But I thought I would have a say when that was happening." I unhooked my necklace and stared at it for a moment, then sighed. "This has a GPS tracker and a transmitter?"

At least, he had the good grace to look sheepish. "Look, once you said you were okay with wearing a wire, I had that made. I would've loved to give you advance warning, but there wasn't going to be time. We had no way of knowing when Rafe was going to try and find you."

"So you thought he'd try on my birthday?"

Noah shrugged. "Well, before he died, he never missed one. Your whole family made birthdays a big deal. Plus, the club was crowded enough, had multiple exits, and is pretty hard to defend. If I were him, and I wanted to make a play for you, I would've chosen a place like that. So, sorry but it needed to be this way."

I planted my hands on my hips. "Fair enough. I get why you couldn't wire me up the traditional way. But that doesn't explain why you didn't tell me. You gave me a gift. At least what I thought was a gift."

He frowned. "I'm sorry. I figured if you knew you would inadvertently draw attention to it. It's not like you're trained for these types of situations. People telegraph all kinds of things they don't mean to. It was easier not to tell you."

I threw up my arms. "This is what I mean, Noah. We have had this conversation a million times. But you keep making decisions without consulting me. You don't give me the opportunity to do things on my own. To figure it out. It's like you don't trust me. That hurts."

"Lulu, I trust you with my life. Yes, I can certainly do better. Yes, I need to figure this shit out. There are women I've dated for covers, there are women who were convenient, but I've never had anybody love me before. I have no idea what I'm doing."

The honesty in his eyes was my undoing. I didn't want to just let it go, but I knew how hard this was for him. "Well, trust is part of being with someone. We need to be partners. I need to know that you're going to be honest with me."

"Can you maybe trust that if I do, there's a reason behind it? And not assume that I don't believe in you or that I'm just trying to fuck with you, or make your life more difficult? Or treat you like a child?"

I opened my mouth to retort, but he had a point. He was right. We'd had that dynamic for so long, I also didn't know how to deal with him in the context of a relationship. "Okay, I can try to do that. We've just had a certain dynamic for a very long time."

He nodded. "Back then, my only job was to protect you. Not protect your feelings, not explain things to you, or check with you. But then, when everything started, that shifted. And it's hard for me to adjust. I'm sorry. I'll work harder on that."

I licked my lips, and then nodded. "I'm sorry too. Tonight was like exposing a raw wound."

"Yeah, tell me about. It was one thing to see him in video footage, but it was another thing entirely to see him in the flesh. After all this time. That's going to take a long time to get used to."

I chewed my bottom lip. "Do you really think he would've shot me?"

Noah laughed. "Absolutely. Somewhere nonlethal, probably more like a graze really. But it would've hurt, and you would've done what he wanted."

I winced. "My own brother would have shot me?"

Noah strode over and covered my hand with his. "He would've done it to protect you. Hell, I would've done it to protect you. If I could've shot you to get you out of the way, so that you didn't risk your life for him, I would've done it."

I lifted my eyes to meet his gaze. "Do not put me in the middle, Noah. Don't make me choose between you and Rafe. I can't do it. I love you both."

Noah's jaw worked. "You mean like he did with you?"

I jutted my chin out. "And I chose you. I wasn't willing to leave you. I'm not willing to let anyone hurt him. Nor am I willing to let him hurt anyone else anymore. We're going to have to work together."

Noah nodded and stroked my cheek gently with his thumb. "Lucia, I promise you no one's going to get hurt. Except for the people that deserve it. We're on the same side. And just so we're clear, you're not the only one who missed him. He was my family, too."

My eyes stung and I rapidly blinked back the tears. "I know. You're okay though?"

"Yeah, I'm okay. But ..." He inched closer and slid his arms around my lower back. "I have some ideas on how you can help me feel better."

I couldn't help the giggle. "Why do I get the impression that if you had your way you'd forever keep me in this room naked?"

"Because that's a fabulous idea."

———

Noah wasted no time getting me naked. But when had Noah ever wasted time? Hell, half the time he didn't bother to take all our clothes off first.

His kiss was searing. His expert tongue slid into my mouth, claiming me and with each stroke making me burn. His big hands slid over my heated flesh and I sizzled with each caress.

Would I ever get enough of this?

I rocked my hips upward and reached for him, sliding my fingers though his hair. "Please hurry."

Noah understood the art of seduction. Knew how to make me want. Knew the buttons to push to make me scream. Or to bring me so close and hold off just enough so I'd hang on the precipice of need. It was enough to make me crazy. Enough to make me beg for what I needed. I was addicted to him. There was no way this would ever be enough.

He had me just where he wanted me. He had my tank off in seconds, the silky material falling to the floor. We both kicked off our shoes. And then the race was on to see who could get naked the fastest.

Noah, of course, didn't have to contend with a pesky bra. But obviously he was more than ready and willing to help me with that.

As he slid the lace from my skin, his fingertips grazed the flesh slightly, making me need him, making me want to beg for his mouth on me. I couldn't help the whimper that escaped.

He picked me up, carrying me to the bed, his lips on mine. But while I was in a hurry, Noah ... was not. He was in the mood to tease. He kissed down my sternum, refusing to kiss me just where I needed. Refusing to give me what I wanted.

With a frustrated growl, I narrowed my gaze at him.

He chuckled. "Something you need, princess? Because I was in the mood to take my time with you. And we're just getting started."

"Damn it, Noah. You know what I want. Why are you torturing me?"

"Don't worry. I'll get there," Noah said with a chuckle.

He grazed along the column of my throat even as his hips rocked into mine, pressing gently. Teasing me with the ridge of his erection.

"Just so you know, I'm going to use my fingers. I'll find your G-spot and touch it just right. Just enough to make you come again. I know you'll be sensitive, but it's going to feel so good."

He sped up his movements, his hips rolling into mine. I rose to meet him, arching my back, begging him to rub where I needed. His lips skimmed over my skin, across my collarbone to my breast. His words alone were driving me nuts. But coupled with his lips, his hands intertwined with mine, I was ready to explode.

His lips brushed my nipple ever so slightly. The motion sent a spear of need directly to my core. Next, he used just his teeth, raking gently. He was careful to keep his full weight off of me. His teeth felt so good and I wondered if it was possible to die from anticipation.

When he laved my distended nipple with his tongue and then wrapped his lips around me, I held on for my life. With tug after deep tug, he sucked on me. It didn't take much, I was so tightly wound. But it was the secondary pleasure when he teased my other nipple with his thumb that sent me over the edge. I came hard and fast, my whole body shaking.

"Noah. Oh my God."

"That's one," he announced with a satisfied grin.

He kissed down my thighs and calves before pulling back to snag a condom out of his wallet. I watched with avid interest as he sheathed himself before settling between my legs.

"Look at me," he growled.

As if I could look anywhere else. Even though I felt like a limp noodle, I still wanted more.

One hand teasing the hair at his nape, the other tracing his pecs, I canted my hips up. "Noah, hurry."

I could see the tension in him as his arms shook. He was having a hard time with control. Would talking to him drive him as crazy as it drove me? He lined his erection up with my opening and I whispered, "I want to know what this feels like bare. Just you and me, nothing between us. Do you think you'll like that?"

He stared down at me, lips slightly parted. "What?"

"It would be a first. I want to know what it feels like to have you come inside me."

He rocked into me in one deep stroke, my name on his tongue. He cursed low and deep, a long drawn out "*Fuuuuck.*"

Noah slid in and retreated, adjusting our position so I sat on his lap. Oh yes, it was so deep like this. Our movements were a frenzy of skin, lips and hands. There wasn't a part of him he didn't touch me with. Body and soul.

My second orgasm was stronger than the first but with a slow build. Once the fire took hold, there was no stopping it and I exploded in his arms. Noah was right behind me. His hips bucked as he came, gripping my ass tight as his muscles corded and his teeth clenched. I wrapped my arms around him, holding tight.

He was mine.

CHAPTER FORTY-FIVE

Noah

The next morning, I set out everything I needed to cook the perfect birthday breakfast. Lucia hadn't even seemed angry that her birthday plans had been so fucked, but I'd apologized anyway. I never wanted to take her for granted or assume that she'd forgive me when I messed up. I'd woken up early and spent a long time just watching her sleep. There in the quiet dark I'd been happier than I knew it was possible to be and it hit me.

This was it.

This was the dream.

I had everything that some men spent their whole lives searching for.

Were things perfect? Not by a long shot. I scowled, remembering that at this very moment ORUS was probably reassigning Lucia's hit contract to another operative. But with Rafe working on our side, I was confident we could keep her safe until we found a way to neutralize ORUS for good.

It was probably hubris to assume I could handle the situation so easily but I'd done it once before. Everyone had told me getting out was impossible but I'd done it. Not only had I negotiated release for myself, I'd also managed to finagle Matthias's freedom in the process. As I knew from that experience it was all about planning and amassing information to use against the powers that be. I'd gathered enough intel to threaten ORUS with exposure, and they'd had little choice but to allow me my freedom.

Somehow, some way, I'd do the same thing for Lucia.

I hummed to myself as the bacon sizzled in the pan next to me while I scrambled the eggs. Cooking wasn't something I was particularly good at, but this morning I paid extra attention to every step. Yesterday hadn't exactly been the ideal birthday celebration but I was going to make up for that today. Lucia deserved the absolute best.

"Look at the little man, making breakfast for the lady of the house."

I startled at the sound of Rafe's voice behind me. "What the fuck? How the hell did you get in here?"

Matthias appeared behind me looking like he'd seen a ghost. He glanced between me and Rafe with trepidation. "I don't know what happened. He didn't show up on any of the cameras."

I hissed when I noticed the eggs had burned slightly. With a flick of my wrist, I turned off the burner. Hopefully I could just discard the edges and wouldn't have to start over.

"It's fine, Matthias. I'm pretty convinced at this point that Rafe is actually a ghost sent here to torment us for our many sins."

The kid left muttering something about firewalls, and I turned my attention back to breakfast. I kept Rafe in the periphery of my vision at all times. It was Rafe and at one time I'd trusted him with my life, but a lot had happened since he'd been gone. For years, I had trusted no one. It was hard to change six years of habit.

"I'm making breakfast for Lucia. Her birthday celebration got a little fucked by all this stuff, and she deserves better. She deserves everything. And we're all going to make sure she gets it."

Hopefully my pointed look conveyed the message that Rafe had better not do anything to interfere with Lucia's happiness.

For a long moment we stared each other down, each gauging the other's sincerity and intentions, until finally Rafe grinned.

"I always knew you had a thing for her."

It was so unexpected to see that smile after so long that I turned away and cleared my throat. Fuck, I'd missed the bastard.

"You wouldn't rather see her with someone else? Someone ... better?"

I would probably later be annoyed that I'd asked the question. The last thing I wanted to do was telegraph my insecurity to Rafe. If you'd asked me a few days ago whether I thought Rafe would have approved, I wouldn't have thought I cared so much.

But it mattered ... a hell of a lot.

Rafe shrugged. "What, like an accountant or something? Some guy with good benefits who'll come home by six o'clock every night?"

"Yeah, someone like that."

"The kind of guy who won't understand what she's been through, who'll have a mid-life crisis at forty and cheat on her with some bitch who works in his office? A guy who can't protect her if we can't get this shit with ORUS settled?"

I swallowed. "I guess there's no normal for her after all this. She deserves so much more."

"She deserves a guy who'd kill for her."

I looked up in surprise at the approval in Rafe's voice.

"Don't look so surprised. I trained you; I'm a little biased. Besides, I don't have to worry about a mid-life crisis with you. Guys like us have been in crisis our whole lives. We've already learned how to deal with our shit."

I chuckled as I arranged a plate for us to share. Lots of eggs, four strips of bacon, fruit on the side. I poured a cup of coffee and then after a moment of hesitation poured another one for Rafe. When I slid it across the counter, the other man took it gratefully. We weren't one big happy family quite yet but it was a start.

"I'll go wake her up and then let her know you're here. She'll be really happy."

I picked up the tray and walked down the hall toward the bedroom. I'd planned to keep her in bed all morning but seeing her brother would be the best birthday present she could ask for.

I set the tray next to her on the bed and then peppered her face with soft kisses. She rolled over and then blinked sleepily. Once she woke up, she wrapped her arms around my neck and pulled me down until I fell laughing on top of her.

After several slow, teasing kisses, Lucia glanced over at the tray on the other side of the bed. "You made me breakfast? That's so sweet."

"Well, things didn't go as planned yesterday so I wanted a do-over. Happy birthday, princess."

She giggled and reached over to snag a piece of bacon. "I like do-overs. And I love bacon. But even I don't think I can eat all of this."

"Oh, don't worry. I plan to help you." I took a bite of the bacon she held out to me. Her soft laughter warmed me all over.

After we'd worked our way through most of the plate, I put the tray on the night table.

"We're going to Nonna's later for dinner but right now, I have a surprise for you. So you'll need to get dressed, which makes me wonder why I'm giving you this gift since I'd prefer you take clothes off instead of put them on."

Lucia squealed and shot off the bed. I watched in amusement as she struggled to get into the jeans she'd discarded beside the bed the night before. She turned in a circle looking for a shirt before giving up and getting one from the dresser.

"I'm ready. Let's go!"

I chuckled. "I forgot how much you love surprises. You're like a little kid at Christmas."

"Hurry up!" Lucia yanked at my hand playfully before racing out the door. I knew the exact moment when she found her brother because she squealed again.

When I found them in the living room, Lucia was wrapped up in Rafe's arms. Our eyes met over her brother's shoulder and even from across the room I could read the words she mouthed.

Thank you.

––––––

Lucia

I glanced over at my brother for the millionth time and smiled. I looked away before he caught me staring again. He was so different now, hard and remote in a lot of ways but underneath all that, I could still feel my Rafe, the one who'd make silly faces to see me smile or take me to Coney Island to cheer me up.

I hadn't really believed it before; it had seemed like a dangerous thing to trust that my brother was really back in my life. But he was here, standing in the living room with all my nearest and dearest looking like he belonged. Even Oskar had stopped giving him the hairy eyeball, although he did rub his shoulder absently every time Rafe was near.

It was going to take time, I thought. They wouldn't adjust to the new way of things overnight, but I was starting to believe that I could really have it all. Noah, my friends and Rafe, all a part of my life. It was almost like things were going back to the way they would have been if that horrible day six years ago had never happened.

Then I thought about the destruction at Noah's old office, being terrorized in my apartment and poor Brent, who'd never done anything but be a nice guy. No, I could never forget about everything that had happened but maybe we could finally start fresh.

I closed my eyes and took a deep breath. This was the first day of my new life and I didn't want to waste a moment.

"Happy Birthday to You! Happy Birthday to You!"

I turned to find the entire group standing around Noah in a loose semi-circle while he held a cake blazing with candles. JJ appeared at my side looking harried but gorgeous as always in skinny jeans and stilettos that looked sharp enough to cut glass.

"Sorry I'm late! Noah just told me we were celebrating this morning."

I hugged her close. "It's no problem. Help me blow out the candles?"

After everyone finished the song, we leaned over together and blew out all the candles amid the cheers and shouts of the group. Noah kissed me on the forehead.

"Did you make your wish?" The husky, intimate tone of his voice made me wish I'd taken him up on his offer of staying in bed this morning.

"I don't need wishes. I already have everything I want," I murmured back.

"God, you two need to get a room," JJ interrupted but she was smiling when she said it. It still made me blush though.

"Sorry about her, Boss," Jonas said, coming to stand next to Noah. "I would have left her in the hallway but I didn't want the neighbors to complain about the barking."

JJ swiped at him, but he moved so her fist just barely glanced off his back. He retreated to the kitchen and JJ crossed her arms, probably trying to restrain the urge to chase him down and punch him again.

Noah tried to stifle his laughter but the twinkle in his eye gave him away.

"Behave," I whispered before turning to JJ. "Thanks for coming. If I'm getting a do-over, I can't do it without my best friend."

JJ poked out her tongue. "That's what I told Captain America over there when he tried to make me wait until you guys were done singing 'Happy Birthday.'"

Jonas scowled at JJ, even though I had no idea how he'd heard our conversation from where he was standing. Unless he could read lips. Although he would have to be watching us pretty closely for that. I looked between the two of them as the idea took root.

"Jonas seems to annoy you a lot lately, huh?"

"Not really. He just thinks he knows everything. All those steroids are impacting his brain."

I decided to save my suspicions for later. Although the sparks coming from the two weren't easy to ignore, I knew better than anyone that when a man annoyed and excited you like that, it was something you had to figure out on your own.

While Noah cut pieces of cake for everyone, Rafe approached.

"Um, I'll just go see if Noah needs any help." JJ beat a hasty retreat. I wouldn't have been surprised to see skid marks where she'd been standing.

"You make my friends nervous."

"I make everyone nervous. Occupational hazard," Rafe replied easily.

He seemed so at ease with what his life had become but I couldn't help wondering how he'd come to terms with it. Had he ever wanted something different? Perhaps he'd once had dreams of being a chef or an artist. Or maybe opening a flower shop. The idea of my ultra masculine brother surrounded by delicate blooms made me smile.

Rafe tipped his head. "What?"

"Just wondering if you ever wished your life could have been different. Everyone seems so focused on making sure that I'm safe and happy, but what about you? I want you to be happy, too."

He turned and looked at the crowd of people in the kitchen. Oskar and Jonas were stuffing their faces with cake. Matthias stood in the background observing them all like he expected the cake to blow up at any moment. Noah and JJ were deep in conversation about something.

I wasn't sure what Rafe saw when looking at them but I saw safety, happiness and love. Did he have those things in his life?

"From the moment our parents died, our life was set to go down a certain path. Poor, young and with limited resources, there weren't too many ways my life could have gone. I knew that eventually I would have to turn to a life of crime to earn enough money to keep you and Nonna safe in our neighborhood. I never expected to have anything more than that."

His answer made me sad. "You deserve to be happy, Rafe."

"I am. My time in ORUS was fucked up, but I'll never regret the way it happened. They gave me skills I couldn't have learned anywhere else. They gave me the skills to protect the only people that mattered to me."

"I wish I could take care of you, too."

He drew in a breath and I was surprised to see something that looked like tenderness in his eyes. "You do take care of me, Lu. If it wasn't for you, I would have gone down an entirely different path. And I think you do the same for Noah."

"You're really okay about ... you know, about us being together?" No matter how old I got, I would never be blasé talking about sex to my big brother.

Rafe pulled me close. "He's been in love with you for years."

I pulled back in surprise. "What? He didn't even know I was alive back then. I had such a crush on him. I would have known if he felt the same way."

Rafe chuckled. "He didn't want you to know. Men like us are afraid to believe in good things. He loved you then, and he loves you now. Plus, I know he'll take care of you. Promise me something."

"Anything."

"Take care of him, too."

I grinned up at him. "I can do that."

CHAPTER FORTY-SIX

Lucia

That evening was spent in a haze of singing, delicious home-cooked food and the warmth of being in my childhood home. Nonna had outdone herself, making one of my favorites, gnocchi that could melt in your mouth with a special pesto made from a secret family recipe that she guarded fiercely. I figured I wouldn't know exactly what was in it until she whispered it to me from her deathbed.

Hopefully that wouldn't be for another fifty years or so.

"Thank you for dinner, Nonna. And the cake." I hugged her and bent slightly so Nonna could kiss my forehead.

"Take care of yourself, *bambina*. You're all I have left. Well, you and Noah, of course." She included Noah in the statement with a soft smile.

Guilt made my stomach churn. Once I'd processed the knowledge that my brother was really alive, I'd been thrilled at the idea of telling my grandmother our prayers had been heard. But Rafe had quickly nixed that plan. According to him, it still wasn't safe for Nonna to know he was alive. He'd only come out of hiding because he'd believed me to be in danger.

"I love you, Nonna. So much."

My grandmother's eyes lit up at the fierce declaration and she hugged me again before going inside and bolting the door as Noah always insisted she do.

I clutched the cake plate in my hands as we walked back to the car. It was a bitter pill to swallow that the only reason I had Rafe back in my life was because of whoever was trying to hurt me. But I had to have faith that Noah and Rafe could figure this whole thing out. Then Rafe could come out of hiding for real and Nonna would have her grandson back. It was almost too much to wish for but I figured why not? After all, the universe had answered my prayers once before.

As if he could sense my turbulent thoughts, Noah glanced over from the driver's seat. "How does it feel to officially be 21?"

"Pretty much the same, except when you drive me nuts, I can officially have a glass of wine. And now, you're less of a dirty old man, so that's a bonus."

Noah's brows snapped down. "I'm not old."

I couldn't help but laugh. "I mean, gosh, you're a whole five years older than me. Ancient. I think I'll upgrade you for some twenty-one-year-old drunken fraternity guy."

Noah laughed as he leaned over the center divide to give me a kiss. His tongue slid past my lips and into my mouth and immediately I was melting. Right into a puddle of hormones. Yeah, he had my number.

When he pulled back, his lips tipped up into a smile. "Yeah, good luck with that. You won't find anyone as sexy as me."

I carefully maneuvered the pound cake on my lap. "Careful. If you make me spill this cake, we'll both be a sticky mess."

His bark of laughter was sharp. And then I realized what I said. Noah gave me his characteristic wolfish, shameless grin. "I have all kinds of fun ways for us to become sticky messes."

I shook my head. "Noah Blake. You are incorrigible."

"Funny. I've heard that before."

I reached by my feet for the custard sauce that went with the cake and frowned. Where the hell did I put that? Crap. It was still in Nonna's house on the counter. "Noah, I need to go back in the house for the sauce."

Noah shook his head. "Stay here in the car. Lock the doors. I'll get it."

I shook my head and handed him the cake. "Don't be silly. We're literally ten feet from the front door. You're parked right in front of the house. You have perfect sight lines. I'm just going to run in and out. I'll be two seconds. Besides, I know you. You'll run in there, take a bite of something, and get distracted on your way out."

"I will not. And it's not safe."

"Noah, can you see who's coming down the street?"

His lips firmed. "Yes."

"Okay. Remember what we talked about. You will not be unreasonable. Right?"

The muscle in his jaw ticked, but I knew that I'd won. I shoved open the door. "I'll be right back."

To prove to him that I wasn't messing around, I sprinted to the front door, used my key and opened it. Jogging past the living room, I called to my grandmother. "Nonna, I forgot the sauce." But my grandmother was nowhere in the living room, the dining room, or the tiny kitchen. "Nonna?"

It was then that I saw the back door open. Had my grandmother run out with the garbage? No. Noah had taken the garbage out already, before we left.

My instincts said run. Every part of me wanted to run out front and call for Noah. Then I saw the smudge of blood on the doorframe, and another instinct took over. The one that wanted to protect. Protect the woman who'd given her whole life to raise me. I grabbed a knife out of the knife holder and ran out the back door.

I was met with pitch black. The back porch light was out. Or, someone had put it out. "Nonna? Are you back here?"

I wasn't sure why I was scared. There was no way into the backyard from any location. The back wall was far too high, and Noah had made sure there was glass and barbed wire over the top of it so no one would dare to climb over. The damn thing was twelve feet tall.

And then I saw it, as the moonlight glinted on a shard of glass. Blood. Oh God. Someone had climbed over. The blood on the doorjamb, it hadn't been Nonna's. I whipped around to run back into the house, mouth open ready to scream. And then someone clamped a hand over my mouth.

"For someone I didn't train myself, you are incredibly difficult to kill. One hit out on one little girl shouldn't be this much trouble."

The voice was low, icy. It sent a shudder through my body. Oh God. This was the guy. This was the guy who was trying to kill me.

"Of course, you have Leo watching out for you. And Perseus. But nearly a month after a hit was issued, you're still alive. How did you do it? How have you turned my own agents against me?"

"I don't know what you're talking about." I struggled in his arms, but he was too strong, overpowering my movements easily.

"Every agent that has tried to move against you has ended up dead and no one can figure out how. You may have convinced them that the ghost of Libra protects you but I know the truth. You're just a scared little girl and you'll bleed red just like any other."

As he talked, his grip on my mouth loosened just a little. My fingers curled around the knife I'd grabbed from the kitchen. He didn't realize I had it and that ignorance was probably my only advantage. The moment he gave me enough wiggle room, I opened my mouth and bit down.

His arm jerked. *Motherfucker.*

I didn't wait. With the knife firmly in my grip, I rotated my wrist and stabbed it backward. I didn't know what I'd hit. All I knew was I hit flesh. As he staggered back, I took off running.

"Noah! Noah! He's trying to —"

Even as my feet hit the back wooden steps, making a *clop clop clop* noise, Noah was charging through the kitchen at a dead run. Instinctively, I turned to the side, making myself as flat against the railing as possible. At his current velocity, he'd run right into me, and I would not survive that kind of hit.

I turned my head to look behind me. The man with the raspy voice was already attempting to make it around the front of the house.

"I stabbed him...somewhere. And bit him. He's bleeding. Did you see Nonna?"

As he ran by Noah yelled, "Nonna's safe. He had her tied up in the closet."

Noah didn't even bother with the stairs, just made the leap gracefully, smoothly, and was rounding the corner of the house in seconds. I shook, leaning against the railing. How could I have been so stupid? I should've listened to Noah and let him come in with me.

I ran back to the house and found my grandmother on the couch. Duct tape still hung from the side of her face as she rubbed her wrists.

"Nonna."

My grandmother sagged with relief. "Lucia, you're safe. Thank God. That horrible man. I hope Noah rips his balls off."

My mouth hung open at my grandmother's use of the word balls. Then her eyes shifted to Noah as he came through the back door.

"Lucia, I need you to get some of Nonna's things. She's coming with us."

I nodded. "Noah, I'm sorry. I should've—"

"Don't. Do not apologize. You did well out there. And I know the rules. I should've come in with you. Or come myself. Something."

"I thought it would be safe. That no one could get into the back. I can't believe he scaled the back wall."

Noah frowned but pulled me close. "That was Orion. He's the head of Orus and he will do absolutely anything he has to do to get the job done."

I shook in his arms. "Oh God. What are we going to do?"

Noah's voice was calm. "I'm going to kill him. Before he ever comes near you again."

His tone was so final, so sure. And I knew he meant it.

———

I was exhausted.

For the time being, we'd put Nonna in Matthias's room and Matthias on the couch. Noah had a place in upstate New York, in a little town called Hope. In the morning, he'd be sending my grandmother there with a friend of his to make sure she was safe. At least for the time being.

We'd both agreed not to tell her that Rafe was alive just yet. We needed to work all of it out first. Although, it killed me not to say anything.

Noah kissed my shoulder. "I know it's hard not to tell her. But that has to be his decision and in the way that he wants to do it."

"I know. But she deserves to know. That's her grandson. She thinks he's dead. I feel like I'm lying."

Noah shook his head. "Let's deal with one crisis at a time. Right now, you're safe. Nonna is safe. And shocker of shockers, so is Rafe."

"Speaking of my brother, has he called?"

Noah shook his head and pulled me to lie down in the bed next to him. "No. But I left a message about what happened. Told him to be on red alert."

This was hard. Too hard.

Noah's phone chimed with a series of beeps. "Speak of the devil."

I sat up. "What is that?"

Noah held up a finger and waited for another series of chimes. "It's Rafe."

A moment later, his phone rang, and Noah answered and put the phone on speaker. "I see old habits die hard."

"Since we've had some trouble, I figured it would be safer."

"That's the understatement of the century. We had some trouble tonight. Orion tried to grab Lucia."

"Motherfucker."

I spoke up. "Rafe, I'm safe. Okay?"

There was a moment of silence. And then my brother spoke. "Where?"

Noah pursed his lips but he still told the truth. "At Nonna's. He tried to take her right out of the backyard. She managed to stab him, so he's hurt."

There was another string of inventive curses from my brother. When he finally spoke, his voice was low. Deadly. "I will kill him."

"I'll fight you for the honor," Noah said. "But first we need to find him. I feel like I've only got half the picture here. I know who would've called in a hit on her, but that doesn't explain why Orion would take the job. That's never happened. At least not as long as I was in ORUS."

"Well, I might have the answer for that," Rafe said. "You know that shell corporation that Perseus is looking for?"

I frowned. "Perseus?"

"Perseus is Matthias's codename," Noah explained.

"Huh." I could only blink. "Okay, carry on."

"The kid has been digging deeper on that Del Tino property. Turns out when we looked even closer at that shell corporation, Holo-Corp, there was another owner. One with ties to cartels all over the world. I started digging through my old FBI case files and some things don't add up. Up until now, every hit we'd taken was essentially because Orion gave it to us. This hit in particular doesn't make sense.

Why would we take this kind of drastic action? They're in the wind. Someone poking around is a loose end, but the family doesn't have anything to lose. They wouldn't care if someone found out they owned that house at some point. But there is someone who would."

Noah frowned. "Who?"

"Think about it. The one person who has everything to lose. The one person who exposed himself tonight."

I wasn't getting it, but clearly Noah was because he stood.

"Fuck. Fuck, fuck, fuck."

Rafe laughed on the other line. "I see you've expanded your vocabulary. Very nice."

Noah ran his hands through his hair. "Orion. All this time. It's been him."

"Right now, that's where my research is pointing. I've gone back through all my old case files to right around the time that I joined. The time the Feds put me undercover, a few of those hits directly threatened ORUS. Yes, those targets were dangerous. Yes, lots of people would have been hurt, but their demise opened up specific strategic holes that ORUS could fill."

I didn't get any of this. "So what does this mean?"

Noah turned to me, his mouth grim. "This means we need to kill Orion. He's a threat to Lucia. We can't just let him live."

At his words, I sat up on the bed. In all the excitement, I hadn't had time to examine everything Orion had said to me. But now that I was looking back on it, none of it made much sense.

"He said something before I stabbed him. About how I'd turned his operatives against him. That no one would take the job."

Noah blinked. "He told you that?"

"Yes. That they were all scared of the *ghost of Libra*. What does that mean?"

On the other end of the line, Rafe chuckled. "Nothing. He's probably going senile."

Noah glanced over at me, the edges of his lips pulled up into a smirk. "So, *Libra*, you have no idea why every ORUS operative is suddenly scared to move against your sister?"

It was quiet. Then Rafe cleared his throat. "Maybe they saw something that changed their minds."

At my confused look, Noah reached over and squeezed my hand. I had so many questions but I wasn't sure if he'd answer them while Rafe was on the line.

"Hmm. Well, even before you died there were people who thought you weren't entirely human. Being a legend has its perks. If they can't get an operative to take the job, that gives us time to figure out what Orion is up to."

They talked quietly for a little bit longer before Noah hung up the phone. I leaned over and brushed a hand over the deep furrow in his brow.

"This is a good thing, right? If my brother has somehow scared them all off, it means I'm safe, right?"

He leaned forward, resting his head against mine. "For now. It's not a perfect ending. It's not tied up with a bow. But you'll be safe for a while."

As we sat there breathing together, I understood why he seemed so troubled. Noah definitely didn't think of himself as good but he'd wanted to be the hero for me. He'd always wanted that, to protect me and hand me everything I wanted on a silver platter. It had to be killing him that he couldn't do that now.

"Noah, you've done everything that anyone could do."

He turned his head, his lips brushing over my cheek. "I want to give you everything. You deserve so much more. You deserve happily ever after."

"Maybe there is no happily ever after," I whispered. "There's just happy right now."

His hand curled around the back of my neck. "Are you? Happy?"

I pulled him down until we fell back on the bed. The steady thump of his heartbeat beneath my ear was the most comforting sound in the world. This would be my life now, going to sleep and waking up with the man I loved. So I gave him my honest answer.

"I'm the luckiest girl in the world. I'm surrounded by an entire team of noble knights, protected by a ghost and the love of my life."

EPILOGUE

Noah

A gentle breeze sent the hair that I had neglected to get trimmed brushing over my forehead. The sky outside our rented hut on the beach was dotted with fluffy white clouds and reflected the color of the turquoise water. When I'd decided to take my lady on vacation, all I'd wanted was a chance to get her away from the stress and bad memories of the city. I couldn't have gotten a better escape.

Although it wasn't usually considered ideal to bring a group of your best friends along on a romantic getaway.

"I'm going to take a shower now that Matthias is done. Then we can go out to eat. I've been dreaming about that fried fish we had on the beach last night."

Lucia stood from her chair next to me where we'd been relaxing and taking in the view while the rest of the team took turns cleaning up. The guys had a hut next door but they still spent most of their time hanging around Lucia. Now that they'd gotten used to protecting her, I suspected they found it just as difficult to turn off their overprotective tendencies where she was concerned. I couldn't blame them for not being able to stay away.

I found her pretty irresistible as well.

"Want me to wash your back?" I wiggled my eyebrows when I said it mainly because it always made her laugh. The joke was on me because her pupils dilated slightly and the look she gave me could only be described as ... hungry.

"Later, once we're alone. Then I'll let you wash anything you want."

She left behind the scent of coconut oil and strawberries, which brought a smile to my face. Briefly, I considered the idea of not going back. Sure, she'd miss friends and family back in the city, but perhaps I could convince her it was worth it. We could travel the globe, beach-hopping, and then we'd always be one step ahead of ORUS.

"You look pretty relaxed for a guy with a target on his back," Matthias commented as he took the seat Lucia had vacated.

I glanced over at him. I was truly out of it if I hadn't heard Matthias approach.

"Not relaxed so much as resigned. Men like me don't get a happily ever after. I've always known that. But I'd hoped I could do better than that for Lucia."

Matthias nodded. "You know I've been trying to crack ORUS's internal security codes ever since we got out. It's some of the most sophisticated encryption in existence and almost impossible to crack unless you have someone on the inside."

"Is that right? Too bad we don't know anyone like that."

He grunted. "That's what I thought, too. Until last week."

"What happened last week?" I kept my voice steady and calm as if we were discussing something mundane like the weather. Any of the other tourists walking the beach would see nothing more exciting than two guys shooting the breeze and watching the ocean.

"A little bird dropped a piece of information in my lap last week that changed everything." Matthias rested his right foot casually on his left knee. "What would you do if you could find Orion?"

The air around us seemed to solidify and I had to concentrate to get my next breath in. Matthias was a straight shooter and not the type to engage in what-if games just for shits and giggles.

"Find him as in know his government identity?"

"Not just his government identity but his fucking street address where he lays his head every night. Where he puts out his trash every Thursday and plants pansies every spring."

I looked him straight in the eye. "I would kill him. Immediately and without hesitation."

Matthias nodded and for a few minutes we continued watching the water without conversation. Just when I thought I'd scream in frustration, Matthias leaned over and handed me a folded slip of paper.

"Don't say I never gave you anything."

Matthias stepped onto the sand and walked toward the ocean, the breeze lifting his dark hair. When he reached the water's edge, he dipped his bare feet in. Then he looked over his shoulder at me and waved.

I waved back.

———

It was all so simple.

A quiet suburban neighborhood. Upscale. If there were cars parked on the street, they were BMWs and Mercedes. A Range Rover here, an Audi there. It was the kind of place that a tech developer might live, or a stockbroker. Refined, elegant. It was not the kind of place people assumed an assassin would live.

I waited until I saw Orion's blond girlfriend climb into her car and drive down the street. I wanted to make sure she was gone and wouldn't be coming back for anything she might've left at the house.

At first, I'd been shocked to see the blonde walking around in the house through the windows. She'd been waiting on him. Taking care of him. Or maybe she wasn't his girlfriend at all. Maybe she was from a home health service, one where you could hire some hot girl to come and look after you. Generally, I'd call that an escort service, but I didn't judge.

I used Matthias's fancy tech toys to turn on the jammer. There'd be no calls out of Orion's house tonight.

Next order of business was to turn off the security system. That was more difficult, and required Matthias's help.

"Kid, you there?"

"I'm reading you loud and clear, Noah. Are you ready?"

"Yep, I'm here."

"Hold up the red remote to his lock and let me take care of the rest."

Since Orion had one of those smart houses, hacking would be

slightly easier. Although, since he would've added his own layer of security, I was ready for all kinds of special booby-traps. I wasn't really interested in Orion knowing I was coming for him.

"Okay, you should be all good."

Riding the razor's edge of anticipation and adrenaline, I tried the door. And sure enough, there was no alarm. And no sound, which suited me just fine.

I found Orion in the kitchen. The guy was cooking. As if he hadn't just tried to take out my girlfriend. The woman I loved. My reason for breathing.

"You know, I'm surprised to find that you cook. I assumed you would get one of those shitty meal delivery services."

Orion seemed completely unperturbed. Considering an ex-operative was standing in his home. With a gun at the ready.

"Noah, I wondered when I'd see you again. I am a little surprised to find you in my home, unannounced, but it's not like me to be a rude host. Would you like a drink?"

"No, I think I'll pass. What I want is the code generator and the sat phone."

Orion laughed. "What do you want those for? Only the director of ORUS has those. You know the rules. And there is no way you're making it past biometric scans to steal it."

I just gave him a slight smile. "So how long?"

Orion didn't play coy. "Since I became Orion. I've always had my own little side projects. I started to see the real advantage of taking out certain players years ago. Before Libra had to go and get involved. But then, he lost his life for that."

"I actually believed in what ORUS stood for. You had us all believing."

"That's because I'm a leader. You think you can run ORUS? You haven't got what it takes. You've gone soft. The fact that I could even get to Lucia tells me you don't deserve this."

Orion might think that I was rusty, but my reflexes were razor-sharp. When Orion sent the knife toward my chest, I sidestepped easily. I fired one shot from my gun, the silencer dampening the sound, and hit my target in the shoulder.

"Fuck you. Clearly you don't even know how to make the kill shot anymore."

Orion sent another knife. This one came slightly closer, but that was how I wanted it. I fired another shot, this time grazing him. He frowned and touched the bloody spot on his ear.

"Oh, so now you're showing off. I'm still not going to give you what you want."

"Yes. You will."

"Oh really? Why would I do that? You'll never have it."

I fought with the part of me that wanted to take my time. That wanted to incapacitate Orion enough that I could tie him to a chair and play. But I suppressed the part of me that liked to kill. I wasn't letting that part of myself out anymore. Not ever.

This was a job.

Clean. Simple.

I had one goal and it wasn't retribution. It was a matter of safety. I took aim and hit Orion's other shoulder. And my former boss cursed again.

"You might not want to give me the code, but I'm taking it one way or the other."

A series of throwing stars came my way, but I saw that they caused Orion significant pain to wield them. One of them clipped me in the shoulder. I barely felt the burn. And bonus, Orion had to step out from around the island to fire them off. And then I saw my opening. With one perfectly placed shot, I hit Orion in the exact place Lucia had stabbed him. My former boss went down in a heap.

Without preamble, I walked over calmly and dragged Orion up by the arm.

Orion writhed and tried to get away, but I was having none of it. Thanks to the schematics Matthias had found, locating the safe was easy enough. When Orion tried to fight me, I calmly but efficiently sent a blow to the back of his skull, not to knock him out but enough to ensure his cooperation. The first biometric scan was easy. One hand-print. Done.

The eye scan was a little trickier as I had to hold Orion up, awkwardly bracing him against the wall with the panel. I leaned his head back and pried an eyelid open. When I had the clear scan, I let Orion fall to the ground as the safe clicked open.

I turned the latch, and inside there were several papers and exactly what I was looking for. I took the sat phone and the code generator, as well as the stack of papers in there. Then I turned back to Orion and fired one kill shot to the head.

I had more work to do tonight.

———

When Ian came out of the shower, he stopped mid-stride when he saw me standing in the middle of his room. Anyone else would have shit a brick to see an uninvited guest in their locked home in the middle of the night, but Ian just shrugged and then walked to his dresser where he calmly selected a shirt and jeans.

"So I guess my number finally came up, huh? Just make it fast, kid. I think you owe me that much."

I chuckled. Ian had always been such a grumpy bastard, but no one could call him anything less than a professional. He wasn't the type to whine and beg for his life. Truth be told, the idea of dying at the hands of a friend was probably Ian's idea of an honorable death.

"I'm not here to take you out. Who would I call when I need advice?"

Ian pushed up his sleeves and leaned against the dresser. "What's the occasion? Don't tell me you missed my pretty face?" He stroked the edge of his scarred jaw absently.

"I was in the neighborhood."

"This place was locked up tighter than the Pentagon. Or so I thought anyway. My guys are good, too."

"Matthias is better."

Ian didn't bother arguing. We both knew it was the truth. I looked around the room, taking in the minimalist décor and looking toward the closet with the military grade weapons that I'd checked out while Ian was in the bathroom. Once I made this decision, there was no undoing it. But Ian had worked alongside me many times and taught me a lot along the way. He was a sonofabitch, no doubt about it, but he was fair and once upon a time had actually believed in the original mission of ORUS.

After a short pause, I pulled up my sleeve to reveal the series of connected dots that formed my ORUS identification. Ian's eyes fell to his own exposed wrists.

"Phoenix," I said. "Your name is strangely prophetic."

"What does that mean?"

My mind made up, I pulled the sat phone and code generator from the interior pocket of my jacket and set them carefully on the desk. Such innocuous items to hold such power.

Ian stood up straight. The items didn't exactly broadcast what they were, but I figured the other man knew something was up just by how strangely I'd been behaving.

"It's time to change your tattoos. You're Orion now."

"What the hell?"

For the first time, I had the supreme pleasure of seeing Ian smile. Just as quickly, his face returned to its usual sullen expression.

"I hope you know what you're doing, kid."

The name reminded me of how I talked to Matthias. It had been so long since I'd felt like a kid, when everything was fresh and new. When everything was possible.

But now it was. And I wasn't going to waste a single moment.

"What I'm doing is something that should have been done long ago. The original goal and purpose of ORUS has been twisted for profit long enough. Now things are going to be different. It's time for control to be back with the people who believed that we could do some good."

Ian held out a hand and when we shook, I could feel it. We were starting something solid. Something right.

"Good luck, kid." Ian paused and then asked, "Do you really think it's possible for men like us to get a second chance? The ORUS I was trained to serve is a shadow organization at its core. You really think we can turn this around?"

"First, I'm not turning it around. You are. And I believe you can do it."

Ian's eyes rounded. "You're really out? For good?"

An image of Lucia waiting for me in our bed, all bright eyes and smooth skin, spread warmth and contentment through me until I felt like I could have actually walked on air.

"Some men can exist in that place between good and evil. But I'm tired of being in the shadows. From now on I'm walking in the light."

With one last handshake, I walked out and into a future where anything seemed possible.

EPILOGUE

Noah

I watched Rafe through the window. My future brother-in-law stood silent sentry over the rest of the clan. Even on the occasion of his beloved sister's wedding, he held himself separate. Not out of reach in case he was needed, but still, not part of the group. An outsider.

Maybe this is a mistake.

No. It wasn't a mistake. Rafe DeMarco was my brother. *Had* always been my brother as much as my teacher. Even if he was different now.

I rubbed the back of my neck. I knew it was true. Rafe had seen things, done things. He'd been out in the cold too long. Without friends, without family. Rafe had never come out and expressed anything, but knowing the kind of undercover work he'd done, I could imagine how he felt.

I didn't want my brother to be separate from us anymore. It was time to do the right thing. The only real question was how the others would take it. They worked for me, but in essence, Blake Security ran like a family. And likely, each of them would have something to say about my decision.

Also, seeing as Rafe had tried to kill them all, some of them might still be holding grudges.

Luckily, it was just that one time. Okay, it might have been a couple of times. Rafe was sorry though, right?

Maybe not as sorry as he should be.

I pushed into the waiting room. Jonas greeted me with a grin. "There he is. We were starting to wonder if you'd executed plan Condor."

I frowned. "What the fuck is plan Condor?

Dylan eyed him knowingly. "It's a plan where you take flight like a bird."

I rolled my eyes. "Do you have any idea how long I waited to have Lucia? I'm not going anywhere." I frowned. "Though, now I feel like I should have one of you make sure *she* doesn't run."

Oskar rolled his eyes. "Well if JJ is planning the escape, they're already gone."

I frowned. Lucia's best friend was a known troublemaker and had a mouth like a sailor, but even *she* couldn't convince Lucia to turn runaway bride. Could she?

No dumbass. They're just rattling your cage.

Rafe frowned. "If she doesn't want to get married, we're certainly not going to force her."

"Have you met your sister? When was the last time she did anything that she didn't precisely want to do?"

Rafe chuckled. "Yeah, you have a point about that."

"Can I borrow you for a minute, Rafe?" I kept my voice low, but the atmosphere in the room changed in a heartbeat.

Rafe gave me a terse nod before saying, "Yeah of course."

Once I had him out of the vestibule and into the courtyard of the church, Rafe was all business. "What's up man?"

"You know what I want to ask you, right?"

Rafe nodded. "I could see you've been working up to it. But I'll tell you the truth, it's a little late for strippers. My sister would kill me."

I chuckled. "As if you would let me get strippers."

"Yeah, of course. I mean I would just hire the same crew of jocks that she hired for you last time. That shit would be funny."

"Man, she told you about that?"

Rafe chuckled. "Yep. Now I know what to get you for every birthday for the rest of your life."

"And here I thought we were brothers."

Rafe grinned, and for a second he looked much more like the man who'd trained me. The man who'd taught me everything I knew.

"That is precisely why I'm getting you strippers every birthday. What are big brothers for?"

I laughed. "You know, that's a good point."

"So what's up, Noah? It's not like you to have cold feet."

I slanted him a look. "You do know me." I rubbed my jaw, unsure what to do with the sudden influx of nerves. "Look, I know you've got your own deal with the FBI and your undercover assignments with Interpol. But I think maybe you've been doing that too long. Maybe it's time to come back into the fold. Family, friends, and all that."

Rafe had always been hard to read. He was an inscrutable bastard. But I pressed on. "Look, it's probably clear to you I need help. I've got more work than I have men for, and I'm spread thin. We've taken a lot of hits this past year. Ryan and Dylan are great, but I need someone who can take them to the next level. Matthias is good, but he's too on edge to be a teacher. I could use someone who actually knows how to train agents. But you know, *not* for wet work."

Rafe sighed. "You try to kill a guy one time, and he never lets that shit go."

I chuckled. "Well, it was more than one time. Let's face it, you very nearly killed me."

"Well, you actually *did* kill me." At my wince, Rafe chuckled. "Too soon?"

I nodded. "Yeah man, too soon. I'm not used to having you back yet."

This felt good. Like those years between us vanished. Up until now, I hadn't known what to say.

"Seriously though. We always think about it." I cleared my throat. "Not just Lucia, but me. I... missed you."

I met Rafe's gaze. I would have sworn I saw a glimmer of hope. Maybe longing.

Rafe rocked back on his heels. "You know, I think I've had enough of the FBI. Obviously, I would never go back to ORUS. I never wanted to be in anyway. But that blood on my hands, Noah... it's not a small thing."

I nodded. "I know. But if I can do it, you can. It's pretty easy actually. The jobs you go on, you're almost guaranteed to come home from."

Rafe shrugged. "Sounds boring. Can't you throw in a starlet or something?"

I chuckled. "I'll see what I can do, man. You might have to wrestle Dylan for starlet duty though."

"To hear Dylan talk about it, it's like he'd rather face a firing squad."

"I don't know what he has against pop princesses. I swear that was one of my favorite assignments."

Rafe nodded. "I've lost too much time with Lucia and Nonna. Other people, too."

I rolled my eyes. "Just say it man, you missed me. Go on, you know you want to."

"Yeah, whatever. You can use some extra training. Next time go for the kill shot."

"Fuck man, *still too soon*."

"Speaking of too soon, how do you think the band of misfits in there is gonna take it?"

I sighed. "They'll follow along. But could you maybe try to refrain from dislocating any shoulders or killing anyone? You know, for a while."

"There you go, ruining all my fun."

It felt good bantering with Rafe. My heart might burst I was so happy. But I sobered quickly. "About Matthias though."

Rafe's good-natured attitude melted off his body. "Is he tight? Because he looks like he's riding that edge."

I nodded. "He had it bad before he even got to ORUS, and I don't know, I might not have gotten him out soon enough. That killer instinct is right below the surface, you know?"

"The way he fights, he's good. A complete natural."

I nodded. "Unless absolutely necessary, I've benched him from any violent shit. Only time I let him out in the field is for his unique expertise or if I really think some people could get killed. He's a good kid, and he's never had a fair shot."

Rafe nodded. "I'll give him a wide berth for a bit. Give him a chance to settle down sand get used to me." He paused for a moment and slid me a glance. "We good?"

I nodded. "Yeah. We're good. You helped me when I was going off the rails, and I've never said thank you for that."

Rafe nodded and drew in a deep breath. "And I never said I was sorry."

I frowned. "For what?"

"You are my brother. And you're about to be my brother-in-law in just a little under an hour —"

I stopped him. "Man, it's not necessary."

"Yes, it is. I feel like I'm in Assassins Anonymous or some shit. But I do need to make amends. I'm sorry for the guilt you had to carry around. If there had been any other way to protect all of you, I would have taken it."

Shit, were my eyes stinging? "I understand. I just wish —"

Rafe's brows drew up. "Yeah?"

"I just wish we didn't have so much time to make up for."

Rafe nodded and swiped a knuckle under his eye. "Yeah. Me too. So, what do you say we get back to the assholes so you can break the news to them real easy, like a couple of anal virgins."

I laughed. "Way inappropriate man. Seems like you'll fit right in."

———

"Okay guys, I wanted to talk to you about something before the wedding. Things have been busier than ever this past year. It's time to expand."

Jonas narrowed his gaze. "Yeah? How many are we taking on? We're spread thin already, and training can be kind of a bitch."

I nodded. "I hear you. That's why we're only taking on one new guy. And I guarantee you, training won't be necessary."

Matthias's gaze ping-ponged between me and Rafe. "Nah, mate. Tell me you're not fucking thinking what I *think* you're thinking about."

Dylan slid his gaze back and forth between me and Matthias. "Huh? What am I missing?"

Oskar crossed his arms and hung his head, shaking it backward and forward. "You don't see it? Noah is asking this one to join the team." He jerked his thumb in Rafe's direction.

Rafe, to his credit, didn't budge. Didn't move, didn't smile, frown or anything.

Matthias however was far less cool. "Over my fucking dead body, mate."

Rafe muttered under his breath. "That can be arranged."

Of course that got Matthias's hackles up. He took a step toward Rafe, and Oskar had to physically stop him.

Dylan shook his head. "No. Not doing it. Not working with this asshole. Dude, have you forgotten he tried to kill us? More than once?"

Rafe smirked. "Trust me, if I'd actually wanted you dead, you would be dead."

I winced. "Rafe, not fucking helping."

Ryan chuckled. "I can't believe this. You're actually thinking about asking him to join the team. I know he's Lucia's brother and all but, I don't like it."

As the members of my team grumbled, I could see the loneliness, the confusion, and what I thought might be a faint glimmer of hope. "Okay, you idiots, you've had the opportunity to express your displeasure. Not that I give two shits. Do you all trust me?"

Matthias was the first to meet my gaze. The kid may not be happy about what I was saying right now, but after everything that had happened between us, I knew I had Matthias's loyalty, no matter what.

When he spoke, his voice was barely above a growl. "Through fire," he said quietly.

I nodded. Honestly, I hadn't even had to ask. Although, it might be one hell of a task trying to keep the two of them from killing each other. Matthias was somewhat untested, but in some ways he was just as deadly as Rafe.

Dylan just threw up his hands. "Are you fucking serious right now?"

Next to Dylan, Ryan clenched his jaw. "Yeah boss, you know I trust you, especially after what you've done for me, but —"

"No buts. You either trust me, or you don't."

Ryan swallowed but then nodded, unable to even look at me. Considering where I had found Ryan, the kid was a sure bet, too.

Dylan was a wildcard. As was Oskar. He always had his own motivation for doing things. But he always wanted to do the *right* thing. And if he thought you were doing that, he'd follow without question.

Then there was Jonas. My best friend. The friend who'd been left to pick up the pieces of my shattered soul. The friend I lied to for years, but who'd still stuck around when I'd eventually been forced to come clean about my past. Jonas was the friend who'd helped me heal.

And you saved him too. There'd been a moment in time when Jonas had been sitting in front of the gates of hell. And then my skills had come in handy. But honestly, if I was being honest with myself, my friend had saved me more than I'd helped him.

Jonas slid his gaze to me and nodded. "I don't like it. I'm not a fan." He glanced briefly over to Rafe. "But he's Lucia's brother, which means he'll do anything to keep his sister safe. And she is our family, so I'm assuming that extends to us. Then, well, you're vouching for him. So I may not understand it, but I'll back your play. Although," he turned to face Rafe and stared him down, "you try any of that shit again, and I will kill you in your sleep."

Rafe smirked. "Again, you're welcome to try."

I could only chuckle. That was Rafe for you. Because at the end of the day, everyone in the room knew that if Rafe wanted to, he could put them all down.

Dylan dropped his hands. "Seriously? Whatever man. If you say he's on the team, he's on the team. I'll work with him. But that's only because I trust you."

I nodded. Oskar only chuckled. "Why the fuck not? Hell, since these guys are pussies anyway, I'll volunteer to train him."

"Like I need your fucking training," Rafe growled.

"See in the real world, you can't go around killing people and shit. I know you former assassins have a problem with that. But it's not really what we do here. So I'm happy to teach you the finer points of security. You know... *not* killing the clients and shit."

Rafe considered this. "Yeah, you might have a point. I am better at killing things."

Oskar just shook his head. "You see, my training skills are at work already."

I turned my gaze to my friend, the man I'd call brother in under an hour.

"Welcome back to the fold."

ANOTHER EPILOGUE

10 Months Later...

JJ

I closed my eyes, exhausted. Day after draining day of pulling double duty while my bestie and partner in crime was on maternity leave was starting to take its toll. Like hell was I going to start complaining, though. If anyone deserved happiness, it was Lucia. My best friend had been to hell and back and deserved the time off.

I could deal. After all Lucia would do it for me. Besides, I wasn't letting a prima donna fashion designer run me into the ground and call uncle. I'd rather burn my Jimmy Choos first. I could handle anything our boss Adriana could dish out.

It felt like I'd only shut my eyes for mere seconds before I frowned in my sleep.

Something was wrong. *Very* wrong.

When I peeled my eyes open again, I was in hell.

"Oh my god," I screamed.

But that scream was my first mistake. It meant emptying out my lungs, which meant I needed to breathe... and that meant lungs full of smoke.

It was so hot my hair plastered against my head and my sheets clung to my naked breasts from sweat. Yeah, I slept topless, so what? It had been so hot lately.

Frantic, I looked around the room trying to find the source of heat. It was so dark I couldn't see anything. But I could feel the smoke all around, cloying and thick, wrapping around me and constricting my lungs.

"Don't panic." The sound of my own voice out loud scared me out of my frozen state. *Fear immobilizes. Anger motivates.*

That's right, get pissed off!

If there was anything I was good at, it was being hot tempered. What the fuck was smoke doing in my room anyway? I'd just had a goddamned blowout. I needed to charge that color and cut to whatever or whoever was the source of this fire.

Move your ass girly.

I had to move because I was *not* dying in this room. I did not survive my past to die like this. Fuck that noise. Besides, if I died Lucia would resurrect my ass and kill me all over again. After Lucia had survived being stalked and almost killed, I had a new appreciation for the meaning of life.

I swung my legs over the side of the bed, letting out a sigh of relief when my toes met the carpet. Now that my eyes had adjusted to the dark somewhat, I could see the faint hint of an orange glow from down the hall. Which meant the fire hadn't reached my room... yet.

But the bedroom door stood open to the hall, which was probably why I could already smell the smoke.

It was weird that the door was open. I always closed the door before going to sleep. It was one of the things Lucia's husband had drilled into me. Noah owned a security company, and his overprotectiveness toward Lucia had spilled over onto me. Now I always had one of the annoying, albeit sexy, guys who worked for him trailing me to and from work, and my apartment had been subjected to a thorough security 'review' by Noah's resident IT wizard. Matthias had deemed my place 'merely acceptable.'

I was pretty sure they'd have asked me to move if they hadn't known from experience that I didn't take suggestions well. The last thing I needed was some man trying to tell me what to do. Maybe Lucia was okay with that, but I wasn't interested. I knew from experience that I didn't want any man having control over my life.

Never again.

That alpha-asshole shit didn't work for me, so they could shove their over protectiveness where the sun didn't shine.

With a quick glance at the open door, I realized it was actually lucky I'd left it open, otherwise I might not have woken up until the flames were closer. What the hell had woken me? *You can think through that shit after you're safe.* Yeah, good point. I grabbed my comforter and wrapped myself in the thick fabric, bringing it up over my head as I stepped into a pair of slippers.

How far to the door? The window might be an option if the fire escape hadn't been welded over some years ago. I looked up and then squinted in the darkness. And then I saw the shadow in the hall. The man-sized shadow.

Fuck me. I opened my mouth to scream then reached into my bedside drawer for the nearest weapon I could find. I'd been aiming for the retractable baton I kept in the top drawer. But instead I'd come up with a gag gift from a bachelorette party. A giant purple vibrator.

What are you gonna do with that? Fuck him to death? Well that was a thought.

"Who the hell are you? And what the fuck are you doing in my apartment?"

He stepped forward slightly, his body still half-hidden outside the door, and I raised my makeshift weapon.

"I'm here for you, Jessica. I'm always here for you."

I clutched the blanket closer, and my fingers curled around the vibrator as his voice washed over me. The low tone of his words sliced through my veins. That voice. It had been so long since I'd heard that voice. I'd hoped to never hear it again, except in my nightmares.

"How did you find me?"

His chuckle was almost as terrifying as the words that followed. "I never lost you."

I screamed and backed up so fast that I stumbled and fell on the bed. The comforter tangled around my legs and I fought against it, certain the next touch I'd feel would be the last.

Strong hands wrapped around my flailing arms.

"Damn it, you crazy woman. I'm trying to help you!"

It took a few seconds before I recognized the voice, my terror distorting it into the one I feared most. When I finally spoke, my voice was tiny.

"Jonas? Is that you?"

The comforter was pulled away from my eyes, and Jonas's handsome face appeared. Jonas Castillo worked for Noah's security company and was a regular fixture in my life. He was routinely assigned to protect Lucia, and by default me, during the workweek. I took great pleasure in giving him hell, and he was usually cursing my name or bickering with me.

"Yes, of course it's me."

Before I could question what he was doing there, I felt myself being lifted. I clutched his shoulders automatically, disoriented after my fall. Now I wasn't sure if that had actually happened. Had I been dreaming? It was so hard to tell.

"Jonas, did you see anyone else in the apartment?"

"Like who? Don't you live alone?"

Was that jealousy in his voice? Even under these circumstances, I couldn't resist the urge to screw with him a little.

"Actually I don't. We can't leave without my favorite guy."

"Who? If you have a boyfriend, where is he? Some help he is during an emergency."

"Well, Fluffy has never been much help during emergencies, but he blows the best wet kisses."

Jonas didn't pause. "I'll come back for your dog, I promise. But I have to get you to safety."

It must have been the smoke affecting my brain, because at first I didn't realize what he'd said. It wasn't until we were at the front door that I understood he meant to leave.

"No! I have to get Fluffy!" I swatted at his massive chest. I must have surprised him because his arms loosened around my legs, giving me the room I needed to jump down.

"Damn it, JJ! This is serious. We don't have time to stop."

"It'll just take a second." I raced back to the guest bedroom and grabbed Fluffy, covering him with the comforter as I ran.

Jonas picked me up as soon as I hit the hallway and ran for the front door. We passed a crew of firefighters in the corridor outside my apartment. The smoke was thicker out here, so I buried my face in Jonas's shoulder, making sure to keep Fluffy covered too.

When we got outside, Jonas set us down carefully on the grass, safely away from the building. An EMT approached, and Jonas pointed at me. I was going to protest, but dissolved into a coughing fit as soon as I opened my mouth. The young man frowned and knelt on the grass next to me. Then his eyes widened when my comforter slipped and I almost flashed an entire boob at him.

"Hey, eyes up, kid." Jonas glared at him before yanking his shirt off. He put it over my head, and I maneuvered carefully to get my arms in without dropping the comforter completely. If I hadn't felt so crappy, I'd have told him exactly where he could shove it. I didn't need anyone speaking for me.

Just to annoy him, I gave the EMT a bright smile that had the young man blushing furiously. Jonas scowled at both of us.

After a flurry of activity, blood pressure cuffs, and oxygen, they finally left me alone. That's when Jonas got a good look at me again.

Me *and* Fluffy.

"A fish? You risked your life to save a *fucking fish?*"

I scooped up Fluffy's bowl protectively. "Fluffy is not just a fish. He's a Japanese fighting fish. A total badass."

Jonas looked like he wanted to strangle me. Normally that was exactly the effect I was going for, but strangely, it wasn't as satisfying as usual.

"Thank you, Jonas. For coming in after me."

He looked as shocked as I felt by my sudden gratitude.

"Of course. It's nothing. The fire department would have gotten to you soon. I just happened to get there first when Matthias said your alarms were triggered."

The talk of alarms brought back memories of the man I'd seen in the smoke. It had happened so fast, and I couldn't be sure what was real and what had been a dream.

"Did you see anyone in there?" At his confused look, I clarified, "In my apartment?"

Jonas knelt and looked me in the eye. "Was there someone in there with you, Jessica?"

It was all such a blur, and I didn't like the way he was looking at me. Noah's entire crew was extremely overprotective, so if I said the wrong thing, I'd end up on house arrest with Jonas as my jailor. Plus, it was likely it had all been a dream. Jonas had been in my apartment.

He would have seen if anyone else was there. The man in the smoke was nothing more than a shadow from a past I'd rather forget.

"No, I meant in the building. I just want to make sure all my neighbors got out okay."

Jonas looked like he wanted to say something else, but Noah arrived just then with Lucia right behind him.

I accepted a hug from my friend, and that was when it really hit me.

"I guess I'm homeless now."

Noah's voice carried from behind Lucia. "You'll stay with us, of course."

My eyes met Jonas's, and I knew he was thinking about my earlier question.

"It's for the best," Jonas said.

I glanced over at Lucia. "Free rent and a house full of hot men. Count me in."

———

Thank you for reading the first book in the *Broken* series.

JJ's past has come back to haunt her but can she rely on the Blake Security crew to keep her safe? Find out in the next book, Broken Ties!

Need more Blake Security? Find out what bonus material is available at malonesquared.com/brokentrust

ABOUT THE AUTHORS

M. MALONE is a RITA® Award winner and a NYT & USA Today Bestselling author of completely inappropriate romantic comedy. She lives with her husband and their two sons in the picturesque mountains of Northern Virginia even though she is afraid of insects, birds, butterflies and other humans.

She also holds a Master's degree in Business from a prestigious college that would no doubt be scandalized at how she's using her expensive education. **mmalonebooks.com**

USA Today Bestselling Author, **NANA MALONE**'s love of all things romance and adventure started with a tattered romantic suspense she borrowed from her cousin on a sultry summer afternoon in Ghana at a precocious thirteen. She's been in love with kick butt heroines ever since.

With her overactive imagination, and channeling her inner Buffy, it was only a matter a time before she created her own characters. Waiting for her chance at a job as a ninja assassin, Nana, meantime works out her drama, passion and sass with fictional characters every bit as sassy and kick butt as she thinks she is. **nanamalone.com**

ALSO BY M. MALONE

Mess with Me

Beg Me

Ask Me

Want Me

Need Me

Blue-Collar Billionaires

Tank

Finn

Gabe

Zack

Luke

Bad Business (The Kingsleys)

Bad King

Bad Blood

RITA® Winner

The Alexanders

One More Day

The Things I Do for You

All I Need is You

Just One Thing

One More Chance

Want to read one of my romantic comedies for free?

Join my VIP list at mmalonebooks.com

ALSO BY NANA MALONE

FREE

Cheeky Royal

Protecting the Heiress

Big Ben

The Heir

Gentlemen Rogues

The Heir

The King

The Saint

The Rook

The Spy

The Villain

Royals

Royals Undercover

Cheeky Royal

Cheeky King

Royals Undone

Royal Bastard

Bastard Prince

Royals United

Royal Tease

Teasing the Princess

Royal Elite

The Heiress Duet

Protecting the Heiress
Tempting the Heiress

The Prince Duet

Return of the Prince
To Love a Prince

The Bodyguard Duet

Bodyguard to the Billionaire
The Billionaire's Secret

<u>London Royals</u>

London Royal Duet

London Royal
London Soul

Playboy Royal Duet

Royal Playboy
Playboy's Heart

London Lords
<u>See No Evil</u>

Big Ben
The Benefactor
For Her Benefit

<u>Hear No Evil</u>

East End
East Bound
Fall of East

To Catch a Thief

Speak No Evil

London Bridge

Bridge of Lies

Broken Bridge

The Donovans Series

Come Home Again (Nate & Delilah)

Love Reality (Ryan & Mia)

Race For Love (Derek & Kisima)

Love in Plain Sight (Dylan and Serafina)

Eye of the Beholder – (Logan & Jezzie)

Love Struck (Zephyr & Malia)

London Billionaires Standalones

Mr. Trouble (Jarred & Kinsley)

Mr. Big (Zach & Emma)

Mr. Dirty(Nathan & Sophie)

The Player

Bryce

Dax

Echo

Fox

Ransom

Gage

The In Stilettos Series

Sexy in Stilettos (Alec & Jaya)

Sultry in Stilettos (Beckett & Ricca)

Sassy in Stilettos (Caleb & Micha)

Strollers & Stilettos (Alec & Jaya & Alexa)

Seductive in Stilettos (Shane & Tristia)

Stunning in Stilettos (Bryan & Kyra)

~~~

In Stilettos Spin off

Tempting in Stilettos (Serena & Tyson)

Teasing in Stilettos (Cara & Tate)

Tantalizing in Stilettos (Jaggar & Griffin)

Love Match Series

*Game Set Match (Jason & Izzy)

Mismatch (Eli & Jessica)

Don't want to miss a single release?

Sign up at http://nanamaloneromance.net

</div>
~~~